Praise for *JUDAS 62*

'Tense and topical, this has all you could want from an
intelligent contemporary spy thriller'
The Times, Books of the Year

'The storytelling is first-rate, with all the minutiae
of spycraft, sense of place and memorable supporting
characters you could wish for'
Sunday Times

'Superbly constructed, it never hurries, but evokes the
world of espionage in a way the late John le Carré
would have much admired'
Daily Mail

'Some of the best writing around on the intricacies of
spycraft and the high price agents pay for doing their job'
Sun

'Intelligent, relevant and engrossing'
NB Magazine

'Cumming adroitly portrays Kite's inner life . . . nail-biting'
Financial Times

'Cumming knows his stuff and has done his research,
giving the novel an admirably authoritative air'
Literary Review

'Charles Cumming knows how to write a good spy novel'
Herald

'The gold standard in espionage fiction'
Kirkus

JUDAS
62

Charles Cumming was born in Scotland in 1971. Shortly after university, he was approached for recruitment by the Secret Intelligence Service (MI6), an experience that inspired his first novel, *A Spy by Nature*. He has written several bestselling thrillers, including *A Foreign Country* which won the CWA Ian Fleming Steel Dagger for Best Thriller and the Bloody Scotland Crime Book of the Year. He lives in London.

@CharlesCumming

/AuthorCharlesCumming

/charlescummingbooks

By Charles Cumming

JUDAS 62

CHARLES CUMMING

HarperCollins*Publishers*

HarperCollins*Publishers* Ltd
1 London Bridge Street,
London, SE1 9GF

www.harpercollins.co.uk

HarperCollins*Publishers*
1st Floor, Watermarque Building, Ringsend Road
Dublin 4, Ireland

This paperback edition 2022
1

First published by HarperCollins*Publishers* 2021

A catalogue record for this book
is available from the British Library

ISBN: 978-0-00-836350-5

Set in Meridien by Palimpsest Book Production Limited,
Falkirk, Stirlingshire

Printed and Bound in the UK using 100% Renewable Electricity at
CPI Group (UK) Ltd

MIX
Paper from
responsible sources
FSC
www.fsc.org
FSC™ C007454

This book is produced from independently certified FSC™ paper
to ensure responsible forest management.

For more information visit: www.harpercollins.co.uk/green

for Andrew Ramsay
and to the memory of James Ramsay (1948–2020)

Index of Characters

Gretchen Jeffreys, a Rhodes scholar
Evgeny Palatnik, colonel in the Red Army
Mikhail Gromik, Russian intelligence officer
Oksana Sharikova, a student in Voronezh
Yuri Aranov, a scientist
Tania Tretyakova, Aranov's partner
Katarina Bokova, owner of the Dickens Institute in Voronezh
Daniil Savin, co-owner of the Dickens Institute
Alexander Makarov, director of the FSB, Russia's foreign intelligence service
Leonid Deviatkin, an FSB officer
Natalia Kovalenko, a businesswoman in Dubai
Andrei Laptev, an FSB officer
Virginia Terry, Russian foreign intelligence (SVR) 'illegal' resident in the United States
Vasily Zatulin, an FSB officer
Valentin Inarkiev, an FSB officer
Khalil Albaloushi, a senior brigadier in Dubai State Security (DSS)
Mark Sheridan, MI6 Controller Middle East

'No man steps in the same river twice. He is not the
same man and it is not the same river.'
Heraclitus

'Voronezh, you are a whim, Voronezh, you are a
raven and a knife.'
Osip Mandelstam

Sverdlovsk, Russia

1979

It began on a Sunday night.

Alexei Nikolayev, a thirty-six-year-old father of two living in the closed Soviet city of Sverdlovsk, was contentedly bathing his son on a warm spring evening when he started to feel short of breath. Sitting back on the floor of the bathroom, he began to cough repeatedly. He could not stop. Alexei's wife, Vera Nikolayeva, came into the bathroom and asked what was wrong. Without responding, her husband stood up, went into the living room and lay down on the sofa.

Vera took the boy from the bath, wrapped him in a towel and carried him in.

'You were drinking last night,' she said, admonishing her husband as she dried the child's hair. Alexei had polished off a bottle of vodka with a friend who lived in a neighbouring street. Vera assumed, with good reason, that her husband had a hangover. 'It's a shame,' she said. 'You're supposed to help me at weekends, to read the children a bedtime story. They look forward to it.'

Vera was not to know that her husband's condition had nothing to do with alcohol. Two days earlier, while conducting a routine check at the end of his shift at the Soviet Army's Biological Weapons Research Facility in Sverdlovsk, an engineer named Oleg Pavlov had discovered a clogged filter blocking an exhaust pipe in Compound 19. Clogged filters were not uncommon, but they were potentially extremely dangerous. Oleg's job was to oversee the drying of fermented anthrax cultures, which would then be ground into a fine

3

powder for use in weaponised aerosols. If these spores ever escaped into the open air, the results would be catastrophic. Oleg had written a note to his supervisor advising him that the blocked filter had been removed and needed to be replaced as a matter of urgency. He had then hurried home for the weekend.

Distracted and short of sleep, Oleg's supervisor, Lieutenant Colonel Nikolai Sorokin, failed to act on the information contained in the note. It was policy for the drying machines to be switched off at the end of each shift so that maintenance and safety checks could be carried out. Seeing nothing of consequence in the Compound 19 logbook, Sorokin had restarted the machines. Settling down at his desk to smoke a cigarette, the lieutenant colonel was unaware that a fine dust of deadly anthrax spores immediately started moving through the exhaust pipes. They were soon expelled into the open air over Sverdlovsk. It was several hours before the missing filter was noticed and the machines shut down. By then, the spores had spread over a wide area, carried on the northerly wind.

Alexei Nikolayev worked in a ceramics factory located just across the street from Compound 19. On his way home on Friday night, he had stopped to speak to a co-worker, Leonid Ionov, who was having difficulties in his marriage. It was a balmy evening and the two men had chatted for some time.

'Just be patient,' Alexei Nikolayev had told him. 'All women want is to feel that we love them. They want to have control. Don't do anything foolish. In a few weeks all this will seem like nothing.'

By Sunday, Leonid was suffering with the same shortness of breath which had afflicted his friend. In the early hours of Monday morning he woke up covered in sweat and coughing wretchedly. His wife, alarmed by these symptoms, mixed honey into a glass of tea and encouraged Leonid to drink. It did no good. By dawn, small black swellings had appeared on his neck and shoulders, quickly spreading to the top of his chest. The swellings became ulcerous as the day went on.

Less than a mile away, in a nearby apartment complex, Alexei Nikolayev's symptoms had also worsened. Vera telephoned for help but doctors were not available. Dozens of employees at the ceramics factory who had left work at the same time were experiencing similar illnesses. Unbeknown to their families, all of them were suffering from acute pulmonary anthrax poisoning. By the end of the week, they would all be dead. As many as one thousand residents lost their lives as a result of the leak from Compound 19.

As a closed city, specific authorisation was already required to enter Sverdlovsk. Any citizen wishing to leave needed a permit to do so. Vera Nikolayeva knew that phone calls were tapped and that news from Sverdlovsk rarely reached the outside world. In the awful days following the loss of her husband, she heard that local hospitals had been overwhelmed by men and women with identical symptoms to Alexei. Two doctors visited her apartment and explained what had happened.

'Your husband's death was caused by a consignment of contaminated meat sold on the black market,' the older of them told her. He wore a white coat and had a stethoscope around his neck. 'Along with many others, he ate the meat and, as a consequence, was fatally poisoned.'

'But I have never bought such food,' Vera replied. 'This is why I don't trust the black market.'

'Unfortunately, the meat was served in the canteen at his factory,' the other doctor explained. 'The authorities are trying as hard as they can to track down the offending vendors. Rest assured they will be caught and prosecuted to the full extent of the law.'

The doctors expressed their condolences, handed Vera Alexei's death certificate and left hurriedly without touching the tea she had prepared for them. They were busy and needed to visit a number of bereaved families in the area. Two days later it was announced on the wireless that several traders in Sverdlovsk had been imprisoned on charges of selling contaminated beef. Officials had also rounded up a number of stray dogs and destroyed them on the grounds that they presented a danger to public health. Flyers were distributed around the city ordering citizens to stop buying food on the black market. Anybody who dared to question the official line was intimidated into silence. In time, fear and suspicion ensured that the disaster was rarely spoken of, even by those who had lost husbands, wives, and in some cases children.

It was only many years later, long after the collapse of the Soviet Union, that Vera Nikolayeva – now remarried and living in Germany – learned the truth about what had happened to her husband. When news of the leak from Compound 19 had reached Moscow, a team of KGB officers had been dispatched to Sverdlovsk. The development of weaponised anthrax constituted a breach of the 1972 Biological Weapons Convention; in typical Soviet fashion, the officers had set about covering everything up. In this task they were assisted by officials from the local Communist Party, including none other than Boris Yeltsin, the future president of the Russian Federation. Under no circumstances could the outside world learn about the activities of Biopreparat, the Soviet Union's secret biological weapons programme. The two men in the pristine white coats who had come to Vera's apartment were not doctors; they were KGB. The death certificate they had given her was a fake. Her late husband's medical records had been destroyed in 1979. Alexei Nikolayev had been just one of many of the victims of what became known as 'the biological Chernobyl'.

The present day

1

'GONE FISHING!' said the handwritten note attached to the refrigerator in Saul Kaszeta's sunlit Connecticut kitchen, sparrows chirping in the trees beyond the conservatory, fresh flowers and a box of chocolates on the kitchen counter. The chocolates were a gift for Kaszeta's daughter, Tasha, who was driving up from Brooklyn to house-sit for the long weekend. Her father, whom she had seen only once since Christmas because of the lockdown in New York, was heading off to the Adirondacks on his annual fishing trip.

A short, compact widower of seventy-seven, Kaszeta was often seen practising tai-chi in the local park. He was known occasionally to jog on the quiet suburban streets of Darien, sometimes in the company of his friend, Ray, who was at least twenty years his junior, but most often alone. Kaszeta had been a general in the Russian army in the last decade of the Cold War, a fact unknown to all but his closest acquaintances in the United States, none of whom were aware that his real name was Evgeny Palatnik, nor that he had been a source for BOX 88, a top-secret Anglo-American spy agency, for the final nine years of his military career. In Darien it was widely believed that Kaszeta had been a schoolteacher in Rostov-on-Don who had taken advantage of a post-Soviet emigration programme to move to Connecticut. A dignified, charming Russian émigré who had lost his wife to cancer late in 2017, he taught chess to the pupils at the local high school, accepting no payment for his time, sang a stirring baritone in the church choir and was famed for an extraordinarily high tolerance for alcohol.

The journey to the log cabin in the foothills of the Adirondack Mountains took approximately four hours in manageable traffic, as much as seven when there was trouble on the roads. Though in robust good health for a man well into his eighth decade, Kaszeta suffered from glaucoma, an eye condition that required the administration of pharmaceutical drops once a day. Driving could sometimes exacerbate the symptoms and Tasha had rung to remind her father not to forget to take his bottle of Xalatan to Lake Placid.

As soon as Kaszeta arrived at the cabin, he carried his overnight bag into the living room, opened the windows, checked that the gas and electricity were working and sat on the porch enjoying the turkey and Swiss cheese sandwich he had bought in town, washing it down with a Heady Topper. The coolness of the beer made him think about his medication, which needed to be kept cold, and he returned to the kitchen to put the Xalatan in the fridge. Having unpacked his clothes, he fetched his equipment from the utility room and called Tasha to let her know that he had arrived safely. She was already at the house in Darien, thanked him for the chocolates and said that she would make a casserole for his return. As a courtesy, Kaszeta then rang his handler at Langley, but the call went straight to voicemail. He sent a text message instead, informing the CIA that he would be staying in Lake Placid for the next four nights.

'Happy fishing, Saul,' came the reply. 'Catch a brook trout, not the virus!'

Kaszeta left the phone charging beside his bed and set out for an afternoon of fishing. In years gone by it had been a matter of pride to the local residents that they did not need to lock their cabins, but times had changed in America. Kaszeta was now careful not only to make sure the windows and doors were secure, but also that the dome lens CCTV camera above the porch was in good working order.

Then he could relax. The lake was the best of his adopted country. In his opinion the calm, sunlit waters and the cry of the loon were as American as apple pie and Nelson Rockefeller. He was never happier than when fishing in summer, breathing the fresh mountain air, listening to the gentle putter of distant motorboats and the delighted laughter of swimmers.

A little more than a mile away, FSB officer Vasily Zatulin, disguised as a US postal worker, approached the front door of Kaszeta's log cabin.

He picked the simple lock with ease and made his way into the kitchen. Confirming that the label on the bottle of Xalatan exactly matched the details on the duplicate in his hand, Zatulin switched Kaszeta's glaucoma medication for an A-234 Novichok dissolved in saline, closed the door of the fridge and returned to his vehicle. At the wheel was Virginia Terry, an SVR illegal, resident in Vermont for more than nine years. It was Terry who had run Palatnik to ground, thanks to a detail in the Snowden files and a chance remark by a CIA officer she had befriended in Washington. With the connivance of FSB director Alexander Makarov and his associate, Mikhail Gromik, Terry had obtained Kaszeta's medical records from a doctor's surgery in Darien and plotted the assassination.

Several hours passed. Kaszeta returned from the lake having failed to catch a fish, drove into town to buy provisions, then cooked himself scrambled eggs for supper while listening to PBS. Just before nine o'clock he changed into pyjamas and climbed into bed, ready to make a start on Vasily Grossman's *Life and Fate*, a novel he had always intended to read and had promised himself he would complete by the end of the year.

He had read only two chapters when he felt the telltale dryness in his eyes, always worse in the warm summer months. As usual Kaszeta had forgotten to take his medication. Setting the novel to one side, he made his way to the kitchen, took the bottle of Xalatan from the fridge, shook the contents and unscrewed the cap. At the kitchen table, he tipped his head back and administered one drop to each eye, blinking to ensure that none was wasted.

He could tell something was wrong almost immediately. It was as though a vast shadow had passed over the cabin, dimming the lights in each of the rooms. Kaszeta had the strange, disorienting sensation that he was losing his sight. Confused and growing dizzy, he walked into the bathroom and checked his reflection in the mirror. He switched on the pop light over the basin but it had little effect. The room was now almost completely dark. Stumbling back to the bedroom, his left eye twitching, he reached for his cell phone. He had taken the eye drops a thousand times without difficulty; nothing like this had ever happened before. He tried to find the number for his doctor in Darien, but he could not focus on the screen. His hands were shaking but he managed to make a call, connecting to the last number he had dialled on the phone. It was Jerry, his handler at CIA.

'Saul? How's all that seclusion? Good fishing?'

The phone was moving uncontrollably in his hand. Kaszeta found that it was almost impossible to speak.

'Jerry.' His voice was very faint. He was trying so hard. It was the feeling of wanting to shout in a dream but being unable to make any sound.

'Saul? You OK? I can't hear you.'

'Help me,' Kaszeta gasped. 'Please, Jerry. Something is happening . . .'

2

Lachlan Kite sat on a wooden bench at the edge of Kew Green watching his first cricket match of the long, disrupted summer. He had a mobile phone in one hand, an Americano in the other, sections of *The Sunday Times* scattered on the seat beside him. It was a blistering July afternoon, the players in caps and crumpled white hats which offered scant protection from the glare of the sun. Kite wished that he was among them, fielding at slip or facing the innocuous medium pace of the opposition bowlers, scoring a quick fifty and taking three wickets after tea. He missed the simple camaraderie of the cricket team: the sense that what was at stake – a frustrating defeat, an honourable draw, a stirring victory – was at once enormously important and yet, in the grand scheme of things, utterly insignificant. Like Kite, the men in the outfield were all in middle age, joking and cajoling one another, clutching sore backs and hobbling on weakened knees. Had he chosen a different path he would have been one of them: a lawyer, a filmmaker, a restauranteur. But BOX 88, even in the quiet summer of 2020, left precious little time for cricket.

Kite was in a contemplative mood. He had come to Kew from the Osbourne & Saxony Care Home in Strawberry Hill, intending to visit the botanical gardens so that he could clear his mind, but instead stopping beside the green to watch the game. His mother, Cheryl, had been diagnosed with Alzheimer's at the beginning of the year, her mental and physical decline described by her doctor as some of the most aggressive he had ever encountered. Due to the restrictions imposed by the pandemic, Kite had not seen her face to face for over two months. In that time she had suffered a fall and now required a wheelchair to move around. He had waited for his mother in the grounds of the care home on a bench wearing a surgical mask and tight latex gloves, a flimsy plastic apron covering his chest and thighs. In order further to protect her from the possibility of infection, an armchair had been brought out from the main house and placed under a small gazebo two metres from Kite. There was a bottle of hand sanitiser attached to the bench and a sticker showing the correct measurements for social distancing. Some lines of scripture had been carved into the wood, a dedication to a former resident:

> 'Their soul shall be as a watered garden;
> And they shall not suffer anymore.'

It had been a grim hour, punctuated by the occasional cries of patients in distress: an old woman screaming for a nurse; a wheezing man begging for pain relief. His mother had been dressed in a pair of blue linen trousers and a pale pink blouse. Her thinning hair was now completely white; it moved feebly in the warm wind like cobwebs. There were moments during their conversation in which Cheryl had seemed lucid, railing against her captivity, bitterly criticising the nurses who cared for her and lamenting the tedium of her long, unchanging days. Kite was to blame, she said. He had imprisoned her. Kite knew that there was nothing he could say or do to challenge this assertion or even to console her; Cheryl had always possessed an irrational shortness of temper which had been amplified by the wretched disease. They had never been close; indeed, it would be fair to say that Kite had spent most of his life trying to get as far away from his mother as possible.

Yet in the sudden twilight of her life he felt a deep responsibility for her wellbeing. She had raised him as a single mother following his father's untimely death; Kite was her only child and, with the exception of his estranged wife, Isobel, and baby daughter, Ingrid, her sole living relative.

'And how is Martha?' she had asked.

Martha Raine had been Kite's on-off girlfriend for much of his adult life. She now lived in New York with her husband.

'I'm not with Martha anymore, Mum,' he explained. 'She married somebody else. A long time ago. Remember? They have two children. She lives in America.'

'I went to America in 1970,' she replied wistfully. Cheryl had been a model in the sixties, riding on the coattails of Twiggy and Jean Shrimpton. 'It was so hot. Hotter than today even.' Her voice, normally so robust, was faint and indistinct. 'What about Isobel?'

'Isobel is in Sweden with her mother,' Kite replied. 'She sends her love to you.'

'Did she have the baby?'

Kite had twice told his mother that Isobel had given birth to a baby girl. He had sent her videos and photographs of the child via WhatsApp. At his request, the home had opened a bottle of Moët & Chandon in celebration of Cheryl becoming a grandmother for the first time. From the Covid-free sanctity of her room they had toasted Ingrid on FaceTime, touching the rim of their champagne glasses against the screens of their phones. This was the new way of family intimacy: distant, pixelated, cold.

'I told you, Mum,' he said, trying not to sound impatient. 'She had a girl. Ingrid. They're both in Sweden. Do you remember the photographs I sent? They're on your phone.'

Cheryl's expression became reproachful.

'Why aren't you with her?' she demanded, the embers of her quick, suspicious temper flaring.

'I've explained that, too,' he said, resenting his mother's disease as he resented the fierce heat of the sun in that bland, ordered garden, the sweat on his hands beneath the tight latex gloves. 'I had to fly back to London for work. Then we were locked down. I haven't been able to get back to Stockholm to see them.'

It wasn't the whole truth, or anything close to it. Kite had not spoken to Isobel in over a month. She was refusing to answer his calls, instead writing to say that she was 'reconsidering her life' and preferred to keep Ingrid 'safe in Sweden'. She had always known that Kite worked for British intelligence; what she had not counted on was the threat to her own safety. At the turn of the year she had been kidnapped by members of an Iranian gang who had targeted Kite. Her ordeal might have resulted in the death of their unborn child; did Kite not understand that he must now leave his job in order to guarantee the safety of their family in the years to come? Kite had refused to countenance such a decision, arguing that the kidnapping had been a one-off, a momentary crisis which would never happen again. Yet the demands of secrecy meant that he could not discuss what had happened in any detail, nor why they would not be seeking justice through the courts. To do so would be to risk exposing the existence of BOX 88, the shadow Anglo-American intelligence service to which he had dedicated his working life and about which Isobel knew nothing. With Ingrid barely a few days old, Kite had retreated into obfuscation, telling his wife that he would soon return to London to resume his work for MI6. This simple breach had been enough to tear the fabric of their relationship; the trust they had built up over more than six years had been broken not by something as commonplace as lies or infidelity, but by the demands of the secret world.

A catch was taken on Kew Green, a looping caught-and-bowled bringing an end to an innings of 65 by a short, barrel-chested South African referred to as 'Savage' by his teammates. There was a smattering of applause from the wives and girlfriends sitting on rugs at the boundary's edge. An elderly couple walked in front of Kite's bench, neither wearing masks, both supported on sticks. In the distance, across the parched outfield, children were throwing a plastic toy for a puppy and delightedly clapping their hands as it jumped and scampered about. A plane roared in descent towards Heathrow. Kite heard the sudden, surprising clack of a seagull and was transported back to his youth, puffins and cormorants wheeling over the beach at Killantringan, the hotel his mother had owned on the west coast of Scotland.

'Lockie?'

Kite set the coffee down and looked up, shielding his eyes from the sun.

Cara Jannaway was standing in front of him wearing sunglasses, wedge heels and a red summer dress. They had made no arrangement to meet, but Kite was not surprised to see her: the fix on his phone meant that BOX could find him twenty-four hours a day. Her unscheduled appearance meant business. She wouldn't have disturbed him on a Sunday if it wasn't important.

'Hello there,' he said. 'Cricket lover?'

'You must be joking.' She had a sharp east London accent and a way of treating him almost carelessly that Kite enjoyed. 'Sporting equivalent of watching paint dry. Makes crown bowls look exciting.'

'That's because you don't understand it,' he replied, gesturing at Cara to sit beside him. 'You don't have to socially distance,' he added. 'I've already had the plague.'

Cara had joined BOX 88 from MI5 after playing a crucial role in freeing Kite from the same Iranian gang which had held Isobel hostage. She was twenty-seven, imaginative but practical, brave without being reckless. With Kite and several others, she had formed part of a skeleton BOX 88 staff during the global lockdown, living in an apartment near the agency's temporary headquarters in Chelsea. Kite had grown very fond of her.

'Funny,' she said, sweeping dust off the bench and straightening out her dress as she sat down. 'So what don't I understand about cricket, Mr Kite? What's so fascinating about a bunch of men standing in the middle of a field for eight hours throwing a ball at each other?'

He liked it that she hadn't immediately told him why she was there.

'Heathen.' He shook his head with exaggerated dismay and gestured towards the players. 'Everything you need to know about our business lies before you.'

'Is that right?' Cara removed her sunglasses. 'Go on then, Gandalf. Enlighten me.'

Kite set his empty coffee cup on the bench.

'You see this man walking to the middle?' A new batsman had come to the crease, replacing the recently departed 'Savage'. 'Chances are the opposition knows nothing about him. He could be their best player, he could be utterly hopeless. It's a mystery.'

The batsman was at least fifty-five, wearing black running shoes and an ill-fitting helmet. His shirt was out at the front and tucked in at the back. Two of the straps of his batting pads hung loose around his legs.

'My money's on hopeless,' she said.

'It's the same for the batsman,' Kite continued. 'He's been watching from fifty metres away, but he doesn't know much about the bowlers, even less about the pitch. Will it bounce or keep low? Will it spin or move off the wicket? Can the bowler move the ball in the air, or is the weather too hot for a swing?'

'Is the weather too hot for what now?' A Labrador had run in front of them, barking delightedly off its lead. 'I literally haven't understood a word of what you've just said. You might as well be talking to that dog.'

'It's a metaphor, Cara. You know what a metaphor is, don't you? Cricket as a version of life. This man taking guard now.' Kite was again referring to the new batsman. 'He has to protect his wicket. He has to score runs for his team. He has to build a partnership with the player at the other end. They have to communicate. They're going to be calling for runs, rotating the strike. They have to learn to *trust* one another.'

18

'What if he's out?' Cara asked.

'Exactly! It could all be over in the next thirty seconds. He might have driven a hundred miles to be here today, to bat in west London, to make some runs he can go home and feel good about. But he could be out first ball. Then he has the rest of the day to regret the shot he played, to stand in the outfield in thirty-five degrees of sunshine with nothing better to do than think about the long drive home.'

'I'm still waiting for the metaphor.'

Kite hesitated. He suddenly wanted Cara to take seriously what he was about to tell her.

'What we do is about making what is unknown known,' he said, fixing her with a stare which snatched all the playfulness from her eyes. 'It's about collective and individual responsibility. It's about loneliness and leadership. Above all, it's about trust.'

She nodded quickly. Kite saw that he had struck some sort of nerve and waited for Cara to respond. But then a wicket fell, popping the tension.

'Oh look, he's out,' she said.

Sure enough, the new batsman had been clean bowled second ball, the sound of the quick, gentle clink of broken wickets travelling across the outfield. The fielders roared in celebration and came together to congratulate the bowler, touching elbows ironically in the contemporary style.

'Not a good shot,' Kite observed. 'Played all round it. Speaking of leadership, what are you doing here?'

'Trouble in America,' she said. 'Somebody on JUDAS. Looks like another Skripal, only this time they were more successful.'

Kite felt his chest tighten. JUDAS was a list of Russian intelligence officers, military personnel and scientists living in the West who had been targeted for reprisal assassinations by Moscow. Alexander Litvinenko had been JUDAS 47, Sergei Skripal, the former GRU officer targeted in Salisbury two years earlier, JUDAS 54.

'Who did they hit?' he asked.

'Evgeny Palatnik.'

Kite stared across the green, the name setting off a chain reaction of memories, each one leading inexorably to Martha, to Voronezh and, finally, to Yuri Aranov. He was back in the long, chaotic summer of 1993, a student sent into the heart of post-Soviet Russia by BOX 88 with instructions to bring Aranov out of the country.

'How did they do it?' he asked, remembering the dying Litvinenko, the miracle of Skripal's survival.

'You don't want to know.'

3

The first seeds of Kite's plan to avenge Evgeny Palatnik were sown in these moments. Kite had seen much in his thirty years in the secret world – violence and limitless greed, abhorrent deceptions and treachery – but few things to compare with Cara's description of what had been done to Palatnik. It was depraved. He was by turns disgusted and roused to furious anger. If the Americans failed to respond to the attack with adequate force – just as successive British governments had done little to deter Moscow from repeated outrages on home soil – then BOX 88 would step into the breach. Kite did not yet know how he would do it, nor what methods he would employ to bring the perpetrators to justice. He knew only that the rule of law would not apply.

They left Kew Green immediately, taking the car which Cara had parked nearby. On the journey to headquarters, Kite explained why Palatnik had been targeted.

'Evgeny was a colonel in the Red Army and first deputy chief of Biopreparat.'

'Biopreparat?'

'The Soviet biological weapons programme. BOX recruited Palatnik in Paris in 1981, codename WALTER. He thought he was working for the CIA. For the next decade he gave us everything he could on Russia's offensive smallpox and anthrax capabilities. What Gordievsky was to the political

21

picture in Moscow, Palatnik was to the threat from biological weapons. He told us about the anthrax leak at Sverdlovsk; he knew about breakthrough research in myelin toxin, which the Soviets had been able to hide inside a common strain of tuberculosis. When Yeltsin took over, Palatnik called time on his days as an agent. Wanted to get out. The idea was to set him up with a new life in the West.'

'Wasn't that straightforward after '91?'

'You might have thought so.' Kite switched off the air conditioning and lowered a window. 'Ten months after the collapse of the Soviet Union, WALTER was still under round-the-clock KGB surveillance, forbidden to leave the country.'

'How come?'

'He was too important. Russia was undergoing a brain drain, scientists leaving left, right and centre. They wouldn't give him a passport.'

'And they had no idea he was working for us?'

'Correct.'

A mother and child stepped onto a zebra crossing on Chiswick High Road. Kite braked, waiting for them to pass.

'Long story short, one of our officers succeeded in spiriting Palatnik across the border into Belarus.'

'*Spiriting*,' Cara repeated, teasing Kite for being unnecessarily euphemistic. 'How did he do that, then? Séance? Hot-air balloon?'

'*She*,' Kite replied, not in the mood for joking around. He kept thinking about Palatnik's last moments, the horror of what had been done to him. 'The exfil was carried out by a woman.'

'I stand corrected.'

'So Mr Palatnik goes to Washington, gets himself a new identity, an American wife, sinecure at the Pentagon, worked there until 2009 before retiring to the suburbs of Connecticut.'

'How do you remember all this so long afterwards?' Cara asked.

'I've always been lucky with my memory.' Kite took his

hand off the gearstick and tapped a temple. 'Stuff goes in, it never comes out.'

'Memory is a talent,' she replied. 'Mine's not bad. I think you're either born with it or you're not. Like being good at chess or playing the piano.'

'Yes, but annoyingly talent is never enough, is it?' Kite swerved around a hubcap lying loose in the road. 'Memory is a muscle. Needs exercise.'

He was playing the boss, trying to teach Cara while at the same time not being entirely truthful with her. Kite remembered so much detail about Palatnik because it was Palatnik who had put BOX on to Yuri Aranov, the brilliant young scientist who had worked on the myelin toxin programme at Biopreparat. Aranov was as much a part of the furniture of his mind as Martha Raine, Cosmo de Paul and his late mentor, Michael Strawson. They had all been principal players in a wretched, chaotic summer twenty-seven years earlier when Kite had been sent to Voronezh to extract Aranov.

'This was definitely a Russian operation,' said Cara. It sounded like a statement, not a question. They had reached a second zebra crossing in Hammersmith and were again obliged to wait, this time for a beret-wearing hipster and an old man in a three-piece suit shuffling in opposite directions. 'I mean who else burns an old man's eyes out with a Novichok?'

'Unless somebody wanted to make it look like a Russian operation, for reasons we don't yet understand,' Kite replied. 'But, yes, we can assume the order came from Moscow. Evgeny survived undiscovered for three decades, but they eventually found him. What's strange is why now? The world is asleep. Why do it when the risk of getting caught is so much greater? Why antagonise the Americans?'

'Maybe this was their only window of opportunity.'

Kite agreed but did not say so. He was busy wondering how Palatnik had been run to ground. The CIA had been responsible for his welfare. Had they become sloppy or was there a breach at Langley? Perhaps the Russians had simply got lucky.

He put these questions – and others – to Azhar Masood, his second-in-command, as soon as they reached the offices in Chelsea.

'How did they find out where Evgeny was living?' Kite asked. 'Post-Skripal, everyone on JUDAS was supposed to be closely watched.'

Masood – known as 'Maz' at The Cathedral – was the tall, good-looking, thirtysomething son of a Pakistani father and Irish Protestant mother who had worked for BOX 88 for more than a decade. Unflappably calm, he expected people to be considerate, principled and kind: when they were not, his natural courtesy became a mask disguising impatience, displeasure and, on rare occasions, ruthlessness. Kite had described him to Cara as the most loyal man he had ever worked with.

'Unsure at this stage,' Masood replied. His voice was quick and thorough. 'Palatnik was well into his seventies. Maybe he got sloppy, started showing off to someone in the Russian community about his mysterious past. Met a woman, wanted to impress her. Who knows?'

Not Evgeny, thought Kite. Palatnik was always methodical, always cautious, dedicated to the memory of his late wife. It was Aranov who had been the reckless womaniser. More likely he was spotted on the street, a face in a crowd on television, and Moscow joined the dots.

'We don't have responsibility for most of the agents on JUDAS,' he explained to Cara. 'Vauxhall were meant to be babysitting Skripal. With Litvinenko they got careless. Palatnik was CIA. But we still need to check our pucks.' 'Pucks' was BOX slang for former agents living under new identities. 'Make sure their security protocols are being observed, let them know what's happened.'

'Aren't they going to find out soon enough?' Cara asked, indicating several television screens bolted to the walls tuned to news channels in six different languages. 'Only a matter of time before the story breaks. Then the whole world goes mad. As if coronavirus wasn't bad enough . . .'

'Didn't you hear?' said Masood.

'Hear what?'

'Langley has taken care of it. Whoever found him was Agency. Realised what had happened, called it in. The cabin was so isolated only a few locals noticed what was going on. Anybody asked why there were guys in hazmat suits wrapping the scene in polythene, they blamed it on Covid.'

'You mean nobody knows this has happened?' Cara asked.

'Nobody in the UK outside these four walls.' Masood picked up a paper clip and pulled it apart in his fingers. 'Better that way. The Cousins knew the White House wouldn't do anything meaningful. They'd say how disgusted they are, the ambassador might be summoned for a rap on the knuckles, Putin would deny having anything to do with it. Same old story. By the time Bellingcat had put the scoop online, the bad guys would have been back in Moscow for a month polishing their Orders of Lenin.'

Kite walked away from the bank of televisions.

'Anything from MOCKINGBIRD?'

MOCKINGBIRD was a high-level BOX 88 source inside the FSB, close to Director Makarov, who had lain dormant for much of the previous year.

'Nothing,' Masood replied, pouring three plastic cups of water from a cooler in the corner of the near-deserted office and passing them around. 'Still keeping a low profile. If he knew Palatnik was a target, he certainly didn't say so.'

Kite absorbed this, wondering why the stream of information which had flowed from MOCKINGBIRD for so long had suddenly stopped. Perhaps he had concerns about security. Perhaps he was laid low with Covid. More likely it was simply agent burn-out. Sooner or later MOCKINGBIRD, like the rest of them, would want out.

'What else does Langley have?' he asked.

'Considering that it's been less than thirty-six hours, quite a lot.' Masood had made a ring of the paper clip, wrapping the wire around his index finger. 'There was CCTV at the cabin. They got a face. Middle-aged male disguised as a postman who entered the property shortly after Evgeny went fishing, presumably to switch the eye solution. Match for an FSB officer wanted in connection with two other Novichok attacks in Russia. Vasily Zatulin. Langley associates him with an SVR illegal, Virginia Terry, living under native cover; she's already on an FBI watchlist.' Masood nodded at Cara, seemed to notice her red dress for the first time. 'Female. Millennial. Your generation.'

'So the Yanks let her go home, they'll keep an eye on her, try to pull down her network?' It was what Kite would have done in similar circumstances.

'We must assume so, yes,' Masood replied. 'If they're doing their job properly.'

'And Zatulin?'

Kite finished his water. He tossed the empty cup into a recycling bucket marked 'SUPPOSEDLY SAVING THE PLANET'.

'Already on his way home. Lands in five hours. Langley wasn't interested in a tail. I've got three Falcons picking him up at Sheremetyevo. They'll house him, see where that leads us.'

'Good,' Kite replied. A 'Falcon' was BOX 88 slang for a surveillance officer. 'We need to know who ordered the hit on Palatnik. Was it Kremlin-sanctioned or FSB off-piste? All the agencies have access to JUDAS, they tick the names off whenever they want Vladimir's attention. Is this the beginning of a new wave of assassinations that's been thought through at a political level or sheer opportunism?'

'I'm talking to New York tomorrow, soon as they wake up.' Masood tugged his earlobe, mentally running through a checklist of all the things he still needed to do. 'Should know more by then.'

Kite had moved beside a window overlooking a deserted residential street. BOX 88 had moved out of Canary Wharf in the spring as a temporary measure: the office workers who usually provided personnel with sufficient natural cover to come and go as they pleased were no longer around. The Chelsea offices, one of several residential blocks in London controlled by BOX 88, were smaller and more discreet. Under normal circumstances, Palatnik's assassination would have been analysed by up to thirty Sunday staff, the room buzzing with reports, rumours, strategies. Now it was just three of them in a slow season. Kite doubted that MI6 even knew that Palatnik had been hit. Langley wouldn't have shared the news with them. Why risk the loss of face?

'Moscow won't like it,' he said, at first to himself, then louder so that Cara and Masood could hear. 'Their people risked their lives handling the Novichok. The operation was a success, they'll be expecting a media blitz. Hitting someone in America is a game changer. They wanted to send a message.'

'And instead they get silence,' Cara observed. 'So what does that mean?'

'It means Moscow will want to know why. They'll be spooked by the American reaction. They can't go publicising it without incriminating themselves. Their bots can start some chatter on social media, but the moment has passed. Either they write it off as a missed opportunity or they take a holiday and go again.'

'Meaning they try someone else.' Masood pursued Kite's line of thought. 'They'll want to know if the media blackout is new Five Eyes policy or if Palatnik was just an anomaly. So next they go to a place that's worked for them before, an environment which gives them the result they're looking for.'

Cara saw what both men were thinking. A softer target.

'They'll come here, won't they?' she said. 'They'll try the UK again.'

'Possibly,' Kite replied.

'Can you give us two minutes?' Masood asked.

Cara seemed surprised but not affronted by the request; several times she had been left out of meetings involving the top brass. It was the way things worked when you were making your way up through the ranks. Nevertheless, Kite was puzzled by the decision to exclude her.

'What's up?' he asked.

27

Masood hesitated, making no effort to disguise his concern. He invited Kite to sit down.

'JUDAS,' he said.

'What about it?'

The younger man reached behind him for a computer printout. Kite saw that it was a list of names typed on two sides of A4.

'I wasn't being one hundred per cent honest about MOCKINGBIRD.'

'He's given us something?'

Masood tapped the piece of paper. 'This came through this morning, possibly as a reaction to the Palatnik hit. The first thing MOCKINGBIRD has sent in months.'

'Go on.'

In the way that you can sense the onset of a sudden storm on a day of glorious sunshine, Kite somehow knew what Masood was going to tell him.

'There's a new name on the JUDAS list at 62. Who is Peter Galvin?'

Masood passed him the piece of paper. Kite studied the list of targets. There was a blank space next to 47, another where Skripal had been listed at 58 before SIS had moved him offshore and given him a new identity. Masood had circled a name next to JUDAS 62.

Kite leaned back, stunned. He understood immediately what had happened. Disguising his disquiet, he folded his arms across his chest and told Azhar Masood what he needed to know.

'A long time ago, BOX sent me to Russia to bring back a scientist. The alias I travelled under was Peter Galvin. Looks as though Moscow wants my head on a plate. JUDAS 62 is Lachlan Kite.'

4

The Aranov operation had cost Kite a great deal, personally and professionally. Peter Galvin was an almost-forgotten name from his past. Now the legend was again in circulation. It had taken him twenty-seven years, but Mikhail Gromik was finally ready to come after him.

'Why now?' asked Masood. 'You're not a traitor to the Motherland. Galvin doesn't fit the profile of a JUDAS target. They're always Russians.'

'A provocation, I imagine.'

Cara knocked on a glass dividing wall to see if it was OK to come back in. Masood shook his head and waved her away.

'How so?' he asked.

'Maybe the Russians realise they've got a leak, that Langley knows who's on JUDAS. They've put Galvin on to spook us.' Kite knew that this theory was fanciful, but caution was preventing him from being forthright with Masood. 'They only have a name, but are counting on British intelligence spending the next twelve months wasting their time trying to protect him.'

'Or,' said Masood pointedly.

'Or what?'

'Or it's more than that. Somebody who was involved in the Aranov operation from the Russian side has always wanted Galvin's head on a block. They are finally in a position to act.

Yet that would go against decades of understanding between the competing services. We never target fellow intelligence officers. It's an iron law.'

'Which makes Galvin's appearance on the list all the more baffling,' Kite replied. He wondered if Masood had read the Aranov file; Gromik's name was all over it. Yet that seemed implausible. If he had done so, why conceal that? 'When MOCKINGBIRD was first recruited, he told me that Moscow had never established the link between Peter Galvin and Lachlan Kite. It was 1993, after all. There was no LinkedIn, no Twitter, no facial recognition. The physical resemblance between the man I am today and the student who left for Voronezh in July of that summer is, I regret to say, minimal. I doubt any of them would recognise me even if I was put into a line-up at the Lubyanka.'

'What about Cosmo de Paul?' Masood replied.

Kite was caught off guard.

'What about him?'

Only three people knew about the BOX 88 investigation into de Paul, a contemporary from his Alford school days who had dogged his personal and professional life for three decades. According to Ward Hansell, the senior American officer leading the investigation, de Paul had revealed the existence of BOX 88 to a suspected SVR illegal in New York.

'Does de Paul know what happened in '93? Does he know that you went to Russia?'

'He knows,' Kite replied. 'At least, he knows that I went to Voronezh in a hurry and came back under a cloud.'

Masood hesitated. He could sense Kite's reluctance to talk about the past.

'And Hansell doesn't yet know if the person de Paul spoke to in New York is SVR?'

'Correct. He's still under investigation. The fact that it's Galvin's name on JUDAS and not mine would indicate that Moscow hasn't yet worked out that we're one and the same person. In other words, whoever de Paul spoke to may not have been as dangerous as we thought he was.'

Masood appeared to accept the logic of this and broke off from the conversation to read a text message.

'Have you read the Aranov file?' Kite asked.

'Should I have?'

'Just wondered.' Kite knew that it would only be a matter of time before Masood, who was as inquisitive as he was thorough, learned everything about the Voronezh operation. 'Perhaps you should. Whoever organised the hit on Palatnik likely knew that he worked with Aranov at Biopreparat. That might have led them to Galvin.'

'Why don't you just tell me what happened.' Masood had a friendly, courteous manner, a way of coating even the most invasive questions in a layer of polite enquiry. 'I don't need to read the file. I just need the famous Kite memory. You know the principal players, the threats we may be facing. If the people who did this to Palatnik find out who you are, they'll come for you. You're on the JUDAS list. That isn't something to take lightly.'

'I'm perfectly safe,' Kite replied, though he did not believe this. The idea that he was vulnerable to Gromik and to the scum who had murdered Evgeny was abhorrent to him. 'They're not going to come knocking on my door.'

Masood looked as unconvinced by this as Kite might have expected. They both knew he was on shaky ground.

'Tell me about de Paul,' he said. 'Where does the animus come from?'

'How long have you got?' Kite walked back to the window. Far below, Cara was talking on the phone, her red dress a dollop of colour against the grey street. 'We met at Alford.'

'That fucking school,' muttered Masood.

'Later he went to Oxford. With Martha. That's when the trouble started.'

There was silence. A member of staff walked past the glass window and raised a hand to acknowledge them. Masood looked as though he was wondering how best to frame his next question.

'Martha,' he said simply.

Kite turned. Did Masood already know the truth?

'What about her?'

'Who is she? What's the story? A lot of rumours flying around.'

'I don't do the personal stuff, you know that, Maz.'

'I'm not interested in your personal life, Lockie. Unfortunately in this instance it's unavoidable. The personal is operational.' He moved towards him. 'Martha is obviously key to all this. So what's the story? Is she the one that got away?'

5

That's exactly who she was, Kite thought, walking home an hour later. *The one that got away.*

He had declined to tell Masood any more than he might find in the BOX 88 files relating to Yuri Aranov which were secured in the vault at The Cathedral. Kite had encouraged him to go to Canary Wharf and to familiarise himself with the details of what had happened in Voronezh. There was no need to speak of Martha, he said, no purpose in telling a colleague what had happened all those years ago. Maz could read the report and draw his own conclusions. Kite's private memories were his to keep; he had never revealed them to anyone, not even Isobel.

He knew that he was being stubborn and obstructive; pride was clouding his judgement. When his relationship with Martha had finally ended and she had moved to New York, Kite had spent years carefully rebuilding his life, eventually finding happiness with Isobel. He had risen to the top of BOX 88, doing the job that Michael Strawson had once done, touring the world, hatching plans, visiting BOX personnel in all five continents to make sure things were running smoothly. There had at last been some semblance of order and balance to his days. Now it felt as though every element of that new life was being pulled apart. Kite was estranged from his wife; he had no access to their newborn child. Thanks to the slippery tongue of Cosmo de Paul, the existence of BOX 88 – and his own involvement with the agency over three decades – was now potentially an open secret in Moscow. Already Kite was living in a version of witness protection, moving between a series of safe houses during lockdown as a precaution against further attacks by the Iranians. If Gromik wanted Peter Galvin dead, Kite would be forced into permanent hiding and his career brought to an abrupt end. In an agitated mood, he texted Hansell in New York.

Any news on our Russian friend?

The American responded immediately.

Hey. Still waiting. No news is good news, right?

Kite slipped the phone into his pocket. He found himself walking past Colbert, the mock-French brasserie on the eastern side of Sloane Square which always made him think of Alford and his teenage years in Chelsea. Back then, Colbert had been called Oriel, an eighties wine bar in the Thatcher style, one part Langan's, one part Colefax and Fowler. On an autumn afternoon in 1986, the fifteen-year-old Kite had come face to face with the appetites of men for the first time. He had been waiting to meet Xavier Bonnard at a table near the window, biding his time with a book and a cigarette, doubtless thinking about girls. Looking up, Kite had spotted Stuart Millar, the father of one of his friends, sitting on a stool at the bar. He had been about to go over and say hello when he saw the young woman beside him place her hand on Millar's thigh. At the same time, Millar put his arm around the woman's back and squeezed her waist. Kite had been profoundly shocked. He said nothing to Xavier when he arrived, by which time Millar and the woman had left. Only in later years did he realise that what he had witnessed was as commonplace as tinsel at Christmas: a man and his mistress riding the merry-go-round of adultery and imminent divorce.

Gazing into the window of Colbert, Kite reflected that he was now, in all probability, older than Millar had been on that not-so-innocent autumn afternoon. Just three years later Kite had been recruited into BOX 88; four years after that, Strawson had sent him to Voronezh.

For Kite to think back to the man he had been in the summer of 1993 was to remember a different person: richer in feelings, hungry for experience and obsessed by the possibilities and complications of sex.

He had matriculated at the University of Edinburgh in the autumn of 1990, telling Strawson that he wanted to take a step back from the secret world. Judging that Kite would benefit from earning a general arts degree, the American had given his blessing. Thereafter Kite had lived the life of a run-of-the-mill undergraduate, sharing a flat with two fellow students, attending half a dozen lectures every week and working in a pub in Leith to raise some extra cash.

Edinburgh was ancient, damp and beautiful. From September to April the city was grey and cold; it rained almost constantly. Kite had grown up on the west coast where the gulf stream warmed the seas; in 'Auld Reekie' there was a permanent chill in the air. The long winter nights smelled of hops and malt. Kite lost himself in books and new friendships, waiting for the clear, sparkling light of summer. It took time to adjust to the fact that he was no longer an Alford schoolboy at the mercy of a callous housemaster; this was a new life with few rules in which he was entirely free. The cobbled streets of Stockbridge and the dilapidated university campus were his new home. Martha, who had been Kite's girlfriend since the operation in France, had gone to Oxford to study English. By spending the holidays together and making regular trips across the border to see one another during term time, they had managed to keep the relationship alive.

As much as any man of twenty-two can understand what it means to love another person, Lachlan Kite loved Martha Raine. She was his closest friend, his confidante, the fulcrum of his life. They wrote letters to one another, spoke on the phone two or three times a week, went travelling around Greece and Turkey in successive summers. Martha sent presents to Edinburgh in the post – mix tapes of the music she was listening to, fluffy dice for Kite's Ford Cortina – and turned up on a whim to surprise him, on one occasion hiding in his bedroom and jumping naked out of a wardrobe. He in turn took the relationship extraordinarily seriously. He read the books that Martha was studying at Oxford so that he could talk to her about them. If she went to a movie at the Phoenix in Jericho, he would seek out the same title at the Filmhouse or the Cameo, then call her about it when he returned home. Martha became friends with his flatmates just as Kite got to know her fellow students at St Hilda's. At first he was secretly glad that she had chosen an all-female college; jealousy of Martha's many suitors had become one of his least commendable characteristics. Fearing that he would lose her if he went abroad to study in his third year, Kite had remained in Edinburgh, much to Strawson's displeasure.

'Wasted opportunity,' he said with his customary bluntness when they met for dinner in 1992 at Chez Jules, a small French restaurant just below the Royal Mile. It was a few days after Black Wednesday and the place was almost empty. 'I know a bit about women, Lockie, and I know this: if you and Martha are going to end up together, you're going to need to break up at some point. No way you go from here, aged twenty-two, to getting married and living happily ever after without one of you blowing a fuse before your fortieth birthday. You should have gone away on Erasmus, lived in Paris or Barcelona for nine months. Got any idea how much you'll regret not doing that by the time you're my age? Martha could have visited you. And so what if she didn't? So what if she ended up dating some Tarquin or Horatio from the Bullingdon Club? Maybe she needs to get away from you before she settles down, have an affair with a Keats-quoting poetry professor with halitosis and a sherry habit. That's what being a student is all about! Same goes for you. You're suffocating yourself, suffocating her. What twenty-two-year-old man of sound mind turns down the chance to live in Paris, for God's sake?'

Kite had felt humiliated. He knew that he had made bad decisions, he realised that he had been too sentimental, too anxious about losing Martha. Strawson had seen the change in him. Kite wondered if he would be welcomed back into BOX 88 after graduation or if the decision makers at The Cathedral would now consider that he had lost his edge. Worse, it was too late to change his mind and apply for a place at a foreign university.

'I've got plenty of time to live abroad,' he said unconvincingly. He had a very rare steak in front of him and prodded the flesh with his fork. 'If Martha and I have to break up, I don't see why it has to be now.'

'You've always had your head up your ass where that girl's concerned,' Strawson told him. He was an imposing, thick-set Virginian with slate-grey eyes and a Hemingway beard. 'In Mougins it was the same thing. Not healthy to have another person cast a spell on you like that. Especially not a woman.'

Kite wanted to protest but knew that Strawson was right. Ever since the BOX 88 operation in France, which had cost the life of his mentor, Billy Peele, Kite had clutched at Martha for stability. Who else was going to provide it for him? His mother was modelling again, living in Dulwich and flying off on a moment's notice to Spain or the Caribbean to shoot campaigns for Next and C&A. His father had been dead for almost a decade.

'We have to learn how to survive as individuals, Lockie.' Strawson had always possessed a talent for reading Kite's thoughts. 'We have to stand on our own two feet in life. Nobody else gets to prop us up. It doesn't work that way.'

'You mean at BOX?'

Strawson seemed surprised that Kite had failed to understand what he was trying to tell him.

'Not at BOX, no.' The American was eating hake. He separated the skin from the flesh with a brisk sweep of his knife. 'I'm talking about a person's ability to function in the world as an adult, period. We are all fundamentally alone.'

'That's bullshit,' Kite replied. 'I totally disagr—'

'Can I finish?' Strawson put his cutlery down, sounding agitated. 'Right now you think your sun sets and rises with Martha Raine. Soulmates. Secret sharers. Bound together like a helix.' He clasped his hands over the table, bending the fingers back to illustrate his point. 'Am I right?'

'I love her, yeah.'

'What does that even mean? You telling me you don't go out at night, to clubs, bars, see a girl you like, want to take her home? You're serving seven-hour shifts in Leith and no customer ever hits on you? I know it's cold in Scotland, but Scottish people still take their clothes off, right?'

Kite knew that it was Strawson's custom to provoke, to take a contrary view as a way of testing him.

'Is this the wild oats conversation?' he asked.

'Excuse me?'

'Is this where you tell me it's important to sow my wild oats while I'm still young?'

'None of my business what you do, Lockie. Just trying to stop you making lousy choices.'

It was late September. Martha was about to enter her final year at Oxford. Kite was not scheduled to graduate for another two years. As he chewed his steak, he reflected on the myriad temptations of student life. There were indeed women – the wild-eyed divorcee who drank in the pub most nights when Kite was working; the Canadian student, Josephine, who had made a pass at him at a party in May; his beautiful neighbour, Vicky, who was in her final year studying medicine and made a point of talking to him whenever they passed on the stairs. Clubbing on weekends at Tribal Funktion and Pure, Kite would get high and dance for hours with girls who wrapped him in their bodies, walked the streets at 5 a.m. with strangers in miniskirts who invited him home for coffee. Yet he had never cheated on Martha. He had developed a system for slipping away, of making last-minute excuses, waking the next day to feel the intense relief of not having succumbed to temptation.

'You kids put so much pressure on yourselves while you're still so young,' Strawson observed. 'But when it comes to Martha, you have a very serious problem.'

Kite wasn't sure that he had heard correctly.

'Excuse me?'

The American speared a chunk of hake.

'Does she know about Mougins? Does she know the truth about Ali Eskandarian? Does she know what happened to Billy?'

Three years had passed since Billy Peele had been killed in France; it wasn't like Strawson to talk about him, to be reminded of the loss.

'No, of course not,' Kite replied.

'Exactly. So she only knows part of who you are. Because you won't show her the rest. You *can't* show her the rest.'

Kite couldn't work out what Strawson was trying to achieve. Was this still a pep talk? Or was he offering him a choice between Martha and BOX, implying that he wouldn't be able to have both?

'I don't understand what you're trying to tell me. That I should break up with Martha? That nobody in BOX can have a relationship? That I have to choose between my private life and my working life?'

'Do you want to choose?'

'You have a wife!' Kite replied, raising his voice sufficiently for the manager of the restaurant to look over at their table. 'I've seen pictures of her. You have children together. Does she know what you do for a living?'

'That's between me and Amy. Got nothing to do with anyone else.'

'What do you tell her?'

'Same as we all do. That I work for the American government.'

39

'So that's what I'll tell Martha when the time is right. That I work for the British government.'

'When the time is right.'

Strawson's reply hung in the air like a lure on the surface of a lake. Kite swallowed it.

'Hang on,' he said. 'I'm on sabbatical. Have been for the last two years. Just trying to live a normal life. That's what we agreed.'

'Indeed it is. But you've been through basic training. If you're going to come back to us, sooner or later you're going to need to address the Martha question. Either you tell her who you are and what you've done, or you spend the next ten years pretending to be one kind of man when in fact you're somebody different altogether. And that's not fair on her. Not fair on you either. It'll almost certainly lead to disaster.'

Strawson had pinned Kite on the impossible hypocrisy of his position. Secrecy was the faultline running between the two halves of his life. He wanted to be in a relationship with Martha, yet he also wanted to have a career with BOX 88 after graduation. Strawson was merely pointing out what had been obvious for some time: Kite was having his cake and eating it. He took everything that Martha could provide – her intelligence, her loyalty, her body, her love – and responded in kind with an incomplete version of himself. He had no wish to tell her about his recruitment, even less of a desire to explain that in the summer of 1989, when they had been falling for one another at Xavier's house in Mougins, he had been spying on his best friend's family. On the surface the relationship was healthy and robust; underneath, it was being eaten away by secrets.

'I don't want to tell her just yet,' he said, resenting the fact that Strawson had made him feel so uncomfortable. 'The timing's not right.'

'And why's that?'

'Because she would leave me.'

'That's not the reason.'

Somebody across the room – one of only six other customers in the restaurant – knocked over a glass of water and swore loudly in German.

'It's not?'

'You don't know that Martha would leave you if she found out who you really are. She might even like the idea. She might find it exciting. How the hell can you anticipate how she'll react?'

'You don't think I know her well enough to predict how she'd feel?'

The American raised his glass in a gesture of solidarity and suggested that they let the subject drop.

'Look. Forget about it. None of my business. I'm just trying to make you think about things in a different way. You're smart, Lockie, but when it comes to women no man of twenty-two is *that* smart. I'm sure you've thought about all this and will do the right thing when the time comes.' They both looked down at their food. Across the room the German was mopping up the spilled water with the assistance of a consoling waitress. 'Have you thought about what you might do after you graduate?'

Kite felt his stomach tighten.

'I don't understand,' he said. 'I thought we'd already decided that I'll come back to BOX?'

Strawson grinned at the misunderstanding.

'Of course you will,' he said. 'But you'll need a cover job. Something that gives you flexibility.'

Finally the reason for Strawson's visit to Edinburgh had become apparent. He was thinking two years ahead, clearing the path for what was to come. The powers-that-be wanted Martha out of the picture so that Kite was unencumbered and ready for action as soon as he graduated.

'Flexibility,' he repeated, trying to gather his thoughts. He dreaded the 'milk round', banks and advertising agencies and law firms selling their wares to graduates; long train journeys to London for tests and interviews; then forty years of the nine-to-five and a comfortable life in the suburbs. No thanks.

'I don't want to get pinned down by an office job,' he said. 'Wear a suit. Commute. Even if it means helping BOX out on the side.'

'No reason you'd have to.' Strawson moved a final chunk of fish around his plate, mopping up the sauce. 'Have you thought about the charity sector? Journalism? Any and every career that might allow you to take a few days off, get on a plane, find yourself in country X or city Y at a moment's notice. You get into freelance work – photography, writing, teaching French or Spanish – that would give you the flex- ibility we require. We'll be paying you, so there's got to be a reason for the money in your bank account, just as there's got to be a plausible excuse for why young Lachlan keeps disappearing for three months at a time.'

Kite was about to express surprise that he might be called away on an operation lasting three months, but thought better of it.

'I'd like to go abroad,' he said, trying to ease some of the strain around Martha. 'Live somewhere outside the UK. I've been studying Spanish since '91, Russian this year. It would be good practice.'

Strawson appeared surprised. 'OK,' he said. 'With the girl- friend in tow?'

'Who knows?' Kite shrugged and poured more wine. 'It's not clear what Martha will do after she graduates. We're just taking things one day at a time.'

6

We were both so young, thought Kite as he turned a corner in Belgravia. Life-size cut-outs of Boris Johnson and Donald Trump were embracing in the window of a dry cleaner. *We took ourselves so seriously.*

He reached the street door of his apartment block. For the previous fortnight he had been using one of the more salubrious BOX 88 properties in London, a top-floor penthouse with a bird's-eye view of the embassies encircling Belgrave Square. It was no remedy for the absence of his wife and child, nor protection against the threats to his career, but better than the damp basement in Neasden and the crumbling maisonette in Greenwich where he had lived during the first weeks of the pandemic. From the rooftop Kite could see the Shard and the London Eye; on most evenings it was possible to make out the blinking lights of Canary Wharf where the shuttered Cathedral lay dormant.

In May, having returned from Stockholm in a dejected mood, Kite had purchased three artworks from his dealer in Mayfair: an etching by Lucian Freud; a charcoal drawing by Frank Auerbach of a standing female nude; and a modernist oil of Edinburgh Castle by Michael Andrews. In all, he had spent almost £150,000, telling himself that Ingrid would one day inherit the pictures and sell them for ten times that sum. He had yet to hang them; they did not belong on the walls of safe houses. Instead they lay against the back of a sofa in the living room, greeting Kite whenever he came home. He would hang them only when he was reconciled with Isobel and they had bought a new house together. It was something to look forward to.

As was his custom in the evenings, he rang Isobel in Sweden; as was Isobel's custom, she did not answer. Instead she sent Kite a WhatsApp message asking him to 'stop calling' and to allow her more time to make up her mind about the future. Seeing that Isobel was still online, Kite seized his opportunity.

Of course. How is Ingrid?

To his surprise, Isobel sent two photographs as well as a video of their child sleeping peacefully in her cot. Kite stared at her in wonder, astonished by how much she had grown. He longed to hold her again. He remembered the sweet warm smell on the top of his daughter's head just hours after she had been born, her fragile, tiny body almost weightless in his arms.

She's so beautiful. Thank you for sending these.

This time Isobel did not reply. Kite forwarded the photos to his mother's carer in Strawberry Hill, asking him to show them to her, and for a wild, illogical instant considered doing the same to Martha in New York. He wanted her to share his joy. Instead he set the phone to one side and fetched a bottle of Corona from the fridge. These days they were discounted by the case at every off-licence and supermarket in London. Kite went out onto the balcony, looked east towards The Cathedral, and lit a cigarette.

Martha. He wondered how she had coped through the Brooklyn lockdown. He wanted to ask her how her job was going, to enquire after her children. He knew that Cosmo de Paul had tried to contact her again; it had come up in Ward

Hansell's investigation. Surely Martha had been sensible enough not to think that sufficient time had passed and that it was now safe to tell de Paul their story? The same people who had murdered Evgeny Palatnik were looking for Lachlan Kite. It was not beyond the bounds of possibility that Martha herself might then be targeted. That thought was unconscionable.

Kite drew on the cigarette, looking down into Belgrave Square. A young couple were sitting on the grass, holding hands, lovers enjoying the innocent freedom of a warm summer night. The sight of them took him back to Edinburgh, his mind still full of memories of those distant student years.

After the 1992 discussion with Strawson at Chez Jules, Kite's relationship with Martha had continued into the following year. They had spent Christmas together in London and celebrated Hogmanay in Scotland, milling with the midnight masses on Princes Street as fireworks blasted in the new year. In March Kite had grown a beard and played Hirst in *No Man's Land* at the Bedlam Theatre, a production described by the university newspaper as 'solid, but posing no threat to Gielgud and Richardson'. In April, Martha had holed up at his flat in Edinburgh to revise for her finals, returning to Oxford in May. For the most part, they had been intensely happy. They argued only if it was about a girl who had shown an interest in Kite or a boy who was sniffing around Martha at Oxford. There was not an absence of trust between them, more an awareness that they were both young and attractive and might one day decide that a future with somebody else was more intriguing than the status quo with one another.

At the start of the summer term, Kite quit his job at the pub to work in a café in the Grassmarket where the hours and pay were better; he was able to see his friends during the day, slipping them cups of coffee and toasted sandwiches on the house. By the beginning of June, university life was winding down. Kite's great friend, Xavier Bonnard, who was studying English at Oxford in the same year as Martha, had arranged to have a fancy dress party in Gloucestershire to celebrate the end of finals. Kite was the only person to make the trip from Edinburgh, leaving at dawn in his prehistoric Ford Cortina and arriving at the house eight hours later.

Built in the eighteenth century by ancestors of Xavier's mother, Lady Rosamund, Penley Park was a seventeen-bedroom Georgian pile with half a dozen full-time members of staff and a seventy-acre botanical garden open to the public five months of the year. Kite had been going there ever since he was a wide-eyed thirteen-year-old schoolboy recently arrived from Scotland. He thought of the house as a place of unmatched luxury, a sealed-off playground where, as a teenager, he had enjoyed immense freedom and privilege. Life at Penley, with its swimming pool and croquet lawn and tennis court, felt like a time capsule of a vanished England, affording Kite a glimpse into a world of upper-class customs and values which would otherwise have passed him by. At the age of fifteen, he had smoked weed for the first time in Penley's labyrinthine wine cellars; two years later, he had dropped acid in the kitchen garden. There was a pub in the local village where he and Xavier were fixtures on summer afternoons and winter evenings, Xavier trying in vain to seduce the landlord's daughter while Kite played darts with whoever happened to be propping up the bar. In July and August they turned out for the village cricket team, a motley crew of local fathers and sons, many of whom worked on the Penley estate. Kite was the star batsman and had twice scored hundreds, earning himself a framed photograph in the pavilion under which Reg, the Penley gamekeeper, had written: 'Posh Lachlan's 174 not out – not bad for an Alfordian.'

To call Kite 'posh' was a misapprehension. Born in Scotland to an alcoholic Irish father and a mother who had been a model to David Bailey and Terry O'Neill, he had been sent to England's most famous boarding school at the age of thirteen, assimilating himself into a world of aristocrats, barristers and stockbrokers' sons as quickly and as seamlessly as he could manage. In his final term he had been recruited by BOX 88 and sent to France to report on an Iranian guest of the Bonnards who was suspected of involvement in the Lockerbie bombing. His efforts had resulted in the sentencing of Xavier's father, Luc Bonnard, to fourteen years in a Paris prison. With her husband's reputation in tatters, and the Penley name shaken by scandal, Rosamund had discreetly filed for divorce. Neither she nor Xavier knew anything about Kite's involvement in the operation which had brought Luc to justice. This was the black secret Strawson had touched upon in Chez Jules.

Martha had promised to come to Penley the night before the party so that she could spend some time with Kite, but at the last moment she left a message on the answering machine saying that she would be staying in Oxford. Kite wondered why. To go to another party? To be with Cosmo de Paul? Just as Martha was wary of the girls Kite encountered in the nightclubs and lecture halls of Edinburgh, Kite was suspicious of the manoeuvrings of de Paul, his Alford contemporary who had befriended Martha at Oxford, making no secret of his desire for her. When she had taken an interest in the situation in former Yugoslavia, for example, de Paul had made himself an expert on the conflict. When Martha revealed that she would be studying Restoration Comedy in her second year, he had angled his way into her lectures. Time and again Martha had reassured Kite that he was 'just a platonic friend', yet Kite suspected otherwise. Cosmo de Paul was a weasel who would stop at nothing to prise Martha away from him. Now she had been vague on the phone, sounding evasive and rushed, saying only: 'See you guys tomorrow, can't wait' before abruptly ringing off.

His suspicions intensified when Martha arrived the following evening. He was in his bedroom looking down at the drive when she pulled up in a black Porsche 907 driven by de Paul. Stylish as an actress on the red carpet, Martha climbed out of the front seat and kissed Xavier, who had been waiting by the front door to greet them. De Paul was next, embracing his host with a cut-glass cry of 'Bonnard!' before exchanging chit-chat pleasantries in his easy, tanned manner. He was barely taller than his trust fund sports car, but pumped up on himself and egregiously self-assured. In an instant Kite saw that de Paul's behaviour at Alford had long been forgotten; Xavier now saw him as a different person, interesting and even passably cool. The short, ambitious snake of their schooldays was now a short, ambitious charmer who had spent time in the gym, thrown money at a new wardrobe and won the respect and affection of the Oxford elite. Kite could hear Xavier admiring the Porsche, Martha saying how fast they had driven from Oxford. Spotting his own rusting, third-hand Cortina parked four hundred metres away near the stables, Kite decided to stay upstairs, a curtain-twitcher spying on his girlfriend, looking for tells in her body language.

There was a passenger in the back seat, a woman wedged in next to an overnight bag with her legs drawn up against her chest. Martha pulled her out onto the drive. This was Gretchen, the Rhodes scholar from San Francisco whom Xavier had reportedly been pursuing for weeks. She was short and pretty and wore ripped jeans, combat boots and a flannel shirt. There was an American looseness and energy about her which Kite instinctively liked. He took a step back from the window, closed the curtains and waited for Martha to come looking for him.

Moments later he heard her on the stairs, taking the old oak struts two at a time, pushing open the door of their room and exclaiming: 'Lockie!' as she wrapped her arms around him. Kite played it cool, acting as if he didn't know that she had arrived, shutting the door with his foot and throwing her onto the four-poster. Within seconds they were undressing each other – it was always like this – Martha whispering as Kite put a chair against the door to stop anybody walking in.

'You got rid of your beard!' she said, unbuttoning his shirt. 'That moustache looks ridiculous!'

Earlier in the afternoon, Kite had shaved off his Pinter beard in preparation for the fancy dress party: he was going as a Mexican bandit.

'Eez for the party, señorita,' he said, lost in the smell of her, the warmth of her skin, wanting to drive away any thought in her head of Cosmo de Paul.

'Just for tonight,' she replied, imitating his accent. 'But then it has to go, my friend.'

'Christ, I've missed you.' Kite was kissing her neck, her shoulders, de Paul braying in the hall downstairs. 'Where have you *been*?'

'I've been right here, my sweetheart,' she replied, pressing her hand to his heart. 'I've been right here.'

They were showering together half an hour later when there was a loud knock on the door of their bedroom.

'Lockie!' It was Xavier. 'Phone for you. It's in the study.'

Kite wondered who could be calling him. His flatmate with news of a leaking ceiling or a break-in? His mother, wondering when he was coming to London? Nobody else knew that he was at Penley for the weekend. He called out: 'Two minutes!', dried himself off and ran downstairs wearing a dressing-gown, his hair still wet. Two guests had already arrived and were milling around in the hall. One of them was dressed as an Oktoberfest beer maid, the other as Arnold Schwarzenegger in *Terminator 2*. A Doors track was coming to an end, Jim Morrison singing 'Break on Through' on a loop as another car pulled up outside. The phone was off the hook in the study. Kite picked it up.

'Hello?' he said. 'This is Lachlan.'

'I get you at a bad time, son?'

It was Strawson.

7

Kite pressed the telephone closer to his ear.

'Michael. Hi. How did you know I was here?'

It was a stupid question. BOX had eyes everywhere. Strawson knew everything.

'What's up at Penley?' he asked.

'There's a party tonight. End of finals.' A droplet of water fell from Kite's hair onto the green leather inlay of the antique desk. 'A lot of Xavier's Oxford friends coming. Fancy dress.'

'So I heard.' A pause. It sounded as though Strawson was gathering together a set of papers. 'Say, what are your movements this summer? How are you fixed?'

Kite knew instantly that he was being weighed up for a job. Why else would Strawson be calling him at Penley on a Saturday evening? He thought of Martha, who was hoping to leave for Croatia before the end of the month. Kite had assumed he would go out and visit her, but otherwise had no summer plans. Just shifts at the café, maybe a week in Spain with some university friends if they could get the money together. At some point he was going to have to write a dissertation about Lermontov's *A Hero of Our Time*.

'No firm plans,' he replied. 'Why?'

Another silence.

Send me on an operation, he thought. *Let me get back in the field and do something useful for BOX 88*. He wanted a break from students and parties and damp days in Edinburgh. More than that, he wanted to know that Strawson still believed in him.

'Can you meet me in London tomorrow?' the American asked. 'Something important has come up. If you can get things straight at your end, we could use your help.'

'Sure.' Kite turned and saw that somebody was standing near the open door of the office talking to Arnold Schwarzenegger. He couldn't make out who it was and wished that he had given himself more privacy. Then he remembered that he was supposed to be playing in a cricket match at midday on Sunday. 'Trouble is I'm meant to be playing cricket for the local village tomorrow.'

'What time would that finish?'

'Depends on the weather. Around six or seven usually. I could be in London by nine. That too late?'

'Not too late.' Kite remembered the exhilaration he had felt in Mougins four years earlier on his first job for BOX 88. Spying was a drug every bit as potent as the powders and pills Xavier had lined up for the party. If getting to London earlier meant pulling out of the cricket match, Kite would do it. 'Let's make it nine thirty in case you hit traffic,' Strawson suggested. He gave an address in Marylebone which Kite didn't recognise. He assumed it was a safe house. 'Call The Cathedral if you run into any problems.'

As he hung up, Kite realised that he would now have to take it easy at the party, do maybe only one tab of Ecstasy, stay off the booze and generally look after himself. He would need to be sharp at the meeting, enthusiastic and cooperative. Whatever Strawson demanded from him, Kite would agree to it.

'Who was on the phone?' Martha asked when he returned to their room.

Kite had come up with a suitable lie while climbing the stairs.

'The café in Edinburgh,' he replied. 'Wondering when I was coming back.'

Martha was naked. She had a leg raised up on a hard-backed dining chair and was applying moisturiser to her thighs.

'How did they have your number?'

'Gave it to them before I left. Told them I'll probably pack it in.'

She looked up. 'Why? I thought you needed the money?'

Kite had sensed an opportunity to lay the groundwork for what might lie ahead. If Strawson asked him to do a job for BOX 88, he would need to have a plausible reason for being out of the country.

'Might go away in the summer. Don't want to be tied down in Edinburgh.'

'Come with me to Zagreb!' Martha suggested.

Kite kissed her shoulder, passing her en route to the bathroom. He was hopeful that whatever task Strawson gave him would allow him the opportunity to go to Croatia at some point in the next few months.

'Definitely,' he replied. 'If you're not too busy. Is it all set up?'

'Looks that way,' she replied. 'I'll tell you about it later.'

He closed the bathroom door. Only then did he realise that Martha had not yet mentioned arriving at the house with de Paul. He wondered when she was going to bring it up.

The gong for dinner sounded at eight o'clock. By then all the guests had assembled downstairs in their costumes. Xavier had made jugs of Pimm's and triple-strength vodka and tonics; Martha and Kite walked around handing out warmed Marks & Spencer sausage rolls and bowls of Walker's crisps. Martha was dressed as Julia Roberts in *Pretty Woman*: knee-high black leather boots, a pale blue miniskirt attached to a cropped white bra via metal loops. Kite was wearing a poncho and sombrero with a plastic ammunition belt tied around his waist. Elsewhere he spotted Gretchen as Annie Hall, two Hannibal Lecters, a Roman centurion and a woman wearing tennis whites with a bloodied knife sticking out of her collarbone.

'Who are you meant to be?' Martha asked.

'Monica Seles.'

At dinner, Martha and Kite were seated at opposite ends of the vast mahogany table. De Paul was somewhere in between. Waitresses spooned *boeuf bourguignon* from porcelain tureens under chandeliers that glinted in the candlelight. By eleven o'clock, the four cases of wine Kite had opened earlier in the afternoon had been drunk; he had to go down to the Penley cellars with his old schoolfriend, Des Elkins, to find more. Every now and again Kite would catch de Paul looking in Martha's direction; he had a habit of glancing quickly at Kite to check that the coast was clear. Kite was aware that his jealousy was becoming corrosive; it was in part a reaction to the close-knit camaraderie of the Oxford crowd. At Alford he had always felt like an outsider, born into a different world, adjusting to the strange customs and traditions of that ancient school. He now understood that the English upper classes were generally harmless and well-intentioned, yet the guests at the party left him with a familiar sense of social isolation. It was perhaps for this reason that he made a beeline for Gretchen after dinner, presuming that an American would be similarly unmoored by the opulence of the party.

'This place is like Brideshead,' she said as they smoked in the larger of the two drawing rooms on the ground floor. A portrait of Rosamund's great-grandmother stared down at them from the wall. 'You know that book?'

Most people talked about the TV series or the teddy bear; Kite could tell that Gretchen had actually read it.

'Sure,' he said, lying. 'Fantastic novel.'

'Look at all this,' she continued, pointing at a stuffed stag's head bolted to the wall. On the marble mantelpiece beside her, a sepia photograph showed various Penley ancestors hunting lion in the Serengeti. 'In the States we have to go to the Smithsonian to see this shit. Or the White House.'

Xavier had told Kite that Gretchen had met the new American president, Bill Clinton, shortly before departing for Oxford.

'Xav told me you went to a Rhodes scholarship dinner in Washington,' he said. 'You met Clinton?'

'I did,' she replied, looking mischievous.

'What did you make of him?'

'Kind of sexy. Intense. Photographic memory. One of those guys who makes you feel like the only woman in the room.'

'If you're a woman, obviously,' Kite replied.

Gretchen's delighted reaction encouraged Kite to push his luck.

'So was there a bimbo eruption? Did anybody sleep with him?'

'Not that I was aware of.' Gretchen paused. 'But I fucked his special adviser.'

Kite laughed. He liked her instantly: she was quick-witted and intense with a quirky, expressive face. This unexpected insight into Gretchen's private life only confirmed his good opinion of her.

'Congratulations,' he said, trying hard to conceal his amazement.

'Why thank you.'

Across the room, Xavier was talking to a beautiful, dark-haired girl Kite didn't recognise. She was dressed as a native American Indian – fringed leather micro-mini, turquoise bead necklace, minuscule suede bra – and had her arm secured around Xavier's waist. Either they were sleeping together or she was trying her luck.

'Are you and Xav seeing each other?' he asked, wary of the answer. Gretchen tipped back half a glass of wine in one shot, emerged wide-eyed and said: 'Well, I certainly thought we might. More fool me!' She directed her gaze at the girl and puffed out her cheeks for comic effect. 'Then I get here this evening and realise your buddy is more interested in Pocohontas.'

'Who is she?' Kite asked.

'I dunno. Gabriella? Mariella? Mortadella? Something like that. Italian. Nice of him to tell me, right?'

It was typical of Xavier in this period of his life. At best he had unconsciously led Gretchen on and she had picked up the wrong signals; at worst he hadn't been expecting Pocohontas to show up at the party and had been keeping Gretchen in reserve. Kite was fiercely loyal to his friend and would say nothing critical of him, but he knew that Xavier's appetites – his greed for distraction and escape in whatever form he could find it – often ended up causing pain.

'I'm sorry,' was all that he said. 'At least you're here, you can experience all this. Sodom and Gomorrah by way of Evelyn Waugh.'

They looked around the room. On a nearby sofa, Gandhi was getting off with Princess Leia. In a distant corner, partly concealed by the raised lid of a grand piano, an old Alfordian from the year below Kite was tapping out lines of coke on the glass of an upturned family photograph; his girlfriend had rolled up a banknote and was bobbing her head to the tune of 'Fool's Gold'. Kite wondered which photo they were using: the one of Rosamund as a deb in *Country Life*, wearing jodhpurs and a pearl choker, or the picture of her father, the Earl of Penley, in his office at Cazenove's?

'Quite a sight,' said Gretchen, biting into an After Eight.

One of Xavier's friends from Manchester University approached them. He had a plastic Kalashnikov slung over his shoulder and was wearing a floppy Christmas hat. Across the front of his pale grey sweatshirt the words NOW I HAVE A MACHINE GUN HO-HO-HO were scrawled in red lipstick. Gretchen asked who he was meant to be, then remembered before he had a chance to answer.

'Oh I get it,' she said. 'You're the dude in *Die Hard*.'

The friend grinned. 'And you're Annie Hall,' he replied. 'Great movie.' From the hip pocket of his trousers he produced a bag of Ecstasy pills. 'Santa's here,' he said, the white bobble of his Christmas hat swaying from side to side. 'You two interested?'

'Not for me, thanks,' replied Gretchen. 'If I get sick and go to hospital, my mom would have a shit fit. Oxford would probably take away my scholarship. And we can't have Cecil Rhodes turning in his grave now, can we?'

Kite took one. 'Thanks,' he said. 'Kind of you.'

The friend moved on with a wave. Kite slipped the pill into his poncho.

'You not going to take it right away?' Gretchen asked.

'Later,' he replied. 'All about the timing, isn't it?'

He was thinking about the meeting in Marylebone, wondering what Strawson had meant when he had said: 'If you can get things straight at your end, we could use your help.' Was he suggesting that Kite end his relationship with Martha? Was that going to be a condition of the operation? Or was he preparing the ground for Martha to be told about BOX 88?

'I don't need Ecstasy,' Gretchen muttered, almost to herself. 'I'm horny enough already.' She shot Kite a confident, flirtatious smile. 'You're Martha's boyfriend, right?'

'I am.'

Right on cue, Martha wandered into the room. The *Reservoir Dogs* soundtrack was suddenly drowned out by the thump of a distant sound system playing Stone Roses. The party was spreading into different rooms; it seemed as though at least another forty people had arrived since dinner. Looking outside, Kite saw that the drive was packed with cars, the lawn covered in people. The house had become a dimly lit emporium of drugs and alcohol.

'There you are,' said Martha. She was drunk and had changed into a pair of denim shorts and a pale-yellow T-shirt.

'What happened to your outfit, Vivian?' Gretchen asked. Vivian was the Julia Roberts character in *Pretty Woman*. There was a tiny edge to the question, as if she hadn't approved of Martha inviting comparisons with the world's most beautiful actress.

'I discovered that if you dress up like a hooker, people will treat you like one.' Martha slipped an arm around Kite's back. 'I had my ass grabbed three times – always by women, by the way. Somebody else offered me two hundred pounds to

56

spend the night with him. I *think* he was kidding.' She kissed Kite on the cheek and said: 'Don't worry. I'm sure it was just a joke.'

Gretchen kept her counsel in a sip of wine. In that moment Kite wanted Martha to have greater self-awareness, to be more modest about her beauty, but she was in a careless, spirited mood and instead encouraged them to dance.

'Come outside!' she urged. 'Did you take one?'

'Just about to,' Kite replied, reaching into the poncho and pressing the pill between his thumb and forefinger.

'Not me,' said Gretchen evenly.

'OK, meet me on the lawn,' said Martha, blowing Kite a kiss. 'Bye, Gretchen.'

In the vacuum left by her exit, the American pulled back a loose strand of hair and attempted to secure it under her hat.

'This hat, man,' she complained, taking it off and throwing it onto the sofa. It landed within a foot of Princess Leia. A man of about thirty with long hair and a straggly beard walked past them; Kite couldn't tell if he was a genuine hippie or someone wearing a costume. When Gretchen said that she needed to use the bathroom, he went in search for Martha.

She wasn't outside. Cosmo de Paul was standing on the far side of the drive smoking a cigarette with Gideon Paine, heir to a banking fortune and a fellow student at Oxford. Both of them were in Bond black tie and giving off a hateful sense of malevolent superiority. De Paul looked over at Kite, held the eye contact and said something to Paine. Kite ignored them. They were the worst of an otherwise decent, blameless generation of privileged young men: entitled, arrogant and without compassion. Kite imagined that he could see their futures: Paine, a physically unattractive man, marrying young for the glamour of a beautiful bride who would settle for his houses and his lifestyle; de Paul using his family contacts to make some money in the City, then snaking his way into diplomacy or politics, anything that would one day serve him with a knighthood and membership at the Garrick.

Surrounded by laughter and music, Kite realised that his mood had become sober and pointlessly cynical; he needed to relax and enjoy the night. He would take the pill, find Martha, dance with her, maybe go out into the grounds of the estate later on and make love in a field as the sun came up. What better way to celebrate this first true night of summer than to fall asleep in the grass with the woman he loved, to play cricket on a Sunday afternoon and meet Strawson in the evening?

A few metres away, two of the lads from the village were drinking beer with Xavier. One of them, Martin, was dressed as Margaret Thatcher: blonde perm, blue dress, black handbag. The other, Nick, was kitted out as her successor, John Major, in a grey suit, grey tie and grey shoes. He wore pale, thick-rimmed spectacles and had covered his hair and face in chalky make-up; in the glare of the lights from the house he looked like a walking cadaver. Kite went over to talk to them. Half an hour later, having solemnly pledged to one another that they would turn up for Sunday's match, no matter how hungover they were, Kite went back inside. He found a bottle of San Miguel at the bottom of an ice bucket, swallowed the Ecstasy and renewed his search for Martha.

She was still nowhere to be found. Kite decided to remain in the larger of the two drawing rooms where guests were dancing to Bowie and Talking Heads; Des Elkins had set up decks on a mattress to stop the needle jumping. Kite saw old friends from school, each of them with plans to go away for the summer, met two German backpackers who had somehow ended up at Penley, but at no point ran into Martha. He waited for the pill to kick in, smoking cigarettes in rotation and swigging room-temperature Smirnoff from a plastic cup. He could feel himself getting drunk but not high. The Ecstasy wasn't working. Instead Kite started thinking about his father, the bottles of spirits hidden in the pockets of his suits, the glasses of orange juice laced with vodka at breakfast.

'You OK, Lockie?'

It was a friend of Martha's from London, coming off the dancefloor in a silver jumpsuit with NASA embroidered on the chest.

'Fine,' he said. 'Totally.'

The girl was high. She kissed him on the cheek then walked out of the room to get some air. Everyone seemed to be locked onto the music except Kite. There was a strange emptiness inside him, close to a sense of dread, a feeling he wasn't used to; he wondered if the pill was working in an opposite, depressive way. Was that possible? He walked out into the vast hall, the stuffed head of a huge stag staring down at him, and again looked around for Martha.

'Must have been going a hell of a speed to end up like that!' said a man in a Darth Vader helmet, gesturing up at the stag. Kite was too cheerless to answer. He heard Xavier's voice on the first floor, shouting to someone, and wondered if he had a joint that would settle his mood or – better still – a different pill that would lift it. Already he was long past any private promises to take it easy, to avoid getting too high or drinking too much. All he cared about was finding Martha, hanging out with her for a while and having a better time. He could wing it at dinner with Strawson.

Kite climbed the old oak staircase, looking down onto a scene of decadent excess: the MPs and captains of industry of tomorrow were stumbling from room to room soaked in dancefloor sweat, smoking and swigging from bottles of water. Two girls on a sofa in the hall, one of them stripped down to her bra and knickers, were necking like teenagers at a school disco. The hippie he had seen after dinner was rolling a joint beneath a priceless oil painting of Venice at dawn. Somebody shouted out: 'Tune!' as Des put 'Is There Anybody Out There?' by Bassheads on the sound system. It felt as though the whole house was shaking. Xavier suddenly appeared, topless and smashed, passing Kite on the way downstairs.

'Lockie!' he shouted, grabbing him in a sweaty hug. 'Come swimming, man. Gabriella's already there.'

Kite reckoned the water would liven him up and said he

would be out in a moment. He asked Xavier if he had another pill but received no answer; it was almost impossible to be heard above the growing soar of the music. For a moment, standing at the top of the staircase in that vast and ancient house, Kite experienced a vivid sense of dislocation not only from the people at the party, but also from himself. It was as though he was suspended between the two worlds in which he lived: his student life – attending lectures, going to the pub, making cups of coffee and cheese sandwiches in a Grassmarket café; and his other, secret existence for BOX 88. The contrast was so stark in his mind that he wondered if the pill was at last beginning to kick in. Yet his feelings were not euphoric: if anything they were uncharacteristically solemn and isolated.

Still no sign of Martha. Kite assumed he would find her outside at the pool. He changed out of the Mexican costume, quickly shaved off the moustache, put on a pair of jeans and a T-shirt and grabbed his swimming trunks. As he was preparing to go downstairs, two people came out of Xavier's bedroom at the far end of the corridor, one of them saying: 'I love this track' as Des put on 'Where Love Lives'. Suddenly Kite heard Martha's voice, a single shouted *'What?'* audible for an instant between the thudding piano chords, exclaimed as if in amused outrage at something somebody had said or done. It sounded as though she was on the second floor of the house. Kite put the trunks back in their room and walked upstairs. There were people smoking on the landing, a stoned pretty girl who gave him the eye and said: 'I liked your Mexican costume'. Martha was nowhere to be seen. Kite went into one bedroom and found five people doing coke off a marble chessboard. Another couple were under a duvet, giggling and kissing. The man was still wearing his socks. Next door, somebody was throwing up in a bathroom. Kite could hear retching and a girl saying: 'Poor you, sweetheart, let it all out.' He wondered if his ears had played tricks on him; perhaps Martha was outside by the pool and her voice had been warped by the Penley acoustics.

He went back down to the first floor, retrieved his trunks and walked along the passage to check Xavier's bedroom. The door had been closed. He turned the handle.

There were only two people inside. Martha and Cosmo de Paul. They were lying side by side on the floor, Martha's head resting on de Paul's chest, their eyes closed, the mellow flute of Herbie Mann playing on a hi-fi. Martha's T-shirt had ridden up and de Paul was softly walking his fingers over her bare stomach. With his other hand he was stroking her hair.

Kite was provoked to such anger that he kicked the door closed and advanced on them. The noise of the slammed door caused de Paul to open his eyes. He saw Kite and instinctively pushed Martha away from him so that he could stand up to protect himself. As he did so, Kite sent a right hook into the side of his head, catching the ear cleanly and sending him to the floor. The muscle memory of the interminable days of Kite's training had come back to him; Ray, the fight instructor, urging him 'not to hit the bloke in the face, not like the films, that just breaks your hand' but instead to target pressure points – ears, eyes, groins – and to inflict maximum pain with minimum effort. De Paul's legs were slightly apart. Kite slammed the sole of his shoe into his groin and pressed down, saying: 'You fucking snake' as he yelped in pain. He pushed harder as de Paul tried to wriggle free, aware that Martha had blinked out of her stoned euphoria and was saying: 'What the fuck is going on?' as she climbed to her feet.

Kite did not reply. He was sickened by her. De Paul tried to twist away and push himself up on one arm. He was stronger than Kite remembered, but it was easy to lean down and to catch him a second time with another hook to the ear, de Paul emitting a small, pitiful cry as Martha grabbed Kite's arms and tried to restrain him.

'Lockie! No!'

'Get the fuck out of here!' he shouted, filled with hatred. But Martha would not leave. De Paul, bleeding from a cut to the head, raised his hands in surrender and said: 'Jesus,

Kite, you've got the wrong end of the stick!' Kite laughed at the use of his surname, at de Paul calling on a spirit of faux public school camaraderie in the hope of being spared. He kicked him in the balls. There was a fractional delay before de Paul howled in pain and rolled over onto his stomach, gasping.

'Lockie, please!' Martha implored.

Kite pushed her to one side. Afterwards he could not remember if he had said anything else before walking out of the room, but she did not follow him. He packed his belongings into an overnight bag and went downstairs. There were large numbers of people sitting around in the hall, drinking and talking, the dancefloor in the drawing room packed. Gretchen passed him on the stairs. She looked sober and bored.

'What's up?' she asked, seeing the bag. 'What happened to your moustache?'

'I'm going to London,' Kite told her.

She didn't express surprise. Instead she said: 'Oh, really? Wait, can I come with you?'

Kite thought of Martha in de Paul's arms, his fingers on her stomach, and said: 'Sure, but I'm going now.'

'What's the hurry? What's happened?'

'Meet me outside. I'm going to get my car.'

Laughter and splashing from the swimming pool, the pop explosion of someone bombing into the water. Kite remembered his first night with Martha beside the pool in Mougins, carrying her weightless submerged body in his arms, then countless summer days on the beach in Greece and Turkey. He knew that he was too drunk to drive, but was determined to leave, to get to London and move on with his life. Fuck Martha. Fuck Cosmo. They had probably been having an affair all year. He lit a cigarette and took out his car keys.

'Hey, Lockie!'

Gretchen had already packed and was behind him on the drive. He waved her towards the Cortina, nobody outside paying them the slightest attention, only his old schoolfriend

Henry Urlwin, his face pockmarked by acne, sloping towards the house with a dishevelled girl on his arm, their clothes stained and untucked from rolling around on the grass.

'How's it going, Lockie?' he said. 'Great party.'

'Yeah,' Kite replied.

'This is Mary. Mary, this is Lachlan Kite. Brilliant bloke, bloody good batsman.'

Mary's lipstick had smeared on her face. She was cross-eyed drunk.

'Hi, Lachlan,' she said, pronouncing it in the Scottish way. 'Drive carefully.'

Gretchen reached the car as Henry and the girl walked away, saying only 'Hey there' as she passed them. There was a smell of perfume. Kite threw his bag onto the back seat.

'What happened?' she asked. 'Martha coming too?'

'Let's just go,' he replied. 'You got everything?'

Gretchen looked unsettled, as if she had signed up for something that she hadn't fully understood.

'You OK to drive?' she asked.

'I'm fine,' Kite replied and he started the engine.

8

They were about a mile from the motorway when the Ecstasy finally kicked in.

'Shit,' said Kite, veering slightly on the road. 'I'm rushing.'

Gretchen laughed. 'You're *what*?'

'Coming up. I took a pill. Ages ago. It just started working. Can you drive one of these? What do you call it? A stick shift?'

'Sure I can. Scoot over.'

Kite pulled the car into a lay-by and they switched seats. He had not yet told Gretchen about Martha and de Paul, but now did so. She listened quietly, at one point touching Kite's thigh with the tips of her fingers, and finally saying: 'Oh man, I'm so sorry, Lockie. Do you think you broke his jaw? That would be beautiful.'

He had not known that she disliked him. Kite was dizzyingly high, aware that his relationship with Martha was almost certainly over, but at the same time in a state of mellow fascination with Gretchen and the night to come. He watched her as she drove, never dipping under eighty miles per hour on the deserted motorway. The car was filled with the smell of her perfume. He was sure that she had sprayed herself before coming out of the house, just for him. His allegiance to Martha faded with every passing second, like a rock he had been holding in his hand which had disintegrated into fine dust. He felt released from any obligation to be faithful.

'You sure you don't want to go back?' Gretchen asked.

They were already more than an hour from Penley. It was almost four o'clock in the morning. Was she implying that he had overreacted by leaving? Kite looked across, surprised.

'Why would I do that?' Suddenly he remembered the cricket game and swore under his breath. He was letting his teammates down. He considered going back, but had no desire to involve himself in what would inevitably become a protracted argument with de Paul and his Oxford chums. The village team would be able to find somebody to replace him. Besides, Kite wanted to enjoy his high. Martha had inadvertently given him exactly what he wanted: freedom to go away for the summer and to work for BOX 88. Strawson would be pleased that they were taking time apart.

'I gotta tell you,' said Gretchen. 'I don't think they were sleeping together in Oxford.' She lit a cigarette and wound down the window. 'Maybe Martha was just really high, you know? Maybe they both were . . .'

'I saw what I saw,' Kite replied.

'Yeah, but what did you really *see*?'

'We're done.' He looked out at a passing field, the Ecstasy surging. 'It's cool. It's fine. It's over.'

'Well I guess that's good news for the rest of us.'

Gretchen turned and flashed Kite a smile that promised him everything. His chest felt full and breathless. He returned her gaze, thinking that her eyes were vast and clear.

'Did you take something?' he asked, but Gretchen just smiled and shook her head, looking out at the glowing road. Kite wished that he had taken more than one pill; the moment this one started to wear off he knew that Martha would be waiting for him on the other side.

'Music,' he muttered and slid a cassette into the player. It was a tape that Martha had made for him, the soundtrack from *The Double Life of Veronique* on one side, Chopin's Second Piano Concerto on the other.

'Easy there, grandpa,' said Gretchen as the first notes

sounded, a slow rolling melody on clarinet. 'Got anything that might keep me awake?'

Kite pressed eject and rummaged around in a case for something that wouldn't make her think he was a secret square. The music for which he had been ridiculed by his Alford friends stared up at him: Dire Straits *Love Over Gold*; Elton John *Too Low for Zero*, Supertramp *Breakfast in America*.

'Leonard Cohen?' he asked. 'Peter Gabriel? Rolling Stones?'

'Stones,' she replied, letting the cigarette catch on the wind of the open window so that it flew off into the night. 'Where are we headed, anyway? You got a place in London?'

Kite explained that his mother was renting a house in Dulwich, but he had no key.

'You can crash at mine,' she suggested.

'You have a flat?'

'Sure. In South Kensington. Belongs to my godmother. She's never there. We wouldn't have to skulk around.'

Skulk. Kite wondered where Gretchen had learned that word. He knew what she was telling him: no godmother, no interference. The Ecstasy took him up onto another plane of euphoria. He saw her hand on the gearstick and longed to touch it, to feel the contact of skin on skin. He remembered de Paul's hand in Martha's hair.

'You OK?' Gretchen asked, as if sensing the switch in his thinking. They were passing the Polish War Memorial, much closer to London than Kite had realised. Where had all the time gone?

'Totally fine,' he said. 'It's an amazing pill.'

'I'm glad,' she said. 'You're very sexy when you're high.'

He tried to think of something to say in response and asked her about the Rhodes scholarship. She said that 'all kinds of weird, famous people you wouldn't expect' had been scholars, 'not just Bill Clinton but Kris Kristofferson, Terence Malick, Naomi Wolf. Even George Stephanopoulos.' Kite wondered if Stephanopoulos was the man Gretchen had slept with at the White House and pictured them together, screwing in the West Wing.

'Is Stephanopoulos a special adviser?' he asked, hoping to lure her into an answer.

'Communications director. Like a press secretary. You know he's only thirty-two or something? Just a baby, six years older than me.' Kite hadn't realised that Gretchen was twenty-six. It made her even more alluring. 'So there you go. All of us have benefitted from the Will trust of a British imperialist diamond billionaire who raped Africa's natural resources and facilitated the slave trade. *Mazeltov!*'

Kite laughed, knowing that when they reached her godmother's flat, they were going to go to bed together. Gretchen would be only the fourth woman he had slept with, the first since Martha in the summer of 1989.

'How much longer do you think?' he asked.

'Almost there,' she said.

And so it came to pass. Gretchen parked the Cortina on Old Brompton Road, fixed them a Famous Grouse from Godmother Mary's drinks tray, went to the bathroom, leaving Kite uneasily waiting around as a clock in the book-lined sitting room ticked towards six o'clock, then suggested they make a snack in the kitchen. Suddenly, but inevitably, they were kissing beside the sink, Kite feeling almost that they should get it over and done with because the pill was wearing off and there was no point in just talking for hours, especially as Gretchen hadn't shown any interest in going to sleep.

It was wrong from the first moment. Her kiss was open-mouthed and devouring, moving her tongue and head in a way that Kite wasn't used to. He was now stuck in a situation with a girl he barely knew, tired and sapped of energy, thinking back to what Gretchen had said in the car: 'But what did you really *see*?' Inexorably she dropped to her knees, unzipped his jeans and went down on him. Kite, still standing, found himself staring at a chart on the facing wall detailing wine *appellations* in Burgundy: *Puligny-Montrachet, Chablis, Côte de Beaune*. He wanted what was happening to him to be happening to another person. He was worried that Martha was tending to the injured de Paul, perhaps even sleeping with him out of sympathy. It occurred to him that what he was doing was pure revenge. Gretchen stood up and suggested that they 'take this into the bedroom'.

Kite followed her – it was impossible to tell her what he was thinking, inconceivable that they should stop. His betrayal of Martha was all the more wretched because it was so joyless. He wanted to say: 'Look, we both know this is a mistake. Let's call it a night and try to get some sleep.' Yet it would have seemed rude, even cruel after what had happened in the kitchen, so they went to the spare bedroom, where Gretchen's godmother had left out a kettle and some teabags, and stripped out of their clothes while facing one another. Naked, Gretchen was white as chalk with black tufts of hair under her arms, a thing Kite had never seen on a woman before. She produced a condom from a drawer, an American brand he didn't recognise. Very soon, like a rushed audition for a play in which neither of them would eventually be cast, they were making perfunctory love. Gretchen seemed to pass into a separate version of herself, stiff and haunted, her eyes rolling up into her head, her gasps not sighs of pleasure but of a strange, wounded neurosis. Kite, perplexed, felt as though he was dancing with a partner who was listening to a different piece of music. Everything seemed forced and insincere. Then finally it was over and they lay beside one another on the narrow bed, sunlight pouring through a gap in the curtains.

Gretchen immediately went to the bathroom and locked the door. The snap of the lock was like an expression of her dissatisfaction. Kite looked down at his naked body and wondered how the hell he had allowed such a thing to happen. He wished that his life could suddenly run in reverse, like the moment in *Slaughterhouse Five*, a book Martha had urged him to read, when the fleet of American bombers over Dresden magically retrieve their bombs from the burning city, sucking the payloads back into the fuselage and returning to England intact. He stood up, pulled on his clothes and went to the kitchen to get a glass of water. He was hungry and searched the fridge for food, finding a jar of duck pâté from Partridges which, when he opened it, turned out to be caked in mould.

Then the telephone rang.

He looked at a clock on the kitchen wall, next to the chart detailing the wines of Burgundy. It was quarter to seven. He knew, with a feeling of empty dread, that Martha was trying to find him.

He heard the bathroom door opening and Gretchen picking up the phone in the hall.

'Hello?' she said. A beat. 'Martha, yeah, hi. What time is it?'

Kite stepped closer to the door. A floorboard creaked in the kitchen.

'Yeah, I did. Needed to get back. He told me what happened.'

If Gretchen says I'm in the flat and passes the phone to me, I'm finished, he thought.

'No, he dropped me here and said he was going on to his mom's place. He's not there?'

Kite's relief was total, but immediately tempered by the thought that Martha was searching for him. It showed that she was worried about him. He had no wish to speak to her until he was back at his mother's house. It sounded as though she had called there first. Kite had no idea if Cheryl was at home or somewhere else.

'OK, sure, if I hear anything I'll let you know.' Gretchen sounded so calm, so convincing. 'Try not to worry. I'm sure he's fine. He was just upset, that's all.'

When the call was over, Kite emerged from the kitchen and thanked her. Gretchen was wrapped in a towel, her skin pale and dry. She said it was no problem. She explained that Martha had called the house in Dulwich and left a message because there had been no answer. Kite seized his chance.

'I'd better go,' he said. 'My mum will be worried about me. I mean, if she listens to her answering machine.'

The plan seemed to suit Gretchen.

'Sure,' she said. 'Sounds like a good idea.' She did not point out that he had no key for the house nor ask what he intended to do if his mother was not at home. They both knew that what had happened had been a mistake. All of the intrigue and excitement they had felt in the car had vanished with the dawn. They were now almost strangers to one another. 'You OK to drive?' she asked. 'You want me to call you a cab?'

'I'll take the car,' Kite replied. 'It's not far.'

He could still taste Gretchen's perfume in his mouth as he walked outside to the Cortina. He lit a cigarette to smother it. He was hungry and tired, driving south to Dulwich along deserted Sunday streets, shops and restaurants shuttered. He reached his mother's house and rang the doorbell. The curtains in her bedroom window were drawn. It was almost eight o'clock.

A light came on in the hall. Kite heard the sound of someone coming downstairs.

'Who is it?'

A man's voice, not someone Kite recognised. The latest boyfriend, no doubt.

'It's Lachlan,' he said. He assumed that whoever was waking up next to his mother on a Sunday morning would know who that was.

'Oh, right.' Surprise tinged with wariness. 'Just a moment.'

Kite heard the rattle of the chain, the clunk of the lock. He could smell Gretchen again. The door opened and he was confronted by a man not much older than thirty, bearded and tanned, wearing his father's dressing-gown. For a sudden, startling moment, Kite thought that he recognised him as one of the staff at The Cathedral, but it was just his mind playing tricks on him.

'I'm Tom,' he said.

He was tall and physically fit. There was a wary look in his eye, dreading the next few moments. Kite put him out of his misery.

'Assume my mum's asleep?' he said.

'Yes.'

'I'm off to bed. If the phone rings, can you tell whoever calls that I'm out?'

'Sure.' Tom closed the front door behind him. 'Phone rang about an hour ago, in fact. We didn't pick it up.'

Kite snagged on the use of 'we', staring at his father's dressing-gown. He wondered why the hell Cheryl hadn't bought a new one in the eleven years since her husband's death. Yet he was too tired to become agitated. Without eating or showering, he climbed into bed, wondering if Gretchen was asleep. He pictured the dawn scene at Penley, Xavier's friends crashed on sofas, in fields, on the floors of bedrooms. Where was Martha? Sharing their bed with de Paul? Already on her way back to London to confront him? He fell asleep to the sound of birds and traffic, hoping that nothing would wake him.

9

'Where's your uniform?' Strawson asked when Kite arrived at the house in Marylebone a little over twelve hours later. It was just after nine thirty on what had become a damp summer night.

'Uniform?'

The American gestured at Kite's clothes.

'Outfit,' he said. 'Costume. What do you call them here?' He searched for the name, spinning a hand in the air like a royal wave. '*Whites*. Weren't you meant to be playing cricket?'

Kite stepped through the door.

'Didn't play in the end.'

'You didn't? Why not? Was it raining?'

'Long story.'

Strawson closed the door, frowning as he intuited Kite's discomfort.

'You OK, son?'

'Absolutely. Came back early from the party. Had an argument with Martha, missed the game.'

'You want to talk about it?'

Ordinarily Kite would have welcomed Strawson's offer, but said: 'No need.' He didn't want to appear unsettled by what had happened at Penley. He needed to look as though he was in control of his life, ready to work, primed for whatever operation was being proposed.

'How about a drink then?' Strawson suggested, apparently setting the issue aside. 'Thought we'd eat here. I went to the supermarket. Bought one of their ready-made lasagnes. You'll eat that, right? One part donkey, one part Red Rum.'

Kite nodded, looking around the hall. He realised, to his surprise, that they were not in a safe house; this was Strawson's home. There was a framed photograph of his wife on a table by the door and a set of racing blades, marked 'Harvard vs Yale 1952', criss-crossed on the wall.

'You rowed at university?' he asked, following Strawson into a living room where the curtains had been closed and various lamps lit on side tables.

'Sure did. Beer OK?'

Kite said that a beer would be great and waited as Strawson fetched one from the kitchen. He tried to do what he always did upon entering a new house: to deduce from the incidental details of a room what sort of person lived there, what they were interested in, how they conducted their lives. It was almost impossible to do so on this occasion. Save for the oars, there were no ornaments nor mementoes from earlier periods of Strawson's life. The books lining his shelves were commonplace classics from both sides of the Atlantic: Austen and Melville, Dickens and Faulkner. Kite spotted the copy of *The Satanic Verses* that Strawson had been reading at Killantringan when they had first met, but there was only one other contemporary novel in view: an American edition of *The Hunt for Red October* with a damaged spine. Strawson had no political biographies in view, indeed only a handful of works of non-fiction: a six-volume set of Winston Churchill's history of the Second World War, Brian Keenan's *An Evil Cradling* and a BBC tie-in edition of *The Living Planet*. With the exception of a reproduction Toulouse-Lautrec, the paintings on the walls were bland watercolours of what appeared to be the New England seaside. Kite surveyed Strawson's matching brown furniture and concluded it had come with the house. There was nothing to discover about his musical tastes, no newspapers or magazines on display other than various inserts from the Sunday papers which had been neatly piled on an ottoman. One framed photograph showed Strawson as a young man in army uniform, another an elderly couple whom Kite took to be his parents, conservatively dressed, steadfast Americans. The carpets and rug had been recently hoovered, the cushions plumped. It was the room of an organised, disciplined man who did not wish to be known.

'Hope you like Budweiser. All I got.'

Kite took the can and a glass, remembering his mentor Billy Peele lambasting him at Alford for drinking Budweiser, calling it 'gnat's piss' and complimenting his mother for refusing to sell it at the hotel.

'Budweiser is fine.'

He sat down with an involuntary sigh. Several hours earlier he had woken up at the house in Dulwich to find it deserted. Cheryl had left him a note:

Gone to. lunch with friends. Why are you back so soon, thought you were with Xav this weekend? Martha rang at six, again at midday. Have you two had a fight? Mum

Kite had taken a shower, made a cup of coffee and gone into his mother's bedroom hunting for information about 'Tom'. He had found a British passport in a drawer, putting his age at thirty-seven, and looked long and hard at the photograph. No, he had never seen that face before, not at The Cathedral, not in Edinburgh, not anywhere. There was a thriller, *Jig*, beside the bed and some medication for insomnia. Rummaging around in Tom's suitcase, Kite had found a set of car keys for an Alfa-Romeo, several rolls of undeveloped 35 mm film, a street map of Thessaloniki and a sealed carton of Greek cigarettes. In those few minutes he had found out more about Tom than he suspected he would learn given an hour to roam free in Strawson's soulless home.

'You look tired, Lockie.'

'Do I?'

In an effort to clear his mind, Kite had gone for a jog around Dulwich, past the Horniman Museum, the Picture Gallery and up to Brockwell Park. He had eaten roast beef and Yorkshire pudding in a pub, drunk a litre bottle of water to rehydrate, then walked home and taken another shower, shaving this time in order to look smart for Strawson. Cheryl was still not back. Martha had left another message on the answering machine asking what the hell was going on. Kite had ignored it. At seven he had taken the Victoria Line to Oxford Circus and sat with a pint in the Barley Mow on Dorset Street. Now settled in Strawson's hard-backed armchair, a glass of Budweiser in one hand, a Marlboro Light in the other, he was irritated to have been described as looking tired. He didn't want the boss to be suspicious of what he had got up to the night before.

'How long have you lived here?' Kite asked, trying to look enthusiastic about the décor.

'About a month. Give or take.'

'And your wife's joining us?'

Strawson stiffened in a way that suggested he didn't like being asked about his personal life.

'Amy doesn't come to London much. She's living in the States. You want to eat now or we talk for a while?'

Kite noted the abrupt change of subject. He wanted to know why he had been summoned, so he lit the cigarette and said: 'Talk first.'

'All right then.'

Strawson lowered himself onto a wide, creaking sofa, shuffling around until he was comfortable. He was drinking whisky and soda.

'I'll dispense with the catching up on old times, seeing how you are,' he said, placing the glass on a coaster. 'Time is a factor. We have a problem with one of our people in Russia. Voronezh, to be precise. Medium-sized city about three hours . . .'

'I know where it is,' Kite replied, still wondering why Strawson's wife was living in America. 'A lot of students

75

from the Russian course at Edinburgh went there to study last year.'

Strawson absorbed what appeared to be a useful coincidence. Kite remembered their conversation in Chez Jules, the American berating him for not going abroad in his third year. He hoped he wasn't going to get a repeat performance.

'What do you know about the Soviet biological weapons programme?' A sip of the whisky and soda. 'I assume not a great deal.'

'Correct assumption.'

'Let's go back a little bit, end of World War Two.' Strawson unbuttoned the cuffs on his shirt and talked as he rolled up the sleeves. 'Western intelligence sniffs the air, realises what's coming. Iron Curtain descending over Europe, East versus West, all that Cold War jazz. OSS doesn't want to leave hundreds of German scientists and engineers behind enemy lines when they could be working for Uncle Sam. So they put together an operation codenamed PAPERCLIP, identified about fifteen hundred Nazis in lab coats and, over the course of the next decade, brought them over to the United States. I take it you've heard of Wernher von Braun?'

The name was familiar to Kite but he knew nothing about him. He nodded and said: 'Sure', inhaling on the cigarette for cover.

'Developed the V-2 rocket for Adolf, eventually shared that knowledge with Washington, helped to build some of our first inter-continental ballistic missiles, then moved to NASA and put Armstrong on the moon. What you might call a full life.'

Kite was wondering where Strawson was headed. What was he going to ask of him? Surely not to research some obscure aspect of PAPERCLIP? That would be no better than spending the summer in the library on Charles Square writing his dissertation about Lermontov.

'So while we were extracting Nazis, the Soviets had the same idea. On a single night in October 1946, they moved over two thousand German scientists out of Russian-occupied

East Germany and forced them to work for Moscow. Now' – another sip of whisky, a minor adjustment to the rolled-up sleeves – 'jump forward to the present day, that same Soviet system collapses, leaves behind two generations of eggheads who've been working all their lives for the Kremlin. What happens to them now? Where do they go? What do they do next?'

A couple in the next house started shouting at one another. Strawson said: 'Ignore them, they're always fighting' just as Kite caught the smell of Gretchen's perfume again. 'What we've come to understand, Lockie, is that while the Soviet system may have collapsed, and new leaders appointed in various branches of the state apparatus, underneath you have the same guys committing the same sins with the same objectives. Only this time they have fewer people telling them what they can and cannot do. Right now in Russia it's every man, woman and child for himself. You've got hyper-inflation, lawlessness, a system which has only ever known tight state control suddenly changing overnight into a market economy. People are being promised a new future, a new country, but in a lot of places all that's happened is the furniture got rearranged while the walls and wiring stayed exactly the same. About a year ago Yeltsin signed a three-way decree with the Americans and the British banning biological weapons research. You may have read about it. Turns out the agreement wasn't worth the paper it's written on. The legacy biological facilities at Berdsk, Kurgan, Penza have been turned into pesticide plants, pharmaceutical factories, but all it would take is a few months for them to switch back to offensive weapons production. Mark my words, when the Russian state emerges from its current predicament, you can bet your ass the Kremlin will want to get all the old chemical, nuclear and biological utilities up and running again. These guys will go on and on, because it's all they've ever known. And when they make that choice, they're going to need scientists, they're going to need technicians to run those programmes.'

Kite felt the insistent pulse of a headache, deep inside his skull, and winced. Perhaps sensing that his guest was growing impatient, Strawson came to the point.

'Bottom line, a lot of scientists have already left, either of their own volition or thanks to foreign intervention, intelligence services sweeping them up, offering them positions at universities, government jobs, pay packets to make their little Russian eyes water. But a lot of the top people have been forced to stay behind. The KGB inserted itself into every corner of Biopreparat – that's the Soviet biological weapons programme – and ran counterintelligence against its directors and scientists for years. Nothing has changed since '91. They've been trying, often successfully, to prevent another PAPERCLIP.'

The couple in the next house were still shouting. Kite thought of Martha: when they argued, they tended to scream at one another then wind up in bed and make the peace. He stubbed out his cigarette.

'Do you have somebody you're trying to extract from Voronezh?' he asked.

'I'll come to that.' Strawson looked behind him, as if somebody had walked into the room. 'In '83 BOX recruited a senior Soviet official, Evgeny Palatnik, name now changed, for reasons which will become obvious. His cover identity was as a scientist, but he was in fact a colonel in the Red Army. Right at the top of Biopreparat, knew all the key players, every move on the board. Eventually became first deputy chief, so the KGB were on him like flies round shit.'

Kite hunched forward. 'They found out he was an agent for BOX?'

'No, no.' Strawson waved away the misunderstanding. 'They never knew. Right from day one, Palatnik was a gold mine. Confirmed to us that at its peak, Biopreparat had fifteen offensive biological weapons facilities in twelve cities across the Soviet Union. Reckoned they were developing a new weapon every year. CIA was on smallpox, so our priority at BOX became the anthrax threat. Andropov was about six months away from being able to arm an SS-18 missile with live, battle-strain spores. If one of those landed in a Chanel city, it would really mess up your weekend.'

'A Chanel city?' Kite asked, trying to remember when Yuri Andropov had been in power. He reckoned it was sometime between 1981 and 1984.

'London, Paris, New York,' Strawson replied. The front door of the neighbouring house slammed with a shouted 'Fuck you!' Kite drained the Budweiser and felt the first tremors of hunger for his host's horse-and-donkey lasagne. 'Anthrax is a really fun way to spend the last few days of your life.' Strawson again turned back to look at the door. Perhaps he was feeling a draught from the hall. 'Person gets exposed, at first they think they're getting a cold, maybe coming down with the flu. You know that little itch you get at the back of the throat, blocked nose, aching muscles? After a few days, you start to feel better. Great, you think. I can go back to work. Only this isn't the flu. The fun hasn't even started yet. Bacteria has gotten control of your lymphatic system, which is the body's way of protecting itself against disease. It gets into your bloodstream, releases a toxin which attacks the liver, the kidneys, the pancreas. Pretty soon your lungs fill up with water, you get oxygen starvation, your skin turns blue. You can't breathe, you're scratching the walls for air. Finally you die, usually within about twenty-four hours.'

'Nice,' said Kite, and felt the headache pulse for a second time.

'Palatnik reckoned that one Soviet SS-18 armed with a hundred kilograms of anthrax would be enough to take out the population of a city the size of Baltimore. Now you'd think a capability like that would satisfy Yuri and he'd go off, maybe concentrate on some other projects, like making his nuclear power stations safe or fixing potholes in the Moscow ring-road. But, no, successive leaders in the Kremlin, including the soon-to-be canonised Mikhail Gorbachev, wanted plague weapons, smallpox that could be fitted on a warhead, even a left-field virus called Marburg, which originates from African monkeys and liquifies human organs. 'You have to hand it to them, the Russians are very resourceful in the ways they think about death. Our scientists only ever developed biological weapons for which there was a vaccine or effective antibiotic. The Soviets went the other way. Each time their scientists came up with a cure for whatever mass casualty weapon they'd invented, they were sent back to the lab and ordered to start all over again.'

'Where's Palatnik now?' Kite asked, smelling food in one of the neighbouring houses.

'Flew a signal, we got him out over the border with Belarus eight months ago. False passport, BOX escort picked him up in Moscow, drove him to the airport in Minsk. Now lives in Maryland, we got him a job at Langley. He thinks the Agency saved his life. So be it. Another?'

Strawson was looking at Kite's empty glass.

'How about that lasagne?' he suggested.

'Good idea.' The American rose from his seat. 'Follow me.'

If anything, the kitchen was even more characterless than the living room. No pictures on the walls, no postcards or magnets attached to the fridge, no recipe books or exotic herbs in pots on the windowsill. In just a few hours, Cheryl had managed to personalise her rented kitchen in Dulwich, putting up a favourite painting of Killantringan, a framed certificate from the AA awarding the hotel two stars, a cut-out from *Nova* magazine in which she was modelling face cream. The soullessness of Strawson's house, the absence of personal touches, was like a warning to Kite of his life to come. There would be no permanence, no chance to put down roots or to build a meaningful domestic life. Everything would be rented, transient, ephemeral. Such a prospect did not dismay him; he wanted freedom, a life without restriction and structure. He thought of Martha and realised that Strawson had been right in Edinburgh: it was far too soon to be thinking about settling down. What had happened at Penley was an opportunity for them to spend time apart. He could now work for BOX as a free man, answerable only to Strawson, moving from place to place, from job to job, without being pinned down by a relationship.

'Have a seat.'

There was a small circular table set for two by the window. A blind had been pulled down and the radio switched on, presumably for noise cover. Strawson put the lasagne in the oven and set a pan of water on the stove, all the while continuing to talk about Palatnik.

'He has no sense of smell and more allergies than Michael Jackson. Can't eat dairy, can't eat processed meat, no chocolate. Every day he has to smear himself in moisturising creams to lubricate his skin.'

'Why?' Kite asked. 'Too much exposure to stuff in the lab?'

'Precisely.' Strawson twisted a corkscrew into a bottle of Valpolicella and levered it out. 'His body's a mess. Too many injections, too many vaccines. Want some of this?'

Strawson held up the wine and poured Kite a glass before joining him at the table.

'So look. Here's the situation. One day in early 1990, Palatnik happens to be paying a visit to a weapons facility in Obolensk. Finds himself sitting in on a lecture being given by a young scientist named Yuri Aranov, who claims to have successfully hidden symptoms of myelin toxin inside a common strain of tuberculosis. Stay with me. The scientific details aren't what's important. What *is* important is that Yuri had tested this next-generation weapon on a bunch of rabbits. Some of them came down with symptoms of tuberculosis, others started twitching their hind legs, eventually becoming paralysed. In both cases it was goodnight Bugs Bunny. But Palatnik realised it was a breakthrough.'

'How so?' Kite asked.

'Because the second set of symptoms – the twitching muscles, the paralysis – are signs of myelin toxin. A single pathogen had produced two sets of diseases, one of which couldn't be traced because it was generated by naturally occurring chemicals in the human body. In other words, the

Kremlin potentially now had access to a weapon that would make it look as though its victims had died of natural causes. Then Gorbachev goes to his dacha, Yeltsin stands on his tank and the Soviet Union collapses. Aranov's research gets mothballed. At the same time the KGB is worried that the world will find out all the charming things Biopreparat had been getting up to since the fifties, so they start shredding documents at Central Committee headquarters, covering up evidence of malfeasance. As the statue of Dzerhinsky is being pulled down outside the Lubyanka, the KGB is busy erasing any link between Russia's state security apparatus and Biopreparat. On the positive side, one of Palatnik's last acts is to order the destruction of formulas and recipes for secret biological weapons so that those programmes will be impossible to resurrect. But certain scientists are still carrying around that knowledge in their heads.'

'Scientists like Yuri Aranov.'

'You got it.'

The water had boiled. Strawson extracted a half-empty packet of peas from the freezer, affording Kite a glimpse of the bachelor lifestyle: boxes of Bird's Eye cod in white sauce; frost-smothered frozen pizzas; a bag of McCain's oven chips. As if in a strange dream whose meaning he could not yet comprehend, Kite suddenly saw his own life as a choice between Martha and Gretchen, an existence of easy pleasures and fun, and the cold, featureless contents of Strawson's freezer. He smiled at the absurdity of the image as Strawson tipped the peas into the steaming pan, turned up the volume on the radio and stood beside the stove. Kite recognised the music: it was the second movement of Mahler's 5th. It always made him think of his father shaving in the morning at Killantringan, his face covered in foam, saying: 'Listen to that, Lockie! Enough to make a man join the French Foreign Legion!'

'When we spoke yesterday, you said you didn't have any fixed plans over the next couple of months.'

'That's right.'

'So you'd be free to go overseas, take off for a while?'

Kite nodded, pushing his glass of wine to one side, trying to disguise his eagerness.

'What about Martha?'

'Don't worry about her. We're taking a break.'

It was the first time that Kite had articulated what he intended to do; he had yet to come to terms with the decision. Strawson looked startled.

'You are?'

'Yeah, just for the next few months. See how it goes.'

'When did this get decided?'

It was as though Strawson, having tasked someone with keeping tabs on Martha and Kite's relationship, had not been informed of this latest vital snippet of intelligence.

'It's been tricky for a while,' Kite told him, not untruthfully.

'She met somebody else?' The American turned to face the pan of peas so that the sharpness of his question might somehow be blunted.

'What makes you think she's met somebody else?' Kite remembered de Paul's fingers on Martha's stomach. 'Maybe *I've* met somebody else?'

'Maybe you have.' Strawson put a lid on the peas. 'I didn't mean to imply . . .'

His words tailed off. There was an extended silence. Strawson filled it by opening the door of the oven. 'Almost done,' he muttered. There was a smell of burnt cheese.

'She's probably going to Bosnia anyway.' Kite felt that he had to justify what he had said. 'Going to Zagreb then heading south.'

Strawson looked baffled. 'Bosnia? What for?'

'Wants to help out. There's an aid agency she's involved with, set up by a guy at Oxford.'

The American turned back to the stove without reply. Kite sensed that he disapproved of idealistic young graduates crusading into the former Yugoslavia thinking they could make the world a better place. He put the lasagne on a heat-proof block and brought the conversation back to Russia.

'You ever done any teaching, Lockie?'

Kite said that he had not, wondering where Strawson was leading him.

'None at all?'

'Some cricket coaching at Alford to the younger boys in my house. That's about it. Why?'

'How would you feel about spending a few weeks in Voronezh teaching English as a foreign language? Everybody in Russia wants to pick it up. You'd have a class full of eager students hanging on your every word.'

Kite was immediately taken by the idea, knowing that it would be a cover job for helping out with whatever problem BOX was experiencing in the region.

'Sure,' he said. 'Sounds interesting.'

'There's just one catch.'

'What's that?'

'You'd have to leave on Wednesday.'

'*Wednesday?*' Kite did not want to appear unwilling, but the timeline was much tighter than he could have anticipated. Strawson took some mismatched knives and forks from a cutlery drawer and put them on the table. 'That's in three days. Last time I had four weeks' prep.'

'Yeah, well last time you were untried and untested. And last time we didn't have the guy who was meant to go in your place break his leg and four ribs in a car accident.'

Strawson, wearing outsized, floral-patterned oven gloves, drained the peas and served the lasagne. As they ate, he explained that a BOX 88 officer using the alias 'Peter Galvin' had been due to take up a teaching position at the Dickens Institute in Voronezh with a view to making contact with Yuri Aranov and getting him out of the country. On Thursday night, Galvin had been driving back from a meeting in Manchester when a van in the fast lane of the M6 suddenly veered in front of him. Both vehicles were well over the speed limit, with several others coming up fast behind them. Galvin was forced to swerve out of the way. He lost control of his Vauxhall Astra, which fishtailed towards the hard shoulder only to be hit by a second car driven by a single mum with two kids in the back seat. Thankfully they were all wearing seat belts. The van driver also survived unscathed, but Galvin was hospitalised. Foul play was not suspected; it was just bad luck.

'So he won't be going to Voronezh. Even if he can walk using crutches, there's no way he'll be able to drive. And driving to Ukraine with Aranov is the key to this thing.'

'So you need me to step in?'

'We do.' Strawson leaned forward, hunched over his food. 'We have a window of opportunity to extract Yuri from under the noses of the KGB. On the face of it, we're talking about something straightforward. You go to Russia, you're just a regular guy teaching English, you're interacting with Aranov, you drive him across the frontier. Easy.'

'If it's that easy, why doesn't he drive himself? Or just fly to Heathrow?'

Strawson made an exasperated gesture, as if to say: 'I wish'.

'Because for one thing, he's not allowed a foreign travel passport. And for another, he refuses to get on an aeroplane. Yuri is kind of a pain in the ass. Needs somebody to hold his hand, talk him into doing the right thing, persuade him that it's safe to leave Russia. We thought it would be easy getting him out, then we found out he doesn't like to fly. On top of that, he thinks every third person he sees on the streets of Voronezh is a KGB officer keeping watch on him.'

'Does he have good reason to think that? Is he paranoid or are people genuinely watching him?'

'Bit of both.' Strawson took a sip of wine. 'His phone is tapped, we know that. One of his neighbours is an informer, tells the locals all about Yuri's shall-we-say colourful private life. At least one person in his class at Dickens is KGB. They call it FSK nowadays, but you know what I mean. Same shit, different day.'

'You mean Aranov is going to be one of my students?'

'Yeah, sorry. Didn't I explain that?' Strawson nodded apologetically. 'Back in March, we responded to a TNT advert

85

looking for a teacher. Got a message to Yuri telling him to sign up for a six-month course at Dickens. It was a nice fit, gives Galvin a reason to spend time with him, to socialise with his group of friends without arousing suspicion. Any foreigner who comes into contact with Aranov is subject to round-the-clock surveillance until Moscow is satisfied they're not a threat. That will include you, just as it will also include anybody sent by Baghdad, Tripoli, Beijing to sound him out.'

'Baghdad, Tripoli, Beijing,' Kite repeated. For the first time, he felt out of his depth. Strawson appeared to intuit this and explained exactly what was at stake.

'We need to get Aranov out of Russia before anyone else grabs him. Simple as that. We have intel that Gaddafi has put a Biopreparat scientist at the top of his shopping list. If Yuri's work on myelin toxin gets into the wrong hands, it's a game changer. Right now he's one of ours, but Saddam, the Libyans, the Chinese – they've all had agents swirling around him for months. Could be gone at any moment. Everybody is competing for Yuri's services. Back in January he was approached by the Koreans, told them to go fuck themselves. So, yes, when you get there you will find there are other interested parties. All of them dangling money, girls, status – whatever they think will work. Gadaffi's people offer him thirty pieces of silver and a virgin in his tent every night, who's to say Yuri might not go with them.'

'Meaning he has no loyalty, no conscience?'

'I wouldn't say that. Yuri's not stupid. He knows that life in the West is his best option. But getting him out was our suggestion, not his. He knows his value. And every man has a price, right?'

Kite was struggling to come to terms with what Strawson was expecting of him. Surely he was too inexperienced to go up against Iraqi or Libyan intelligence officers? He could not say this, because to show weakness or concern for his own safety was unthinkable, yet he was filled with doubts.

'You mentioned earlier that Yuri is one of ours,' he said. 'In what sense? You mean Palatnik helped to recruit him?'

Strawson swallowed a mouthful of food and said: 'Exactly.'

'Somebody is running him in Voronezh?' Strawson shook his head. 'From Moscow?'

'From Moscow, yes.'

'So why don't *they* get him out? Why do you need me? Yuri could go to Moscow, his handler drives him to Minsk, just like Palatnik . . .'

'You think we haven't thought of that? Since we got Evgeny out, the KGB has squeezed all remaining senior Biopreparat personnel. Those guys can't take a shit without someone sitting in their laps while they do it. Moscow is not a place you want to be running an exfil. There's no way one of our agents could get close enough to Aranov for long enough that the KGB would drop their guard. Same in Voronezh. Somebody they don't recognise shows up out of the blue and gets in a car with him, starts driving towards Ukraine, the Russians will pull them over quicker than it would take to reheat this piece-of-shit lasagne.' Strawson looked down at his plate. 'Bottom line, the teaching cover is the best we've got. Galvin will have regular contact with Aranov five days a week. They can socialise, go to parties, sooner or later the KGB will ease off.' Strawson looked more closely at Kite. 'You having doubts, son? No shame in thinking this might be above your pay grade.'

'No, no.' Kite tried to act tough. 'No doubts, none at all. The way you describe it, it sounds straightforward.'

At the back of his mind was the memory of what had happened in France four years earlier: Strawson and Peele had withheld vital information about Xavier's father, keeping Kite in the dark until the operation was all but concluded. He wanted to be certain that they couldn't pull the wool over his eyes a second time.

'What's the angle?' he asked.

'What do you mean, what's the angle?'

'I mean what aren't you telling me?'

Strawson looked affronted. 'Is this about Xavier's father?'

'In part, yes.' Kite's heart was thumping. He didn't want

to land on the wrong side of his boss, but he knew that it was vital to have as much information as possible before he agreed to cooperate. 'I just want to understand what the deeper story is,' he said. 'If there is one.'

'The deeper story?' Strawson inhaled loudly through his nose. 'The deeper story is that if you're caught, you'll end up in prison for ten years on charges of espionage. You know the rules, Lachlan. BOX 88 does not exist. Six has no idea who you are, ditto Langley. We won't come for you, we won't vouch for you, you're somebody we've never heard of.'

'Deniable,' Kite muttered, staring at his glass of wine. 'I need to know more about Yuri,' he said. 'How do BOX make contact with him?'

'With difficulty. Last time was in Moscow. He was visiting one of his girlfriends. Wendy had about a half-hour with him, was able to tell him about the language course, persuade him that this was the safest way for him to leave Russia.'

'He didn't want to go?'

Strawson looked down at the table. 'Wasn't ready. Said he needed time to put his affairs in order. We didn't know if that was true or if he was playing for time, waiting for a better offer. You might get to Voronezh and discover he's ready to leave for Ukraine, you might find out he's already in business with the Iraqis. Your job is to persuade Aranov that coming to the West is his only viable option. He starts getting ideas about a better life in Beijing, you remind him about the shitty food and tell him we've got a job waiting for him at Porton Down, tax-free salary, three-bedroom house, new identity, whatever he wants. If he says he's had an offer from the Libyans, you improve on it. Not hard to do. Who the hell wants to live in Tripoli?' Strawson fixed Kite with a hard stare. 'Always be aware that individuals in your classroom may not be who they seem. Could be KGB keeping an eye on you, an eye on Yuri. Suffice to say, getting him out may not be as easy as jumping in a car and driving to Dnipro.'

'No shit,' Kite replied, smiling as he caught Strawson's eye. 'One problem, though.'

'Only one? You sound confident. I like it.'

'If I'm going to pretend to be Galvin, but your guy with the broken leg already got the teaching job, don't they know what he looks like from his application form?'

Strawson scratched his jaw. 'They never saw a photograph. Language schools have been springing up all over Russia. They don't care what people look like. They're not concerned with security. They just need teachers from the West who are prepared to come to places like Voronezh, live in cockroach-infested accommodation and work for minimal salaries. Not that many people are into that. Why go to Russia and queue for bread when you could be teaching English in Rio, Bangkok, Paris? They only wanted Galvin's CV and some passport details.'

'What was his legend?' Kite didn't mind that the job wasn't taking him to the beaches of Rio de Janeiro or the streets of Paris. A backwater city in Russia sounded like an adventure. 'Who do they think is coming?'

'Galvin is just a regular joe.' Strawson adjusted the position of a pepper grinder on the table. 'British citizen, unmarried. Degree in English literature from, uh, Bristol University, I think it was. Born in Wokingham, spent four years teaching in Malawi, which is the only part of the legend which might cause you problems. That and the fact we made no mention of Galvin speaking Russian, so don't let on that you know any. It's all in a file I've prepared for you.'

Kite wondered if Strawson was going to go next door to fetch it, but he remained in the kitchen and cleared the plates. Kite offered to help but was told to stay put.

'What about my visa?' he asked.

'All done. There's a photograph of Galvin on file with the Russians, but we're going to switch it out. We can have one of our people in Moscow substitute it for your picture.'

'The Turings can do that?' Kite asked.

'The Turings can do that.' Strawson seemed surprised that Kite was not aware of their capabilities. 'As long as the director at Dickens hasn't seen the visa application – and there's no reason at all to think she would – you're home and dry.'

'And if she has seen it and wonders why I look nothing like Galvin?'

Strawson turned. He had been putting a bottle of ketchup back in the fridge.

'Then you do what we've trained you to do. You say there's been a glitch in the application process, you have no idea why Galvin's photograph is associated with your visa, you had no trouble at Sheremetyevo, etcetera, etcetera.'

Something in the tone of Strawson's reply caused Kite to think that he should sound more bullish. He was reminded of moments during his training when the American had become frustrated with his progress and his patience had suddenly snapped. It was out of the question to refuse what Strawson was offering. If he was going to work for BOX 88 after university, this was exactly the sort of operation which would secure his future.

'I don't see anything stopping me,' he said, his eagerness running ahead of his common sense. 'I'll do it.'

Even Strawson seemed surprised that Kite had so readily agreed.

'That's great!' he exclaimed. Kite saw that a speck of mince had become trapped in his Hemingway beard. 'I knew I could count on you, Lockie. Just the answer we were looking for. No ifs, no buts. Great attitude.'

It was like agreeing the sale of a second-hand car; Kite immediately sensed that he had made a mistake. They formalised the arrangement with a toast, their wine glasses – which Kite recognised as freebies claimed on petrol station vouchers – clinking to the strains of Bach. After that there seemed little else to say. The rest would be made clear to Kite at The Cathedral first thing on Monday morning.

'We'll have a whole team ready to prep you,' Strawson assured him. 'How does eight o'clock sound?'

'Done,' Kite replied, looking at his watch. It was already

close to eleven and almost an hour by taxi to his mother's house in Dulwich. Thinking of her, he realised that he would need a cover story for suddenly vanishing to Russia without notice. 'What do I tell my mum?' he asked.

Strawson didn't hesitate.

'Always get as close to the truth as possible. Say you're going travelling around Russia and Eastern Europe. Meeting friends from Edinburgh, back by August. From what you've told me, Cheryl doesn't pay all that much attention to your comings and goings, am I right?'

'True,' Kite replied.

He knew that Martha would be a different proposition. He was scheduled to be in Voronezh by Wednesday night. With so much to get through in the next two days, he doubted there would be time to meet her face to face, yet to write her a letter, or to end their four-year relationship over the phone, was unthinkable. He was not even sure if ending the relationship was what he wanted to do.

'Shall I call you a cab?' Strawson asked.

'Thank you,' Kite replied, perplexed by the best course of action. 'That would be very kind.'

'Get some rest, son.' The American laid a paternal hand on Kite's back. 'You're gonna need it. We've got less than seventy-two hours to turn you into Peter Galvin.'

10

By the time Kite reached the house in Dulwich, his mother was asleep. Somebody had left a pair of worn Docksiders by the front door. Kite could hear a man – presumably Tom – snoring in the master bedroom. There was a note on the stairs saying that Xavier was trying to get hold of him and that Martha had called again. Kite threw it in the bin, slept for five hours and was at The Cathedral by seven thirty.

It was the first time he had been back to BOX 88 headquarters since his training three years earlier. He ate breakfast alone in the first-floor canteen, wondering when he would get a chance to speak to Martha. By now news of his fight with de Paul would be all over town. Kite assumed that in normal circumstances, de Paul would have gone to the police and pressed charges. Not this time. He wouldn't have wanted to look petty in front of Martha.

Strawson kept Kite on site until midnight. The file on Peter Galvin ran to forty pages. Kite had a photographic memory, but a limit on how much enthusiasm he could muster for Galvin's phantom childhood and adolescence in Wokingham. There was a page on the family home in Bishops Drive, exam results from two separate schools, the names of the pubs he had frequented as a young man, even a paragraph about the cinema where Galvin had supposedly kissed a girl for the first time after watching *Superman II*. The level of detail was overwhelming and, in Kite's view, gratuitous. His fictional father was a plumber named Ron, his mother, Miriam, a housewife three years Ron's senior. Kite was told that the BOX 88 officer who had been injured in the car crash, referred to only as 'Chris', had built the file from scratch, using fragments of his own life story. The long section dedicated to Galvin's four-year stint in Malawi sounded particularly authentic, even including phrases in the local language, Chichewa, which Kite was obliged to commit to memory. He assumed that Chris had spent time there.

'Is all this absolutely necessary?' he asked Rita Ayinde, who had helped to prepare him for Mougins and was now doing the same in the build-up to Voronezh. Her response was unequivocal: it was BOX 88 policy to be thorough, to build a legend as comprehensive and meticulous as an actual life. Kite duly read through the document a second time. When Ayinde tested him on its contents soon afterwards, he failed to answer only one question correctly. Galvin's girlfriend in Malawi had been called Yomo, not Yolanda.

Yet the file was just the tip of the iceberg.

For two further hours on Monday, Kite was given a crash course in car mechanics, specifically relating to the Lada Niva, the vehicle he would be driving from Yuri Aranov's dacha outside Voronezh to Dnipropetrovsk in Ukraine.

'From St Petersburg to Vladivostock, the Lada is still the car of choice for your average Russian,' said Tony, his affable instructor. 'To say they're unreliable would be a masterpiece of understatement. It's not like home. There aren't too many repair shops in that neck of the woods, so if your vehicle happens to break down, chances are you're going to have to fix it. Switch a tyre, change the oil, replace a broken headlight.'

'Make sure you concentrate,' Strawson insisted, sticking his head into the room just as Tony was demonstrating how to clean the oil filter. 'Last thing we need is you breaking down and being forced to spend the night in Stary Oskol or Belgorod drawing attention to yourselves while some local mechanic with a vodka habit promises to have you back on the road by Thursday. Once you leave the dacha, you'll have six hours, no more than that, before the KGB find out Yuri has disappeared. After that they'll seal the border.'

Stary Oskol was the first major town on the road south from Voronezh. Kite's job would be to persuade Aranov to invite a group of friends to his family dacha for a weekend, then to slip away shortly before dawn on a Saturday or Sunday morning without arousing suspicion. On a signal from Kite, a local BOX 88 agent would leave a Lada Niva parked in a prearranged location close to the dacha. Inside there would be enough hard currency for bribes, as well as false passports for Kite and Aranov. The route would take them south-west via Stary Oskol on a potholed minor road. Belgorod was the last Russian city before the frontier. Strawson estimated that the journey would take about five hours.

After mastering the finer points of the Lada, Kite was taken to a room in the basement of The Cathedral and shown detailed road maps of the area immediately to the south of Voronezh. He noted the locations of petrol stations and restaurants and looked at surveillance footage of the border crossing at Zhuravlevka. It was then time to learn more about Aranov. Between eleven o'clock and twelve thirty on Tuesday morning, Kite was given a presentation by the BOX 88 officer who had been running Aranov since his recruitment. Her name was given as 'Wendy', a rotund woman in her early forties who spoke to Kite in a careful, solicitous manner which made him feel like an astronaut about to embark on a perilous mission to the moon.

'Yuri is . . . fun,' she said, though the slight hesitation she employed before choosing that word indicated that her definition of 'fun' was perhaps closer to 'unusual' or even 'difficult'. 'A sort of man-child, an eternal teenager. Brilliantly clever when it comes to facts and figures, numbers and data, not so clever when it comes to holding what you and I might characterise as a normal conversation. Nor is he reliable about the amount of alcohol he consumes or the wide variety of young women he takes to his bed. There's a sexual revolution going on in Russia, Lachlan, and Yuri has decided to take full advantage.'

Kite thought of Gretchen and wondered if she had spoken to anybody about what had happened between them. He didn't think she would go to Martha, but if de Paul found out he would surely have no hesitation in telling her.

'Aranov isn't always punctual,' Wendy continued. 'Doesn't know the meaning of "please" and "thank you". Thinks anybody who lives west of Warsaw isn't aware of how lucky they are and shouldn't be complaining about anything other than the weather. Married at twenty, local girl called Masha, now estranged though she still lives in Voronezh. No children, which is obviously going to make your job a lot easier. Fear of flying, which isn't. Like most men of his personality type, Yuri responds well to flattery, to being placed centre stage. Loves presents, expensive meals, western cigarettes, Levi jeans, that kind of thing. Just keep an eye on the women and the drinking. Both are liable to get out of hand. Here are some photographs.'

Wendy opened a folder and passed five photographs of Aranov across the table.

He was thirty-five, but looked a decade younger. Not a physically fit nor particularly handsome man, but unquestionably striking. Building on what Wendy had told him, Kite guessed at a strong, possibly bullying temperament, proud and stubborn. Aranov's narrow, rather surly features reminded Kite of certain clever boys at Alford to whom sharp ideas and academic success had come easily: some of them developed an impatience with lesser mortals, a lofty intellectual arrogance which usually concealed thumping sexual insecurity. It made sense that Aranov was a womaniser.

'He doesn't look much fun,' he said, taking mental photographs of Aranov's face.

'Oh, Yuri can be great company,' Wendy countered. 'I agree, the pictures make him look a bit pleased with himself.

He's a terrible poser. Knows he's cleverer than ninety-five per cent of the people with whom he comes into contact, and that's bred a bit of self-importance.'

Kite wondered what was stopping Wendy from getting Aranov out of Russia herself. Why was BOX using a relatively untested twenty-two-year-old who had been out of the game for three years? He knew that such questions could not be asked and tried to trust in Strawson's judgement. Nevertheless, he could not shake the feeling that some vital piece of operational information was being held back from him. Was he again being manipulated?

When the meeting was over, Kite found Rita Ayinde in the canteen and asked if he could be excused for an hour so that he could telephone Martha.

'What are you going to tell her?' she replied, looking concerned.

'Just that I'm going travelling. Eastern Europe. Russia. I'll leave it vague.'

'She won't be suspicious?'

Kite knew that whatever answer he gave would be reported straight back to Strawson.

'She'll be surprised I'm leaving so soon,' he admitted. 'But she knows I have my reasons for wanting to go abroad.'

He left the building through the tunnel which connected BOX 88 headquarters to a church across the square, eating lunch in a pub half a mile from The Cathedral. The closer Kite came to picking up the phone and dialling Martha's number, the closer he came to the realisation that he still yearned for her, that he had acted too hastily leaving Penley and was being foolish – possibly even cowardly – in going to Voronezh. He found a phone box on a quiet residential corner, dropped two twenty-pence pieces into the slot and dialled Martha's parents' house in Swiss Cottage.

An answering machine clicked in. Kite spoke in the hope that somebody might pick up.

'Martha, hi. It's me. Lockie. Are you there?'

He had been so submerged in the Galvin alias that he had

almost given his name as 'Peter'. He waited, picturing the Raines' sitting room, the place where he had spent Christmas Days, dinners with Martha, family celebrations. Where was she? In Oxford with de Paul? Perhaps in Dulwich waiting with Cheryl for the errant Lachlan to return home. Kite had told his mother that he was going to the Russian embassy to organise a visa.

'It sounds like you're not there,' he said. 'I'll call later.'

He walked back in the direction of The Cathedral, smoked a cigarette in the grounds of the church and made his way to Strawson's office. The American was busy at his desk, giving off an air of impatience. Kite checked his watch. He was three minutes early for their meeting.

'Everything OK?' he asked, closing the door behind him.

'Lots to get through,' Strawson answered, gesturing Kite into an armchair. There was a half-eaten sandwich on the desk and a can of Diet Coke. 'This time tomorrow you'll be on the plane.' He reached for a document. 'Make notes if you have to. Here's what's left.'

Kite took a notepad and Biro from the inside pocket of his jacket. He felt like a cub reporter scribbling down shorthand at a hastily arranged press conference.

'We need to set up a signal,' Strawson began, 'for when you're ready to go to the dacha. Could be as soon as next weekend, but Yuri won't want to be rushed. He knows we want to get him out, but if he doesn't like you, chances are he'll stay behind.'

'Great,' said Kite, with an edge of sarcasm.

'Commit this to memory.' Strawson passed Kite the eight-digit telephone number for a secure line in Moscow. 'As soon as you know you're heading out to the dacha, call the number from a payphone. When somebody picks up, they'll answer you in Russian. Ask if they speak English. They'll say they do. Ask if you're connected to the Hotel Metropol. They'll tell you it's a wrong number and hang up.' Kite wrote 'Hotel Metropol' on the pad though he knew he would remember the name. 'Once we have that signal, the Lada will be driven down to the dacha and left within a hundred metres of Yuri's property on the afternoon of your arrival. Keys in the exhaust, full tank of gas. First two letters of the licence plate TX, last two MX.'

'How will you know what day we're going to be there?' Kite asked. 'What if Yuri wants to head out on a Tuesday or Wednesday?'

'Not allowed,' Strawson replied, wagging his finger in a way that reminded Kite of a teacher at Alford who had been a stickler for school tradition. 'He still has work commitments during the week. So do most of his buddies. Dachas are for weekend fun. You might get there on a Friday night, but you don't leave until the early hours of Saturday or Sunday morning.'

'That's how Burgess and Maclean got away,' Kite observed, trying to sound knowledgeable. 'MI5 surveillance stood down over the weekend and they crossed on the ferry.'

'Indeed they did, indeed they did . . .' Strawson was picking at something on his forearm and his voice briefly tailed off. 'You won't be that fortunate, but with any luck there won't be so many cops on the roads, fewer eyes on you at the house.'

Kite looked down and studied the phone number, working out a way to remember it. He knew the area code for Moscow. The next two digits were 71, the year of his birth, then a 9, the month of his mother's birthday. After that, the secure line had a sequence of zeros, ending with another 7. It was simple.

'Goes without saying, this time round you aren't going to have a BOX team just down the road that you can talk to.' Strawson was referring to the safe house in Mougins, close to the Bonnard villa, which Billy Peele had rented in 1989. 'If at any point you need to pass an urgent message to us in Voronezh, you're not going to be able to use the telephone. In order to make an international call, you have to queue at the Telegraph Office and obviously can fully expect that any conversation will be tapped. Instead make an item of red clothing visible in the window of your apartment. Somebody will check the site twice a day for the duration of your visit. They will then make themselves known to you on the street.'

'In what way?' Kite asked.

'You recognise the theme from *The Godfather*?' Strawson whistled the first few bars. Kite knew it well. 'So if you hear that, you follow the guy, you do it in brush contact.'

'It'll be a man? You have somebody in Voronezh working for you full-time?'

'That isn't your business. We have people everywhere, Lockie. All you need to know is that somebody will check your windows twice a day for the signal, just like we did in Mougins. Once you've flown it, keep your ears open. Vito Corleone will come to the rescue, either in male or female form.'

From a drawer in his desk Strawson produced a British passport and an envelope with the word DICKENS typed in large block capitals on the front.

'These are yours,' he said. 'Official letter of invitation from the Dickens Institute, faxed to us several weeks ago. And a passport. You are now officially Peter Galvin. Congratulations.'

Kite flicked through the passport. There were stamps for Malawi, one for Ethiopia, one for South Africa, and what looked like an authentic Russian tourist visa.

'Says here Galvin has been to Addis Ababa and Johannesburg. There was nothing about that in the file.'

'Don't worry about that.' If Strawson was impressed that Kite had noticed the anomaly, he did not show it. 'You were just in transit. They ask, you say you had to stay overnight in Jo'burg on your way to Malawi. Bullshit if you have to, same as always.'

Whoever had put the passport together had done a good job. It was supposedly three years old and looked suitably weathered; even the photograph of Kite – taken first thing on Monday morning – had somehow been altered to make him look slightly younger.

'Are you Pete or Peter?' Strawson asked. 'What did Chris go for?'

'Peter,' Kite replied. 'Pete to his close friends.'

'No nickname?'

There hadn't been one in the file. 'Not that I saw.'

'So, worst-case scenario, you see somebody on the road who calls you 'Lockie', that's a Galvin nickname from childhood. You just got to think of a reason why your friends call you that.'

'Easy enough,' Kite replied.

'Shit hits the fan, you need to abort, you call the same number I just gave you. Ask if they speak English. They'll say they do. Then ask if you're connected to the American embassy. When they say wrong number and hang up, we'll know you're not coming out with Yuri. How you get home is your own business. You'll only have the Galvin passport.'

'Understood.'

Kite wrote 'Abort / American embassy' on the notepad and chewed the end of the Biro. Strawson stood up and opened a window. There was the sound of a drill in a nearby street, dust and pollen visible in bright shafts of sunlight.

'What's next?' he muttered, returning to the desk and consulting a checklist. 'Oh yeah. Right. Obviously Yuri doesn't know what you look like. Doesn't know if his new teacher has been sent by Wendy or is just some guy from Wokingham wants to summer in Voronezh. So as soon as he shows up in class, you steer the conversation towards Winston Churchill. Talk about the war, cigars, the state funeral, whatever works. He knows to listen out for that. He'll know you're the guy we've sent to get him out. After that, it's a question of how you approach one another. Yuri understands basic anti-surveillance, but obviously the guy isn't formally trained. Better you speak when there are people around, snatches of conversation, nothing that looks suspicious to anyone who might be watching. Don't treat Yuri any differently to the way you treat other people in the class. If he insists on meeting you one-on-one, do it out of town in the forest or by the river, tell him to clean his tail and wait for you in a particular spot. Maybe you put on your running shoes and go for a jog, bump into him accidentally on purpose. Keep the cloak and dagger to an absolute minimum.'

'I know what to do,' Kite replied. Agent running had taken up ten days of his training course.

'There's also this.' Strawson held up a book. It was a pristine hardback copy of *The English Patient*, the Michael Ondaatje novel which had won the Booker Prize the previous year. 'You read this?'

'No,' Kite replied, omitting to mention that Martha had raved about the book and talked about it endlessly at Christmas. 'I hear it's really good.'

'Whether it's any good or not is of no importance. Inside the binding you'll find an official letter offering Yuri the job, the house, the car, the status. You're to give him the letter if he doubts who you are, starts getting second thoughts. Otherwise it stays in there.'

'Hopefully it won't come to that.'

'Hopefully.' Strawson checked the clock on the wall behind Kite's chair. 'Now you've got another session with the language teacher, then Rita wants to go over your cover one last time. Am I correct?'

'Sounds about right,' Kite replied.

He was beginning to grow weary of the flood of information to which he was being exposed. He grabbed a cup of black coffee from the canteen and took the lift to the fourth floor, where he was treated to two hours of classes on prepositions and tenses, articles and gerunds. The teacher handed him a cheat sheet booklet containing enough lesson plans to get him through the first two weeks at the Dickens.

'It's all about confidence,' she told him. 'Get the students to do the work. If you run out of ideas, just set them a test or watch a video.'

'Will do,' Kite replied, wondering if they had video recorders in post-Soviet Russia and doubting that it would be as straightforward as the teacher was making out.

It was seven o'clock by the time he made it back to Rita's

office. She had changed into a tight-fitting yellow dress, explaining that she had a dinner reservation with her husband at eight thirty.

'Before that, we've got to get you packed,' she said. There was a large suitcase in the centre of the room. 'Open sesame.'

Inside the case was everything Peter Galvin would need – and would have thought to have packed – for a two-month stint in Voronezh. There were packets of tea from Fortnum and Mason ('gifts for your boss'), a coffee percolator, a jar of Marmite, several packets of dried soup, several more of noodles, a bottle of multi-vitamins, a padlock, a combination chess and backgammon set, paperbacks of *War and Peace*, *The Idiot* and *The Brothers Karamazov*, a travel pillow and even a large box of Durex.

'In case you get lucky,' said Rita, grinning as she locked her desk. 'Boss told me you broke up with Martha. Apparently Russian girls are crazy about sex. You've always been a randy little sod. You'll be to the manor born.'

Kite picked up a bar of Imperial Leather soap from the case, wondering why Rita thought of him that way. What had she sensed about him? He had always been faithful to Martha. He suddenly remembered the hair in Gretchen's armpits, the strangeness of her body after four long years with the same woman.

'Also this, of course,' she said.

Rita passed him a worn leather wallet. Inside were several credit cards in the name Peter Galvin, some Tube and railway tickets, various shop and restaurant receipts, about three hundred pounds in sterling and a National Insurance card. Standard wallet litter.

'You'll find a thousand dollars in traveller's cheques in there which need signing.' Rita nodded at the suitcase. 'Also five hundred US dollars in cash. Everybody loves the dollar in Russia.'

'What about clothes?' Kite asked. 'I just take my own?'

'You do. But for goodness' sake don't take any pants from

that posh boarding school of yours with your nametape sewn into the waistband.'

They both laughed.

'What's funny?' Strawson asked, walking into the office.

'I was just testing Peter on his Chichewa,' Rita replied, straightening out the hem of her dress. 'How do you say "Hello" in Malawi?'

'*Moni*,' said Kite after only a fractional hesitation.

'Where did you go to school at the age of seven?'

'St Teresa's.'

'Who was your boss in Malawi?'

'Jenny Muldaur.'

Rita looked at Strawson, who seemed impressed.

'Not bad, son,' he said. 'Not bad at all.' He indicated the open suitcase. 'This all the junk you're taking tomorrow? Noodles and Tolstoy?'

Kite wondered if Rita would make a crack about the condoms but she spared him the embarrassment.

'I have to go to dinner,' she said. 'You're taking our boy out for a last supper, am I right?'

Kite did well to hide his frustration. He had been hoping to slip away and have the chance to telephone Martha, perhaps even to meet up with her. Now there was no chance of that: he couldn't get out of dinner with the boss. Strawson would want to go over every last operational detail before sending him on his way.

'Thought we'd go to Langan's,' he said. 'See you off in style.'

'Sounds great,' Kite replied, wondering if he could take a cab to Swiss Cottage afterwards and at least see Martha for half an hour. 'Always wanted to go there.'

'That's if you don't have plans?' said Strawson, perhaps sensing Kite's hesitation.

'No, no,' he replied. 'No plans at all.'

Rita came towards him. She smelled of the same perfume she had worn at Colenso's the first time they had met.

'Good luck, handsome,' she said, embracing him. She was much shorter than Kite but her high heels almost brought her up to his height. 'Look after yourself. Don't do anything silly. And bring yourself back in one piece.'

'Amen to that,' Strawson added. 'With Yuri Aranov in your hand luggage.'

11

Langan's was packed. Kite and Strawson drank martinis and a bottle of Gevrey-Chambertin, spotted Michael Caine dining at a table near the bar and were mistaken for father and son by the waitress. After coffee and cognacs, Strawson settled the bill and they went outside to a waiting taxi.

'Remember what I've taught you,' he said, pulling Kite into a sudden embrace. 'One. Trust your cover. Two. *Breathe*. Three. Whatever happens, never admit to . . .'

'I know, I know,' Kite replied. He was touched that both Rita and Strawson had hugged him as they said their goodbyes. Increasingly he thought of BOX 88 as a kind of surrogate family. 'Don't worry. I won't. I'll get out there and bring him back. This time in six weeks you'll be buying me dinner again.'

'Let's hope so.' Strawson pumped Kite's hand. 'Fly well, Mr Galvin. Good luck.'

Kite had brought the suitcase to the restaurant. He put it in the front seat of the cab and gave directions to Dulwich; it was too late to doorstep Martha and he was worn out after the long day. Driving south, drunk on vodka and wine and Courvoisier, it felt to Kite as though he was seeing London at night for the last time; he kept thinking about Strawson's warning: 'If you're caught, you'll end up in prison for ten years on charges of espionage.' He wondered who would come first to visit him in his Voronezh prison cell: Martha or his mother?

As the cab pulled up in front of Cheryl's house, Kite saw that the light in her bedroom was already out. Tom's Docksiders were again in the hall. He listened to Martha's increasingly fraught messages on the answering machine, carried the suitcase up to his room, packed some clothes into an overnight bag and went to sleep.

When Kite came downstairs at seven, Tom was already up, sitting on a stool at the kitchen counter buttering a slice of toast and reading the *Independent*.

'Going somewhere?' he asked, indicating Kite's luggage.

'Travelling,' Kite replied.

'Oh that's right. Your mum said you were off to Russia, getting a visa or something? Crazy over there at the moment.'

'Have you been?' Kite asked.

Tom tapped the shell on a boiled egg and said that he hadn't. He had huge hands and was too well-built to fit comfortably on the stool. The small portable television beside him had been switched on with the sound set to mute. As Kite pressed the kettle, Cheryl walked in from the garden.

'Oh look,' she said. 'My two favourite boys. Did you get your visa, Lockie?'

'I did,' Kite replied. 'Flight's at eleven.'

'You're off already?' She was astonished. 'To Moscow?'

'That's what the ticket says.'

Tom detected the surliness in Kite's reply and went back to his newspaper.

'It all seems to have happened so quickly,' Cheryl continued. 'What will you do over there?'

Kite had not slept well and gave a sluggish reply.

'Just look around. See the place. Sharpen up my Russian. Might go to Poland on the way home, the Baltic States . . .'

'What will you do for money?'

'Dunno. Work in a bar. Pick fruit. I've saved enough from the café for the first couple of weeks.'

'Doesn't sound very stable, Lockie.'

'Might get a job teaching English,' he added, seeming to pull the idea out of thin air. 'Apparently there are lots of schools popping up in and around Moscow.'

It was more information than he should have given out, but where was the harm in telling his mother a version of the truth? He sat opposite Tom, poured himself a bowl of Shreddies and turned up the sound on the TV. Chris Evans was standing outside the Lockkeeper's Cottage on *The Big Breakfast*, fooling around with a drag queen.

'Your girlfriend left another message.' Tom's tone was over-familiar, as if he had lived at the house for years. Cheryl caught Kite's eye, aware that her lover had overstepped the mark.

'Thanks,' Kite replied. 'It's all taken care of.'

'You've kissed and made up?' she asked. She was smartly dressed, her hair in a bun, bustling around the kitchen making tea and toast for Tom. Kite wondered why he couldn't do it himself. 'Is she taking you to the airport?'

He swallowed a mouthful of cereal and went with what he had told Strawson.

'We're taking a break for a bit. Seeing how it goes.'

'Oh no, Lockie. That's awful for you both. When did this get decided?'

Kite was surprised by the force of his mother's reaction. Usually she was so wrapped up in her own affairs – romantic as well as professional – that she didn't appear to give much thought to what was going on in his life. He knew that she liked Martha, but they had never been particularly close. Perhaps she was just worried that he was running away from his problems.

'Recently,' he replied, irritated by the way Tom was pretending to read an article about the Channel Tunnel while earwigging their conversation. It occurred to him that his mother might try to call Martha as soon as he had left for the airport.

'Mum?'

'Yes?'

107

'Can you not call Martha and ask her about it? Don't make a big deal . . .'

'Why would I do that?' She had adopted that faux-innocent tone he knew so well. It meant: 'I'll do exactly what I want, thank you very much.'

'It's just we're still trying to work it out.'

'And you think deepest, darkest Russia is the best place to do that from, do you?'

Tom turned a page on the newspaper.

'Can we drop it?' Kite asked.

He had ordered a minicab for seven thirty. To his relief he saw that it had already arrived. The driver was parked in view of the kitchen window.

'My taxi's here,' he said, not bothering to finish the cereal. 'Might as well go.'

'How do I get hold of you in an emergency?'

'Just call the British embassy in Moscow. I'll ring you when I get the chance.'

'Not easy making international calls from Russia,' Tom interjected. Kite wished that he would stay out of his business. 'You might have more luck in Estonia or Latvia.'

'I'll write then,' Kite replied. It had not occurred to him that his mother might want to contact him. Perhaps she was just putting on a show for Tom; she was always nicer when there was a new boyfriend on the scene. 'Or put one of those emergency messages on the World Service.' In an attempt to lighten the mood, he imitated the voice of a BBC announcer: 'Would Mr Lachlan Kite, of Edinburgh, please contact his family in London, where his mother is gravely ill.'

'Oh thank you!' Cheryl exclaimed.

They looked at one another. Tom had the tact to slink into the garden for a cigarette.

'I'm going to miss you,' she said.

It was an uncharacteristically affectionate thing for her to say. Kite assumed that she was secretly relieved to be seeing the back of him: it meant that she and Tom would now have the house to themselves all summer.

'I'll miss you too,' he replied.

She rushed to her handbag, pressing two fifty-pound notes on him, saying: 'Here, take these.' Kite thanked her with a kiss, stuffing the money into his pocket; he hadn't wanted to take out the Galvin wallet. 'That's really generous of you.'

They carried his suitcases to the taxi. Tom was already back in the kitchen, watching them.

'Just you look after yourself,' she said. 'Dangerous out there. They're not like us, the Russians. Different values.'

'That's not true,' Kite told her. 'They're exactly like us, just with a different history. Everybody says they're kind and hospitable, not at all like they're portrayed in the movies. Besides, we're all friends now. I'll see you in a month or two.'

He could hear Rita's voice in his head as the taxi pulled away from the house: 'As soon as you leave your mother's place, you'll become Peter Galvin. Get into the role, live the cover. You're Peter Galvin to the driver, Peter Galvin to anyone who talks to you at Heathrow, Peter Galvin to the bloke sitting next to you on the plane.' Yet Kite could not yet take on the alias. He wanted to call Martha from the airport, to try to explain why he had dropped off the radar for three days and to tell her he was leaving the country. All the way to Heathrow the traffic was bumper-to-bumper. Thanks to roadworks in Richmond and a car crash in Twickenham, it took almost two hours to reach the terminal. By the time Kite was queuing at the British Airways desk, it was already nine thirty. He put the suitcases into the hold but kept *The English Patient* for his hand luggage. If Customs went through his bags and found the letter to Aranov, Kite would have no idea that he was blown. Better to take it through security rather than risk being tailed by the KGB all the way to Voronezh or – worse – thrown into prison.

'Have a good flight, Mr Galvin,' said the man behind the check-in desk. 'You'll be glad to hear we're on time.'

Kite passed through security, found a payphone and dialled

Martha's house. As soon as she had picked up and said 'Hello', there was an announcement on the tannoy for a flight to New York.

'Martha, it's me.'

'Finally!' she said. 'Where the fuck have you been, Lockie?' She sounded baffled rather than angry, relieved that Kite had at last made contact. 'Where are you? Sounds like a train station.'

'I'm at Heathrow,' he said.

A woman came up behind him, queuing to use the phone.

'Heathrow? Why?'

'I'm going away. To Russia.'

Martha's voice faded as she said: 'Russia? I don't understand . . .'

Kite had known that he would have to give her some sort of plausible excuse. He couldn't just say that he was leaving England on a whim. She might ask him to delay his trip, to come back into London so that they could talk. There was even a possibility that she might want to join him in Moscow.

'It's a last-minute thing. I've been told I can get a job.'

'A job?' She sounded surprised. 'Where?'

Kite didn't want to give Voronezh as his destination so he said: 'Moscow. Teaching English.'

'You've got an interview? I don't understand. When did you decide this? Since when did you want to teach? Don't you need a visa for Russia?'

Each of her questions sounded more astonished than the last.

'Got one yesterday. Just need to go away for a bit, Martha. Get my head straight after what happened.' He hated lying to her, but lies were all that he had left. Kite turned and eyeballed the woman in the queue, annoyed that she was standing close enough to hear what he was saying. 'We need time apart.'

'No we don't! I wish you'd answered my messages. Why are you running away? It's not like you.'

At the insult to his courage Kite's temper flared.

'I'm not running away,' he said. 'You're the one having an affair.'

'Lockie, I am not seeing Cosmo, for Christ's sake. We were high. I didn't even know what I was doing, what *he* was doing. Our pills had been cut with smack. Everybody was monged out.'

'Nobody else was on their own doing what you were doing.'

The retort sounded petty. Kite realised that Gretchen had been right. There was no affair; de Paul had just been taking advantage of Martha's blissed-out state to feel her up. There was another announcement on the tannoy, making it harder for him to hear what Martha was saying.

'You were right to be angry,' she said. He pressed the phone tighter to his ear. 'But you weren't right to leave and just disappear like that. You should have stuck around. You almost broke Cosmo's jaw.'

'Good,' Kite replied, and waited to see how Martha responded. If she defended him, or demanded an apology, he would hang up. To his surprise, it sounded as though she was amused.

'Don't say that,' she said, clearly suppressing a laugh. 'Poor Cosmo. He didn't know what had hit him.'

'It was me. I hit him. And I'll do it again if he comes anywhere near you.'

Kite looked at the screen on the phone. There were likely only a few seconds left on the call. He slid a fifty pence piece into the slot but it fell through, clattering into the tray. He tried again with the same result, saying: 'We're going to get cut off.' He scrabbled around in his pockets for more coins, but each one slid through the mechanism.

'Try 1471,' he said. 'Call me back.'

The line went dead. Kite waited by the phone, indicating to the woman that he was waiting for a call, but it did not ring. There were now two people in the queue, the woman at the front eyeing him impatiently. Kite looked at his watch. He realised that the tannoy announcement must have been the last call for his flight.

He dialled the operator and asked her to reverse the charges to Martha's number. The woman behind him swore under her breath.

'I'm afraid that number's engaged, sir,' the operator told him. 'Do you want me to try it again?'

'Don't worry,' Kite replied and hung up. Perhaps there would be a way of getting a message to Martha once he was in Moscow. Or he could write a letter to her on the plane and ask one of the British Airways crew to post it when they got back to London.

'At long last,' said the woman pointedly as Kite walked away. 'Took your sweet time, didn't you?'

12

The airport at Sheremetyevo was everything Kite had hoped it would be: filthy, chaotic and semi-criminal. His last brush with western *politesse* came at the door of the Boeing 737, which had landed on a humid Moscow afternoon shortly before four o'clock local time. A fussy flight attendant with a blonde bob wished him good day and thanked him for flying British Airways. She was on her way back to London; Kite was heading into the heart of post-Soviet Russia.

There were no problems with the Galvin visa. A dishevelled immigration official, who looked as though he was working four different jobs and hadn't slept in as many days, wearily stamped the passport and seemed to think Kite was certifiably insane for wanting to head into Moscow. In the baggage area, slipping a dollar bill to a porter in a dirty uniform, Kite was given a trolley with only three functioning wheels and shoved his suitcases through Customs. There was an overpowering smell of industrial bleach. A distracted official in a torn jacket conducted a cursory search of his belongings. Finding nothing worth confiscating, she waved him through.

Strawson had warned him that the arrivals hall at Sheremetyevo was 'like the fourth circle of Dante's Inferno'. Kite thought of this as he emerged from the Customs area to be surrounded by a phalanx of unsanctioned taxi drivers, imploring him in broken English to accompany them to the car park and to pay five times the going rate for a journey into Moscow. Kite was en route to Domodedovo for his connecting flight to Voronezh and had been tipped off that the canny traveller would find cheaper, quasi-official drivers on the first floor. So it proved. Having thrown his suitcases into the back of an antediluvian Lada, Kite was at last free of the airport and looking at Russia with his own eyes for the first time.

His driver was a moustachioed, middle-aged Muscovite with a faded colour photograph of his wife and children tacked to the dashboard. He had been a politics professor, hence his good English, and treated Kite to an unbroken monologue about the contemporary political situation so that he might go home and 'tell the world about the chaos in Russia'. The Lada inched along the ring road under a clear blue sky, passing identikit Soviet apartment blocks, broken-down cars, forlorn hitchhikers and old women selling sunflower seeds at the side of the road. The landscape reminded Kite of the outskirts of Glasgow, but it was somehow crueller and more dilapidated. There was no hope in it.

'Yeltsin is puppet of the CIA,' the driver declared. It was at least an hour by car from Sheremetyevo to Domodedovo. Kite had accepted that he was in for the long haul. 'Moscow changing. Everything for sale. Two years ago you arrive on your aeroplane from London, we were all good Communists. Today you arrive on your aeroplane from London, we are all good capitalists. But what has changed? I am the same person.' The driver was a passionate, tactile man. Eyes flared, he turned to face Kite, touching his moustache, pinching his chin and squeezing a cheek to illustrate his point. 'My friends are also the same people, no? My children are the same children they used to be.' He tapped the photograph on the dashboard. 'But the old KGB, they are mafia now. They sell the same things they used to sell in Soviet times, they make the same bribes they used to make when the stock market was not here, but now they are allowed to be openly rich, openly greedy. These people are buying my country for free.'

Kite had been told to conceal the fact that he could read Cyrillic and speak Russian with a degree of fluency. In Strawson's view, there was an obvious operational advantage to being able to understand what others were saying if they assumed they were speaking in confidence. However, as Kite was now discovering, there was also a social disadvantage in not being able to practise his Russian. He was instead obliged to ask questions in English, most of which the driver ignored.

'We had seventy years of Communist rule. People like Yeltsin and his "young economists" think they can change this in less than two years. They are idiots.' He gestured at an unspecified traffic violation in the distance and leaned angrily on the horn. 'Now Michael Jackson is coming to Moscow. Does this prove we are all good capitalists? No, it only proves Russians listen to shit American music.'

The Lada was passing an unlit neon sign for Mercedes-Benz. The stench of disinfectant had come with him; just as Kite had still been able to smell Gretchen's perfume on his skin hours after they had parted, the bleach of Sheremetyevo was on his clothes, in his nostrils, somehow even on his hands.

'Cigarette?' he suggested. The driver shook his head and carried on talking as Kite wound down the window and lit a Marlboro Light.

'You remember what I tell you.' The Lada swerved to avoid a pothole. 'There will soon be civil war in Russia. Riots and protests on the street. The old Communists will not give up control. They have many millions of voters to support them, families without money, bread, clothes. A country cannot continue when people are queuing to buy products from empty shops.'

On that blunt observation, the driver braked hard in a sudden queue of traffic. One of Kite's bags tumbled off the back seat. He had bought a bottle of Johnnie Walker Black in duty-free and checked that it hadn't smashed. He wondered how Martha had reacted to their conversation and assumed she had now spoken to his mother. What would Cheryl have told her? That he was planning to work in a bar in Moscow, to pick fruit in the countryside, to teach English at a language school? He had not written to her on the plane, on the assumption that the risk to his cover, however small, was not worth taking. Presumably Martha would now go back to Oxford, pack her belongings and leave for Zagreb. Kite hoped to be home before August. That would leave plenty of time to patch things up. In the meantime he could enjoy his freedom, just as he was sure that Martha would enjoy hers.

They drove for some time through forests of birch and pine, eventually reaching Domodedovo just after six o'clock. Kite's flight was scheduled for eight fifteen. He paid the driver in dollars, told him to look him up if he ever came to Wokingham, and entered the airport, searching for the Aeroflot counter to Voronezh. There was an identical smell of bleach in the terminal, the same frenzied crowds, but the building was even more run-down. Sheremetyevo had been built for the 1980 Olympics; Domodedovo dated back to the Soviet Brutalism of the 1960s. The queue for the check-in counter was a winner-takes-all scrum of travellers waving tickets and residence papers which Kite managed to circumvent thanks to the intervention of an astonishingly beautiful Aeroflot stewardess who opened up a new line and waved him to the front.

'You are spending long time in Voronezh?' she asked, smiling at Kite in a way that no woman had ever smiled at him before.

'About three months,' he replied, his throat suddenly dry. She was clear-skinned and blue-eyed, a goddess out of a catalogue.

'Please, take this brochure about the city,' she said, handing him a booklet with a colour photograph of a pink-domed Orthodox cathedral on the cover. Kite noticed long, slim fingers, perfectly manicured nails.

'Thank you,' he replied.

'I see you on the plane, Mr Galvin,' she promised, smiling again as she labelled his suitcases.

'See you there,' he said, aware that the woman's interest in him was opportunistic rather than romantic, but flattered nonetheless. He watched his suitcases disappear into the bowels of the airport, picked up his satchel and went in search of something to eat.

There was a café open on the departure side offering not much more than tea and coffee, some dehydrated pastries and a few open sandwiches which looked as though they'd been on display since the 1991 putsch. Kite was famished, buying whatever looked vaguely edible: a croissant, a square of white bread covered in slices of salami, another slathered in butter and red caviar with a mournful sprig of dill on top. As he was eating the croissant, waiting for a cup of radioactively hot black coffee to cool down, he looked up and saw, to his consternation, that a boy he had known at Alford was walking past the café. Kite hoped to God that he hadn't been spotted.

'Lockie?'

His name was Rupert Howell, better known by the nickname 'Lazenby', a sports jock two years his senior who had scored a hundred against Harrow and famously seduced the daughter of a particularly odious housemaster.

'Rupert. What a coincidence.'

No matter where you were in the world, there was always an old Alfordian just around the corner. Kite stood up, wiped his fingers on a paper napkin and shook Howell's hand. Kite did not get the sense that Howell was rushing for a flight.

'Are you heading to Voronezh?'

He looked down at the booklet. Directly above the picture of the cathedral was the word 'Voronezh' in Cyrillic.

'I am,' Kite replied. 'What about you? Where are you off to?'

The way his luck was running, Kite expected Howell to tell him they were on the same flight. He was relieved to discover that Lazenby was in fact en route to Rostov-on-Don.

'A lot of money to be made down here,' he said, lowering his voice to a conspiratorial murmur. 'Lot of palms to be crossed with silver, know what I mean?'

Kite said that he knew exactly what he meant and looked down at his coffee, hoping Howell would leave him in peace. The longer he stuck around, the more of a risk he would present to his cover.

'And you?' he asked, failing to take the hint. 'What does Voronezh hold for Lachlan Kite? I've never been.'

'Meeting a friend,' Kite replied. He did not want to say that he was teaching English, nor that he was simply travelling around Russia for the hell of it. 'He's been studying at the university, invited me out.'

'Ah.'

The conversation continued in this vein for some time. Kite learned that Lazenby was working for an American bank, had a Russian girlfriend in Rostov, another in Moscow, and 'hadn't thought about Alford since the day I left'. As they said farewell, he gave Kite the number of his office in Moscow, urging him to get in touch if he was passing through.

'You should stay out here longer,' he called out. 'Or come back once you've graduated.' Kite flinched at the breach in his cover story. 'Have a good flight, Lockie.'

He sat down at the table, the coffee now at room temperature. There were half a dozen people within earshot, any one of whom could be an FSK tail having a look at him. Kite took their photographs with his eyes. If he saw them on the flight to Voronezh, he might have a problem. Finishing his coffee, he picked up his bag and made his way to the departure gate.

The hour before take-off was pure theatre, beginning with a shakedown from a group of predatory police officers demanding to see residency papers; continuing with a drunken argument between two overweight Russian men quarrelling over who had stepped on who as they were stowing their bags in the overhead lockers; and ending with the beautiful stewardess bringing Kite a balloon of cognac as a

pre-flight aperitif. She deliberately kept her perfectly manicured hand on his arm as she placed the glass on a coaster.

'In case you have fear of flying, Mr Peter. My name is
Elena. If you need anything, let me know.'

For reasons Kite assumed were particular to Russian
hospitality, the cognac came with a small white plate on
which Elena had placed a slice of lemon and a sachet of
sugar. The cabin stank of stale summer sweat and tobacco,
overlaid by a pungent chemical air freshener which hissed
through the valves of the air conditioning. Every passenger
towards the back of the aircraft was smoking, flicking ash
onto a worn, scorched carpet. Kite fell asleep soon after
take-off, waking to find they were flying in darkness. The
engines sounded strained, the plane bouncing around like
a tractor in a pitted field. Holding onto the seats, he walked
the length of the cabin, checking every face, but saw nobody
that he recognised from Domodedovo, only those passengers
who had watched him being ushered to the front of the
queue at the Aeroflot desk. Elena squeezed past him, saying
'turbulence' in a breathless whisper. At the end of the aisle,
a second stewardess, almost as striking as Elena, emerged
from the galley and told Kite to sit down and buckle his
seat belt. Fifteen minutes later the plane was landing in
Voronezh.

Kite had been told that somebody from the Dickens
Institute would be waiting for him. He was not required to
show his passport and collected his bags without difficulty.
In the arrivals hall he was indeed greeted by a very tall man
in a cheap brown suit who introduced himself as Daniil.

'Like Defoe,' he said. He had a high-pitched voice, lively
eyes and chest hair running all the way to his Adam's apple.
'You know Daniel Defoe?'

'Of course,' Kite replied, shaking his hand.

The Russian had been holding a piece of paper with the
name PETER GALVIN written on it in large black letters. He
now scrunched this up into a ball and tossed it into a wire
mesh bin. The airport was a wide, two-storey building not

much bigger than the out-of-town Cash 'n' Carry in Stranraer where Kite had spent many a teenage afternoon buying supplies for his mother's hotel. It was after ten o'clock and the poorly lit car park was almost full. Daniil explained that he would be taking Kite direct to his accommodation and then collecting him at eight o'clock for his first day at the Dickens. He asked if he had enjoyed a good flight and made friendly conversation about the new Russia. Kite had the impression that he was embarrassed about conditions in the apartment block where Galvin had been billeted.

'You will have electricity, but sadly there are power cuts. These are common and not to be a concern to you. Also hot water. There is shower in your apartment. The sheets were changed by my wife this afternoon. They are clean now. I advise you to lock the door at all times and to be careful walking at night.'

It was Kite's first real opportunity to test the Galvin alias. At first he had believed that he might have to assume a completely new character, but had decided that there was no reason for Galvin's attitudes and manner to be any different from his own. Galvin was twenty-eight, not twenty-two. He had lived in Africa; Kite had never been further south than Izmir. Galvin had been raised in suburban England, the only child of a happily married couple from Wokingham; Kite had grown up in rural Scotland, the son of a widowed fashion model whose husband had drunk himself to death. These were the principal biographical differences between them, yet there was nothing to stop Kite and Galvin sharing the same values and sense of humour, the same outlook.

'Do you teach at the school?' Kite asked. He already knew the answer: the Dickens Institute had only one classroom and two permanent teachers. The first was Daniil's boss, Katerina Bokova; the second was Peter Galvin, who was expected to remain in post for several months.

'No,' Daniil replied, shaking his head as though he lacked the necessary skills to succeed as a teacher. 'You are the only one. My superior, Katerina Vladimirovna, has been teaching your classes while we waited for you.'

'How many students will I have?'

Again, it was a question to which Rita had already provided an answer.

'At present we have fourteen enrolled. Some come for the entire course. Others are less . . .' Daniil searched for the correct word: 'Reliable.'

Kite could tell little about Voronezh as they drove away from the airport along a narrow highway on which the headlights of passing cars were the only meaningful source of light. Eventually they passed a children's playground and turned towards an estate of cookie-cutter apartment blocks similar to the *khrushchevki* Kite had seen on the road from Shermetyevo. Daniil parked in front of a dimly lit five-storey block of flats and helped Kite with his luggage. There were torn flyers attached to the rusting metal door as they went inside. The building was hot and smelled of cat urine; an elderly couple were sitting in the lobby on plastic chairs, presumably because it was cooler than in their own apartment. They greeted Kite in Russian. He said: '*Dobryy vecher*' in return but indicated that this was the extent of his knowledge of their language. They looked at him in surprise, clocking the foreign clothes, the foreign accent. Daniil informed him that the lift had temporarily broken down.

'It is normal,' he said with a knowing smile, carrying Kite's bags up several flights of stairs. 'Just in here.' He opened a door on the third floor marked '9' and switched on a bright overhead light inside the flat. 'I hope you will at least be comfortable.'

Kite looked around. He concluded that Daniil was being optimistic. The apartment comprised a small living room, a narrow kitchen and a bathroom with a chipped sink and stained shower curtain. The linoleum flooring throughout was sticky underfoot. Chicken wire had been meshed across the bathroom window. There was a black leatherette sofa in the living room and a chair with orange sponge leaking out of the armrests; it reminded Kite of the honeycomb inside a Crunchie bar. A pair of French windows led out onto a tiled balcony where the mosquito guard had been punctured several times. It was uncomfortably hot and stuffy. Inside the bedroom, the sheets did indeed look recently changed, but a small section of wallpaper was hanging loose from the ceiling and there were marks on the bedside table where somebody had stubbed out a cigarette. In the kitchen Kite found a bowl of fruit, a box of Alionka chocolates and a small bottle of vodka with an envelope leaning against it. He opened it up as Daniil went in search of a fan.

Dear Peter
Welcome to Voronezh! We hope that you enjoyed a good flight and your journey here was most comfortable.
Please accept these gifts from everyone at the Dickens Institute. We are excited that you are here! Tomorrow we will show you the city and you will commence your first classes.
I look forward to meeting you in the morning. Please enjoy a refreshing sleep.
Sincerely
Bokova E.V.

Daniil found a small electric fan and plugged it into a socket in the living room. Kite offered him a glass of vodka but the Russian shook his head.

'Only drink at weekends,' he explained. 'As soon as I start, I do not stop.'

Kite hadn't eaten since Domodedovo and was famished, but assumed that any restaurants in Voronezh would be shut. He opened the fridge. There was some fresh cheese and processed meat inside, two large bottles of water, a packet of butter, some plain biscuits and a cube of black bread.

'So everything is fine, Peter?' Daniil was obviously keen to return home. 'You have everything you need?'

'Everything is fine.'

Kite confirmed that he would be ready at eight o'clock, bid Daniil farewell and locked the door. In a cupboard in the kitchen he found some sugar cubes, a packet of black tea and a tin of corned beef marked 'EC Humanitarian Aid'. There was no sign of a kettle or tin opener. He boiled a pan of water on the stove, retrieved a packet of dried noodles from his suitcase and ate them with a glass of vodka while he walked around the apartment. There was a radio in his bedroom and a black-and-white television in the living room. Kite could hear conversations in the neighbouring flats, the occasional screech of a cat. Having eaten the noodles, he boiled more water and made a cup of tea, smoking a cigarette on the balcony as he watched the traffic on the road into Voronezh. In the distance he could see the blinking lights of the airport and the dark outline of a forest. The balcony would be the best and most obvious place to fly the red signal for BOX in the event that it was needed; there were tram stops on both sides of the busy road from which the clothing would be easily visible.

He finished the cigarette and went back inside. It bemused him to think that only five days earlier he had been living the high life at Penley, sleeping in Egyptian cotton sheets, eating *boeuf bourgignon*, watching Sloanes snorting coke to the tune of 'Fool's Gold'. Now here he was in a Soviet apartment block, digesting ready-made noodles and black tea, thinking of Martha and the long weeks to come. He unpacked his suitcase, took a shower in a trickle of lukewarm, sulphurous water, and climbed into bed. The mattress was hard, the pillow soft and slightly damp. Kite had little sense of his new surroundings; it felt as though he had been wheeled into a hospital in the dead of night and been left to sleep in the darkness of an empty ward. There was no friend or colleague he could turn to for advice or conversation, no way of contacting the outside world. Lying in the darkness, he was not lonely but felt an acute sense of isolation similar to the first night he had spent at Alford as a thirteen-year-old boarder recently arrived from Scotland.

'What am I doing here?' he muttered to himself. 'This is a strange life you have chosen, Mr Galvin.'

13

Though he had seen photographs of its landmarks and studied a detailed street map of Voronezh, Kite's new home came as a surprise to him. He had pictured a bland, medium-sized Russian town of identikit tower blocks, potholed streets and rusting trams, far from the cosmopolitan bustle of Moscow and St Petersburg. His first morning in the city showed Voronezh to be a much larger, more sophisticated place than he had imagined. His apartment may have been situated in a dull suburban housing project three miles from the centre of town, but his route into work passed along the sweeping banks of the Voronezh River into an old town of wide boulevards and pretty nineteenth-century buildings finished in pale yellow stucco. It was not too much of a flight of fancy to imagine Lermontov's Grigory Pechorin pulling up in a horse-drawn carriage at the edge of Petrovski Park, or to picture the dome of the Annunciation Cathedral shrouded in ice in the depths of winter. Voronezh wasn't exactly the Russia of Tolstoy and Zhivago, but nor was it merely a drab Soviet town of concrete and food queues.

'Ninety per cent of what you see was destroyed by the Nazis fifty years ago,' Daniil explained as they drove into the city. 'This is to compare with between fifty and seventy per cent of the great cities of Germany such as Berlin, Hamburg, Dresden. Our city was rebuilt in the Soviet style,

125

the churches and historic monuments restored to former greatness. In parts of Voronezh you can see how the city looked one hundred years ago, before the Communists.'

Ekaterina Bokova was waiting for them outside the Dickens Institute wearing a fixed smile and a simple blue suit. She was a diminutive woman of his mother's generation with a brisk, official manner. She spoke good English, but it was the language of the trade delegation, formal and humourless.

'I take it that you slept well?' she asked, shaking Kite's hand.

'Very well, thank you,' Kite replied, lying through his teeth. Cars had come and gone all night from the parking area beneath his window and it had been stuffy in the airless bedroom.

'And your trip from London was pleasant?'

'Extremely pleasant.'

They entered a three-storey building via a shared entrance on Pushkin Street. Bokova led Kite up three flights of stairs, stopping halfway to adjust a small vase of dried flowers on a windowsill. There was a travel agency on the first floor, an accountancy firm on the second; both looked as though they had been in existence for less than six months. The Institute was on the third floor, occupying four rooms in a converted apartment overlooking the street. Bokova showed Kite into an office lined with bookshelves and filing cabinets, inviting him to leave his satchel by the window. There was a sofa behind the door, a pot of freshly brewed coffee on a side table, a kitschy picture of a Tsarist officer kissing the hand of a girl.

'This is where you can come between classes if you desire it, Peter. Otherwise you will find some cafés within walking distance of the school. You may choose to take lunch there. Please follow me.'

They walked along the corridor to the classroom itself. The first thing Kite noticed was a map of the London Under-ground and, beside it, a medley of flags – a Union Jack, the Stars and Stripes, the red maple leaf of Canada – on the facing wall. He walked up to the map and put his finger on South Kensington, thinking of Xavier in Onslow Square, of his friends from Edinburgh and Alford setting out on summer holidays to Greece and Ibiza. There were sixteen desks arranged in rows of four facing a large table at the far end of the room. On a whiteboard somebody – presumably Bokova – had written: 'Welcome Mr Galvin'. On either side of the whiteboard were photographs of various western celebrities and politicians – Clint Eastwood, Madonna, Margaret Thatcher, Ronald Reagan – as well as photographs of famous landmarks in the English-speaking world: the Sydney Harbour Bridge, the World Trade Center, Big Ben. For the first time Kite felt a sense of anxiety about what lay ahead. He had never taught a class in his life yet was masquerading as a man who had spent four years in Malawi teaching the locals to speak English. How the hell was he going to get away with it?

'What do you think?' Daniil asked.

'Very nice,' Kite replied, craving a cup of coffee. 'Just like my classroom in Lilongwe. Although in Malawi there was also a picture of the Queen on the wall.'

Bokova smiled benignly. 'Yes. We are looking forward to hearing about Africa. First I take a copy of your passport.'

Kite had brought the Galvin passport and handed it over. Bokova looked at the front page, walked with him back to the office, studied Kite's photograph closely and made a note of his details on a typewritten sheet of paper. It was like going through Immigration again.

'You look much younger than we were expecting,' she said, eyeing him with apparent suspicion. 'I had imagined you as a grown man. You seem more like student.'

Kite wondered if she had seen the photograph on Galvin's original visa application, but dismissed the idea as fanciful. More likely she was concerned that Galvin had lied about the depth of his teaching experience on the CV.

'I used to have a beard,' he said as she continued to fill in boxes on the form. 'Shaved it off. People say it makes me look younger.'

'I see.'

Daniil came into the office. He handed Kite a map of the city, a booklet detailing times for the local bus and tram networks and a copy of *Horizon*, the textbook used by language schools across Russia which had already been shown to him at The Cathedral. It became clear that Daniil and Bokova were in business together as joint owners of the Dickens. Kite was required to fill out various forms, told that he would be paid 215,000 roubles per week – the equivalent of about $200 – and given a list of useful local telephone numbers.

'We begin at eleven o'clock every morning, Monday to Saturday,' Bokova told him. 'You will teach for two hours then take a lunch break. After that you will teach from three o'clock until five o'clock. Halfway through each class you can break for five minutes so that the students may smoke or use the bathroom. I trust this will be convenient.'

'Very convenient,' Kite replied.

'I insist on certain rules from my staff.' Bokova's inflexible, moralistic tone was sounding alarm bells. She reminded Kite of Joyce Blackburn, the Rosa Klebb lookalike who had run his house at Alford. 'First, you must arrive for work fifteen minutes early each morning and tidy the classroom last thing at night before you leave. Second, any books that you take from the library must be signed out on this form.' Kite wondered what library she was referring to and assumed that the English-language paperbacks in the office were made available to students as loans. 'The fax machine is not for your personal use. You may only take advantage of the telephone in my presence or in the presence of my fellow director.' She nodded in the direction of Daniil, who shot Kite a look of grave seriousness. 'Additionally,' she said, 'you are forbidden to have relationships of a romantic nature with our students. Under the terms of your employment, you may also not leave Voronezh. This is because your medical insurance will be forfeit. You are forbidden to give private lessons. All professional work must be carried out on the premises of the Dickens Institute. Is this satisfactory?'

'Entirely satisfactory.' Kite didn't like being ordered around, especially by dour, box-ticking bureaucrats. His impulse was to push back, to have an affair with a student and to teach private lessons, but he told himself that Peter Galvin was the quiet, biddable type, a yes man who wouldn't make waves. Daniil suggested that he might like to eat breakfast and Kite gratefully excused himself, finding a canteen three blocks away where he ordered a watery omelette and a cup of tea. It was evident that the job was going to be a drag, that life in Voronezh would be almost entirely devoid of the basic comforts of home. Strawson had dumped him in the back of beyond working for an unreconstructed Soviet authoritarian who would be watching him like a hawk. He told himself that all that mattered was making contact with Aranov. He could turn out to be the world's worst English-language teacher, but if he got Yuri out of Russia, he would be a hero at The Cathedral. As soon as Aranov showed up, Kite would set in motion the plan to go to the dacha. With any luck, they would be in Dnipropetrovsk before the end of the month.

He returned to the Institute and waited in the classroom for his students to arrive. It was like being the first guest at a party, pacing the room to no purpose. He stared at the map of the Tube, picturing Martha boarding a train at Swiss Cottage, moving on with her life in his absence. He recalled Strawson's warning that any student attending his class could be FSK. Kite would need to be alert to anyone who asked him too many personal questions; one slip and the operation could be over. For the first time, he realised that he was going to be trusting his life to a man he had never met. What was to stop Yuri Aranov betraying him to the Russians if he thought he could gain personal advantage from doing so?

That thought was interrupted by the arrival of his first students, a hand-in-hand couple in their late teens who wished Kite a cheery good morning in Russian.

'Hello there,' he replied in English, asking their names.

The man had close-cropped hair and puppy fluff on his

pale freckled cheeks. He was wearing a denim jacket with chinos and a set of Walkman headphones looped around his neck. The girlfriend was a similarly pallid, shy-looking woman, also wearing a denim jacket. She had piercings in her ears.

The next student arrived alone. A grey-haired woman who might have been sixty, might have been forty, she was seemingly of a different class to the well-tended Bokova. She wore old clothes, no make-up, and carried an expression of infinite weariness. She reminded Kite of the women he had seen selling sunflower seeds at the edge of the Moscow ring-road. As she sat down, she greeted her fellow students in Russian but showed no interest in her new teacher. Kite dubbed her 'Auntie' in his mind as he searched in the drawer of his desk for a board marker.

Aranov was not among the group of three students who now entered the classroom in quick succession. The first was a very young man in a black bomber jacket who introduced himself as Lev and shook Kite's hand, welcoming him to Voronezh in surprisingly good English. The second was a tall, stunning blonde in her mid-twenties in brown leather cowboy boots, skintight blue jeans and a yellow T-shirt. She knew where her power lay and immediately settled a flirtatious glance on Kite. He nodded at her, stunned, and gave silent thanks to Strawson for sending him to Voronezh. The last of the three was a thick-set man of about forty-five carrying a copy of *Izvestia*. He had the surly, impassive manner of a long-distance truck driver and chose a desk in the back row, directly beside the beautiful woman. There was an audible grunt as he sat down.

Still no Aranov. Bokova entered the classroom and stood beside Kite as the last of his students hurried in. Another young couple, both with a sharp, intelligent air about them, headed towards the front row. The woman was wearing torn jeans and an Iron Maiden T-shirt. Her partner was in a brown leather jacket and said 'Hi' to Kite as he sat down. Kite doubted that the FSK would go to the trouble and expense of putting two role-playing officers into the classroom at the same time, but would keep an eye on them nonethe-less. A much older woman, at least seventy, with thinning grey hair and a loose-fitting dress, now entered the room, apologised to her classmates for being late and settled at the nearest available table. She produced a notebook from a plastic shopping bag and sat with an air of patient expectation on her face. She was soon followed by a man of a similar age who walked with a slight limp. The two did not appear to know one another, though the man sat beside her in the third row. Either could be FSK retreads, brought out of retire-ment for the simple but time-consuming task of reporting on Yuri Aranov. Kite dubbed them 'Granny' and 'Grandpa' and glanced at his notes. Bokova closed the door on the stroke of eleven o'clock and announced in Russian that the class would now proceed.

'This is everybody?' Kite asked. There were still several empty desks and no sign of Aranov.

'There may be more,' Bokova replied. 'Some of our students do not always attend every class. They have other responsi-bilities.' In Russian she added: 'Sometimes they also oversleep' and everyone laughed. Kite had to pretend not to have understood what she had said.

He was introduced to the class as 'Mr Peter Galvin, recently arrived from London.' There was a round of muted applause. Kite had the impression that Bokova had been talking him up as an experienced, resourceful teacher who had travelled widely. He was worried that the students might be surprised by how young he looked.

'So now I would like to hand things over to you, Peter, and you will begin,' she said.

Kite stepped forward.

'Thank you. Good morning, everybody. My name is Peter Galvin.'

'Good morning, Mister Galvin!'

Kite was taken aback by the force of the collective greeting and took a moment to compose himself. *Go for it,* he thought. *You have nothing to lose*. He remembered what the teacher at

The Cathedral had told him: 'Speak slowly and clearly. Impose yourself on the class from the very first moment.'

'As a rule,' he began, 'I always speak English in my lessons. Even if you cannot understand everything that I am saying, I think it is important for you to hear spoken English as much as possible. To tune your ears to the words, to adjust your brains to the rhythms.' Kite caught Bokova's eye. She was looking at him with an air of uncertainty. 'When I first started out as a teacher, in Africa of all places, I tried to use some of the local language whenever my students found it too difficult to understand what I was saying. But I concluded that it was best always to speak English. So that is what we will be doing over the next weeks and months. I will try to speak slowly and clearly, and to avoid using slang, so that you can recognise as many of the words that I am using as possible.'

It all seemed to be going well. The *Izvestia*-reading truck driver was nodding in apparent understanding of everything Kite was saying. The beautiful girl was dutifully writing notes in a pad. Bokova slipped out of the room, leaving Kite to his own devices.

'I was born in England in 1965,' he said, 'in a small town called Wokingham. I have been a teacher for the last five years. Why don't we start by going around the room? You can tell me your names, where you were born and what you hope to do after qualifying from the Dickens Institute. Lev, let's start with you?'

And so it began. For the next two hours, Kite learned the names of his pupils, was able to gauge the level of their spoken English and concluded that teaching them was going to be relatively straightforward. The truck driver, Dmitri, turned out to be a former factory worker. Granny and Grandpa were, respectively, a retired shopkeeper and a lawyer. Kite doubted their stories and wondered if one, or both of them, were retreads. 'Auntie', who grew more friendly towards him as the class progressed, revealed that she had once been a violinist with the St Petersburg Philharmonic. Her name was

Maria. The beautiful, mysterious girl in the cowboy boots was called Oksana Sharikova. She was due to study law in the autumn and wanted to be fluent in English in order to enhance her prospects of working overseas. She had a low, smoky voice and a way of looking at Kite that drove every thought of Martha from his mind.

'My dream is to go to America,' she told the class, tapping her cheek with the tip of a pencil. 'New York. Chicago. Los Angeles. This is where I want to live.'

The rest of the day passed quickly. Kite was surprised by how easily he took to teaching and was not concerned that Aranov had failed to show up. He was sure that he would appear the following morning. After classes had ended, Daniil gave him directions to a local store where he stocked up on some basic provisions for his flat. There had been more on the shelves than he had expected from watching news footage of the food queues in Russia: he was able to buy a bag of rice, a tin of tomatoes, some dried macaroni and a packet of boiled ham. Having eaten a tin of sardines and some processed cheese with the block of black bread for dinner, Kite drank more of the vodka and wandered the corridors of his apartment block, stopping briefly to greet a married couple on the top floor, neither of whom spoke English. The next day he went back to the Dickens, but there was again no sign of Aranov. He taught a full day's classes before heading into Voronezh for dinner. A pizza restaurant had opened near the school and there was a kiosk in Petrovski Park selling Heineken from plastic cups. Kite decided to walk the three miles back to his apartment and was asleep by midnight.

It was the same on Saturday: no Aranov. Kite assumed that he was either sick or out of town, but was nevertheless frustrated that they had not yet made contact. He spent the rest of the weekend walking the humid streets of Voronezh so that by Sunday evening he had more or less familiarised himself with the layout of the city.

An entire week then passed with no sign of Yuri. Day after day, Kite dutifully commuted to the Dickens, taught his lessons and returned home wondering when the hell Strawson's scientist was going to show his face. Granny and Grandpa stopped coming to his classes; it was as though they knew that Aranov was no longer in Voronezh and were wasting their time by being there. Kite listened out for the whistled theme of *The Godfather*, expecting somebody from BOX 88 to explain what had gone wrong, but heard nothing. Only once, while waiting at a tram stop carrying several shopping bags stuffed with tinned food and Georgian wine, did he hear a man humming a tune, but it was just a few jaunty bars of Tchaikovsky, not the contact signal from London.

A glance at the Institute's list of students in Bokova's office showed that Aranov was still enrolled at the Institute, yet Kite could not ask about him without arousing suspicion. He assumed that somebody in the class – Lev, perhaps, or Dmitri – knew something about him socially and resolved to find a way of asking them which would not seem odd or out of character. Yet when he enquired about the students who were missing from the class, mentioning Aranov by name as well as another individual, Misha, who had never shown up, neither man was particularly helpful.

'Maybe they were here before,' said Lev, smoking with Kite outside the Institute on a roastingly hot Wednesday afternoon. 'Maybe somebody else teaches them now. I do not know.'

Dmitri was slightly more forthcoming, mentioning that he had seen Yuri at the Institute in May, but had heard that he was busy with other 'opportunities' and perhaps did not have time to attend class.

'He was kind of a crazy person anyway,' he said. Kite had wanted to delve deeper into this, but could not do so for fear of seeming unusually preoccupied with one particular student. Better to respond as though he had no interest in the idiosyncrasies of Yuri's personality and to continue to keep a low profile.

To pass the time between classes, Kite took to running in

the forest and swimming in a freshwater lake on the edge of town. With some of the money given to him by Rita, he bought a bicycle which gave him the freedom to explore parts of the city that might later become useful as meeting places for Aranov. In the evenings he would watch old European art-house films at the cinema or go to Café Anna, a quiet, cosy restaurant where it was possible to eat passably well. Strawson had told him to keep a journal, recording Galvin's impressions of Russia, his feelings towards his parents back in Wokingham, his day-to-day thoughts about life in Voronezh. It was all part of building up his cover. After dinner he might have a whisky at the bar of the Hotel Brno, his fellow drinkers providing some sense of connection with the world beyond Voronezh. Local girls wearing stockings and miniskirts would flirt with businessmen from Kazakhstan and the Baltics. After a couple of drinks – sometimes after only a few minutes – the men would withdraw to the lobby with a girl and head for the lifts. Kite had never seen prostitutes before and was fascinated by them; he wondered if what happened upstairs was any different to what happened between ordinary couples when they went to bed. He could only imagine that the sex was false and depressing, like a re-run of what had happened with Gretchen. The girls were about the same age as Oksana, which only intensified his desire for her. In class, she had taken to wearing high heels and miniskirts of astonishing brevity, regularly catching Kite's eye as he declined an irregular verb or tried to explain the difference between 'there', 'their' and 'they're'. Only a sense of professional obligation prevented him from asking her out: if he was fired by Bokova for seducing one of his students, Strawson would never forgive him.

Teaching was all that Kite had. He designed his lessons so that they became celebrations of British achievements – the discovery of DNA and penicillin, the invention of the jet engine and television. He tried to teach the laws of cricket to a room of befuddled Russians who seemed interested only in learning about tennis. He was asked to explain the reason for Paul Gascoigne's tears at the 1990 World Cup and to give his opinion on the divorce of Prince Charles and Lady Diana Spencer. (Bokova had found a photograph of the Queen and tacked it up in the classroom on the assumption that Kite was a staunch monarchist.) Every afternoon he took classwork to a café near the school and dutifully marked spelling tests and grammar modules, passing the halfway mark in *War and Peace* and wondering when – if ever – he would be able to speak to Martha. It was fascinating to experience Russian life at first hand, to live in a way that was completely new to him, but without Aranov, Kite felt as though he was walking alone in a dense forest, moving forward to no purpose, never knowing when, if ever, he would emerge into the light.

After ten days he began to wonder if Strawson was testing him: perhaps there was no Aranov, no exfiltration plan. BOX 88 simply wanted to know how he would cope with the Galvin alias for long days in a strange and distant city. Or perhaps he was being used as a decoy, pulling FSK surveillance away from a more pressing operation in the region. Yet at no time had Kite felt that he was being watched; on the contrary, when he ate in the canteens and restaurants of the old city, or swam in the lake after work, he did so with a sense of absolute anonymity. Nobody seemed interested in him. No stranger approached him on the street, nobody knocked on the door of his apartment looking to strike up a friendship. Far from being informers for the FSK, his students seemed blamelessly industrious. As far as Kite could tell, his flat had not been searched, nor was he followed when he went for runs or biked along the banks of the river. He was just another random star in a crowded night sky – obscure, indistinct, solitary. Hour by hour, it felt as though his former identity as Lachlan Kite was receding from him and he was being replaced by another person: a loner called Peter Galvin, a man without friends or purpose for whom each day was eerily similar. Kite's life in Russia was a blank canvas. Without Aranov in circulation, he had no reason to be there. He was not himself; he was not even a spy. He remembered something Billy Peele had told him at Alford: 'Character is how you behave when you think nobody is watching.' There was no director of studies, no flatmate, no Martha, to keep an eye on him. For the first time in his adult life, Lachlan Kite was completely free.

How to use that freedom? Oksana had given him every encouragement to ask her out, but Kite was trying to remain professional. His self-discipline lasted only until Lev invited him to a Saturday-night birthday party in a suburb of Voronezh at which Oksana was one of the guests. She turned up with two older women, both Russian, and did not seem at all surprised when she spotted Kite in the kitchen. He had been standing over a table of fried cheese, jellied fish and room-temperature red caviar blinis, wondering what was safe to eat.

'Professor,' she said, touching his arm. It was her nickname for him in class. The contact of her fingers against his skin was like a signal she was sending which pulsed through his body. She was wearing denim shorts and a cropped T-shirt and smelled as though she had just stepped out of a long, hot shower. 'I am so glad you are here.'

'I didn't know you'd been invited,' Kite replied, trying to play it cool. Lev had given him a shot of Bulgarian brandy when he arrived and he was feeling slightly drunk. 'Are those your flatmates?'

'My sister and a friend,' Oksana replied, as if she was confessing something to him.

Kite wondered if Lev was deliberately setting them up, perhaps on her orders. Either way, he at last had a chance to get to know her away from Bokova's all-seeing eye. There was a case of cold beers in the fridge and he fetched her one, taking Oksana out onto a terrace overlooking the city. He asked about her past and learned that she was one of five children; her father had walked out on his family when she was six years old, never to be seen again. As soon as he understood this about Oksana, Kite could see her character more clearly. In class she was diligent and attentive, with an air of mystery and self-assurance particular to Russian women, which he found extraordinarily attractive. Now he saw the survivor in her, the young woman determined to make the most of her opportunities, to work hard, to self-improve and – yes – to use her beauty to her advantage. It was as though she could see her own future with absolute clarity and knew how to get there. Kite might just be a stepping stone along the way.

One beer led to three, four beers led to six, and by eleven Kite and Oksana were huddled together in the living room of the spacious apartment smoking a joint and listening to The Clash. Kite wanted to touch her skin, just as de Paul had walked his fingers along Martha's stomach while they lay together in a stoned embrace. 'Lost in the Supermarket' gave way to 'Should I Stay or Should I Go?' and Kite put down his beer.

'I never understood the lyrics of this song,' he said. Oksana had taken out a pair of sunglasses. She put them on Kite's face as he spoke. 'If he stays, there will be trouble. If he goes, it will be double. So why doesn't he just stay?'

'Are you teaching me all the time, Professor Peter?'

'All the time.' Kite peered over the top of the sunglasses. 'I take my responsibilities towards my students very seriously.'

'How old are you?' she asked.

Kite almost said 'twenty-two' but checked himself and remembered that Galvin had been born in 1965.

'Twenty-eight,' he said. 'How about you?'

'Twenty-five. My last boyfriend thirty-five. You are baby compared to him.'

She reached out and touched his nose with the tip of her finger, the joint still in her hand and close enough that Kite felt the heat of the ember. His entire body surged with desire.

'I look younger than I am,' he replied, resenting the need to lie to her.

'So how is it you never invited me out?' she asked, making a face of mock outrage. Her mouth was so beautiful Kite wanted to photograph it.

'Because it is illegal.'

'*Illegal?* What is this please?'

Kite searched for equivalent words in English: 'Outlawed. Banned.' He knew one in Russian – '*zapreshcheno*' – but could not use it.

'Forbidden,' he said.

Oksana looked genuinely offended. 'I do not understand. What does it mean, please, forbidden? You are married?'

Kite laughed. 'No, no. I'm not married.'

'You have girlfriend then? Back in England. I think she is very beautiful, no?'

Again he lied, this time for his own benefit. 'I don't have a girlfriend.'

Oksana looked relieved. Kite wondered if he was being played, but there was surely something genuine in her apparent desire for him. She said: 'I am happy to hear this,' and he felt his neck flush.

'I would lose my job if we are caught having dinner together,' he explained. 'Katya Bokova warned me not to date any of my students. It is against the rules.'

'And you are afraid of this woman?'

A flash of defiance in Oksana's eyes. Kite took the sunglasses off and looked at her. 'Of course I'm not afraid of her. In fact I was going to ask you out to dinner on Monday.'

'You were?' She fixed him with a quizzical look, at once delighted and suspicious. 'And where will we have this dinner, Professor?'

'Wherever you like,' Kite replied quickly, noticing an improvement in Oksana's English. Her friend walked into the room, saw that they were deep in conversation and immediately left. 'I'm forbidden to leave Voronezh,' he explained. 'My medical insurance won't cover us if I take you to Moscow or St Petersburg.'

Oksana giggled. 'Medical insurance? What you think I do to you? Give you heart attack?'

'You would give any man a heart attack, Oksana.'

'You are just flattering me,' she said, touching his chest. The music changed abruptly from The Clash to The Beatles. In the sudden change of mood, Kite leaned foward and tried to kiss her.

'Not here,' she said, turning her lovely eyes towards him. 'Let's go somewhere else.'

They walked back to his flat along the banks of the Voronezh River, occasionally stopping to kiss, Oksana teasing him that they would be seen by 'one of Bokova's spies'. A cockroach scuttled across the lobby of Kite's apartment block when they walked in, but they were both too stoned and too full of desire to care, tearing at each other in the shuddering lift which had now been fixed and smelled of engine oil. Kite fumbled for his key, pulled Oksana into the apartment and took her straight to bed where they remained for the next thirty-six hours, emerging only to make scrambled eggs and a pot of coffee or to smoke the occasional cigarette on the living-room balcony. She was by turns passionate and unrestrained, yet also tender and funny, tuning into Kite's reckless spirit, his need for intimacy, so that at times a dangerous tenderness grew up between them. By dawn on Monday, he was physically exhausted, watching Oksana sleep in the strengthening light of a new summer day, frustrated that he had to go into work but convinced that they would now be together for the duration of his stay in Russia. He felt awkward about Martha but not guilty; he told himself that she was now almost certainly involved with Cosmo de Paul and that what had happened was an acceptable corrective. He wrote Oksana a note, telling her to stay as long as she wanted, then biked into town. Bokova was not yet at the Dickens, but Daniil buzzed him inside.

'Student waiting for you already,' he said, sipping a cup of coffee in the office. 'He come early.'

Normally the students arrived just before eleven o'clock, giving Kite ten minutes or so to think about what he was going to teach. He walked down the corridor and entered the room. A man was sitting in Oksana's seat with his back to the door. He was eating an apple and reading an article in *Novaya Gazeta*.

'My name is Yuri,' he announced, turning around. 'I have been student here since March. What is your name, please?'

14

Aranov was thinner than Kite had expected, but wiry and fiercely alert. His eyes were bright blue, cunning and clear, the skin unhealthily pale; it was the complexion of a man who had spent too long in the laboratory. He did not appear to recognise Kite nor give any indication that he had been waiting for him. Their conversation was matter-of-fact to the point of being dull. Aranov asked the questions, Kite gave the answers.

'You are English, Mr Galvin?'

'That's right.'

'When did you arrive in Voronezh?'

'About ten days ago. Were you coming to classes before then?'

'I have told you that already. I began in March.' Aranov's English was good, possibly too good for him to be plausibly enrolled at the Dickens. 'So who is left in class now? Viktor? Dmitri? Is Oksana still a student here?'

Kite was startled to hear Oksana's name. He thought of her asleep in his hard, narrow bed, the sheets crumpled after hours of bliss.

'Oksana?' he repeated.

'Yes.' Aranov made a cupping gesture, weighing Oksana's breasts in a mime, and said: 'Looks like the witch.'

'The witch?' Kite felt the criticism as a personal insult. 'What do you mean?'

'The film. The Witch of Eastwood. One of the women. The blonde. Michelle . . .'

'Oh! Pfeiffer. Michelle Pfeiffer.' Kite didn't see the resemblance but ran with it. 'Yes, *The Witches of Eastwick*. She does look a bit like Michelle Pfeiffer. You're right.'

'Of course.' Aranov's tone suggested he was rarely wrong. 'Who else comes? The woman playing the cello?'

Kite realised Yuri was asking about each of the students in turn because he was concerned that one of them was FSK.

'Yes, Maria still comes in.'

Aranov folded up his newspaper. He had still not given Kite any indication that he knew who he was.

'How do you like my city?' he asked.

'I like it very much . . .'

'They give you shit apartment?'

Kite laughed. 'It's not the Palace of the Kremlin, but it's OK.'

Aranov was confused. 'Kremlin? What do you mean Kremlin?'

Kite clarified what he had meant, but his explanation was laboured; by the time he had finished, Aranov had moved on.

'What time lessons begin?' he asked, pointing at the clock above the door.

'Same time as always.'

'Then I go for cigarette,' he said, and left the room.

Kite had waited so long to make contact with Aranov that their first encounter felt strangely anti-climactic. He could only assume that he had been playing the innocent for Daniil, who might be listening in, or for the benefit of any FSK microphones secreted in the classroom. The first of Kite's students filed in. Any elation he might have felt at Aranov's appearance was further curtailed by his hangover; he craved a decent breakfast and a strong cup of coffee. To make things

143

worse, Kite realised that he had left his students' homework back at the apartment; there was no phone in the flat and therefore no way of contacting Oksana and asking her to bring it in. As he stood at his desk, remembering that he needed to begin the class with some words about Winston Churchill, Granny and Grandpa walked in and sat at their usual seats. Were they back because of Aranov? The other students soon followed, most of them wearing long-suffering, Monday-morning expressions of resentment at the long day to come.

'Good morning, everybody.'

'Good morning, Mr Galvin.'

'We have a new student with us today.' Kite looked over at Aranov, who had returned from smoking his cigarette. 'I'm sorry. Can you remind me of your name, please?'

'Me?' The Russian touched his chest, as if nobody who met Yuri Aranov ever forgot him. 'I already tell you. My name Yuri.'

Kite was extraordinarily thirsty. He had meant to bring a bottle of water to class but had been in too much of a rush to buy one.

'Thank you, Yuri,' he said. He suddenly pictured Aranov in his place of work, cooking up death in a lab coat. The mental image distracted him and he briefly lost his train of thought. 'I am afraid to say that I have left your exercises at home,' Kite continued. There was minimal reaction to this. 'My apologies. I will bring them in to class tomorrow. Everybody did very well, especially on the spelling test.' Granny looked up and gave a relieved smile, as though she had been expecting to fail. 'So instead of going over the mistakes some of you made, why don't we talk about Winston Churchill, the prime minister of Great Britain and an ally of Russia during the Second World War?'

It was as though Aranov had touched an electric fence. Unseen by his fellow students, he flinched in his seat and blushed. Had he been so caught up in himself that he had forgotten what Wendy had told him? Perhaps she had not explained things clearly enough.

'Winston Churchill is the most famous and respected man in my country because of his leadership during the war.' Granny and Grandpa looked intrigued; the younger students appeared to be tuning out. All Kite cared about was Aranov's reaction: there had been a complete change in his expression, a new-found respect for the mysterious Mr Galvin. 'Born into an aristocratic family, he only became prime minister after the war had begun . . .'

Kite continued in this vein for about five minutes, far longer than was necessary for the purpose of conveying the signal to Aranov, but a plausible amount of time for any listening FSK officers to be hoodwinked. Feeling the effects of his hangover more seriously with every passing minute, he encouraged the students to turn to a section in their booklets about government and walked them through several key words – 'politician', 'minister', 'election' – before setting yet another spelling test. It was hard going. By the time the lunch break came around, he was desperate for something to eat. He packed the tests in his satchel and headed to his regular canteen on the next block, wondering how best to make a formal approach to Aranov.

The food in the canteen did not change from day to day. Under bright strip lights, Kite picked up a metal tray and queued for soup, the ubiquitous sprig of dill and dollop of sour cream floating on the surface. The main course was a lump of unidentifiable meat with boiled potatoes and a helping of pickled cabbage. It wasn't Langan's, but it was the first substantial meal he had eaten in almost two days and he wolfed it down. He had sat at his usual table by the window, looking out at the narrow, cobbled street. The unmarked tests stared at him like a rebuke for the excesses of the weekend. What to do next? Aranov knew who he was; it was now up to him to make the next move.

Kite finished eating and pushed his plate to one side, wiping his fingers on a paper napkin so that the grease wouldn't transfer onto the tests. One by one, he worked through his students' answers, noting that everybody misspelled 'government' and only one pupil – Lev – knew how to write the word 'election'. Aranov's was the last paper Kite marked. He picked it up and quickly scanned his answers:

1. **Prime Minister**
2. **Vote**
3. **Electin**
4. **Adolf Hitler**
5. **Downing Street**
6. **Winston Churchill**
7. **Polticians**
8. **Goverment**

So far, so unremarkable. Aranov, the genius scientist, had scored five out of eight. But at the bottom of the page, in an almost illegible hand, the Russian had written a note.

Nice to meet you Peter Galvin. You are good teecher. I am interested private leson. Maybe you no place we talk cost of this?

Of course. Kite's sleep-deprived brain had been slowed by the excesses of the weekend and the interminable morning. By setting the test he had unwittingly given Aranov an immediate opportunity to contact him.

He now knew what to do. As soon as the class resumed, Kite returned the tests to the students and ran through the correct answers. This took the better part of half an hour. As he was talking, Kite noticed that Aranov slowly tore off chunks from the bottom portion of his test paper, quietly scrunched them up and stuck them in his mouth like chewing gum. Leaving no trace, no trail. Wendy had taught him well.

'So, what I would like to do now is carry on where we stopped off on Friday and continue our work on gerunds,' Kite announced. The class, including Aranov, looked hugely bored. 'Don't despair!' he said. 'Specifically I want to look at the use of "to" plus the infinitive.' Kite turned to the whiteboard and wrote the word 'to' in huge letters. 'Can anyone give me an example of the infinitive?'

Various examples were volunteered: 'to walk', 'to eat', 'to drive', 'to kill'. Kite nodded along enthusiastically, encouraging his students to keep making suggestions. Thus far, Aranov had remained silent.

'Good!' he said, as Granny called out 'to cook'. 'Now we add the gerund.'

'Mister Galvin,' Aranov interrupted. 'What is gerund, please?'

Kite was glad that he had asked. It meant that Yuri was paying attention and would realise what he was about to do. He explained that a gerund was the -ing form of a verb and gave examples: 'walking', 'cooking', 'killing', 'driving'.

'OK,' Aranov replied, looking as though he had grasped it. 'So what's next?'

What's next is that I'm going to tell you how to make contact with me, Kite thought. He smiled benignly at the rest of the class.

'Let me give you some proper examples.'

He turned again to the whiteboard, only this time he was writing messages in plain sight intended only for Yuri Aranov. Kite spoke each of the sentences aloud, making frequent, glancing eye contact with the Russian.

I want to start meeting new people as soon as possible.

Every evening I like to go swimming in the lake near the old windmill.

My mother agreed to try dancing for the first time.

My sister hopes to stop smoking in the winter.

I like to go drinking in the bar at the Theatre of the Young Spectator.

Kite scanned the faces of his students. Some looked

confused, others were nodding along in their customary way. He was interested only in Aranov's reaction. Surely he had grasped the very basic code?

'Does everybody understand?' he asked.

Aranov stuck up his hand.

'Swimming,' he said. 'This is when you go in the water?' He mimed a front crawl, to the amusement of his classmates.

'That's right, Yuri.' Kite smiled at him encouragingly. He pointed to the sentence on the board, giving Aranov another chance to understand what he was trying to tell him. 'Every evening I like to go swimming in the lake near the old windmill. This is an example of "to" plus the infinitive, adding a gerund.'

Aranov was seated at the back of the class. Only Kite could see the particular look of satisfaction on his face as he said: 'Yes, I understand.' For an instant it was just the two of them in the room, speaking privately, making a secret plan.

'I'm glad to hear it,' Kite replied. 'Now we can proceed.'

15

Kite returned to his apartment in a buoyant mood, elated at last to have made contact with Aranov. They would meet at the lake in two days' time; Aranov had muttered the Russian word *Sreda*, meaning 'Wednesday', to him as he left the class. Whoever else happened to be there – or happened to be watching – would witness an apparently innocent, accidental meeting between teacher and pupil.

It had been a hot, stuffy day in Voronezh. A group of Kite's neighbours were gathered outside the apartment block, escaping their cramped breezeblock flats for the cooler evening air. Though he had been living in the building for some time, Kite was still a stranger among them; they stopped talking as he pulled up on his bicycle. He wanted to befriend them, to find out about their lives, but could not converse in Russian because of the Galvin cover. Kite nodded at the elderly lady he had spoken to on his first night in the city, but she blanked him. As he reached the rusted steel door at the front entrance, he heard one of the older men say, in Russian: 'I don't trust him.' He wanted to confront him but had to keep walking, crossing the lobby with its torn flyers and stench of stale cat piss. The remark had the effect of sucking away some of Kite's optimism. Once again he felt the acute sense of isolation of his first days in Russia.

Oksana had left an unfinished glass of tea on the kitchen

table. He was glad not to find her slumbering in bed; he needed some time to himself. She had left the balcony doors open. The voices of his neighbours were audible below; Kite wondered if somebody had seen Oksana leaving the building or had heard them making love at the weekend. The walls were as thin as the boys' rooms at Alford. Kite was regularly treated to the clatter of dropped saucepans, the miaow of cats, the screaming rows between the middle-aged couple who lived above him.

He went to the fridge and drank two glasses of orange juice in quick succession, then switched on the shower and stood under a two-pronged stream of cold water which did little to cool him down. He should have gone for a swim in the lake. On the handrail in the bathroom was the red T-shirt he had set aside before the weekend. Had Aranov not shown up at school, Kite had been ready to fly the signal.

He wondered if Oksana had gone home and, in the same thought, tried to imagine what Martha was up to. He had no photograph of her face, only his own memories and the constant worry that he had abandoned her without explanation. He imagined that she was bewildered and angry. Perhaps she too felt that same strange mixture of liberation and longing with which Kite had been wrestling since Penley. He poured himself two inches of vodka from the freezer, drank them as a shot and waited for the mellow kick of the alcohol to lift him, smoking a cigarette on the balcony out of sight of the neighbours below. A bird flew in low over the road and settled on the next balcony, pecking briefly at the chipped concrete floor before flying away. He planned to eat the last of Rita's dried noodles and to get an early night. No sense in pining for Martha or feeling guilty about what had happened with Oksana. He was young and a thousand miles from home. The weekend had been magical. Nobody, least of all Martha, would have expected him to live like a monk.

Switching off the light an hour later and lying back against the pillow, Kite heard the crackle of a piece of paper under his ear. He reached for it, turning the light back on, and saw that Oksana had written a note.

Thank you for making me feel so good, baby.
I like you. I can talk to you.
See you Tuesday for dinner after class? Meet me at ice cream cafe near puppet theatre at 7?

She had pressed her mouth to the page leaving a lipstick kiss. Kite experienced a jolt of desire. It was good that she was confident enough in what they had shared to write to him so candidly. He had felt something similar, an understanding between them. He wondered if feeling this way was a function of his loneliness or something more meaningful. Tiredness took away the question and he again switched off the light, lying on his back in the sweltering bedroom.

Yet he found that he could not sleep. He listened to the old electric fan turning uselessly, the noise of his neighbours laughing far below. After fifteen minutes, Kite decided to read and padded out into the living room in search of *War and Peace*. He had left the book beside the television along with the other novels Rita had packed for him in London.

He flicked on the light and immediately noticed that *The English Patient* was missing. He had placed it beneath *The Idiot* and *The Brothers Karamazov* and not moved it since. He was certain that he had not shown the book to Oksana, nor taken it to work in his bag. It was possible that she had picked it up at some point on Sunday, but he could not remember her doing so.

He searched everywhere in the flat but with no success. Gradually the realisation that he was facing a serious problem settled on him. He knew, as he peered beneath the bed, that the book was gone. He was sure, even as he searched in the cupboards and the chests of drawers, that someone – presumably Oksana – had taken it. Anxiety smothered him like a shroud. He looked on the balcony where he had smoked the cigarette, behind the cushions on the sofa where he had eaten the noodles, but of course the novel was not there. Why had she taken it? And why had she not mentioned doing so in her note?

Kite sat alone in the living room, trying to reassure himself that Oksana could not have known about the concealed letter to Aranov. Nothing else had been taken from the apartment; there had been no sign of a break-in or disturbance. The disappearance of the book was surely just an unfortunate coincidence. Oksana wanted to improve her English, perhaps to be seen by her friends and family reading a contemporary British novel in an expensive hardback edition. She had taken something that belonged to Kite, assuming that he wouldn't care. She had borrowed it without asking, but perhaps this was perfectly normal in Russian culture. His flatmate in Edinburgh was constantly taking his stuff.

There was another possibility which Kite tried to ignore, in the same way that he might have refused to believe the diagnosis of a terminal illness. If Oksana was an FSK honeytrap who had been playing him from the first minute she set eyes on him at the Dickens, he was finished. If Strawson's book was now in the hands of the security services, the hidden letter would be enough to put him behind bars for a decade.

Breathe, he told himself, remembering Strawson's advice. *Breathe*. He wished that he could call Billy Peele and confide his fears to him. He was exhausted, hardly able to think straight, at once convinced that there was nothing at all to worry about, then certain that Oksana had played him for a fool. With nothing to do but pace the apartment, Kite went back to bed, lying in the dark with his mind in turmoil, eventually falling asleep to the sound of birds singing in the trees beyond his window.

16

Kite woke up from a dream of captivity long after dawn, jolted from sleep not by his alarm clock – which he had forgotten to set – but by the sound of a siren pounding on the highway. Realising he was late for work he dressed quickly, weaved his bicycle through a mile of impatient traffic and reached the Dickens just as Bokova was making her way down the stairs shortly after eleven o'clock. She made a huffing noise and pointedly looked at her watch as she passed him, saying 'You are late' without stopping to hear Kite's explanation.

For the second day running, Oksana was not in class; worryingly, Aranov was also absent. Kite continued teaching a lesson on gerunds, scraping the barrel of his knowledge and setting yet another test as a way of killing time. After lunch there was still no sign of them. He had packed a spare shirt for dinner with Oksana but wondered if their date would even take place. Though he had not been arrested, nor noticed anything unusual en route to the Dickens, Kite could not shake off the fear that he had been fooled. Perhaps Oksana was waiting to meet him at the ice cream café so that she could hand over the book. Kite would have no choice other than to take it, at which point his guilt would be proven, he would be surrounded by a team of plain-clothes security officers and bundled into the back of an FSK van.

Keep the faith, he told himself. It's just a book. She's just a girl you slept with who wanted to improve her English. Maybe Oksana read the first few pages in your apartment, realised she could understand fifty per cent of the meaning and took the novel home so that she could look up the difficult words. Kite was leaning on his training, remembering that he had been taught not to stress about things which were beyond his control, to gather evidence and not to ruminate. In a more bullish and determined mood, he washed his face and chest in the sink in the cramped Dickens bathroom and set out towards the Puppet Theatre.

Oksana was waiting for him in the shade of a pine tree. She was wearing a pale blue summer dress and yellow plimsolls. Kite had never seen her dressed so conventionally. It was as though she was sending him a message: 'I seduced you with my miniskirts and heels, now let me show you that I can be demure and conservative, a suitable girlfriend for a young man from England.' She had a pair of counterfeit Chanel sunglasses pushed up on her forehead and was holding a loose-strapped shoulder bag. Kite reckoned it was large enough to contain the book. They did not kiss, nor did he touch her hand or any part of her body when they met. He was still drawn to her, despite the doubts and paranoia that pecked at him like the birds which scavenged for food on his balcony. As they caught up on the news of the previous two days, Kite could not bring himself to believe that Oksana was anything other than the beautiful, enchanting woman she appeared to be.

'Your bed is very comfortable, Professor,' she said. 'I sleep until three o'clock if you can imagine this!'

'Yesterday was hard work,' Kite replied, wondering when to bring up the subject of the book. 'I ended up talking about Winston Churchill and politics in the United Kingdom. You missed a fascinating lesson.'

Oksana did not pick up on the sarcasm and produced a glassy smile. They bought ice creams and headed for a nearby park. Kite felt that she was distracted by something. Was it merely that she was anxious to make a good impression or was she under orders to behave in a certain way? He looked behind them to see if they were being followed but saw only a babushka bustling along the pavement and a young mother chasing after an errant toddler. Somewhere in the park Ace of Base was playing at top volume; 'All That She Wants' was the song of the Russian summer.

'So did you miss me?' Oksana asked.

She looked unpredictably nervous as she anticipated Kite's response.

'I loved what happened this weekend,' he replied, looking ahead into the trees on either side of the wide path. Four people were walking directly towards them. 'Why did you not come to class today?' he asked. 'I thought I would see you.'

'You do not answer my question, Peter.' Oksana settled her beautiful wide eyes on him as the group passed. 'Did you miss me?'

'Constantly,' he said and almost reached for her hand. 'I can't touch you,' he said. 'What if Bokova is watching?'

'You are afraid of her?'

It was the second time she had asked that question. Kite gave up trying to assess if they were being watched; there were now too many people in the park, too much natural cover.

'It's not a question of fear,' he replied. 'I like you. I like living in Voronezh. But if I lose my job, what will I do?'

'Do you need the salary?'

She had never mentioned money before. Was she trying to find out if he was going to be a suitably well-financed western boyfriend or just making casual conversation while the FSK closed in?

'I need the salary,' he replied. 'Although I came here with some savings from my job in Malawi.' Suddenly stumped for something to say, Kite saw a child coming towards them, cycling delightedly on a blue plastic tricycle. He said: 'I want to buy you a present, Oksana. What would you like?'

The question had a remarkable effect. Much of Oksana's apparent nervousness seemed to slip away and she fluttered those eyes again, lashes on a cartoon kitten.

'What would you like to buy me, Peter?'

Perhaps all she had been waiting for was a reassurance that he was serious about her. Kite felt a layer of anxiety falling away from him like dead skin.

'Well it's too hot for a fur coat,' he replied.

Again Oksana did not pick up on the sarcasm. Instead she jumped at the suggestion.

'No!' she exclaimed. 'You can still buy fur coat in summertime. They cheaper now. I want one very much, Peter. This would be wonderful present. Thank you!'

Kite saw that he had been needlessly paranoid. Oksana wasn't FSK. She was just a beautiful Russian girl who wanted to wear nice clothes, to live well, to be happy in summer with an English boyfriend. Perhaps one day she would expect him to buy her more than a fur coat; maybe she hoped that he would fall in love with her and take her away to London.

'Shall we get a drink?' he suggested.

They sat at a brand-new wooden table beside a café, talking for almost half an hour. At no point did Oksana mention *The English Patient*. Kite at last resolved to draw it out of her. He was by now certain that she had taken the book in all innocence.

'What kind of novels do you read?' he asked. 'It's such an interesting time in this country. Who are the best Russian writers at the moment?'

That was all it took. As Oksana raised a glass of vodka to her lips, she remembered that she had taken the book.

'Oh, Peter!' she exclaimed, touching her lips with her fingers. 'I forget to tell you. I take your book. From apartment yesterday. I sorry. I want to read it.'

'Really?' Kite feigned not to know what she was talking about. 'You did? Which one?'

'English Patients.' She knew that she had mispronounced

the title but didn't make a second attempt. 'I start to read in bed with coffee after I wake and I like the words. They are so . . . beautiful. So I take home. You will forgive me?'

She reached across the table and touched his cheek. If she was an actress, trained and tutored by the magicians at the Lubyanka, they had conjured a Streep. Kite looked down at her shoulder bag. He wanted to ask if she had brought the book with her but did not want to seem too eager to have it back.

'Of course, I forgive you!' he said and reached for her waist. Even the simplest contact with her body provoked him. He had a flash memory of something Oksana had done with her mouth in the small hours of Monday morning and immediately wanted to go back to his apartment and get straight into bed. 'It's a great book. Perhaps I could read it to you and explain when it becomes confusing. Would you like that?'

She moved her hand along his leg and gave his thigh a discreet squeeze. 'I would love this, Peter,' she said, then looked across the square at a kiosk next to a public toilet. 'If we leave for restaurant soon, you will allow me to go for one moment, please?'

The timing of her sudden exit revived Kite's feelings of dread. Why not wait to use the bathroom at Café Anna? Was she making herself scarce so that her FSK pals could close in and make an arrest? Yet Oksana had not brought the book with her nor offered to give it back to him in such a way that the interaction might be photographed. Kite looked around the park. It was packed with locals walking in the warm summer air, hundreds of people sitting at tables, on the grass, gathered around a fountain, talking and smoking. The fear was surely all in his head.

'Of course!' he said, remembering his training. *Play the situation, Lockie, not what you think might be happening.* 'I'll wait here.'

Smoothing down the hem of her dress, Oksana stood up and walked across the dusty square towards the public toilet.

Two other women were queuing ahead of her. Kite took a sip of vodka and tried to suppress his paranoia. He had been so long out of the game that his constant anxiety came as a surprise to him. Had he been this unsettled in France? He knew what he would say if they accused him. That the book had been tampered with en route to Moscow; that he was just a patsy, an unwitting courier for whoever was trying to lure Aranov to the West. He could hear Strawson urging him on, the mantra that had kept him sane in Mougins. *Never confess. Never tell them what they want to hear. Never admit to being a spy.*

'Mr Galvin?'

Kite felt a hand on his shoulder. His body liquified. He turned to see who had come for him.

'I thought it was you.'

To Kite's astonishment, Daniil, the director of the Dickens, was standing over him holding an ice cream and a child's plastic toy.

'Daniil!' It was like waking from a dream in which he had been shot in the chest to find that all was well, the bed drenched in sweat, but the dawn sun peeping through the curtains. 'What a coincidence!'

'Yes, isn't it?' The Russian had a habit of sounding haughty and suspicious even in the most benign circumstances. It was a characteristic he had perhaps borrowed from Bokova. 'You are passing a pleasant evening?'

'Very pleasant, thank you.'

Kite knew that they had been spotted: Oksana's fingers on his cheek, her hand on his thigh, his arm encircling her waist. Daniil had the look of a beak at Alford who had caught him infringing a petty and infuriating school rule.

'You're here with your family?' Kite asked, indicating the toy in Daniil's hand. The Russian was wearing a stained polo shirt and badly fitting stonewashed jeans. 'I was just having a drink with . . .'

'Yes, we saw.' Daniil exhaled heavily, apparently crestfallen. Kite would have laughed if the situation was not potentially so serious. This pale, vacuous, entry-level capitalist had the power to kick him out of Voronezh. It was vital to kiss his ass.

'Is everything OK, Daniil?' he asked.

In his peripheral vision, Kite saw Oksana coming back from the public bathroom. She pulled up as she saw who Kite was talking to.

'You are drinking with student.'

Kite longed to send a decent reply back over the net, but instead swallowed his pride and said: 'I am. Although I believe she is no longer a student.'

Daniil was caught off guard. 'Oksana Sharikova?' He frowned. 'She is enrolled at the Dickens. She is your student.'

'She has stopped coming to class.' The plausible excuse for Kite's behaviour had materialised out of thin air. 'I thought that because this was the case, I would be permitted to take her out for dinner. I apologise if this has upset you, Daniil.'

The Russian looked as though he had a lot of thinking to do. A dumpy, put-upon woman with dyed auburn hair was watching them from nearby, an undernourished child clinging to her arm. Kite assumed this was Daniil's wife.

'Upset?' he replied. It wasn't clear if he had failed to grasp the meaning of the word or was taking issue with Kite's interpretation of his mood. 'As we told you when you arrived, it is not permitted to socialise romantically with students. This is an iron law.'

Kite almost laughed. He could see Oksana at the edge of the seating area waiting for the exchange to end; by holding back she was perhaps adding fuel to Daniil's accusations.

'Let me talk to her at dinner,' Kite replied. 'I'll find out what her intentions are. If she wants to come back to class, then this will be the last time I ask her out. Will that satisfy you?'

He had been entirely reasonable, but Daniil wasn't one to go quietly. This was the highlight of his day. He needed to prolong his moment of authority over the Englishman.

'There has also been a complaint,' he said.

'A complaint?' Kite was suddenly aware of the size of Daniil's head. It was vast, out of all proportion to his body. 'About what?'

'About the teaching.'

Kite was stung by this. He had done his best in the classes and felt that he had built up a rapport with his students. For somebody to complain about him behind his back was behaviour worthy of Cosmo de Paul.

'What about it?' he asked. 'What do you mean?'

'I was discussing it with my colleague, Katerina Bokova. We feel there is too much focus on the history of your country. Industrial Revolution. Invention of jet engine. This game you call cricket.'

'Somebody has *complained* about that?'

'We are the directors of the school, Peter.' It was suddenly obvious that nobody had filed a complaint. Bokova was the one who was dissatisfied. 'We ask you please to stick to the book we have given you which our paying students expect you to follow, day after day . . .'

'I *am* sticking to the book,' Kite insisted. 'All That She Wants' started up again in a distant section of the park. 'We are all making excellent progress. Talking about British history was a technique I used in Malawi . . .'

'Malawi is a former British colony in Africa. The Russian Federation is not a British colony. You tell your students that the steam train was invented in England. This is not true. Penicillin was discovered not by Alexander Fleming but by the Ermolyeva Sisters. If you continue with these false stories, we will have difficulties.'

Kite was so flabbergasted that he could not find an adequate response. Oksana came back to the table, shot Daniil a nervous smile and settled in her seat.

'Have a good evening,' he said in Russian without formally acknowledging her.

'You too, Daniil, thanks for stopping by,' Kite replied.

'What happened?' Oksana asked when he was out of earshot. 'Are you in trouble, Peter?'

'It's nothing,' he told her. 'Let's go for dinner.'

Café Anna was closed so they ate in the big, gloomy dining room at the Hotel Brno. Oksana said that she had never been there before. To Kite's surprise, she asked for the most expensive things on the menu – French champagne, black caviar, beef Stroganoff. He thought of his mother, who had always told him that greedy ordering was a sign of bad character. Kite was more forgiving: Oksana had grown up with food queues and bread shortages. Perhaps she believed that the most costly dishes on a menu were also the most delicious; or that by eating caviar and steak in what passed for luxurious surroundings she was celebrating the freedoms of the new Russia. He did not feel that she was being vulgar or taking advantage of his generosity; in fact there was something exhilarating about Oksana's desire to enjoy herself.

Afterwards, drunk and full of food, they slow-danced to a band playing Sinatra covers and were offered slices of cake by a middle-aged woman celebrating her birthday in the restaurant. Oksana laid her head on Kite's shoulder as they swayed on the dancefloor, not because she was drunk or tired but because they had developed an intimacy which made such a gesture natural, even inevitable. Kite wanted to go back to her apartment, both to retrieve the book but also to spend the night with her. But when he suggested this, Oksana said that her sister's boyfriend was staying the night and they would have no privacy. So they took a taxi to his flat, kissing in the back seat and holding hands while the driver complained about the unusually high radioactivity levels from Chernobyl.

Many of the same neighbours Kite had seen the previous night were gathered outside once again. When they saw Kite and Oksana approaching the building, they stopped talking and stared. Kite felt like an exhibit in a cage. Oksana greeted them cheerily in Russian, but only one person responded, a man with a yellowing moustache and stained white shirt who mumbled a quiet hello.

'*Sovki*,' said Oksana as they entered the lobby, a term of

abuse for craven, judgemental Russians who clung to the old Soviet ways. 'They think I am prostitute.'

'No they don't,' Kite replied, realising that his reputation in the building had taken a nosedive since the weekend.

'They judge me. And they judge you.'

'Then let them judge,' he said.

'It was the same with Yuri.'

They were getting into the lift. Kite stopped and turned. He felt as though Oksana had suddenly prodded him in the back.

'What do you mean?' he asked.

'I have boyfriend before you. His neighbours same. *Sovki*. Small people, jealous. Not kind.'

Kite said nothing until they reached the flat. Perhaps the name was just a coincidence. He switched on the television to provide noise cover for their conversation.

'Who was Yuri?' he asked, remembering the way Aranov had mimed cupping Oksana's breasts.

'It is not important.' She stepped towards him, gave a doe-eyed flutter of those vast eyes and began to unbutton his shirt. 'He say he love me, but he cheat on me with other woman. So I end it. He get mad.'

'Yuri from my class?'

Kite dreaded the answer. Oksana stepped back, a look of surprise on her face.

'Yes!' she exclaimed. 'How did you know this?'

Kite did well to disguise his consternation.

'Just a guess,' he said.

'But everything over between us now.' Oksana was happily tackling a final button on the shirt. 'He has somebody else in his bed.'

'So do you,' Kite replied, knowing that he should immediately break up with her. The operation demanded it. His relationship with Aranov was of paramount importance; if Yuri discovered that Peter Galvin was seeing his ex-girlfriend behind his back, there was no telling how he might react. Yet as Oksana lowered the strap of her dress, swept her hair to one side and raised her head so that her beautiful neck was exposed to him, Kite was powerless to resist. They went into the bedroom. He told himself he would enjoy one last night with her and then confront the problem in the morning.

17

Again Aranov did not come to class the next day.

By the time his afternoon lesson had ended, Kite was concerned that the Russian was not going to show up at the lake. In a moment of distilled paranoia, he wondered if Aranov had somehow found out about his affair with Oksana and, enraged with jealousy, would now refuse to accompany him to Ukraine. Realising that he had no choice other than to go to the arranged meeting point, Kite tidied the classroom and cycled out to the lake.

It had been a cloudy day in Voronezh and there were fewer swimmers gathered on the narrow strip of shingle at the edge of the water. On a previous visit Kite had witnessed the unusual sight of an elderly Russian couple sunbathing while standing up; it was apparently a local tradition. Somebody had set up a makeshift stall selling *shashlik*; thin clouds of charcoal smoke and smells of grilled meat wafted across the swimming area. Kite followed his usual routine, laying out a towel on a narrow expanse of grass about fifty metres from the shore and folding his clothes to make a pillow. He took out his dog-eared copy of *War and Peace*: Nikolai had just married Maria Bolkonskaya. An old man with very tanned, leathery skin gave him a perfunctory wave; Kite had seen him several times before on previous visits to the lake. He waved back and lay down on the towel, trying to behave as he always did while at the same time keeping an eye out for Aranov. He had waited so long to make contact with the Russian that the coincidence of his relationship with Oksana seemed like a cruel trick. Kite was absorbed in memories of the previous night; when his thoughts should have been operational, they were distractedly carnal. That Oksana had potentially been as impassioned with Aranov revived in Kite some of the same feelings of jealousy he had felt about Cosmo de Paul. He knew that he was in danger of risking the operation because of a summer affair but told himself that the damage was probably already done; even if he ended things, Aranov might still find out that he had slept with Oksana.

A bearded man was leaning against a sycamore tree strumming a guitar, singing hits from the Russian back catalogue. Children were splashing in the shallows, couples up to their waists in water, kissing and chatting. There was suddenly an intense, industrial smell of pollutant carried on the wind from some unseen factory to the north. Nobody seemed to notice or care. Kite continued to read – or, rather, to read the same paragraph in *War and Peace* over and over again while looking around for Aranov. It was almost half-past six; the sun would set in less than two hours. He looked back in the direction of the city, convinced that the Russian was not going to show. Had he fully understood the message Kite had conveyed in the classroom or had Kite only imagined that his tactic had worked?

He decided to go for a swim. Just as he was putting his feet into the chill water of the lake, he turned to find Aranov standing near the sycamore tree. He was smoking a cigarette and held a blue swimming towel under his arm. When he saw Kite, he waved enthusiastically, stubbed out the cigarette and came towards him. Purely for the benefit of any interested parties who might have been keeping an eye on them, Kite waved back, feigning immense surprise at this chance encounter.

'Yuri!'

'Mr Galvin!'

Aranov was a decent actor who knew how to play the role. His manner perfectly conveyed a mixture of surprise and delight, his words fitting the cover story Kite had concocted for their encounter.

'You say you swim here every day after class. I want to come down talk to you. It is very nice coincide . . .' He stumbled on the word. 'How do you say?'

'Coincidence,' Kite replied, shaking Aranov's hand. 'Have you swum here before?'

'Never,' the Russian replied. 'I don't have time.' He took off his shirt to reveal a pale, unexercised torso. 'I join you? We talk?'

'Of course. Are you here with anyone? Do you have a family? Friends?'

Aranov played along with the question. There was always the danger of a directional microphone, even of somebody lip-reading their simple English conversation through binoculars.

'I come alone. I want to discuss private lessons of English.' Kite moved towards the water. 'I know that the Dickens Institute does not allow this, but perhaps we come to . . . arrangement? Arranging?'

'Arrangement, Yuri,' Kite replied. 'Why don't we go for a swim and talk about it?'

Covered by the noise of laughter and music, of parents chastising their children, the two men began to swim towards a small island on the far side of the lake. When they were safely clear of dry land, Kite encouraged Aranov to tread water while he told him who he was and the nature of the plan to extract him from Russia. He did not bother with social niceties or enquiries about Aranov's wellbeing. He had only a limited amount of time to impart a huge amount of information.

'We need to socialise. We need to become friends,' he said. 'You have to be the one who makes that happen. When we get back to my towel, say what a great guy you think I am and invite me to dinner with your friends. Set it up in somebody's apartment. I can meet you any day you like.' Aranov suddenly stopped and coughed. A small amount of water had entered his mouth and he had spat it out.

'You OK?' Kite asked.

'I am fine.'

They carried on swimming towards the island, Kite continuing to issue instructions.

'Invite a small group of friends to your dacha outside Voronezh for the weekend of the nineteenth then extend the invitation to me whenever the time feels right. I'll signal London, a car will be left for us outside the dacha, we will leave at around one o'clock in the morning on Sunday, reaching Ukraine by six or seven.'

'You know the road?' Aranov asked. It was the first time he had asked a question; to everything else Kite had told him, he had simply muttered 'Yes' or 'OK' while trying to keep his mouth clear of the water.

'I've studied it in detail,' Kite replied. 'We'll be fine. Act normally for the next ten days. Don't pack anything for the weekend that you would not normally pack. Don't say your goodbyes. When we get to the dacha, do as I tell you.'

'Fine.' Aranov's reply sounded curt. Kite could not tell if he was affronted or merely out of breath. A woman in a red bikini was lying on the far side of the island. She shielded her eyes to watch Kite and Aranov as they emerged from the water.

'So I could teach you five hours per week in my apartment, or I can come to your home,' Kite said, continuing with the ruse. 'Whichever is more convenient.'

The Russian looked at him, glanced at the woman as if to say: 'Come on, we don't have to be careful in front of her,' and wiped his eyes with the back of his hand. His skin was milky white and dotted with moles. Kite looked at it and thought of myelin toxin being injected into rabbits.

'Both are fine.' Aranov had clearly been tired by the swim and apologised for his lack of fitness. 'Sorry,' he said. 'I do not swim very often. I am not adjusted.'

'It's fine.' Kite knew that they should keep talking about the lessons. If the woman was later interviewed by the FSK, she would confirm that their conversation had been anodyne.

'I charge fifty roubles per hour for private lessons.' Aranov made a noise in the back of his throat. 'But I can make every sixth lesson free of charge. Does that sound good?'

Aranov nodded with slightly exaggerated derision and said: 'Yes, Peter. Sound good price.'

Accepting that they would make no meaningful progress until they were again alone, Kite sat in silence, listening to the high-pitched laughter of the distant children. A bird circled the island and a lone fly buzzed around his head. Having finally regained his breath, Aranov stood up and stared down at the woman, who seemed to sense that she was being watched. She turned to face him. When Aranov continued to look at her, she muttered something in Russian and went back into the water. Kite wondered what she had said. The woman submerged herself and swam away in the direction of the shingle beach, surfacing several seconds later to swim a fast front crawl.

'So you are the one they sent for me,' said Aranov, seemingly oblivious to the fact that he had driven the woman away. 'You are the one who gets me out.'

'That's right.'

'You are young, Peter.'

'I'm not as young as I look.' Kite didn't want to get drawn into a conversation about his suitability for the exfil. If Aranov was serious about leaving Russia, he would go even if he was being driven across the frontier by Ronald McDonald. 'Are you OK with all the instructions?' he asked. 'The dinner, the invitation to the dacha?'

'Yes, yes, I am clear.' Aranov sounded impatient. 'But I have problems.'

'What kind of problems?'

'My girlfriend. She pregnant.'

If a dolphin had leapt out of the water, executed a pirouette against the evening sky and splashed down into the lake, Kite would not have been more shocked. Had Oksana slept with him to make Kite think he was the baby's father?

'Girlfriend?' he said. Would she claim that Kite had got her pregnant, then insist on coming to England to have the child? Christ, he had been so stupid. 'Who is she?' he asked, dreading the answer. 'Where did you meet?'

Aranov hesitated. 'Her name Tania,' he said. The name instantly released Kite from a private torment. He almost gasped in relief. 'I meet her at work.'

'I see.'

Presumably Tania was the woman Aranov had been two-timing with Oksana.

'I cannot leave her behind,' he continued, speaking more forcefully. 'I cannot leave my child.'

'No, of course not.'

There was silence. It seemed to Kite that all of Strawson's carefully laid plans now lay in tatters. He would have to improvise. Without properly thinking through the consequences of such an offer, he presented a solution for which he had no authorisation.

'She can come with us. Would she want to do that?'

Aranov was taken by surprise. In the time it took him to respond, Kite noticed that the woman who had been lying next to them on the island had reached the shore.

'It is possible,' said the Russian. He walked into the shallow water around the island, looking down at his submerged feet. 'But how do I ask her this?'

'You don't,' Kite replied, still improvising. 'What's her situation? Does she have family here? Brothers, sisters?'

'Only mother. They hate her, Tania hate her. How do you say this?'

'They hate each other.' For some reason Kite thought of the famous opening lines of *Anna Karenina*, the next book on his reading list: 'Every unhappy family is unhappy in its own way.'

169

'OK, so they hate each other.' Aranov bent down and flicked a handful of water out onto the surface of the lake. 'Older brother in Moscow. Sister married, lives near Rostov.'

'How old is Tania?' Kite asked.

'Twenty. Twenty-one next week.'

Even younger than me, he thought. *Younger than Martha.* 'And she loves you?'

'Of course.' Aranov's tone suggested that no sane woman east of Kiev had ever been able to resist his charms. 'Yes, she love me. I cannot leave her.'

'You don't have to leave her. I'll organise it.'

Aranov looked at him, squinting against the low summer sun.

'British intelligence do this for me? MI6?'

'Exactly.' To Aranov, as to so many others, there was no such thing as BOX 88. 'If Tania agrees to come with you, we will provide her with a new identity, a new job. Your child's medical expenses will be taken care of. If she doesn't like it, she can go home, say we kidnapped her. She'll be perfectly safe in Russia.'

'Education,' Aranov replied.

'Excuse me?'

'Education. I want it paid for. The famous British private schools.'

Kite smiled, picturing Yuri Junior pulling on a tailcoat at Alford.

'You'll get that too,' he said, again without any clearance from Strawson. He wondered how London would react when they learned that Kite had tripled the cost of Aranov's move to the UK in the space of five minutes.

'You promise this, Peter?'

'I promise.'

Two middle-aged men were swimming towards them, side by side. In the distance Kite could see the woman in the red bikini talking to a man wearing trousers and a white shirt.

'We should wait for a couple of minutes after these two

arrive, then head back to shore,' he said, indicating the approaching swimmers. 'Let's buy a *shashlik*, get to know each other, talk about life in England, my experiences in Voronezh. I'll ask you what you do for a living. You lie in the way I presume you have always lied when people ask you that.'

'Sounds good,' Aranov replied.

'On the way back we'll talk procedures.' Kite had had many days to think about what he was going to say to Aranov. Despite the complication presented by Tania's pregnancy, it felt good finally to be working through the various elements of the operation.

'Procedures?' Aranov seemed not to have understood the word, despite the fact that its Russian equivalent – *protsedury* – was almost identical.

'Procedures,' Kite repeated. 'Things that you must do if you are concerned about anything or need to speak to me.'

There was a strange and unexpected look of repulsion on Aranov's face. Perhaps to be answerable to Kite, to have placed his fate in the hands of such a young man, had made him feel vulnerable.

'I am not concerned about anything,' he said quickly. 'You seem intelligent. You are obviously a good liar. I only hope that MI6 has sent somebody who has enough experience to get me out of Russia without the authorities putting me in jail.'

Then get on a fucking aeroplane, Kite thought. But he put his best face on and reassured Aranov that he had been working for British intelligence for several years.

'Why does Wendy not take me?' Aranov asked. 'Why they send you?'

'You can ask her that when we get to London.' Kite had always assumed that Wendy was too senior at BOX to spend the summer teaching in Voronezh; she had bigger fish to fry. 'Last thing,' he said. The two middle-aged men were now less than ten metres away. 'Your English is very good. You need to pretend to be less fluent whenever we're talking.'

'You think I don't know this?' The petulance of Aranov's reply surprised Kite. 'What do you think I was doing on Monday? You think I don't know a word like "swimming"? You think I don't know how to spell simple word like "election"?'

Kite reflected that in less than half an hour he had seen the full range of Aranov's personality: his quick temper, his sentimentality, his facility for deceit, his fragile ego. This was not a man who was going to be easy to handle. Before he could respond – he was about to offer a profuse apology in order to smooth the Russian's ruffled feathers – the two swimmers stood up, steadied themselves on the muddy shoreline and walked towards them. They greeted Kite and Aranov in Russian before embarking on a conversation about classical music which was too complex for Kite properly to understand. After a few moments he suggested that they return to the beach, telling Aranov, for the benefit of their listening audience, how much he'd enjoyed bumping into him and hoping they could do it again one day.

'Yes, this would be very good,' Aranov replied, wincing as he submerged himself in the water.

They swam back. With Aranov slightly ahead of him, Kite continued to issue instructions. He had the impression that the Russian was either too proud, or in some other way distracted, to pay proper attention.

'If there's a problem with the arrangements at the dacha, if you're concerned about Tania or anything else, ask me a question in class about Paul Gascoigne.' They were close to the shingle beach. The woman in the red bikini and the man to whom she had been speaking were nowhere to be seen; Kite was irritated with himself that he hadn't noticed them leave. Aranov, who was breathless again, stopped swimming and said: 'Wait. Who?'

'Paul Gascoigne. The English footballer.'

'I hate football. I ask instead about President Bush.'

'Fine.'

He started swimming again.

'What about surveillance?' Kite asked, drawing alongside. 'Do you feel you are being watched?'

'It is not a feeling, Peter. It is a reality.' Aranov stopped and trod water again, plainly to have the opportunity to catch his breath. Kite found that the water was shallow enough to allow them to stand up. 'I am watched from the moment I wake in the morning to the moment I go to sleep beside Tania. This is not an imagination.'

'Are we being watched now?'

'Of course we are being watched! This is Russia. Nothing has changed. You are so naïve.'

Kite looked back at the island. He was suddenly cold, the weak sunlight offering little warmth.

'What about in class?' he asked. 'Who do you suspect is FSK?'

'I think maybe Arkady and the old woman. I see them always.'

Arkady was 'Grandpa', the old woman was 'Granny'. Aranov's suspicions chimed with Kite's.

'Who else?' he asked.

But the Russian was too tired to respond. He pushed off again towards the shore without answering Kite's question, covering the remaining distance with the speed of a doggy-paddling toddler taking a swimming lesson. When they reached dry land they retrieved their towels and headed to the makeshift barbecue where a man in torn denim jeans sold them *shashliks* and two bottles of Baltika, a local beer. It was only now that Aranov fully regained his composure and reverted to the role of the friendly student proudly showing off his city. For almost half an hour they sat on the grass, eating the kebab and chatting amiably about nothing of any operational interest or importance. Kite noted Aranov's quick mind and natural self-confidence, concluding that it was these which had attracted Oksana. Doubtless his salary, many times larger than a man of equivalent age, and a dacha provided by the government, were also factors. In this one-horse town, Yuri was a catch. As they were finishing their beers and preparing to leave, Aranov broached the subject of his love life, telling Kite that he had been involved with 'one of the girls at the Dickens'.

'Oh?' Kite replied, feigning innocence. 'Who was that?'

It was a chance to come clean. Aranov surely wouldn't blame him for being attracted to Oksana. It wasn't as though Kite had known about their relationship or encouraged Oksana to cheat. Yet as he listened to the Russian's paean to his lost love, he realised it would be impossible to tell the truth. He clearly still pined for her, despite all that had transpired with the pregnant Tania.

'She was incredible,' he said. 'They say that the most beautiful women in Russia come from Voronezh. Peter the Great, he ordered his best engineers to the city to build ships so the finest girls in Moscow were sent here to keep them happy. They marry, they have beautiful children, and so on down the centuries. But none as beautiful as Oksana.'

'Your English is too good, Yuri,' Kite muttered, wanting him to speak less fluently.

'Oksana the most beautiful,' he replied, rolling his eyes. 'This woman, I never recover. Like a wild animal. But a bitch. Eat me up, spit me out.'

A wild animal. A bitch. It was not how Kite would have chosen to describe her: she had been by turns extraordinarily passionate and unexpectedly tender. There and then, he decided that he must break things off with her. Even if it would cost him in terms of his personal happiness, it was too risky to continue to be involved with a woman whom Aranov felt had treated him so badly. The prospect of upsetting Oksana, of losing her from his bed, was frustrating, but it would be a price worth paying if it guaranteed the stability of the operation.

'We have a dinner!' Aranov announced, suddenly standing up and speaking loudly enough for everyone on the narrow shingle beach to hear him. For all of his idiosyncrasies, he was at least reliable when it came to playing a role for any watching spooks. 'I am going to big party Saturday night and invite you. Some Swedish man, owns big apartment – I get others from class to come. Not her. Not Oksana. Only the ones I like.'

'Sounds great,' Kite replied. 'Just let me know where and when.'

They parted soon afterwards. As he mounted his bicycle, Kite told Yuri that he would see him in class the next day. Aranov dutifully repeated the invitation to dinner, adding that he hoped they could go swimming again very soon. Kite then headed off along the path while Aranov walked in the direction of the tram station a few hundred metres away.

The meeting had gone as well as Kite could possibly have hoped and he cycled through the forest in a buoyant mood. Yet his elation was short-lived. He had covered about a mile when he became aware that he was being followed. A black Volga had been on his tail ever since he had emerged from the forest. The driver was making it obvious, holding back at a distance of about thirty metres as they moved in single file through a suburb at the edge of the city. Several times Kite turned to see the vehicle tucked in behind him, a man in the passenger seat staring at him through reflective sunglasses. It was obvious they were FSK. The boys from Lukhanov Street wanted to know who he was, where he lived, why he had gone swimming with Yuri Aranov. Kite could not run anti-surveillance nor attempt to elude them: he was Peter Galvin, not a trained intelligence officer. The meeting with Aranov had made him radioactive. He must play the innocent and wait for the Russians to make their move.

At last they stopped him, the driver accelerating quickly and pulling across Kite's bicycle at such a sudden, sharp angle he almost toppled off.

'Hey!'

The two men got out of the car. Kite had seen one of them at the lake and clocked him as a possible threat: fit, early thirties, trimmed beard and mirrored shades. His partner was older, physically slower, closer in appearance to KGB central casting. He was wearing a white shirt with a cheap leather jacket slung over his shoulder, despite the humidity of the midsummer evening. Kite realised this was the same person he had seen talking to the woman in the red bikini. He was also wearing sunglasses with reflective lenses. It was evidently the house style.

'What is your name?' he asked in Russian. He stuck a match in his mouth and started to chew it, like he'd seen Sylvester Stallone in *Cobra* going through the same routine and thought it would play well on the street. Kite acted dumb, telling the men in tourist Russian that he did not speak their language.

'You are American?' asked the one with the trimmed beard. It sounded as though he could speak English with a reasonable degree of fluency.

'I'm from the UK,' he replied. 'United Kingdom. Great Britain.' He was amazed by how quickly his contact with Aranov had drawn them on. They hadn't even bothered watching him for a couple of hours. 'What's going on? Who are you?'

'Passport.'

On day one Daniil had advised Kite to carry his passport with him at all times. Kite duly produced it from his bag, feeling past his damp towel and swimming shorts. He handed it to Cobra, who took it and flicked through the pages. The younger man asked the questions. He reminded Kite of a cricketer whose name took time to pop into his head: Kepler Wessels.

'What is your name?'

'Peter Galvin.'

'What are you doing here?'

Kite channelled his alter-ego, the nervous, faltering teacher from Wokingham. 'Here?' he said, looking around. 'I'm on my way home.

What's happened?'

'I ask you again, Mr Galvin. What are you doing here?'

'Oh, you mean in Voronezh. I'm an English teacher.'

'You have permission?'

Kite gave an innocent shrug. 'Of course. Yes. I have permission. Who are you? All the papers are in my apartment. I've been teaching at the Dickens Institute for the last two weeks.'

Cobra moved the match to the other side of his mouth. He had the build and rhythm of a low-level thug and didn't look as though he understood what was being said.

'Foreign language teachers are unusual in Voronezh,' his colleague replied. Kite sensed that he was smarter and more capable than Cobra. There was an edge of cruelty to both men, but the Wessels lookalike was lean and ambitious, radiating a slick malevolence.

'They are, yes. The owner of the school, Katya Bokova . . .'

Wessels took off his sunglasses, stopping Kite mid-sentence. 'I know Bokova.'

Cobra raised a hand. In Russian he said something about Africa which Kite did not understand.

'What were you doing in South Africa?'

Cobra had seen the stamps in the Galvin passport. As he turned the pages, he chewed the match, moving it from one side of his mouth to the other.

'In South Africa?' He remembered Strawson's advice: *Bullshit if you have to. Say you had to stay overnight in Jo'burg.* 'Oh that. I used to teach in Malawi. It's a small country between Mozambique and Tanzania. I had to connect via Johannesburg, so they stamped my passport.'

'When was this?'

It had been almost three weeks since Kite had committed the Galvin file to memory but the date came to him as though he was recalling his own birthday.

'God. I don't know. Wait.' A suitable pause. 'Pretty sure it was the winter of 1989 because I remember Mandela was still in prison. They released him a few months later while I was in Malawi. Why?'

No reply. The two men spoke to one another in Russian,

but so quietly that Kite was only able to pick out the odd word: 'Malawi', 'teacher', 'Moscow', 'bicycle'.

'Where this?' Cobra asked, touching the saddle of the bike. Kite assumed he was asking where he had bought the bike, but with a confused shake of the head made out that he had not understood.

'My colleague asked where you find this bicycle,' Wessels explained. 'You pay for it?'

'Of course I paid for it!' Kite tried to look suitably outraged at the implication that it was stolen. 'I bought it in Voronezh. Somebody who works at the Dickens helped me find it. I can give you his name . . .'

Cobra spat out the match. A small amount of spittle remained on his lower lip and he was obliged to wipe it away with the sleeve of his shirt. He handed back the passport and returned to the driver's seat of the Volga. His colleague carried on staring intently at Kite; his clothes smelled faintly of patchouli oil, like the rooms of mock-hippies at Alford who smoked weed and listened to Neil Young records but ended up doing work experience at Daddy's bank.

'Make sure you look after your bicycle, Mr Galvin. We have problems with thieves in this city. Gypsies. Georgian gangs.'

'Yes, I was warned about them.' Kite laid a private bet with himself that he would find the bike gone by the end of the week. It would be an FSK signal to him. 'Is everything OK? Was I riding illegally?'

There was no answer, just an unnerving silence. Then:

'Do you like swimming?'

Kite felt a fizz of unease. He would have to answer carefully. He knew not to touch his face or adjust his hair, to do anything that might be read as evidence of deceit.

'Yeah. I go most evenings after work,' he said. 'It cools me off.'

'You swim today?'

That struck Kite as a bad question, a sign that his interlocutor was running out of road. It was obvious that he had been swimming. His hair was still wet and there was a damp patch on the bag from his towel.

'Yeah, I just came from there actually.' He decided to risk telling them what they already knew. To hold back on Aranov might look suspicious. 'Bumped into one of my students, we had a good swim.'

The Russian rolled his head to one side and frowned. 'Convenient, no?'

'Excuse me?'

'That you meet where you can talk.'

Kite's heart punched against his chest. 'I don't understand,' he said. He now understood why Wessels had asked if he had been swimming.

'What was your business together?'

'I'm sorry?' *Be Galvin*, Kite told himself. 'Convenient? What do you mean what was our business together? You mean me and Yuri?'

Taking a step forward, the Russian said: 'You know exactly what I mean, Peter.'

Rats scampered in Kite's stomach. He opted not to respond. He tried to convey with his expression that he did not understand what was being asked of him.

'Am I in trouble?' he said eventually. 'I don't understand your questions. Who are you? Can I see some identification?'

The Russian laughed. He moved from threat to contempt as easily as someone changing gear in a car.

'Who I am is not important,' he replied. 'What is important is why you meet one of your students when that student does not swim.' Kite saw his mistake. In all the time they had been watching him, Yuri Aranov had never set foot anywhere near a body of water. He had behaved out of character. They had nailed him. 'So what were you doing?'

His chest tight with nerves, Kite opted for a version of the truth.

'Lessons,' he said. 'He wants me to teach him privately. English. I'm an English teacher. What do you mean about swimming? Yuri was fine. We swam out to the little island.' Kite told himself to think of the men as Russian mafia, to suspect that Yuri owed them money or was in some way under threat. That was what Galvin would have concluded. 'Who are you guys?' he asked, taking a step backwards. 'What's the story with Yuri? Why are you so interested in him?'

'Thank you, Peter.' A look flashed across the man's face like a snake vanishing into long grass. He made no attempt to answer Kite's question. Instead he closed the notebook and climbed back into the car. 'We will be seeing much of each other in the future, I think,' he said, leaning out of the window. 'A foreigner is never alone in Voronezh.'

18

Kite watched the black Volga disappear behind a screen of birch trees. In the space of a few minutes everything in Russia had changed for him. Though he had been warned to expect the attentions of the FSK, the sudden appearance of the two men was as disconcerting as it was frustrating. Kite had believed that he could spirit Aranov out of the country without anybody noticing; now he was faced with a different set of challenges altogether. He told himself that this was what he had been trained for, that the FSK were handing him a priceless opportunity to prove his worth to Strawson. Yet for some time after the men had gone Kite felt unbalanced and angry: the encounter left him with a sense of isolation which was like a stain on his character. Only after he had returned home and smoked a cigarette on the balcony did he begin to feel more like his usual self. He knew what to do. He knew how to behave. From this moment onwards, it would be Moscow Rules.

Kite must assume that he was being watched twenty-four hours a day, seven days a week. If it was not already bugged, his apartment would now be rigged with microphones. Every letter and postcard BOX 88 were sending from London, purportedly written by Galvin's friends and family, would be steamed open. If he took the bus or rode the tram, there would be surveillance teams ahead of him and behind him at every stage of the route. When he cycled to work or went for a walk, the old woman selling sunflower seeds at the side of the road, the young couple kissing on a bench, the old men playing chess in the park, any of them could be mobile surveillance.

Kite duly behaved as Peter Galvin would behave, writing a letter to his mother in Wokingham saying how frightened he had been by the two men who had followed him while he was riding his bicycle back from the lake. He didn't want Mummy and Daddy to worry about him – he was generally having a fascinating time and enjoyed teaching enormously – but he had heard that the local police were corrupt and they had certainly scared him a little bit. Perhaps they had wanted a bribe. Maybe they were Russian mafia? It was hard to say. Kite sealed up the letter and sent it on its way.

Next he booked an international call to the family home in Wokingham giving a number in the UK which would reroute to The Cathedral. Whoever was on duty would role-play the part of a Galvin family member, speaking to Kite on the understanding that the FSK was listening to every word. Kite would again complain about the encounter with the two men who had followed him from the lake. He would talk about his students at the Dickens, ask for any news from the UK and tell his phantom parents that he was intending to be home for Christmas.

The call was scheduled for the following day and went ahead without a hitch. Kite spoke to Rita Ayinde, who effort-lessly slipped into the role of Miriam Galvin, expressing concern that her beloved son had been scared by the nasty Russians but untrammelled delight that he would be home for the festive season. The conversation lasted about ten minutes, cost Kite the equivalent of a day's salary, and left him with the feeling that he could still pull off the impossible. Aranov had come to class that morning confirming that the party was going ahead on Saturday night: Kite knew that an invitation to Aranov's dacha the following weekend would be forthcoming. After that, he must call the number in Moscow and alert BOX to his imminent departure. He would need to tell Aranov to ensure that Tania took her internal passport to the dacha so that she could cross into Ukraine. Otherwise Kite just had to behave as naturally and as blamelessly as possible. The Peter Galvin alias had become second nature to him, but the risk from microphones and surveillance made it vital that he did not slip up or give any indication that he was living under an alias.

Having originally planned to break things off with Oksana, Kite now came to the conclusion that it would be a mistake to do so. Why would Galvin, a lonely Englishman from Wokingham, stop sleeping with one of the most attractive women in Voronezh, unless it was to avoid upsetting her ex-boyfriend? The FSK surely knew about Aranov and Oksana's relationship; if Kite dumped her, it might look suspicious. Indeed, it wasn't beyond the bounds of possibility that the FSK would haul Oksana into their headquarters on Plekhanov Street and ask her all kinds of questions about Peter Galvin. No, better to keep things just as they were.

Kite was honest enough to admit that his decision to keep seeing Oksana was also coloured by the fact that she had invited him to stay at her apartment on Thursday night. Her sister was going to be away and she wanted to cook 'chicken under the press' for him. Her flat turned out to be a small, two-bedroom conversion in a nineteenth-century block in the old city. She greeted him at the door in bare feet, denim shorts and a loose pink T-shirt, immediately handing him a glass of Cagor, the lip-staining communion wine which was the drink of choice for anyone who lacked the budget for imported Georgian reds. Kite had brought a bunch of wild flowers, which Oksana placed in a vase. Her apartment, which smelled of cats and laundry, had competing decorative styles: the living room was crammed with old furniture, Soviet encyclopaedias and boxed jigsaws, a corner of orange wallpaper peeling from the ceiling; the bedroom, on the other hand, had been newly decorated, the freshly painted white walls adorned with photographs of Madonna, a mid-moon-walk Michael Jackson and Matt Dillon in *Drugstore Cowboy*. Oksana's bed was a small double and there was a desk in a corner by the window on which she had arranged various bottles of French perfume in neat lines. Kite was working his usual trick of trying to read Oksana's personality through the idiosyncrasies of her taste and style when she started unbuttoning his jeans and pulled him down onto the bed. They were still there after sunset. It was only towards ten o'clock that she finally cooked the chicken, setting a simple table in the kitchen with the vase of flowers, serving him the food wearing nothing but a pair of knickers and a man's pale blue shirt. Kite was in paradise. To complete an almost perfect evening, Oksana remembered the borrowed copy of *The English Patient* and gave it back. She said that she hoped the professor would read to her from it the next time she came to stay at his apartment. Kite had not been aware of the extent to which the book had still been playing on his nerves: he felt he could breathe again. While she washed up, Kite sat in the living room sipping a glass of vodka and casually checked the bindings. He could tell immediately that the book had not been tampered with. He decided that he would destroy it as soon as he could. Aranov was compliant enough; there was no need for the official letter of invitation.

Suddenly the lights went out in the apartment. Power cuts in Voronezh were common, particularly at night, and at first Kite did not think there was anything suspicious about the timing. Oksana cursed in Russian, brought more candles from the kitchen and placed them around Kite's chair. In the flickering light she looked bewitching and he took her back to bed, amazed that he had even considered denying himself the intense pleasure of being with her.

Yet his guard was down. Lying naked beside Oksana on the low, soft bed, soaked in sweat from sex and the humidity of the midsummer night, Kite made a needless mistake.

'Can I ask a favour?' he whispered, turning to face her.

'Of course,' she replied, touching his mouth. 'What is it, Peter?'

'Don't mention that we are seeing one another to Yuri Aranov.'

Oksana immediately sat up. The look she gave him was not one of confusion but instead of shock, as though Kite had confirmed a suspicion she had been harbouring for some time.

She said: 'I do not understand.'

Pulling the sheet over his chest, Kite realised his error and scrabbled around for a plausible explanation.

'It's just that he's invited me to a party on Saturday night. I like him. He's become a sort of friend. I think he would be upset if he knew that we were dating.'

Oksana frowned. Kite knew the look: it was the same one his mother showed to men when they had disappointed her. He was obliged to repeat his excuse, this time in more straightforward English. To his relief, Oksana appeared to accept the logic of his reasoning and lay back on the bed.

'Why you care about that man?' she asked. 'He more important than me?'

'Of course not!' Kite touched her stomach. 'I just don't like upsetting people, that's all.'

Yet the needless damage had been done. He thought of the swimmer on the island who had been spoken to at the edge of the lake. If the FSK interviewed Oksana, Aranov's name would now come up. There would be nothing to prevent her telling them about Kite's request. He lay back, trying to think of a way out of the trap he had set for himself, but there was no magic bullet. To make matters worse, he realised that he had again left his students' textbooks at his apartment and would need to collect them before going to work the next day. He waited until Oksana was asleep, wrote her a note explaining why he had not stayed the night, then slipped out of her building and cycled back to his apartment.

To prevent it being stolen, Kite always left his bicycle in the passage outside his flat, carrying it upstairs with one arm gripping the handlebars, the other under the frame. He was tired and drunk but managed to drag the bike to the fourth floor, setting the front wheel down on the landing and pausing to catch his breath.

Two men were waiting for him.

They were both well-built, one in combat trousers, the other in a tracksuit. Something hit Kite on the back of the head and he fell over, shocked and disoriented, the bike going with him. The taller of the two men saw that Kite's leg was trapped in the chain and pulled the bike away from him, ripping his trousers. The bike clattered against the wall.

They could now come at him without obstruction. Kite covered his head saying: 'Get the fuck off me!' as they swore in Russian, raining kicks and punches into his neck and stomach. There was a thick smell of sweat and unwashed clothes. If they were errand boys sent to scare him, Kite knew that he would have to take the beating. If he got to his feet and used what Ray had taught him, the FSK would know that he had been trained. Peter Galvin would have no idea how to fight or to defend himself; all he was capable of was screaming for help and whimpering like a cornered animal. It was humiliating.

A well-aimed kick landed in Kite's ribs, sucking the air out of him, then a follow-up in the balls which caused him to yelp in pain. Spittle landed inside Kite's mouth. He spat it out, making a retching sound, his face turned to the floor. He longed to bring the beating to an end. It would be so simple. To reach out and grab a stray leg, to pull one of the men to the ground, to stamp on his face and groin and drive an elbow into the face of his accomplice. Yet there was nothing he could do.

'Please stop!' he begged, the pitiful cry of a simple man from Berkshire who had never thrown a punch in his life, never been mugged, never hit out in sorrow nor in anger. 'Please!' he repeated, this time in Russian.

They responded in English, muttering: 'Go home' and 'Fuck you'. Then suddenly they sounded exhausted, drained of energy and purpose. It had been too easy for them. Kite continued to cover his head, the pain in his balls like a clamp. He was gasping for breath. Taking advantage of their tiredness he crawled away, dragging himself across the stained, torn linoleum towards a door at the end of the landing. One of the men kicked him lazily in the back of the thigh, the toe of his boot connecting with the top of the hamstring so that it felt as though he had ripped the muscle.

'Please!' Kite shouted.

Suddenly he heard the sound of an old woman at the top of the stairs; she was calling out in Russian. Kite recognised it as the voice of his elderly neighbour, the woman he had spoken to on his first night. She was walking downstairs, chastising the men, telling them they should be ashamed of themselves, that they were a disgrace to their families.

'Fuck off, old lady,' hissed the younger of them, the other picking up the bicycle. He spat on the ground.

'Don't take my fucking bike!' Kite shouted, but both of them were now at the top of the stairs, carrying it between them. The old lady reached the landing. By the time Kite had clambered to his feet, they were almost at the lobby.

'Disgraceful,' she said in Russian, looking at Kite with a strange kind of contempt, as though he had brought shame on the building by becoming involved in a fight.

'Thank you for helping me,' he gasped.

'You should not have come to Voronezh,' she muttered, a phrase Kite understood word for word. 'You are too far from home.'

19

Kite did not particularly care about the bike, nor was he badly injured. He woke up with a slightly blackened eye and some bruised ribs; there were marks on his legs and arms where the men had kicked him. The damage was mostly to his ego. He wished that he had been free to take on his attackers, to fight back and defend himself, rather than hiding feebly behind the shield of the Galvin alias. For appearance's sake it was necessary to spend Friday filing a report with the police and to visit a doctor's surgery. Kite waited for over two hours in an airless white room with bars on the windows. He was eventually seen by an unshaven Armenian in a filthy coat who charged him twenty dollars for an emergency appointment, sending him home with some suspicious -looking ointments and a packet of threadbare bandages. Kite threw them in the bin.

By Saturday morning he was feeling more like himself again. He carefully removed Strawson's letter from the binding of *The English Patient* and burned it in the kitchen sink, mending the damaged binding with tape to make it look as though it had come apart in his bag. He put on a pair of Ray-Bans to disguise his black eye, went outside and finished *War and Peace* on a bench in the sun. The old lady who had come to his aid returned from buying food at the market and stopped to ask how Kite was feeling. He had the sense that she knew what everybody else in the building suspected: that the heavies had been hired by the FSK. Kite thanked her for her assistance and watched her shuffle off through the front door, stooped and alone. He thought of all that she had lived through in her lifetime: the deprivations of war, the terror of Stalin's purges, the grim stasis of the Brezhnev years. He assumed she had been alive as far back as the Revolution of 1917.

Just after eight o'clock, Kite left for the party, riding the tram to the address Aranov had given, an elderly man in the opposite seat staring at him for a long time without expression, as if Kite's black eye was somehow a mark of poor character. He heard music as he approached the building, climbing to the top floor past broken plant pots and dried cigarette butts, a smell of alcohol in the stairwell. The party was being held in a large, deserted apartment which had been cleared for renovation. The place was packed. Kite counted at least twenty people in the kitchen, helping themselves to vodka and Fanta and Baltika lager, two of them already passed out drunk near the front door. The parquet floors were stained, some of the windows cracked, the only furniture in the place a few fold-up tables and the odd lamp without a shade. At the entrance to a wide balcony, a group of young women had set a table with paper plates and every kind of traditional Russian food – dried fish, cheeses, cornichons, even chunks of dark chocolate. There was a grungy atmosphere of smoke and unwashed clothes, of cheap alcohol and loud imported music. Kite realised that it was exactly four weeks since the party at Penley. He thought of the Bright Young Things of Oxford sipping vodka and tonics in Rosamund's elaborate eighteenth-century drawing rooms; the contrast was stark.

'Russians know how to throw good party, no?'

Aranov had materialised beside him wearing a clean white shirt and pressed denim jeans. It looked like his party uniform. He was holding a plastic cup of kvass, a Russian summer drink made from fermented bread which looked like Coca-Cola but tasted to Kite like cold mushroom soup. In the crowded room, thumping to the sound of a bootlegged version of 'Back in Black', they were able to speak freely. Aranov asked about Kite's black eye and he described the fight. They also discussed his encounter with the two men who had tailed him from the lake.

'I know them,' the scientist revealed. 'We have spoken many times. They hire the men to beat you up, no question. They think I am planning to leave Russia. I tell them: "Where am I going to go? I have pregnant girlfriend. I have an ex-wife who needs my house. I have good job in a country no longer ruled by fucking Communists. Why would I leave?" But of course they do not believe me. Mikhail Gromik is the one with the power.' Aranov took a sip of kvass. The room was noisy and Kite was not concerned about being overheard. 'He runs FSK in Voronezh. Only thirty years old. True arsehole. Eyes everywhere in the city. Likes to scare people. He only paid these guys to give you a beating because he doesn't have the courage to do it himself.' Aranov slapped his chest with a fist in imitation of a gorilla. 'All these old KGB sadistic. They were humiliated when their coup against Gorbachev failed, humiliated when Soviet system collapse. They make themselves feel strong by giving an Englishman a black eye and stealing his bicycle. They will also come out to the dacha.' Aranov searched Kite's face for a reaction. 'He will follow us. You know this, right? Do you have a plan for how we get away when Gromik is awake at one o'clock in the morning and sees us leaving in your car?'

'Let me take care of that,' Kite replied with more confidence than he felt. Strawson had suggested that any FSK surveillance on the night of the exfil would be neutralised, but Kite knew that he couldn't take anything for granted. 'The only thing you have to worry about is persuading Tania to come.'

'She will come,' Aranov promised, raising his cup and meeting Kite's eyes. 'She hate FSK as much as I do. We leave

Russia to get away from animals like Mikhail Gromik and the men who beat you up.'

'I'll drink to that,' Kite replied.

With the party swirling around them, they kept talking. Kite knew that these were important moments: not only was he able to confirm further details of the exfil, he was also building a relationship with Aranov, exactly as Strawson had decreed. Every now and again they would be interrupted by one of Aranov's friends stopping by to say hello. As their conversation continued, Kite became aware that one of his students, Lev, was looking over at them. When he saw that Kite had noticed him, he turned and walked outside onto the balcony.

'Tell me about Lev.'

Aranov seemed confused. 'Lev?'

'The guy from my class. He was over there a moment ago.' Kite nodded in the direction of the balcony. 'He was watching us. He always seems to be around. Any chance he's not who we think he is?'

Aranov shook his head animatedly, as if the idea was preposterous. 'No chance. He's just a kid.'

'What about Oksana?'

Kite had not meant to bring up her name, but wanted to be rid of the last vestiges of his doubts about her.

'What about Oksana?'

'Is she the real thing or is she FSK?'

Aranov tipped his head back and laughed. 'The real thing?' He lowered his voice as the music changed to The Beatles. 'You have to be joking with me, right? Oksana fucks like she was trained by FSK. She dresses like she has money provided by FSK. But she is too smart to work for FSK.' The Russian took a long drag on his cigarette, seemingly relishing the opportunity to talk about Oksana. 'She is ambitious. She knows her own value. She wants to find nice intelligent man who will give her comfortable life in the West. She wants to live in New York. She is dumb, in fact. If she had stayed with me, maybe it is Oksana comes in the car with us to Ukraine, not Tania, and she makes nice life in England with Yuri Aranov!'

If ever there was a chance to tell Aranov that they were sleeping together, this was it. Yet Kite ducked the opportunity. Yuri was being friendly and cooperative; there was no point in rocking the boat by provoking his jealousy.

Speak of the devil.

Right there and then, walking into the living room wearing her favourite denim miniskirt, was Oksana. She did not see Kite, instead heading through the crowds to the balcony where she greeted a friend with a hug and a yelp of joy, helping herself to a bottle of lager.

'She's here,' said Kite.

Aranov did not react. He appeared to be looking around for something to drink, distractedly mumbling the chorus of 'Hey Jude'.

'Oksana is here!' Kite shouted over the music. 'I guess somebody else invited her?'

Then it clicked. Kite understood why she had come. She wanted Aranov to see that she was involved with another man. She didn't care that Kite had asked her to be discreet; the party was the perfect opportunity. Sure enough, she came back into the living room, walked up to Kite, slipped her hand around his waist, kissed him full on the lips and said: 'There you are, Professor. I was searching everywhere' while staring at her former boyfriend. 'Oh, baby. What happened to your eye?' She looked concerned and touched Kite's face. 'You get in fight?'

Kite said, 'It's nothing, don't worry,' as Aranov's narrow features contorted in surly disbelief. Kite looked at him apologetically but was met with more contempt than he had seen in the faces of the men who had beaten him up. It felt in that moment as though there would be no coming back: Aranov had ceased to trust him. Unless Kite could somehow reel him back in, the operation was effectively over.

'What the hell is this situation?' Aranov asked, refusing to look at Oksana. 'You fucking her?'

Before Kite could respond, Oksana said: 'So what if he is?' in Russian. 'You got your little girlfriend pregnant. I am free to do what I like.'

Aranov continued to ignore her.

'You are snake,' he said to Kite. 'Get fuck away from me.'

Kite knew that he needed to act quickly or all would be lost. This was the moment to turn Aranov, not after a day or two when he had been allowed to stew in humiliation and resentment.

'Yuri, you misunderstand. We got together before I knew about your relationship. I didn't know you, we hadn't even met.'

Lev had come in from the balcony. He was close enough to hear what was being said.

'What do you mean you didn't know me?' Aranov looked disbelieving. 'You knew me. You knew the man I am.'

It was an extraordinarily dangerous thing to say. Kite tried to warn Aranov with his eyes.

'I knew nothing about you except that you were a good student, Yuri. I met Oksana before you came to my classes. I had no intention of upsetting you. I didn't think you would care.'

Aranov noticed Lev and stared at him watchfully. In the circumstances his presence was the best thing that could have happened; it made Aranov more judicious with his words, not perhaps because he shared Kite's doubts, but because he did not want to lose face in front of him.

'We swim,' he said. 'I tell you about this bitch.' Oksana swore in Russian and walked away, leaving the men to fight over her. 'Why you no tell me then, huh? Why do you not say you are sleeping with my girlfriend?'

'She's not your girlfriend, Yuri. *Tania* is your girlfriend! That's what you told me when we met at the lake. You told me she was pregnant. So why would you care about anybody else?'

'Hey Jude' was ending. All around them people were singing 'Na na na na, Hey Jude!', arms around backs, bottles and cigarettes raised in the air, the room swaying back and forth. Aranov did not answer Kite's question. Shaking his head, he walked off in the direction of the kitchen. Oksana was standing nearby. Kite went over to her.

'Why did you do that?' he demanded. 'I asked you not to say anything. I knew it would upset him.'

'Why you care so much?' she asked, and Kite saw that this wasn't just a game to her. She had been testing his loyalty, assessing the depth of his feelings.

'I told you,' he replied. 'I like him. I don't like hurting people.'

'You hurt me.'

'How?' Kite asked, genuinely puzzled.

'You will be friends with a man who treat me so badly? How is this possible?'

Lev was there, a few metres away, still tuning in. Kite shot him a look, as if to say: 'Mind your own business' and the little Russian scuttled off.

'I'm sorry,' he told Oksana. 'I met Yuri accidentally on Wednesday evening after class.' He had to explain the word 'accidentally' because Oksana had never heard it before. 'We went for a swim. Yuri was very friendly. He invited me to this party. He's a good person to have in my class because he asks a lot of questions. He makes my job easier. But if you don't want me to be friends with him, fine, I won't be friends with him.'

Oksana fell for it. To make a demand like that on Kite was beneath her. She could tell that he cared for her, that he was serious about their relationship.

'It is OK, Professor,' she said, leaning towards him and touching his mouth with the tip of her finger. 'As long as you come back to my bed and do the things you do to me, I do not care about this Yuri. You make me forget him, Peter. You are better man than him in every way.'

Kite knew that he should get away from her and talk to Yuri. An androgynous Russian girl with a rough peroxide crewcut greeted Oksana. She spoke no English. Feigning frustration at his inability to understand what was being said,

Kite excused himself. He found Yuri chatting to a young girl in a red leather jacket who immediately walked away when she saw Kite coming towards them.

'Great,' said Aranov. 'So now you stop me talking to all women.' He sounded like a spoiled schoolboy. 'You are not happy just to take Oksana from me, you also drive off this one as well.'

Kite was mystified. 'What about Tania?' he asked. 'What's going on there? You told me you loved her.' He gestured towards the girl in the leather jacket. 'If you want me to get her back, I'll go and get her.'

'Forget it.' Aranov tried to push past him. 'Forget everything.'

Kite did not want to be seen having an argument with Aranov, but it was vital to get him back onside. To lose the window for the exfil would be catastrophic. How would he explain himself to Strawson? Furthermore, to delay his departure, to hang around for another two or three weeks, would be extremely dangerous. The more time he spent in Voronezh, the more time Gromik would have to expose Peter Galvin and to put Aranov in front of a firing squad.

'Let's talk,' he said, putting his arm around the Russian in what he hoped would seem like a gesture of semi-drunken camaraderie. At the same time he grabbed two bottles of Baltika. 'Come back to the other room.'

Oksana and her friend were now on the balcony. People were dancing to Blondie, shouting and kissing. A whippet-thin youth in sagging jeans took off his top and swung it round his head in a state of delirium. There was a smell of fresh sweat and warm summer air.

'Look,' Kite began, back in the safety of noise. 'I don't think you realise how serious this situation is. I am risking my life. You are risking yours.'

'How am I risking *my* life?' Aranov shot back. 'I have done nothing wrong.' He looked pleased with his answer. 'I can stay here. What will you do then, Peter Galvin? You will have to go home as a failure.'

'Is that what you want?'

195

'For you to fail? Yes.'

Kite looked up at the ceiling and shook his head, amazed that a grown man of thirty-five could be so petulant.

'Not me,' Kite replied. '*You* to fail. Is that what you want? To stay here? Because if it is, I'll go back to London tomorrow. You think I want to stay in Voronezh when I could be in Athens or Rio or New York? You think I enjoy spending my summers teaching English for two hundred dollars a week waiting for you to make your mind up?'

Aranov said: 'Don't make an enemy of me, Peter,' but his eyes lacked the force of his words.

'If I go back to London, that's it. Nobody comes for you again. No life in London, no life in America. Forget Australia, Canada, New Zealand. All of them would be off the table.'

'What do you mean?'

'I mean you would be in the hands of the Libyans, the Iraqis, the crazies from North Korea. Those are the people who will take you. Nobody else. Is that what you want? A life in Tripoli, Baghdad. A job in Pyongyang making rockets tipped with anthrax for Kim il-Sung? This isn't a time for acting like a teenager just because you're jealous over a girl. Your entire life is at stake. Your future. You don't go now, you don't go at all.'

'Maybe I can trust them better than I can trust you.'

Kite was glad that he had drunk some vodka. It loosened his tongue.

'You think?' He laughed contemptuously. 'Fine. Go ahead and trust them. Go ahead and spread death for the rest of your life. Be watched wherever you go, have a security guard outside your bedroom door in Tripoli, closed-circuit cameras in your living room in Iraq. Get thrown in prison for sleeping with the wrong woman or just for being in the wrong place at the wrong time. What if there's a revolution in these countries, a change of government and they want to make an example of the political elite? You happy to survive or die on the whim of a maniac like Colonel Gaddafi?'

196

'Life in your country would be no different. I will be watched. I will be followed.'

'Bullshit. Nobody will give a crap who you sleep with, where you eat and drink, who your friends are. It's called *freedom*. You get a new identity, a new passport, go anywhere you like – if you could just get over your fucking fear of flying.'

A tremor of a smile. Kite knew he was winning.

'Tania,' said the Russian.

Kite wanted to laugh. It was always women with Aranov. If it wasn't Oksana it was Tania. If it wasn't Tania, it was some random girl in a red leather jacket who gave him five minutes of her time beside a kitchen sink at a party. The neediness and insecurity were risible.

'What about her?'

'She not come, I no see my child.'

'Why wouldn't she come?'

To Kite's relief, Aranov appeared to have no plausible rationale for Tania not wanting to get in the car. He explained that her life in Voronezh was wretched. She had no money, no job, a baby due at Christmas. He knew that if he told her they were leaving on Sunday night, she would probably be packed and ready to go in less than an hour.

'But it is not so easy for me.' At first, Kite didn't understand what Aranov was talking about. 'Youngest director of operations in Russian history. I can pick my team. They give me apartment in Moscow, new dacha, expense account.'

Kite hesitated. He could see that the Moscow offer sounded enticing to someone who had grown up with Soviet privations. He wondered how to play his hand.

'Sounds better than Pyongyang,' he began. 'But you'd still have men like Mikhail Gromik all over you for the rest of your career, making sure you don't talk to any foreigners, don't go on holiday, checking out who you're sleeping with, pushing away anybody they don't like the sight of. Look what happened to me.' He touched the mark around his eye. 'If that's what you want, go for it.' Kite took a swig of Baltika. 'If you want to spend your working life stalked by men like Mikhail Gromik while thinking of ways to kill tens of thousands of innocent people in Europe and America, do that. Trade in death. Everything you love – the possibility of freedom, to live in a world without fear, without hate – you would be destroying that.' At the last moment Kite remembered a documentary about the Manhattan Project he had watched one night in Edinburgh. 'You've heard of Robert Oppenheimer, the man who invented the atomic bomb?'

'Of course I have.'

'Did you see that press conference he gave, talking about the aftermath of Hiroshima? *Now I am become death. The destroyer of worlds.* That's you. That's who you have been for the past ten years. That's who you'll continue to be if you stay in Russia. A chemist of death, as haunted as Robert Oppenheimer.'

Aranov considered Kite's words. A group of young Russians, arm-in-arm and steaming drunk, swerved past them. One of them fell over and had to be helped up by a man standing nearby. Aranov waited until they were out of earshot.

'You are clever, Mr Galvin. You make things sound so logical. But you miss one thing.'

'What's that?'

'I kill for them, I kill for you. What's the difference?'

Kite was startled by the question.

'You think that's how we operate? Is that the extent of the brainwashing the fucking Soviets did on you? You would be coming to us to *stop* weapons of this kind, to teach us what you know and anticipate what might happen in the future. The West has no interest in creating biological weapons. We only have an interest in *stopping* them. You can make the world a safer place, Yuri. You can make *Russia* a safer place by not being here and cooking up death.'

Kite looked around. He half-expected to catch sight of Lev watching them from a darkened corner of the apartment, but the little Russian was nowhere to be seen. There was only a spotty, undernourished teenager holding a paper plate; it sagged under the weight of some boiled beetroot and a tuft of sodden lettuce.

'You want to eat this food for the rest of your life?' Kite pointed at the paper plate. The lettuce looked as if it had been left out in the rain. 'Drink Armenian brandy when you could be drinking Courvoisier, Communion wine instead of Rioja? You want power cuts, holes in the road, your phone calls bugged, FSK heavies beating up your friends? These people who are offering you the apartment in Moscow, the expense account, the dacha – they will make you do things you don't want to do because you will have no choice. Eventually they will make you ashamed to be the man you are. They know your value, Yuri. They know what's inside your head. They are desperate to keep you.'

'I want to leave,' he said. 'But I don't want it to be you who takes me. How can I trust you?'

'There is nobody else! You want to get yourself to an airport and risk flying on a false passport? Go ahead. I'll get one for you. You'll be arrested before you make it out of the car park. I am your only option. Nobody else will come for you. Why would we bother to try again when you mess us around like this?'

Oksana and her friend were coming towards them. A good-looking man in a loud shirt was trailing after her; Kite had a mental image of a panting cartoon dog dragging its tongue on the floor. Aranov said: 'Here comes your girlfriend, Peter,' but did not walk away.

'What do you two talk about?' she asked.

'I was explaining to Yuri how you feel,' Kite replied. 'I was hoping we could put this misunderstanding behind us and be friends.'

She looked taken aback and glanced at Aranov. She seemed not to believe what Kite had told her. The Russian remained impassive.

'And can you?' she asked.

The good-looking man gave up the chase and sloped off. Appearing out of thin air, Lev took his place.

'Can we what?' Aranov replied, as though he hadn't been listening.

Oksana repeated what she had said, this time in Russian: 'Can we be friends, Yuri? Will you be kind to me? Will you accept that you hurt me?'

Kite did not expect her words to have any meaningful effect. Aranov was surely too proud, too wounded, to concede ground. And yet as he looked at Oksana he seemed to be softened by the memory of what had passed between them.

'Of course!' he said. 'Of course we can be friends!' He put a hot, sweaty arm around Kite's neck, squeezed the muscle then moved it up and down on one of the bruises left by Gromik's thugs. 'Come to my dacha next weekend. Both of you. We can be friends!' In Russian he added: 'Lev, you also want to come? Tania will be there, you can meet her. Bring a girl if you have one.' Lev looked delighted. 'We have good time, teach this Englishman about the *banya*.'

They all laughed. Kite caught Aranov's eye. That he had issued the invitation in front of Oksana and Lev was an unexpected bonus.

'I would love to come,' he replied. 'Always wanted to go to a dacha. What a great thing to look forward to.'

20

As soon as you know you're heading out to the dacha, call the number from a payphone. When somebody picks up, they'll answer you in Russian. Ask if they speak English. They'll say they do. Ask if you're connected to the Hotel Metropol. They'll tell you it's a wrong number and hang up.

During his lunchbreak on Monday, Kite found a payphone near the railway station and dialled the number Strawson had given him. A woman answered.

'*Privet?*'

'Hello. Do you speak English?'

There was a pause. Then:

'Yes, sir. I speak English. How can I help you?'

'Am I connected to the Hotel Metropol?'

'I am sorry, sir. You have the wrong number.'

The woman hung up. Kite felt a rush of exhilaration. The message had been received; there was now no going back. On Saturday he would make his way to the dacha. On Sunday morning he would drive to the border with Aranov and Tania.

He telephoned Oksana the next day from the office at the Dickens. She had stopped coming to classes, not because she was trying to avoid Aranov, but because it was the only way Kite could legitimately continue to see her without losing his job. Her decision to switch schools gnawed at his conscience;

it showed how serious she was about their relationship. On the phone she told him that she was going to Rostov for two days but would be back by Thursday. They arranged to have a drink that night at the Brno Hotel. Kite would meet her in the bar at seven o'clock.

'Don't be late,' she told him. 'I don't want to be mistaken for one of those girls.'

Having given himself twenty-four hours to think about it, Kite was now determined to tell Oksana that their relationship could go no further. He would just have to think of a plausible reason for ending things. It was necessary to be cruel in order to be kind. If she came to the dacha, it was even possible that she would be accused of aiding and abetting a British agent. Above all, he did not want her to suffer as a result of his treachery. I'll break it off over dinner on Thursday, he told himself. I'll tell her that I've got to go back to England because of a family emergency. Mention the reservation at the Metropol Hotel so that she knows I was serious about her. I'll tell her there's a chance I'll be back in Voronezh in August, depending on the situation at home. Suggest that maybe we can still meet up in Moscow.

The fluency with which he conjured these deceits unsettled Kite. He was becoming a new kind of person: an opportunist and manipulator. *Just tell her part of the truth*, he thought. Say you had a girlfriend in England. Tell her you don't want to get into another serious relationship so soon. Explain that you won't be in Voronezh forever and it's better to break off now before both of you get hurt.

The lies and excuses were still spinning around Kite's mind as he walked towards the river after work. He was close to the neighbourhood where he had been tailed by Gromik. Gradually he became aware of someone whistling in the distance. As the sound grew nearer, Kite recognised the tune. It was the melody from *The Godfather*. BOX 88 had at last sent his contact.

He felt his breath quicken, his senses tuning to every element of the surrounding environment. The whistling was coming from the next corner. Kite heard the seven mournful notes once again as a stray dog darted out from behind a car, brushing against his leg as it passed him.

A man crossed the road. He was in his thirties wearing cotton trousers and a white shirt, lips pursed as he whistled. Without looking at Kite he continued on his way, trying out different phrases in the melody. Kite followed, skirting around a pile of fetid garbage, turning to check that he was not being tailed. The street behind him was deserted. Up ahead there was a woman pushing a pram, an elderly man waiting at a bus stop, a teenager leaning against a wall smoking a cigarette.

The whistling man turned left, away from the oncoming traffic on Ulitsa Kirova. Kite had no logical reason to follow him, so he stopped on the same corner, took a street map from his bag and looked around vacantly, pretending to be lost. Then he turned in the direction taken by the man and found himself on a deserted street. He soon heard the melody again. It was coming from a narrow passage close by. Kite glanced quickly behind him, then ducked down the passage. The man was waiting for him. His hair was cropped close and he was tanned and stocky. He asked the signal question.

'Do you have the cigarettes from London?'

'I left them in my apartment,' Kite replied.

They were standing in dead ground between two abandoned buildings. Kite put his satchel on the ground and said: 'Is everything OK?'

'My name is Pavel,' the man replied.

He was evidently Russian with an easy, avuncular style, sharp eyes and a ready smile. He could have passed for a bus driver, a medical doctor, a PE teacher, a piano tuner. He looked like everybody and nobody. 'Everything is fine,' he continued. His gentle, reassuring tone was deliberate. Kite knew that he had been trained to put agents at their ease. 'I am happy to confirm that your message was received. The car and the passports will be waiting. Are you all right? Is there anything we need to know, anything we can do for you?'

203

Pavel spoke quietly and respectfully, making Kite feel that he admired him for what he was doing.

'There's one hitch,' he said. 'Yuri has a girlfriend.'

'Tania, yes.'

'She's pregnant. He wants to bring her across.'

Pavel looked down at the ground, nodded, looked back up and said: 'OK, fine. She comes. She has passport?'

'Can you fix one?'

'It will be difficult at short notice. Residency stamps and so on. But it can be arranged. Nothing is impossible. Leave it with us.'

Kite wondered how BOX would get hold of a photograph of Tania but reckoned it was someone else's problem. He stared at Pavel and his mind went blank. He knew that there were a thousand things he wanted to ask, but all he could think about was how long Pavel had been risking his life for BOX. Was he based in Voronezh or had he travelled down from Moscow? Why wasn't he taking personal charge of the operation and escorting Yuri across the border? Kite supposed that he was too useful as a long-term, deep-lying agent facilitating BOX 88 operations inside Russia. He would only ever leave if he requested to do so.

'I was beaten up,' he said, finding something to say.

'Your face is marked,' Pavel replied. 'This is because of the FSK who spoke to you.' It sounded like a statement of fact rather than a question. 'You did well not to fight back.'

'Thank you,' said Kite, wondering how Pavel had learned about the attack. 'What about my classes?' he asked. 'Who is informing on Yuri? Who do I need to look out for?'

Hearing something, Pavel looked back in the direction of the street, but it was just the sound of a passing bicycle.

'The older man, Arkady. He is connected.' Arkady was 'Grandpa'. 'He meets people he should not meet. It's possible he talks about your classes, but I have heard nothing to concern us. They think Peter Galvin is Peter Galvin. You have done well.'

Kite let the compliment pass over him; he was still feeling

uncertain about Oksana and guilty for messing her around. He wanted to ask this seemingly wise and experienced man for advice on affairs of the heart. He was sure that Pavel would know the right thing to do.

'What about this weekend?' he said. 'Gromik tails me to the dacha, he works shifts outside the house, the FSK might see us leave . . .'

Pavel smiled beatifically. 'All this is possible,' he confirmed. 'They may follow you. Their pattern is to stand down when it gets late. I will be there. You will not see me. If they are a threat, if they will prevent you getting away, there are procedures.'

'What kind of procedures?'

Pavel did not respond. His expression gave nothing away. Was he going to slit Gromik's throat or simply let down the tyres on his Lada? Both seemed equally likely.

'If it is dangerous for you to leave, if we consider that you should remain in Voronezh, I will come to the house and ask to borrow something. A ladder. A bowl of sugar. Some onions. Then you will know for certain not to leave. But the chances of this happening are very small. What about the girl?'

At first Kite thought Pavel was asking about Tania but quickly realised that BOX knew about Oksana. Of course they did. They knew everything.

'Yuri has asked her to the dacha. I need to break up with her to keep her safe. I'll do it on Thursday. We're going for a drink at the Brno.'

Pavel gave a man-of-the-world shrug and with the single word 'Yes' conceded that this was indeed the best plan of action. He did not comment on Kite's relationship with Oksana nor suggest that he had taken a risk in trusting her.

'What will happen to her after I leave?' Kite asked. 'Will she be in trouble for associating with me?'

'Anything is possible,' he replied. 'She might be brought in for questioning, they might use her as bait to get you back.'

'How?' Kite asked.

'If they are stupid, they send her to London to try to seduce you all over again.'

'But how will they know where to find me?'

'Exactly.'

With that, the Oksana problem was set to one side.

'So I have news from England.'

Kite instantly thought of Martha, longing to hear what had become of her.

'You do?' He realised how much he had craved even the simplest snippet of information from home. He had been told that he would be able to listen to the BBC World Service but had never been able to get a signal on the radio in his flat.

'Your mother is well,' Pavel told him. 'She has been on holiday with her boyfriend.'

'Tom,' Kite muttered, remembering his Docksiders in the hall. 'Rita she says hello. This next section I have not memorised.' To Kite's surprise, Pavel took a piece of paper from his trouser pocket and began to read. '*England lost the first Test against Australia by 179 runs. Australia have a new bowler.* Is that the correct way to pronounce this word?'

'Bowler, yes,' said Kite, amused and touched that Rita had gone to the trouble of sending him the cricket scores.

'*His name is Shane Warne. He bowled his first ball in Test cricket* – does any of this make sense? – *which pitched outside Gatting's leg stump.* What does this mean? *It turned very sharply and bowled him at the top of off stump.*'

'Wow,' said Kite.

Pavel looked up from the sheet of paper, bewildered. 'I have no idea what any of this means. I am assuming you understand?'

'Perfectly,' said Kite, who was suddenly back at Lord's with Billy Peele watching Malcolm Marshall steaming in from the Pavilion End.

'*Warne was man of the match,*' Pavel continued. '*He takes eight wickets. England also lose second Test against Australia by an innings and 62 runs. Mick Atherton . . .*'

Kite corrected him: 'Mike Atherton.'

'Mike Atherton was run out at Lord's for 99.'

'Shit. Poor guy.'

Again Pavel asked: 'What does it all mean?' while burning the aide-memoire with a Zippo lighter and letting the fragments fall to the ground.

'It means England are probably going to lose the Ashes,' Kite replied. 'It's bad news. But please tell Rita I'm very grateful.'

Pavel wiped his hands on the back of his trousers and indicated that they should go their separate ways.

'Will you be following me on the road?' Kite asked.

The Russian cleared his throat. 'Of course. But you will not see me, you will not react to me. I am to escort you and to help if something goes wrong. You understand that in the event you are arrested, there is very little I can do.'

'I understand that,' Kite replied.

The Russian slapped him affectionately on the side of the arm, hitting yet another bruise from the fight. 'But you will not be arrested,' he said warmly. 'Nothing will go wrong, my friend. This time in one week you will be back in London watching Mick Atherton play this strange game you love so much which makes no sense to a man like me. I wish you good luck.'

21

Kite arrived early on Thursday night at the bar of the Brno Hotel. He wanted to mark out a discreet corner where he could speak privately to Oksana about his decision to end their relationship. He was going to tell her that he had a girlfriend back in England, that he intended to leave the Dickens before the end of the summer and that he didn't want to string her along and make her think that they had a future together.

He was going to need a drink first. He went to the bar and ordered a fantastically expensive imported French wine with a shot of local vodka to chase it. The barman knew him and asked in English how life was going before uncorking the Beaujolais and pouring it into a long-stemmed glass.

A woman was sitting three stools away from Kite. She had the darker skin and hair of the Caucasus and was more striking than any of the women he had seen before in the hotel. She was older, for a start, more smartly dressed with an air of Mrs Robinson sophistication. The smell of her perfume drifted across the bar like a guarantee of worldly experience and refinement. Kite told himself that she was a businesswoman visiting from Spain or Italy. The Brno was the only decent hotel in the city and she was having a drink after a long day of meetings.

Then she turned and looked at him. It was not an ordinary look, good-natured and polite, but a glance of invitation, private and mischievous. The intent was obvious. She was saying to him: 'I am alone. You are alone. I am yours if you can afford me.' Kite hurriedly turned to face the wall of spirits ahead of him, his heart racing. Having paid for his drinks, he nodded at the woman and retreated to his table, continuing to watch her as she plied her trade. A bald man walked into the bar and sat two stools away from her. She glanced at Kite, ascertained that he had taken himself off the market, and proceeded to welcome her new admirer with the same quiet smile. The man moved across to sit beside her. It was that easy. He was in his mid-thirties, closer in age to the woman, and doubtless had picked up girls in bars around the world as easily and as calmly as he was doing now. The two spoke in Russian and, when the barman was free to serve them, ordered a bottle of champagne.

Kite sank his vodka shot and took a first sip of the wine, mentally checking off the things he was going to say, hoping that Oksana would not be too upset or make a scene in the bar. When she eventually arrived, she was wearing a dress Kite had not seen before, heels that accentuated her long, exquisite legs, her hair tied up. She looked older and more refined than usual.

'Hello, Professor.'

He stood up to greet her and Oksana kissed him. She had been smoking a cigarette. Her lips tasted of tobacco and the warm summer evening.

'How are you?' he asked.

'I am very well. I looked forward to seeing you.'

'I did too.'

Kite took an audible deep breath as he sat down. Oksana looked at him as if she immediately suspected that something was wrong. He smiled at her reassuringly and felt a stab of guilt at what he was about to do. Raising his hand to summon the barman, Mrs Robinson clocked Oksana and smiled knowingly, doubtless concluding that Kite preferred blondes. He ordered two glasses of Russian champagne, waited until they had been served, then delivered the coup de grâce.

When it was over, Oksana rose from the table, tears in her eyes, and said in her best English that she felt used and angry and hoped that he would never contact her again. She left in a hurry, passing two drunken businessmen on her way out. One of them, an American, said: 'Hey! Don't leave, beautiful!' and tried to grab her by the arm. Oksana swore at him in Russian and went out onto the street.

Kite sat back in his chair. He had not broken up with a girl since 1988, awkwardly dumping Gaynor Hamilton-Andrews in a branch of Dome on Windsor High Street while they drank hot chocolates under a reproduction Toulouse-Lautrec. She had taken the news better than Oksana. He felt wretched, wondering how often in the future he would have to cause unnecessary pain and to sacrifice his own pleasure for the sake of an operation.

Kite looked up. The woman at the bar was again alone. He had not noticed the bald man leaving. Perhaps he had gone to the bathroom or to book a room at reception. A younger Russian in fishnet tights and what looked like a blonde wig had taken a seat at a table near the door and was scanning the male customers as they entered the room. She looked over at Kite and gave him the customary come-hither stare. He lit a cigarette and looked out of the window. He wondered if he would see Oksana on the street, waiting for him to emerge from the hotel. She might try to change his mind or even attack him physically for his heartlessness. But there was no sign of her, just the usual evening bustle of ageing Soviet trams and rusted cars, babushkas pulling shopping trolleys, a skinny kid with spiked hair gawping at the Brno and catching Kite's eye through the glass.

Oksana had hardly touched her champagne. Like a drunk at a wedding Kite knocked it back in three quick mouthfuls, finished the cigarette and looked for the bathroom. Leaving his jacket and a packet of Marlboro Lights on the table, he walked out of the bar and crossed the busy lobby. He did not see the bald man at the reception desk, nor in the bathroom. Perhaps he was already upstairs, waiting for the woman to join him. Perhaps she was simply too expensive and he had left the hotel. Kite washed his hands, stared at his reflection in the mirror and let out a deep sigh. He wanted to call Oksana back to the Brno and tell her that the whole thing had been a huge mistake.

He came out into the lobby. A bellboy was pulling an empty luggage trolley towards one of the lifts. Two Russian heavies in black leather jackets were sitting on a sofa keeping an eye on the street. Kite assumed they were protection for an up-and-coming Mafioso or security looking after a visiting politician. He stopped to adjust his shirt. He was about the length of a cricket pitch from the reception desk. A woman was checking in.

It wasn't the wine. It wasn't the champagne. It wasn't the vodka. Kite looked at the woman more closely. She was filling in a form at the desk. Surely it wasn't possible? With a feeling of elation which quickly turned to profound disquiet, Kite realised who had come for him.

It was Martha.

22

Kite was ashamed to confront an impulse to turn and run. A perfect spy would have done so. He knew afterwards that he should have left the hotel and trusted that Martha would leave Voronezh without ever finding him. Yet he was rooted to the spot. Even as he stared at her in disbelief, he realised how it had happened: Rupert Howell, the old Alfordian who had spotted him at Domodedovo, had gone back to London and told somebody who knew Martha that Lachlan Kite was headed for Voronezh. Martha would have rung every hotel and boarding house in the city trying to track him down. When that hadn't worked, she had jumped on a plane and flown out to surprise him.

He was on the point of retreating to the relative sanctity of the bathroom when she looked up and saw him.

'Lockie!' she cried incredulously. 'You're here!'

Too late. She rushed forward, wrapping her arms around him. It was as if what had happened at Penley with Cosmo de Paul was a false memory. Her cheek was against his cheek, her hair in his mouth and eyes, the smell of her like the comfort of home and the promise of his own future.

'What are you doing here?' he whispered, kissing her.

'I came to find you.' She looked at him, tears in her eyes. 'I thought we needed to talk. And I've never been to Russia before. What happened to your face?'

'It's fine. Nothing.' There was still a slight cut and some faint bruising around his eye. 'Needed to *talk*?' he said. 'So you came all the way to Voronezh?!'

They hugged again, Kite hoping to God that nobody had heard Martha calling him 'Lockie'. The heavies on the sofa didn't appear to be paying them any attention. Only the receptionist seemed put out because Martha had not yet finished checking in.

'Why are you in this hotel?' Martha asked. 'Are you staying here? Is this where you live?'

'No, no,' Kite replied, and the lies came flooding in. 'I just had a drink in the bar. It's the only place in the city where you can get decent wine.'

She gave him an appraising look, as though Kite's timing was off and more had gone wrong between them than Martha had been prepared to admit. She said: 'Hang on a minute' and went back to the reception desk where she filled in the last of her forms and was handed a key to a room on the second floor.

'Did you know where to find me if I hadn't been here?' Kite asked, hiding his consternation.

'No,' she said. 'I rang all the hotels from London but hardly anybody spoke English. I assumed you were in a flat. The Russian embassy gave me a list of all the language schools in Voronezh. A friend of Sammy's saw you at Moscow airport, so I knew you were here. That's what you said you were going to do, right? Teach English. So I was going to go to all of the schools and hope to find you. There are only five.'

She seemed pleased with her strategy, talking excitedly, oblivious to the chaos she had caused which Kite knew he now had to put right.

'Why didn't you just ring them up?' Kite asked. He prayed that Martha had not spent the previous two weeks showing his photograph to officials at the embassy in Kensington and asking their help in tracking him down.

'I tried,' she said. 'But I only got through to one. The

person on the line didn't even speak English, which was a bit crap for a language school!'

'What if you didn't find me?' It occurred to him that Martha might not be telling the truth. Her story sounded far-fetched, too detailed, almost desperate. Had Strawson sent her? Surely not. 'It's such a long way to come . . .'

Some of the joy went out of her eyes. Something wasn't quite right with her elusive boyfriend.

'Aren't you happy to see me, Lockie?' She touched her face. 'Aren't you glad that I came?'

'So happy,' he replied, wanting to beg her not to use his name again, to call him 'Peter' or 'Pete' or better still nothing at all. 'I'm just in shock. It's so amazing that you're here. You look fantastic. How long are you planning to stay?'

She took her room key from the desk and waited before answering, asking if Kite could help with her bags. He picked them up and carried them to the lifts, then said he had to pay his bill at the bar and would meet her in the room.

'I can wait,' she said, as if he was being presumptuous inviting himself upstairs. 'How much have you had to drink?'

It wasn't like Martha to be pious, but she had smelled the alcohol on his breath. Perhaps she thought Kite looked anxious and dishevelled. Looking at himself in the bathroom mirror earlier, he had felt washed out.

'A bit,' he replied. 'Not that much. Give me two minutes.'

He walked off, all the time calculating the best strategy. He knew that his ability to think quickly and to make split-second decisions was prized by BOX 88, yet in this moment, when the operation had become infinitely more complex, he could not work out the best way to protect Martha from harm. If he told her the truth, she might leave on the next flight to Moscow. If she was then interviewed by the FSK, he was finished, and Aranov a dead man. If on the other hand he told her to leave, that he wanted nothing to do with her, Martha would be devastated and might anyway face the same interrogation, with the same outcome. No, he was going to have to work out a way of keeping her in Voronezh while not compromising the exfil. There was no safe option. At least he had had the good sense to break up with Oksana. If Martha had come across them in the bar just half an hour earlier, his two secret lives would have collided in plain sight.

Mrs Robinson was still on her stool. She was now like someone he had met many years ago whom he was determined to avoid. Kite picked up his jacket and cigarettes, handed the waiter a fifty-dollar bill from Rita's stash, told him to keep the change and left without so much as a glance towards the bar. Returning to the lobby, he noticed that the two security goons had vacated the sofa and were now outside on the street. Martha was waiting for him, standing beside her suitcases and rucksack, watching Kite coming towards her.

'You've lost weight,' she said matter-of-factly.

'Food here is shit. Let's go up to your room. I really need to talk to you.'

He could tell that she knew something wasn't right. Martha would have played out their reunion in her mind a dozen times, but now that it was happening it wasn't fitting the script. As they rode the lift together, holding hands but not speaking, Kite formulated the story that he knew he needed to tell her right away. He leaned on Strawson's observation in Chez Jules: *You don't know that Martha would leave you if she found out who you really are. She might even like the idea. She might find it exciting.* Yet he feared her anger and her disappointment. He had been lying to her since the moment they met. He was going to have to find a way of telling Martha about his secret life without her ever suspecting that he had been operational in France.

The lift doors opened onto a narrow, carpeted corridor which smelled of furniture polish and decades of cigarette smoke.

'It's not the Ritz,' Martha observed.

'Sure isn't.'

Kite knew that certain bedrooms in Soviet hotels had been bugged for foreigners. It was possible Martha had been given one. He could not risk telling her about Aranov with microphones potentially picking up his every word.

'Are you all right, Lockie?' she asked.

They passed an open door to a room which had not yet been cleaned. The sheets were on the floor and there was a full ashtray near the television. Kite could hear a hoover running in the distance and saw a chambermaid's trolley parked at the far end of the corridor.

'Come in here,' he said, pulling Martha into the room.

'But that's not the right one,' she protested, checking her key.

'Doesn't matter.'

He closed the door behind her, ran the taps in the bathroom, switched on the radio beside the bed and opened a window.

'Lockie, what the fuck are you doing? Not in here. Are you pissed?'

He pulled her towards him, whispered: 'Please don't call me Lockie. My name is Peter. Call me Peter. I can explain everything.'

She looked at him as though he had lost his mind. He pulled the dirty sheets clear of the bed and indicated that she should sit down.

'Just listen,' he said. He knew they didn't have long before the chambermaid interrupted them. 'I need to tell you something.'

A bewildered Martha sat at the end of the bed looking as though she had just been woken from a deep sleep. Kite fetched a chair and sat down facing her. He spoke as honestly and as plainly as the circumstances allowed, keeping his voice low against some Rachmaninov on the radio.

'I'm sorry I didn't explain to you before I left. I wasn't allowed to. It's wonderful that you've come all this way to see me, but it's very dangerous.'

'Dangerous? Dangerous how? Lockie, what's happened? Is this about the cut on your face? Are you in trouble? Who the fuck is Peter?'

'You can't call me Lockie,' he said firmly. 'You have to

forget everything about me, everything we've ever done. It's going to sound unbelievable, and I need you to understand that I wasn't allowed to share this with you, otherwise I would have confided in you.' He took her hand. BOX 88 was a secret too far; he could not tell her about that. He opted instead to break his cover. 'I've been hired by MI6 to work for them after we leave university. They've sent me out here to Russia as a test.'

Martha broke into disbelieving laughter. She muttered: 'What?' very softly, as if Kite was involving her in some kind of tasteless practical joke.

'I'm serious. Somebody else was supposed to come here and teach at the Dickens.'

'What's the Dickens?'

'It's the language school where I work. His name was Peter Galvin. He also works for MI6. He had an accident and wasn't able to come. I had to take over his identity at the last minute, which is why I left in such a hurry. I only found out on the Saturday we were at Penley.'

'Is that why you drove off with Gretchen?'

For the sake of simplicity, Kite said: 'Yes. I'm sorry. I had to leave in a hurry. The phone call. You remember I had a phone call just before the party?' Martha nodded. She no longer looked shocked. It was as though she was weighing things up in her mind: can any of this possibly be true, or has my boyfriend turned into a deranged fantasist? 'Well that was the signal. That was to tell me what was happening. I had to leave, fast.'

Martha broke into disbelieving laughter. Kite realised how absurd what he was saying must sound to her, but he continued.

'Martha, you need to hear this and remember it. I'm here teaching and my name is Peter Galvin. I'm twenty-eight. A professional teacher of English. I spent four years working in Malawi. My parents live in Wokingham.'

'Wokingham?'

'If anybody asks who you are,' he continued, 'we met a

few months ago in London at a party. I'm Peter. You're Martha. We don't know each other very well, but you've come out to surprise me. Have you shown my photograph to anybody in Moscow or Voronezh, saying my real name? Did you show it to the people at the embassy?'

Martha looked worried. Kite dreaded what she was going to tell him. It felt as though Aranov's life depended on her answer.

'I told them that my boyfriend was in Russia and I wanted to visit you. I don't think I told them your name. I definitely didn't show them your photo. I don't have one, I don't carry one around . . .'

'Good. What about in Moscow? What did you tell them about why you were here?'

Again Martha hesitated. Kite knew that she wouldn't lie to get herself off the hook, but he could see that she was struggling to recall exactly who she had spoken to and what had been said.

'Same,' she replied. 'They asked why I was in Russia. I said my boyfriend was teaching in Voronezh. They said where, as in what school or university, and I said I didn't know. I gave them this hotel as my kind of forwarding address.'

'That's good,' Kite replied as he tried to work out their next move. Martha whispered: 'MI6, fuck' under her breath and for a moment neither of them said anything. A vacuum cleaner moved past in the corridor.

'We're going to have to go to your room soon, pretend we got the wrong one,' said Kite. 'Don't say anything about this when we're there. Hotel rooms for foreigners can be bugged. Call me Peter. *Never* Lockie. That's the most important thing. Don't mention my mum or anything to do with Edinburgh or Xavier or Penley. Ask me the questions you would have asked about Russia. How have I been? What's the job like? Am I enjoying myself? I'll ask you the questions I would have asked you. I'm supposed to be leaving in two days. We won't have to keep up the masquerade for long, I promise.'

The hoover stopped. Martha stood up. 'This is so fucked

up,' she said. 'I've made things impossible for you. Are you in danger?'

'No,' he replied, though this was plainly untrue. 'Your coming here has made things slightly more complicated.' He wanted to reassure her. 'If you leave, there's a chance you might be stopped at the airport and people would ask how you know me. It would be impossible for you to answer their questions without putting everything at risk. So I'm afraid you'll have to stay.'

'Of course I'll stay.'

She's not fazed by this, Kite thought. Strawson was right: she likes the idea of me working as a spy. She instinctively finds it exciting.

'But,' Martha continued, halting Kite's thought in its tracks, 'when we get back to London, I'm going to have a lot of questions that need answers.'

'I understand,' he replied. He was far more concerned about their present predicament than any future conversation he might have to have with Martha about BOX 88. 'We can stay here tonight,' he said. 'In the morning I'll go to work.' He was making things up as he went along, trying to find the best way to keep Martha hidden until it was time to go to the dacha. 'You'll have to lie low, stay at the hotel. Pretend to have a stomach problem, be ill or something.'

'Why?' she asked, as if Kite was being unnecessarily para- noid.

'I can't risk being seen with you too much,' he replied. 'We both get stopped and interviewed, you won't know what to say.'

'Has that happened to you? Is that why your face is marked?'

Kite decided to elide the two incidents – the conversation with Gromik and the fight with his thugs – and said: 'Yes, they've already questioned me.'

'Jesus.'

There was a knock at the door. A short, exhausted-looking woman of at least sixty walked in wearing the uniform of a chambermaid. She saw Kite and Martha and stopped dead, screwing up her face. In Russian she said: 'What are you doing here?' to which Kite replied, in English: 'Sorry, we got the wrong room.' He played the confused tourist, switching off the Rachmaninov, picking up Martha's key and showing it to the woman. 'Where do we go?' he asked, turning off the taps in the bathroom. 'Which room?'

The number was stamped on the key. The chambermaid looked at Kite as if he was congenitally stupid. She walked to the door and indicated a room several metres along the corridor.

'There!' she said in Russian. 'Not here. This is the wrong room.' Then she cursed 'foreigners' with a swear word Kite didn't recognise.

'Thank you,' he said. '*Spasibo, spasibo bol'shoye.*' Martha joined in, picking up her rucksack and saying: '*Spasiba*. Sorry. We won't make the same mistake twice.'

Their new room was identical to its predecessor, though with a stronger smell of old tobacco and a view out onto the street. Kite played the role of the overjoyed boyfriend, saying all the things he might have been expected to say upon arrival in Martha's hotel room.

'What's the bed like? I still can't believe you're here. I wish you'd told me. It's the most fantastic surprise.'

To his amazement, Martha immediately played along. It was almost as if she had been trained for the task.

'I wanted to surprise you, Peter. And I've never been to Russia before. I was jealous. Wanted to see what all the fuss was about.'

They talked for a little while about her journey to Voronezh, her efforts to obtain a visa, falling into conversation with surprising ease. Kite asked about her family, about Oxford, reassuring her every now and again with an exaggerated gesture of gratitude that she was doing brilliantly and playing her role to perfection. In due course they left the room and went downstairs to eat. The waiter tried to insist that they take one of the tables by the door. To his frustration, Kite asked to be seated near the window, where the noise from passing traffic would have deterred the FSK from planting microphones. The waiter had no choice but to grudgingly comply.

Nevertheless Gromik's goons kept an eye on Kite and his new friend; only a few minutes after they had sat down, a lone man in middle-age took the table next to theirs. Martha was aware of his presence and understood that he was a threat. Over blinis she asked Kite questions about life in Voronezh, his job at the Dickens, his flat in the shitty apartment block where Bokova was putting him up. Not once did she call him 'Lockie' or talk about the past, though he could tell that over time she was straining to maintain the facade.

At around nine o'clock, a live band struck up in the bar. Now unable to hear what Kite and Martha were saying, the man at the next table stood up and left.

'Thank God for that,' said Kite, watching him go. 'We can talk more freely now.'

'Yes, yes, I get it.' Martha touched his hand across the table. She puffed out her cheeks and looked around in case the waiter might be watching them. 'This whole thing is slightly blowing my mind. I'm sorry I've come out here and made everything so complicated. I thought it would be romantic and adventurous, a way for us to get back on track, but it was stupid. I feel embarrassed as much as anything.'

'You couldn't possibly have known,' Kite replied.

'True!' It looked as though she wanted to forget, however briefly, the pressures they were under. 'But even without that you may not have wanted to see me. You could have a new girlfriend out here. I should have waited until you got home.'

'I don't have a girlfriend out here,' he said. It was technically true. He had been single since Oksana had walked out of the hotel three hours earlier.

'I'm glad to hear it.'

'And you? What happened with Cosmo? What was the story?'

221

'The story is that I don't want to talk about it. Cosmo is a creep. I thought he was a friend but he turned out to be a snake.'

Kite felt a surge of vindication, tempered by a sense that Martha had only seen de Paul for who he was after sleeping with him.

'Is that why you didn't go to Croatia?' he asked.

She nodded, clearly wanting to change the subject. 'Why are you here?' she asked. 'How did it happen?'

Kite knew that the question had been coming and constructed a lie about being tapped on the shoulder at Edinburgh by a tutor who had invited him to appear for interview in a room at the Balmoral Hotel. He said that he had done some exams in Stirling in the spring of 1992, attended two training courses, one in Edinburgh, the other in London, but had been forbidden to tell anybody about his application. He said that 'Six' had asked him to come out to Russia to get a VIP across the border into Ukraine. He wasn't allowed to say any more to Martha about the identity of the VIP or the method by which they would leave the country. He revealed that it would be in the early hours of Sunday morning and hoped that she would come with him.

Martha shrugged: 'Sure, I've already said I'm sticking around.' There was a fantastic spirit of audacity in her which delighted him. 'I'm not going to abandon you.'

'You wouldn't be abandoning me.'

'Well, putting you at risk then. If I go, they'll get suspicious.'

'So what if they do?' Kite was trying to sound courageous. 'I could handle it.'

'What? After two training courses and a prawn cocktail at the Balmoral?'

He laughed. 'It was more than that,' he said. 'I know what I'm doing.'

They had both ordered breaded pork chops which were tasteless and chewy. Kite looked down at his half-eaten food and felt calm for the first time in hours.

'You know, it's funny,' said Martha.

'What is?'

'My great-aunt died just after you left. My granny's sister.'

'I'm sorry to hear that.'

The waiter passed their table and looked at them. The noise of the band was now so loud that Kite could hardly hear what Martha was saying.

'Before the funeral, Dad told us she'd been in the Special Operations Executive during World War II. Have you heard of that? The SOE?'

'Sure,' Kite replied.

'Turns out quiet little aunt Sophie was a war hero. Parachuted into occupied France, cycled around passing messages to the French resistance, sabotaged a telephone exchange just before D-Day. She was only twenty, a year younger than me.'

'Amazing,' said Kite, drawing the obvious conclusion. 'So maybe some of Great-Aunt Sophie's DNA has been passed down to her great-niece?'

'Why not?' Martha replied delightedly.

In that moment Kite saw that she was not afraid of what might happen to her. She trusted him. She was naturally optimistic, an adventurous free-spirit, and knew that Kite was tough and clever. They would get through it together. Kite had made the operation sound relatively straightforward; they would need only to keep a low profile for another thirty-six hours, reach the dacha and make a run for the border. What could possibly go wrong?

'Look,' he said. 'We should pay and go upstairs. The waiter keeps hovering. But we don't have to do anything tonight . . .'

He stopped himself, aware that he was being tactless. Under normal circumstances they would have gone to bed the second they had reached the hotel room, but the operation – not to mention Oksana and Cosmo de Paul – had come between them.

'Go on,' Martha replied, not wanting to show her hand.

'What I mean is . . .' Kite chose his words carefully. 'We haven't talked about what happened at Penley.'

'I told you. Nothing happened. Far as I'm concerned Cosmo can go fuck himself.'

'Did he hurt you?'

'No, of course he didn't hurt me. He's just a liar and a creep.'

'I'd been trying to tell you that for years.'

A female singer had taken over the live act and was belting out a Russian-language version of 'My Way'.

'Come on, let's go,' said Kite.

'But what about the microphones in our room?'

He saw the mischief and longing in Martha's eyes. It was the same look she had given him beside the swimming pool the first night they had made love in Mougins.

'Fuck the microphones.'

23

Kite left the hotel at dawn. Beneath the covers, whispering in Martha's ear, he told her to stay in the room for the rest of the day and to pretend to be suffering with food poisoning. If anybody rang or knocked on the door, she was to tell them that she was sick. On no account was she to let anybody into the room. If she could be heard retching in the bathroom from time to time, so much the better.

He walked the two miles back to his apartment, buying a loaf of fresh bread and some cheese on the way. He planned to put a change of clothes into a bag and to go to work as normal. He would spend Friday night with Martha at the Brno then they would leave for the dacha on Saturday. As had been agreed in London, the bulk of his personal belongings – his clothes, his books and traveller's cheques, the photos of his phantom friends and parents – were to be left behind at the apartment. Kite must make it look as though he had every intention of returning to Voronezh after the weekend.

He passed several neighbours on the stairs making their way to work. None of them greeted him. Kite was about to put his key in the lock when he heard movement behind the door. He stopped. Whoever was walking around the flat was making no attempt to keep quiet. He went in.

'Peter! I wasn't expecting you home so soon.'

Mikhail Gromik was standing beside the sofa, Kite's journal in his hand.

'What the fuck are you doing here?' His heart was racing. 'Get out of my flat!'

Gromik laughed. He set the journal down on the table. He was wearing black trousers and an open-necked red shirt. A cheap metal chain nestled in the hair on his tanned chest. Kite smelled the same sickly-sweet odour of patchouli oil he remembered from their first meeting.

'It is not your flat, Peter. It is an apartment. An apartment which belongs to the Dickens Institute.'

Kite checked himself. He must not be too confrontational. He must maintain the Galvin persona, make his replies respectful and nervous. 'Who let you in?' he asked. 'What's going on?'

'Sit down.'

Gromik pulled back a chair and indicated that Kite should take it.

'I don't want to sit down,' he said. 'I want to know why you're in my flat. I'm late for work. I need to get to work.'

'Sit down.'

This more firmly. Kite saw that he had no choice. He pictured Gromik's colleagues hauling Martha out of bed, asking her how she knew Peter Galvin. As smart and brave as she was, he did not think she would be capable of withstanding even the most basic cross-examination.

'Fine,' he replied, doing as he was told. 'Are you a police officer? KGB?'

The Russian's eyes flicked towards him. His hair was slicked back and he was wearing what appeared to be a fresh pair of Air Jordans. Kite assumed they had been stolen or confiscated.

'What makes you think I am KGB? Are you MI6, Mr Galvin? Is this your concern?'

'Am I *what*?' Kite tried to look suitably stupefied. 'Am I in MI6? What the fuck are you talking about? I'm asking if you're KGB.'

'We do not call it KGB anymore. Times are changing in Russia. You know this. We are FSK now.'

Kite dug deeper into Galvin's timid, fearful personality.

'FSK,' he whispered, mindful not to overplay his hand. 'Jesus. What do you want? What have I done wrong?'

Gromik picked up Rita's copy of *The Brothers Karamazov*.

'You have read this?'

'Not yet, no.'

'Me neither. Why don't you take better care of your books, Peter?'

'Excuse me?'

He knew that Gromik had seen the damaged bindings on *The English Patient*. It was the only explanation for his remark. Sure enough he crossed the room and picked it up.

'This one,' he said. Kite had hidden the novel among a pile of books and magazines beside the television. 'What happened to it?'

Breathe, Kite told himself. *Trust your story*. 'A friend borrowed it,' he said. 'It got pulled apart in my swimming bag. I had to tape it up. Why?'

Gromik pursed his lips and examined the cover for evidence of Kite's claim.

'Your friend borrowed it or it got pulled apart in your bag? One or the other?'

'What?' Kite reacted as though Gromik was being pointlessly obtuse. 'My friend borrowed it. She didn't look after it. Then it got water on it after I went swimming. Hence the tape.'

Gromik, unconvinced, placed the book back in the pile.

'Speaking of girlfriends,' he said. 'What happened at the hotel last night?'

It was not clear whether Gromik was referring to Oksana or Martha. Kite knew that he must seem outraged at the revelation he was being watched.

'How did you know I was at the Brno Hotel? Are you following me?'

'I am free to do whatever I choose.'

'Yes, I can see that.'

The Russian smiled, amused by Kite's riposte. He continued to pick up various objects in the room and to examine them, all the while peppering Kite with questions.

'You spent the night at the hotel?'

'Yes, I did. Is that illegal in the new Russia?'

'Not illegal. Not illegal at all. But you were not with Oksana. Who were you with?'

Kite tried to work out how much or how little Gromik knew about Martha.

'If you're KGB or FSK or whatever it is you say you are, wouldn't you already know who I was with last night?'

'You tell me, Peter. Would I know that?'

Kite had no choice other than to offer a version of the truth.

'My girlfriend came over from London. I was staying with her.'

'At the Brno? Really? Your girlfriend?' Gromik's tone was sceptical to the point of derision. 'It's OK, Peter. I am a man of the world. I know what happens at night in this place. Did you take a girl from the bar? Did you go to a room and pay her?'

Kite wished that he had adopted this simple excuse but could not risk lying about Martha. If Gromik had asked to see her registration details at reception, he would already know exactly who she was.

'I don't know how much of this is your business,' he replied. 'But no, I didn't pay a prostitute. My girlfriend flew over to see me from London as a surprise. We're staying at the Brno because it's nicer than this shithole.'

Mikhail looked around the apartment and appeared to share Kite's assessment of his lodgings. Right on cue a cockroach scuttled out in the kitchen, vanishing behind a skirting board.

'We did not know you had a girlfriend in England.'

'Excuse me?'

'I said we did not know . . .'

'I heard what you said. Why would you know that? What's going on? Have you mistaken me for somebody else?'

Gromik turned towards the kitchen, picking the lock on Kite's cover story.

'Does she know about Oksana?'

The question was a veiled threat, yet it brought with it an odd sense of relief. If Kite's affair with Oksana was the only hold that Gromik had over him, he was on slightly safer ground.

'Does she know *what*?' he replied.

'That you have betrayed her with another woman? With Oksana Sharikova. Your student.'

Kite played the outraged foreigner.

'Are you blackmailing me? Is that what this is about?'

Gromik ran a hand over his slicked-back hair and gave a faux-innocent shrug.

'Why would I do such a thing?'

'I have no idea.' Kite reminded himself to stay within the Galvin persona, not to allow guilt or fear to provoke his anger. 'Funnily enough I didn't think that telling Martha about Oksana after her eight-hour journey from London was the best way of welcoming her to Voronezh.'

Gromik produced a man-of-the-world smile. 'Probably right,' he said, picking up a glass from the counter. 'Women can be very emotional.' He came out of the kitchen and approached him. 'So you'll spend this weekend together?'

He knows about the dacha, Kite thought. Or was the question merely a test? Again Kite steered close to the truth.

'Actually I've been invited away by a friend tomorrow,' he said, taking a step backwards. 'The guy I was swimming with. Yuri Aranov. Martha wasn't feeling very well this morning so we may not go. But presumably you already knew that. You seem to know everything else about my private life.'

Gromik did not deign to respond. Instead he turned his head, as if distracted by a noise in the bedroom. Kite felt a droplet of sweat run down his back.

'I am sorry to hear Martha is sick so soon into her visit,'

229

he said with feigned concern. 'Does she require the attentions of a doctor?'

'No thank you.' Kite moved from one side of the small living room to the other. 'I think she just ate some bad pork. We both had it. Neither of us feels very well this morning.'

'And yet here you are.'

'Yes. Here I am. And late for work.'

Gromik faced the living-room window. He had developed a habit of asking Kite questions while not looking at him.

'Your friendship with Yuri is interesting,' he said. 'The timing of your girlfriend's arrival is interesting.'

'How?' Kite asked. His voice almost cracked on the word. To busy himself, he began gathering up his belongings, putting exercise books and some pens into his work satchel.

'She is helping you?'

It was the first question Gromik had asked which caught Kite completely off guard. It seemed to imply that the FSK knew about the exfil. He had to assume it was a bluff.

'Helping me with what?' he replied, trying to look as baffled as possible.

'Never mind.' Gromik's reply was nonchalant, yet it disguised a sucker punch. Picking up another book and turning to Kite so that at last he was looking directly at him, the Russian said: 'I'm just confused about something, Peter. Or should I call you Lockie?'

Kite's stomach dissolved in fear. It was only through determined force of will that he found a viable response.

'You don't call me Lockie,' he said. 'Nobody calls me Lockie.' Gromik was about to interrupt when Kite cut across him: 'Only Martha calls me that.'

'She does? And why, please?'

'In English we call it a nickname. Do you have those here?'

Gromik did not respond. He was studying Kite's face for the tell, waiting for the moment when he would break. Kite continued to pack the satchel, busying himself to look as relaxed as possible. He realised that he had forgotten to ask the obvious question.

'How do you know Martha calls me Lockie?'

Again Gromik declined to answer. It astonished Kite how much he wanted to confess the truth; anything just to be rid of the constant, gnawing suspicion that his cover was blown, that Martha would be arrested, that Aranov would be sent to his death. He longed for some relief from Gromik's interrogation.

'I said how did you know Martha calls me Lockie?'

At last Gromik spoke: 'We have eyes in the city, ears in the city.' It sounded like a translation of a more sophisticated Russian expression. 'Why "Lockie"?'

'That's private.' Kite stood his ground. 'It's between me and Martha.'

Without being conscious of doing so, he had done what the instructors at BOX had taught him: to refuse to answer certain questions on the grounds that they offended his sensibility.

'Private,' Gromik repeated.

'That's right. Private. As in, you're invading my privacy. I'm a British citizen trying to work in Russia. You have taken away my privacy. You're obviously following me around, listening to my conversations . . .'

'Tell me. In all the time you have been in Voronezh, why have you not telephoned this Martha? Why have you not written to her?'

The second question gave Kite the time to come up with an answer to the first.

'Why do you think? Because of Oksana. I thought Martha and I had broken up.' He paused, summoning another burst of faux outrage. 'Wait a minute. Have you been opening my letters? Have you been listening to my phone calls?'

Gromik shrugged, like a thief who has been caught red-handed yet shows no remorse.

'Nobody mentions her when they speak to you. You don't ask about Martha when you call home. Your mother does not tell you how she is. How do you explain this, Lockie?'

'Please don't call me that.' Kite took a gamble based on

231

Gromik's obvious sense of machismo and added: 'It's quite a sexual nickname between us, so it just sounds weird if a man says it.'

Kite's lie had the desired effect. For the first time Gromik looked slightly uncomfortable and backed away from the exchange.

'Peter, then,' he said. 'I call you Peter. This is what your mother calls you. This is what your friends call you.'

'That's because it's my name.'

The Russian stared at him again, watching as Kite zipped up his satchel and placed it on the ground by the door.

'So you didn't want to see her yesterday?'

'Who, Martha? No, not particularly.'

'But she is very beautiful, no?'

'So is Oksana. Everything isn't always about looks.' He was on the point of saying 'Mikhail' but stopped himself at the last moment. 'Martha's a pain in the arse. She's sort of followed me here. I was trying to get away from her.'

To his relief, Gromik appeared to believe this. With an odd sense of camaraderie, he asked: 'So what will you do about it?'

'About what?'

'About Martha coming to Voronezh?'

An idea came to Kite, a plausible way of trying to bring an end to Gromik's questions.

'To be honest, I was thinking of going home early. I was beaten up the other day by some people in my building. They stole my bike. Now I find out everything I do and say is being recorded by the FSK. I don't feel safe here. I'm not happy at the Dickens Institute. I'm going to hand in my notice.'

Gromik indicated that he did not understand what Kite had said.

'Hand in my notice,' he repeated. 'It means I'm going to tell Katya Bokova that I'm going back to London. If I can get a flight, I'll go with Martha when she leaves next week.'

To Kite's gratification, the ruse appeared to work. Gromik

walked towards the door, looking as though he had achieved what he had set out to achieve: if he could not prove that Peter Galvin was a foreign agent, he had at least succeeded in scaring him out of Russia.

'Unfortunately, Voronezh is not always a safe place,' he said, though it was obvious from his expression that he knew about the attack on Kite. 'I hope you were warned not to walk at night, not to wait for the bus in the darkness.'

'I was warned.'

'Katya Bokova will be disappointed that you are leaving. We will all be sorry to see you go home.'

'I doubt that. You'll find somebody else to inconvenience.'

It wasn't a word Kite would ordinarily have used, but it suited the Galvin vocabulary.

'Try to enjoy yourself this weekend.' Gromik adjusted the collar of his shirt. 'It will be your first time at a dacha?'

'First time, yes.'

'How interesting,' he replied. 'Well, I look forward to hearing all about it.'

24

If ever there was a time to abort, this was it. Kite knew there was too much heat on him, too much attention on Martha and Aranov. Gromik would undoubtedly be sending officers to watch Yuri over the weekend and planting informers among his friends, any one of whom would sound the alarm as soon as they saw the car leaving in the small hours of Sunday morning. What was the expression the Russian had used? *We have eyes in the city, we have ears in the city.* The same would apply to the dacha, to the road from Voronezh to Dnipropetrovsk, to the frontier itself. It would surely be impossible to get away without being stopped.

Yet Kite would not quit. He was determined to finish the operation, to get Aranov, Tania and Martha safely into Ukraine; if he could humiliate Gromik into the bargain, so much the better. Riding the bus to work, having left his apartment for what he hoped would be the last time, carrying only his work satchel and an overnight bag containing a change of clothes, some toiletries and a copy of *Anna Karenina*, he told himself there would be no going back. To abort would be to betray Aranov; to fail would surely bring an end to his career in BOX 88.

Neither Aranov nor Oksana were at the Dickens. Lev was the first into class, talking animatedly about the weekend to come, telling Kite that he hoped to meet a girl and boasting

234

about his prowess with a barbecue. It became clear that many more people would be at the dacha than Kite had anticipated: Aranov had other friends with houses in the area, all of whom were planning to descend on the neighbourhood for two days of drinking and singing.

'I bring pork for *shashlik*,' said Lev excitedly. Kite listened to him, alert for any indication he was Gromik's man. He was always so slick, so cheerful, never far away. 'Also the bread from Georgia. Yuri ask me to prepare it. You bring Oksana?'

'We broke up,' Kite replied, wondering why Lev was nosying around in his private life. 'My girlfriend came over from England as a surprise. She'll be there. I'll introduce you. You can practise your English.'

He left the Dickens just before six, having spoken to Bokova about the possibility that he might go back to England. If she was reporting to the FSK, it was important that Kite make good on his threat to leave Russia. He explained that he was shaken up by the beating he had taken and upset at the attentions of an FSK officer who had been opening his mail, listening to his telephone calls and even breaking into his apartment. Making no secret of her annoyance, Bokova insisted that Kite should ignore the activities of the security service – 'They are always like this at first with foreigners' – and trust that everything would calm down in due course. Kite assured her that he would think things over and give her a final decision after the weekend. This seemed to satisfy her and they parted on good terms.

Kite was back at the Brno by dusk. He'd stopped en route to buy charcoal tablets and some potassium permanganate at a pharmacy; it was important to give any interested parties the impression that he was caring for his sick girlfriend. As he walked across the lobby towards the lifts, the receptionist who had checked Martha into her room called to Kite in English.

'Excuse me, sir! Excuse me, please!'

He approached the desk. 'Yes?'

'You must change the room. You must move. The lady. She does not allow it.'

At first Kite did not understand what the receptionist was trying to tell him. Had something happened to Martha?

'What do you mean she doesn't allow it? Allow what?'

'The lady in your room, she does not want to move.'

'Move where?'

'Move room. You must move. It is necessary.'

The receptionist was a diminutive blonde in her late twenties, nervous and neatly turned out. Sensing her unusual levels of anxiety, Kite quickly understood what had happened: Gromik had instructed the hotel staff to move Martha to a different room so that her conversations with Kite could be eavesdropped. It was exactly the same tactic that the waiter had employed in the restaurant. The FSK was trying to move them towards the house microphones.

'Why?' he replied, playing dumb. 'Why is it necessary?'

As he expected, there was no plausible explanation, only a half-baked lie about 'hotel policy' and a suggestion that Martha had been given a larger room than her nightly rate warranted. The receptionist informed Kite that Martha had not only bolted the door but told no fewer than three members of staff to leave her in peace. Kite was amused, but in suitably sombre tones revealed that his girlfriend was suffering with food poisoning and would not have wanted to be disturbed.

'I am sorry to hear this,' the receptionist replied. She looked agitated as she said: 'But I must insist that you go to the new room.'

'Bad pork in your restaurant,' Kite replied, pointing accusingly in the direction of the kitchen. 'If she's feeling better, we'll move tonight. OK?'

Of course he had no intention of switching rooms; they were already making life difficult for the FSK. If they stayed where they were, they could speak freely, albeit with the usual noise cover from the television and radio.

'Thank you, sir,' she said, oozing gratitude. 'Thank you so much, Mr Galvin.'

Kite assumed that the receptionist had learned his name from whichever FSK officer had ordered the switch. He rode the lift to the second floor and found Martha sitting up in bed watching an old black-and-white Russian movie on the television. A paperback of Ian McEwan's *The Innocent* was open on the bed beside her.

'Hi, honey, I'm home,' he said, setting his bag down.

Martha played along with the joke, putting on an American accent and saying: 'How was your day, dear?' as he lay on the bed beside her.

'Good film?'

'Don't understand a word of it.' She muted the television. 'Book's good though.' She lowered her voice to a whisper: 'All about spying.'

Kite turned the sound on again and pushed the volume up one notch.

'We probably don't have to be so careful anymore.' He explained that the hotel had wanted to switch their room for one which was likely rigged for surveillance. As long as they kept the radio or TV switched on, they could talk about whatever they wanted to talk about and Martha would no longer have to pretend to be sick. The sudden release from restriction acted on her like a shot of vodka and she was soon out of bed, opening the window onto the warm Voronezh evening and asking Kite if he could get her something to eat.

'Haven't had anything all day,' she said. 'I'm starving. Took a sleeping pill when I woke up at four, slept till midday, but since then it's just been half a packet of Hobnobs and some fruit gums from Heathrow.'

'Since when did you use sleeping pills?' Kite asked.

'Since never. But Mum gave me some for the trip just in case.'

He went down to the restaurant and ordered a tray of food, telling the receptionist that his girlfriend was feeling slightly better but would prefer to remain in her room overnight. He explained that Martha would be checking out in

237

the morning but wanted to leave some luggage at the hotel which she would collect on Monday. All this was for the benefit of the FSK: the more it looked as though Kite and Martha were intending to return to Voronezh, the less concerned Gromik would be that they were planning to bolt.

Kite carried the tray of food upstairs. They sat on the bed eating borscht with stale black bread, then a mutton stew with dumplings and sour cream, all of it washed down with the remains of a bottle of vodka he had brought from his flat. With a radio station playing western pop music, Kite was free to tell her about Yuri and to explain why it was so important that Aranov left Russia. He gave Martha more information about the Galvin alias and constructed a plausible backstory which would explain their relationship to anyone who happened to ask. To Kite's amazement, Martha was neither particularly concerned nor confused by anything he told her; indeed she was gratifyingly calm, as if she had always known that Kite was hiding something from her and was relieved that his secret was finally out in the open. Only when he mentioned Tania did she seem worried that things might not go according to plan.

'She's pregnant?'

'Yes.'

'How long?'

'About four months, maybe slightly less.'

'And she has no idea that the father of her child is defecting and wants her to go with him?'

Kite shrugged. It was possible that Aranov had already broken the news to Tania, though he hoped he would wait until the last moment.

'So she just packs her things, gets in the car with us and abandons her life in Russia?'

'Apparently.'

Martha's puzzled reaction embodied Kite's own private doubts. Yet he had been unable to think of a viable alternative: Aranov had made it clear that he would not leave Russia without Tania. Kite had to trust that she would embrace the chance to start a new life in the West rather than throw the entire exfil into chaos.

They slept until ten and ate breakfast in the restaurant. Back in the room, Martha separated her belongings into two piles, putting anything she was prepared to leave behind – some old underwear and T-shirts, several books and a pair of jeans – into a suitcase which Kite deposited with the concierge. They checked out and took a taxi to the dacha. Yuri was expecting them at some point in the early afternoon.

Driving along Prospekt Revolyutsii, Kite had the same feeling he remembered going to Alford for the first time as a thirteen-year-old; the sense of heading into the unknown, to a strange place with new rules which he barely understood. He tried to disguise his concern from Martha, yet she did not seem worried by what lay ahead. Kite knew that she was patient and strong-willed with a streak of recklessness; perhaps she had taken her great-aunt's example closer to heart than he had anticipated. She wasn't going to complain or lose her nerve. She certainly wasn't going to make Kite's life any more complicated than it already was. They would get to Ukraine, it would be a triumph, and she would have a story to tell her grandchildren.

'You OK?' he asked.

'Hundred per cent.' She took his hand and squeezed it tightly. 'You?'

'Never been better.'

It was only the second time Martha had seen the city in daylight. She commented on the beauty of the pale stucco buildings, the ancient churches and grey cobbled streets. For a moment Kite was able to imagine that they were just another student couple on their summer holidays, exploring a new country, spending time away from their parents, from the demands of university and the pressures of finding a job. It frustrated him that he would not properly be able to share Voronezh with her, to show off what he had learned about the city, the places he had been. Everything was now operational.

They were soon in a low-lying labyrinth of Soviet-era dachas on the outskirts of the city, the houses not much larger than the pebble dash bungalows Kite remembered on the road into Stranraer. There were picket fences in front of most of the properties and smoke rising from barbecues above a patchwork of multi-coloured roofs. Chickens pecked in patches of dried earth at the side of the road. The more he saw of the neighbourhood, which had the atmosphere of a sleepy, slightly run-down village, the more Kite understood why Strawson had picked it for the exfil: there were as many as thirty dachas on each narrow street, unsurfaced roads intersecting from all directions, plenty of natural cover provided by trees and winding paths. Unless Gromik put ten vehicles at every road exit and another twenty men on foot inside the maze of houses, it would be relatively easy to slip away under cover of darkness. The difficulty would come in getting Yuri and Tania into the car.

'Where is the house?' the driver asked. In London Rita had shown Kite a satellite photo of the street, Yuri's dacha circled in red, but even with his near-photographic memory, picturing it was like trying to calculate a route around Hampton Court maze. He decided to risk speaking some rudimentary Russian.

'I don't know,' he said. 'We've never been here before.'

It was only by chance that on the next block they drove past Lev walking along the road carrying two heavy carrier bags. He stopped to talk to a group of half a dozen young Russians standing in front of a small wooden house. Kite spotted two of his students among them and realised they had found Aranov's dacha. As Kite was paying the driver, he heard Yuri's voice coming from the house.

'Professor Galvin is here! Students, gather around! Time for another lesson to improve our spoken English.'

Martha was fetching her favourite black leather jacket from the back seat of the cab. She closed the door of the taxi. Kite saw the mixture of confusion and mischief on

Aranov's face and realised what he was about to say. There was no stopping it.

'What happened to Oksana?' he said. He was walking towards them with his arms wide open. 'You have a new girlfriend now, Peter?'

25

Aranov realised his mistake immediately. He had assumed that Martha was Russian and would not have understood what he had said.

She turned to Kite, a sudden hardness in her eyes, and said: 'Who's Oksana?'

'Not my girlfriend,' he replied, disguising his anxiety with a reassuring smile. 'She was a pupil of mine at the Dickens. She was meant to be coming today.'

'That's right, that's right,' said Aranov, trying to make the situation better but with every word and gesture making it worse. 'She was with me before I am with Tania. I thought Peter was giving her lift.'

Kite tried to change the direction of the conversation by introducing them.

'Yuri, this is Martha. She flew over to surprise me. Martha, this is our host, Yuri.'

'*Dobryy den*,' said Martha pointedly. 'I'm Peter's girlfriend from the UK. Not his girlfriend from Voronezh.'

The Russian laughed awkwardly and shook her hand. 'Please excuse me,' he said. Kite had never seen him behave in such a solicitous, apologetic manner. 'My English is not good. I make mistake.'

'Perhaps it's your teacher's fault,' she replied, shooting Kite a look. 'You should ask for your money back.'

Kite could think of nothing constructive to say so he picked up their bags. He had been living a double life for weeks, staying in character, never getting trapped in a lie. Now at last he had been caught, not by the FSK but by the man he had been sent to help. In that moment it felt as though he had blown everything: the operation, his relationship with Martha, even his future with BOX. Martha would have had every right to take her suitcase, get back in the taxi and drive to the airport. He wouldn't have blamed her. Yet something in the way she reacted suggested that she was prepared to be sanguine about his indiscretions, at least for the time being.

'I show you around,' said Yuri, yet to recover from his embarrassment. 'Let me take you inside.'

The dacha was tiny, just a living-room with a small kitchen and a wood-burning stove, a bedroom at the back, another upstairs. The wood-panelled walls were newly varnished and there were various science-related books on the shelves. A pot was bubbling on a single gas ring near the stove and there was a metal pestle and mortar drying beside the sink. In the corner of the room, muddy vegetables, pots of home-made jam and an old iron kettle were crowded onto a wooden table. There was a smell of fried garlic and mushrooms, a warm breeze blowing in through the window.

'What a charming house,' said Martha, sounding as formal as an aristocrat clutching a copy of *Baedeker* in nineteenth-century Florence. Kite had not dared to look at her since their exchange beside the car.

'Thank you,' Yuri replied. 'I hope you will be comfortable here.'

'Oh very,' said Martha.

'You prefer to sleep upstairs or downstairs?'

It was a pointless question – they would be gone within twelve hours – but Kite knew why Yuri had asked it. He was speaking for the microphones.

'Whichever is easiest for you,' he replied, and pressed a finger to his mouth to indicate to Martha that the dacha was bugged.

'Yes,' she replied immediately. 'Wherever you want to put us. It's so nice of you to have me. I've never been to Russia before, coming to your house is an amazing experience.'

'You will drink!' Aranov announced, recovering something of his customary bullishness. 'Most of us arrive here last night. We do not sleep very much when we come to dacha. We like to eat well, to sing songs. Isn't that right, Peter?'

'Yes, I heard that,' Kite replied. 'It's my first time, too. Where's Tania?'

Aranov pointed outside. 'She go to shop to buy fish.' He fixed Kite with an eager grin. 'She very much looking forward to meeting you and to spend our special weekend together.' He raised his eyebrows comically and mimed steering the wheel of a car just in case Kite hadn't got the message. 'I tell her all about you. She very excited.'

Kite felt a wave of relief: Tania had been told what was happening and raised no objection. It was one less thing to worry about.

'Let's start the party,' he said. 'I brought some cake and a bottle of vodka.'

'I go light fire,' Aranov replied.

Tania arrived half an hour later on a bicycle so similar to Kite's that he half-wondered if Gromik's thugs had sold it to her. Her pregnancy was showing very slightly through the fabric of a plain summer dress and her skin was luminously healthy. When Aranov introduced them, she squinted at Kite while shaking his hand as though she didn't quite trust him. Her attachment to Aranov was plain to see: he was her ticket out of Voronezh, the baby a guarantee of his commitment. In her company Yuri was kind and patient, protective even; it was the best of him. Tania was neither pretty nor garrulous, charming nor curious. She spoke no English. When Kite tried to understand why Aranov was so taken with her, he concluded that it was because she was so bland. No man would ever desire her, she would always look after him, she was young enough to bend to his will

244

and to be shaped into the sort of wife Aranov had promised himself: hardworking, faithful, uncomplaining. Oksana wouldn't have fitted the bill: she was too strong-willed. If Yuri had proposed marriage to her, she would have found a lover and moved on within a year.

Lev had been carrying a three-litre jar of marinated pork in one of the carrier bags. His *shashlik* became the centrepiece of a long, delicious lunch eaten in the garden of the dacha with fresh cucumbers and tomatoes from the garden. Kite and Martha sat on rickety wooden chairs talking to two of Kite's students, Viktor and Vera, who were staying in a house two streets away. They had been conscientious pupils, quiet and withdrawn, but always on time to class and intelligent enough to make steady progress. Kite had always assumed they were too young to be reporting to the FSK, but was suddenly wary of them, just as he was wary of Lev. In a quiet moment in the garden, he took Aranov to one side and asked why they had been invited.

'What do you mean?' The Russian looked confused. He was wearing a stained white apron and holding a pair of metal barbecue tongs. Nobody would have believed from his sprightly mood that he was spending what was likely his last day on Russian soil.

'I mean did you invite them or did they invite themselves?'

'I invite them.' Aranov could see why Kite was concerned and put a sweaty, reassuring hand on his shoulder. 'I know they have dacha nearby. It is good for us to have more people here, no? Make everything look natural.'

Kite nodded in agreement, only to look along the street and see another of his students, the retired factory worker Dmitri, climbing out of an old Lada wearing a Spartak Moscow football shirt. He retrieved a case of beer from the back seat.

'What the fuck is he doing here?'

Aranov shrugged. 'I invite him too. I see him at the water when I go swimming. We become friendly.'

Kite knew something wasn't right. In class, Dmitri had

245

described Yuri as 'a kind of crazy person' in such a way as to suggest that he did not like him. Yet here he was at the dacha, having befriended Aranov down at the lake. Kite had never seen him swimming. To judge by the voluminous beer belly spilling out from beneath his shirt, he was a stranger to exercise. Had Gromik paid him to keep an eye on the FSK's favourite scientist?

'Relax,' Aranov told him, waving the tongs in the air. 'You worry too much, Peter. Nobody cares. Dmitri is good guy, I am promising you.'

Paranoia clung to Kite like the sweat induced by the hot summer afternoon. He could not shake off the feeling that there was a ghost at the banquet. *I look forward to hearing all about it.* Gromik's remark had sounded a warning: he knew that there would be a reliable agent at the dacha who would keep an eye on Kite and raise the alarm if Aranov behaved suspiciously. Kite looked along the narrow street. None of the cars on the road was occupied. If there was an FSK surveillance team watching Yuri, they would surely be camped out in one of the dachas across the street. Yet three of the houses looked so decrepit he doubted they were inhabitable. Two others were occupied by elderly couples, neither of whom seemed capable of lifting a pair of binoculars, far less tailing Yuri Aranov if he suddenly drove off in the middle of the night. No, the warning was going to come from a guest at the party. But who?

To clear his mind, Kite went in search of the BOX 88 Lada. Once he knew that the vehicle was in position, he could wait for nightfall, watch the guests more closely and immobilise anyone who threatened the exfil. He explained to Aranov that he wanted to go for a walk 'before the serious drinking begins' and invited Martha to join him. Dmitri had gone to find out if they could use the large *banya* belonging to a friend a few streets away; Lev was eating the last of the *shashlik*. Juice dripped onto the dried ground as he leaned forward to catch a stray chunk of pork.

'I come with you?' he said, his mouth still full.

'Leave them alone!' Aranov responded in Russian. 'Can't you see they want time to themselves?'

'Fine,' Lev muttered.

Kite took Martha's hand and led her down the street. As soon as they were out of earshot, he made his suspicions plain.

'I think Lev might be reporting on us. What kind of person invites himself to join a couple on a romantic walk when he's still eating his lunch?'

'Funny you should say that,' she replied. 'He was grilling me about you. Where did we meet? How long have we been together? Did I go to Malawi when you were teaching out there?'

Kite felt a shiver of anxiety. 'Subtle questions or nervous?'

'What do you mean?'

'Did you get the feeling he was short of things to say and couldn't think what else to ask you, or was he probing for information, trying to catch you out?'

'Hard to say.' Martha tucked a loose strand of hair behind her ear. 'I told him we'd only just met, that I didn't know you when you were in Africa, that we got together at a party in London.' It was the basic cover story they had agreed at the hotel. 'How the hell are you supposed to work out who might be watching us, informing on us?'

Kite shrugged his shoulders. 'We could ask Angela Lansbury to fly in,' he replied. 'She'd work it out in ten minutes.'

Martha smiled half-heartedly, but did not seem in the mood for jokes. Kite turned to her.

'You're being amazing,' he said, holding her arms. 'This must be so strange for you.'

'It's fine,' she replied. 'I don't find it difficult. I just want it to be over. I want to get home.'

It was the closest she had come to suggesting that she was worried. Kite kissed her. Then they hugged one another for a long time, saying nothing. He knew that what Aranov had revealed about Oksana had upset her; there was a separateness in the way Martha was holding him.

'Look,' he said, deciding to confront the problem but not at all sure how he was going to frame his confession. 'I need to tell you something.'

'Don't,' she said. Tears suddenly welled in her eyes.

'I need to,' he said. 'It's important.'

'For you maybe.' She stepped back. 'Not for me. You've become too used to lying. Let's not ever lie to each other. You were here. You thought I was with Cosmo. You were upset about Penley. I get it. It's OK. It would be weird if you hadn't been involved with someone. But I don't want to know about it. I don't want to hear her name or think about you being together. Can you understand that?'

Kite nodded. 'Of course,' he said. He had the rotten, shameful feeling of being let off the hook. Then it dawned on him that Martha was only taking such an emollient line in order to disguise her own indiscretions.

'So you were with Cosmo?'

She took his hand. She suddenly looked as unknown and mysterious to him as the girl he had first met at a party in 1988, many months before the summer in Mougins. Beautiful, complex, unattainable Martha Raine.

'I'm sorry,' she said. 'It was only once. I want to forget it ever happened.'

Kite felt the sickness of sexual jealousy, a renewed fury with de Paul.

'Right,' he said.

She touched his face.

'Let's forgive each other,' she said. 'Things are going to be hard enough for the next twenty-four hours without us being at each other's throats.'

'Yes.'

'I love you. You know that, don't you?'

She kissed Kite without waiting for a reply. He wondered how that love had allowed her to be free of him; how his own had led him to be a different man in the company of Oksana. The situation confused him. How was it possible to

248

love a person and yet to betray them? Martha was the most important person in his life, yet he had left something of himself with Oksana which he feared he would never retrieve. What was that exactly? A sense of liberation? An absence of responsibility? It was too complicated to analyse and certainly something he would never be able to discuss with Martha. Instead he said: 'I love you too' and they continued along the road, hand in hand, just another young couple taking time away from the city on a peaceful weekend afternoon. Kite was again operational; the switch was as unconscious as breathing. As they turned into the street running parallel to Aranov's dacha he checked that they were not being followed, all the time scanning the number plates of every Lada they passed. It was Martha who eventually spotted the exfil vehicle opposite a poster of a grinning cat advertising breakfast cereal.

'You said TX at the start, MX at the end?'

'Yes.'

He saw it too, a bashed-up Nova parked on the street beside a dacha with six months of weeds growing in the front garden.

'Great,' said Martha. 'Michael J. Fox got a DeLorean. We get a fucking lawnmower.'

'Watch the street,' Kite replied. 'I'll get the documents.'

He found the keys in the exhaust pipe and opened the passenger door. There was nobody else around, not a sound from the neighbouring houses. The car stank of tobacco and sweat: it was the smell of his grandfather's car, an old Marina he used to drive over on the ferry from Larne when Kite was a child. There were three passports in the glove box, a British driving licence in the name 'Simon Hobson' and about five hundred dollars in twenty and fifty denomination bills. As soon as he had taken them out and locked the car, Kite noticed a man emerge from beneath the poster on the opposite side of the street. He was pushing a bicycle. Martha saw him too. It was Pavel. He had been watching the car to make sure that nobody interfered with it. Now that he was certain Kite had the cash and the documents, he could move to his next position.

'Who was that?' Martha asked, noting the expression on Kite's face.

'Our guardian angel,' he replied.

26

They were drinking back at the dacha. Dmitri was dancing with a middle-aged widow who happened to have been passing the house. He seemed reluctant to let her go. As he sang the words to an obscure Russian folk song, the woman laughed and allowed him to turn her around the narrow garden, eventually walking away when Dmitri broke off to find his glass of vodka. Kite was reassured that he was not an informer; sobriety was surely one of the prerequisites of the job. Occasionally Tania poked her head out of the kitchen to enquire if anybody wanted tea. Kite noticed that she kept herself to herself: she seemed happiest indoors preparing yet more food for the evening. It wasn't possible for him to speak to her except with Aranov operating as a translator; once they were on the road he would be able to use his Russian. Viktor and Vera had informed Yuri that they would not be staying after dark; they had a young baby who was being looked after by Vera's mother. That surely left only Lev as the cuckoo in the nest.

Kite remembered the first time he had set eyes on him at the Dickens, the charming, easy-going young man in the expensive bomber jacket, already speaking surprisingly good English. He had invited Kite to a party and thereafter always seemed to be on his shoulder, listening in, hanging on. Was he just a young Russian on the make who wanted to spend time with the cool teacher from England? Had he been smitten with Oksana? Or was it something more sinister? Kite realised there was no point in driving himself crazy with theories and notions: even if Lev was just an innocent kid caught up in the exfil, he was going to have to take him out of the picture.

He took Martha to one side in the garden.

'How many of those sleeping pills did your mum give you?'

'I dunno. About ten. Twelve. Why?'

'Did you bring them here or leave them at the hotel?'

'They're upstairs in my suitcase. Do you want one? Do you want a siesta before we go?'

'Not that.' Kite asked if it would be OK to go through Martha's luggage.

'Sure,' she replied. 'They're in my washbag. I'll come and dig them out.'

They went indoors. A trout was poaching on the stove and there was a smell of gutted fish. Tania was putting the finishing touches to a potato salad, adding the bowl to an already heaving table.

'Check out the local food,' said Kite, pointing to a plate of bright pink salami. 'The one that's slathered in beetroot is called "herring under a fur coat".'

He wondered who Tania was cooking for: there was enough to feed thirty people. Perhaps it was just her way of keeping herself busy while she thought about the days to come.

'Looks wonderful!' said Martha. Tania stared at them blankly. Spotting the pestle and mortar on the bookshelves, Kite sought a distraction. 'Do you have chocolate?'

'What?' Tania replied in Russian.

'Chocolate. *Shokolad*. You have?'

She nodded, saying only: '*Biskvit*' and turning to rummage through a cupboard. While she was looking for what he wanted, Kite slipped the pestle and mortar off the shelf and handed it to Martha, indicating that she should take it to their room.

'Perfect,' said Kite as Tania closed the cupboard door and

handed him a packet of chocolate cookies. 'Can I take these? I have a craving.'

Tania looked mystified, but nodded and shooed him away. She had something of the same terse impatience as his mother; everything was a burden to her, every request an encumbrance.

Kite walked quickly upstairs to find Martha sitting on the floor next to her open suitcase. She had unzipped the washbag and taken out her mother's sleeping pills. Silently, Kite took the bottle and tipped some of them into the mortar, crushing them very gently until they had disintegrated into a fine powder. Without even being asked to do so, Martha switched on the wireless beside the bed.

'What's this for?' she whispered.

'I want to get it into Lev's food. Knock him out for a bit.'

'How many is that?' she asked. 'Looks like loads.'

'About six.'

'Jesus, Lockie.' Martha's voice was slightly louder now. 'That's enough to sedate Shergar.'

'He'll be fine. Wake up with a headache. It's either this or we get him drunk, but that means all of us playing Russian drinking games until it's last man standing. I can't do that. I have to drive.'

'I could do it.'

He looked at her. 'That's a kind offer but if you start drinking then Yuri's masculinity will be affronted and he'll have to tuck into the vodka as well. Then I've got two pissed passengers asleep in the back seat and Tania moaning about being made to leave.' He turned towards the radio. 'What *is* this music?'

'Polka, Peter!' Martha exclaimed in a mock Russian accent. 'You want dance?'

Kite smiled, but he wasn't yet finished. 'I'm going to get the men out of the house for a bit. While we're gone, I need you to tuck into the food. The "herring under a fur coat" I showed you.'

'I hate herring.'

'I know. Doesn't matter. You don't have to eat it. Just bring a dollop of it upstairs on a plate. Obviously don't let Vera see. If Tania notices, mime the steering wheel in the same way Yuri did when we arrived. She'll get it.'

Martha nodded. 'OK.'

'Mix the powder into the mayonnaise and keep the plate upstairs,' he continued. 'When we get back, I'll give everyone a blini with a spoonful of herring on it and a shot of vodka. I'll give the drugged one to Lev. He won't suspect a thing. The fish will kill the taste of the pills.'

Martha was silent for a while. Kite had not hesitated to ask this favour of her; he knew that she would be able to pull it off.

'How long will you be?' she asked.

He looked at his watch. 'I dunno. Three hours? Plenty of time. I'll get them to take me to the *banya*.' He tried to think of what might go wrong. 'If there's a problem when we get back, if you're worried that it hasn't worked, just say "Fiddlesticks" and I'll know something's wrong.'

Martha burst out laughing. '*Fiddlesticks?!*'

'You know: something weird, a signal word. I don't want Yuri or me getting sedated. Makes driving a car a lot more difficult.'

'I get it.' She kissed him. 'Leave it with me. I won't poison you.'

'You sure you're OK to do this?'

'Hundred per cent. I'll channel the spirit of Great-Aunt Sophie.'

Kite poured the fine dust into a glass and put it in the drawer of the bedside table, covering the top with a book. The rising warmth from the kitchen and the unrelenting sunlight on the windows had made the bedroom hot and stuffy. Martha looked out of the window.

'We'd better go downstairs,' she said. 'Mess up your hair and make it look like we've been shagging.'

It was now almost five o'clock. The sun would set at around

nine thirty. Dmitri was still drinking steadily, Aranov playing chess with Lev, Tania taking a break in the sun. They still had at least seven hours to go before it would be safe to leave. The worst of it was the waiting. Kite stared up at the brilliant sun and thought that it might never set; he was reminded of the final, painstakingly slow days of his first term at Alford, desperate to get home and yet held back by endless empty hours of hanging around.

The plan emerged among the men to go to the *banya* with no one noticing whose idea it had been. They would stay there for a few hours, then come back to the dacha to eat. Kite was glad that he would have something to do. Aranov gathered together some towels and they set off on foot, leaving Tania, Vera and Martha behind at the house.

'Germaine Greer would have a fit,' said Martha, taking a photograph of the men lined up on the road holding their towels and swimming trunks. 'You boys go off and enjoy yourselves. We'll be here doing the washing-up and making sure dinner is ready for when you get back.'

Lev did not appear to understand that Martha was being sarcastic and offered to stay behind to help. Kite reassured him that she was joking and cut her a look. He had absolute confidence in her that she knew what to do.

27

All through his time at the *banya*, Kite kept thinking about Martha and how easily she seemed to have embraced her new existence. As he sat in the baking chamber, clamped between the broiling Lev and the vast, sweating Dmitri, he pictured her calmly making her way upstairs and mixing the powder into piles of semi-congealed beetroot mayonnaise. It was a bedroom farce that was both comic and extraordinarily dangerous. Had he been crazy to involve her? He was still not certain that Vera was bona fide; what if she became suspicious and mentioned what she had seen or heard to Viktor?

Eventually Kite emerged from the *banya* to find that dusk had settled on the neighbourhood. He felt rested but fiercely alert, sipping water from a plastic cup as Aranov searched for his shoes. Mosquitoes wheeled in the glare of a streetlight. The camaraderie of the *banya* and the huge quantities of vodka they had consumed had left Dmitri and Viktor in a state of stupefaction. Lev was still relatively sober, as quiet and watchful as ever. Aranov was drunk enough for Kite to be concerned; the last thing he needed was his prize scientist passing out.

'You've got to stop drinking,' he told him as they walked back in the direction of the house. Lev, Dmitri and Viktor were several metres behind them, singing a mangled version of 'New York, New York'. 'If something happens on the road, I need you sober.'

'I know, I know,' he said, putting his arm around Kite. 'I just worried.'

'Worried about what?'

'About everything. Maybe we get stopped.'

It was Kite's job to reassure him.

'We're not going to get stopped. The car's there. I've got the passports. There's five hundred dollars for bribes. This time tomorrow we'll be in Ukraine.'

'You promise?' Kite caught a blast of alcohol on his breath. 'This is what will happen?'

'I'm sure of it,' he replied.

Behind them, Viktor stumbled on the road. Aranov turned and ordered him to go home.

'You are drunk!' he called out in English. 'I send your wife to look after you!' Then he repeated himself in Russian, adding: 'All of us need to go to bed!'

'Nonsense!' cried Dmitri in his mother tongue, but the effort of objecting also caused him to lose his footing. At the last second Lev grabbed his arm to prevent the fall. Kite surveyed the scene, wondering what Strawson or Billy Peele would have made of it. He was just a few hours from driving one of the world's top biological weapons specialists out of the country and yet here he was wandering around in shorts and flip-flops with two boisterously drunk Russians.

'What about Lev?' Aranov asked as they continued along the road. 'I don't trust him. He doesn't drink. Asks too many questions.'

'I don't trust him either,' Kite replied.

The neighbourhood was noticeably quieter. Children had gone to bed, daytrippers returned to the city. Kite felt restored by the exertions of the *banya*, the twin poisons of paranoia and suspicion partly expunged from his body. Even if Aranov succumbed to fear or Lev threatened to turn them in, he felt ready for what lay ahead. It was a blind faith in his own ability, a sense that all risks were worth taking because there was nobody in Voronezh capable of stopping him.

At that moment he saw Martha and Tania coming towards them. They were carrying plates of food and a bottle of vodka. Kite was confused. What were they doing? For what seemed like the first time all day, Tania had a smile on her face. Kite could see that she was carrying two small glasses and a handful of paper napkins.

'We've all decided that you need to sober up, so we came to find you!' Martha announced. As she drew closer, Kite could see two beetroot-red blinis perched on the plates. Aranov translated what she had said into Russian.

'I *am* sober!' Lev insisted.

'Then you shall be first as a reward for your moderation,' Martha replied, walking towards him. 'Nobody comes back into the house until they've had something to eat. I've been told how much vodka gets consumed in the *banya*! You must all try Tania's delicious herring in a fur coat.'

Kite could hardly believe what he was seeing. How did she know which blini was which? Were they colour-coded? Then he spotted it. One was decorated with a sprig of dill, the others were not.

'Take this one, sweetheart,' she said to Kite, passing him the blini with the dill. 'Lev, this is for you.'

Lev dutifully and entirely unsuspectingly picked up the blini from the plate.

'Wait!' said Martha. 'Tania! Vodka!'

Tania proceeded to pour two small shots of vodka into the glasses. She handed each in turn to Lev and Kite.

'Cheers!' said Kite, eating the food. Lev did the same. He did not even seem to chew it, instead swallowing the doctored blini whole and then gratefully chasing it with the glass of vodka.

'Who's next?' Martha asked, catching Kite's eye. He was exhilarated by her. 'We have more in the house, gentlemen. Yuri, can you translate?'

Lev walked past her, following Viktor and Dmitri as they grunted and stumbled towards the dacha.

'You're a genius,' Kite whispered to Martha, grabbing her by the waist and kissing her. 'How did you pull that off? I was meant to do it.'

'Maybe I gave you the wrong one,' she said and winked. 'Fiddlesticks, Peter.'

28

Lev was out like a light within forty minutes. Sitting outside with Kite and Martha, he suddenly complained of feeling very tired.

'It must be the heat of the *banya*,' he muttered. 'I should drink more water . . .'

They helped him to his feet and walked him to the back bedroom where he lay down, apologising for causing trouble.

'Don't worry about it,' Kite told him. 'You'll feel fine in the morning.'

By then, Vera and Viktor had gone home, leaving Dmitri as Aranov's only other guest. The combination of a hard day's drinking, three hours in the *banya* and several helpings of Tania's poached trout had him snoring on the sofa by eleven o'clock.

'And then there were four,' said Kite.

This time it was Martha who pressed a finger to her lips, reminding Kite to be careful with the microphones. Yuri put Duke Ellington *Live at Newport* on the record player while Tania washed up; Kite occasionally checked that Lev was still breathing and each time reported back that he was sleeping like a lamb. He found a piece of paper and a pen in a drawer, took down a framed picture from the wall and wrote Yuri and Tania a simple note in Russian on the glass.

I am going to get the car. Be ready to leave at midnight.
Tania needs both passports. I have passports for Yuri.
Do you have any questions?

Tania read the note and looked astonished that Kite was able to write in Cyrillic. She took the pen and the glass frame from him and wrote beneath his note.

I am very frightened. Is it safe?

Aranov made a clicking noise at the back of his throat. Kite shot him a look. He smiled at Tania and took the pen. For the benefit of the microphones he said: 'My uncle heard Duke Ellington playing live,' then leaned over to write his reply.

You are safe. Nobody is watching the house.
The road will be empty. We won't be followed.

A saxophone was playing gloriously in the night. Martha caught on to what Kite needed.

'Saw him live! Lucky uncle. Where was that? In Europe or the States?'

'New York, I think.'

Tania studied what Kite had written. She looked confused. He had most likely misspelled a word or made a grammatical error. Eventually she nodded and stepped back.

Now it was Yuri's turn. As he took the pen, Dmitri let out an ear-splitting snore which caused all of them to start. Martha muttered 'Jesus' and grabbed Kite's arm. Tania glanced at Martha affectionately. While Kite had been at the *banya* they had formed a curious bond; despite being unable to communicate in anything other than basic sign language, they seemed to trust one another.

Yuri put the picture flat on the table and wrote in English:

'Who am I? Who are we?'

In less stressful circumstances, Kite might have made a joke about the philosophical complexity of Yuri's questions, but he understood what Aranov was asking and turned the paper over to begin at the top of a fresh page.

Martha is Martha Raine. A student from Oxford.
I am her boyfriend, SIMON HOBSON. Also a student from Oxford.

Aranov nodded. Kite had already told him that he would be travelling under a false identity. He had learned his new name after taking the documents from the Lada.

Tania is Tania.
You are KONSTANTIN BABURIN. Same age. Born in KIEV.
You work in a pharmacy in Voronezh.

Kite looked up. He was struck by the difference between Tania's reaction and Aranov's: she looked relatively relaxed; Yuri was almost shaking with anxiety. He put a hand on his back and said: 'This is such a great record. Let's have another drink and dance with our girlfriends!' At the same time he wrote what he hoped would be the last of the messages.

Martha and Simon are travelling in Russia. We met you at a party in Voronezh.
You have invited us to meet your parents in Kiev.
We plan to fly home to London from Ukraine next week.

Tania and Aranov stared at the message. They looked like a couple on a gameshow deciding whether or not to go for the jackpot. For a long time they stared at the words on the paper, absorbing the new information, coming to terms with what it all meant.

'Everything OK?' Kite whispered as 'Jeep's Blues' came to an end.

'OK,' Aranov replied uncertainly as Tania nodded.

Kite duly burned the piece of paper and tossed it into the sink. He ran the tap and pushed the charred remains down the plughole. They were all watching him, waiting for his next move. Kite pointed at himself, then mimed starting the engine of a car and moving the steering wheel. They understood that he was going to fetch the car. Then he tapped his wristwatch and held up five fingers on both hands. All they had to do was wait.

29

The neighbourhood was absolutely still. Kite walked to the same corner where he had kissed Martha and turned down the road, heading in the direction of the parked Lada. There was only the sliver of a moon to light the way; the street-lamps emitted a feeble glow. No cars passed. He heard faint laughter and song in the distance, a sudden burst of gunfire on a television in a dacha across the street. Then nothing. Just the gentle whirring of cicadas, the hum of the night.

When the road began to bend to the south, Kite worried for a moment that he had taken a wrong turn but then saw the poster up ahead, the grinning cat and the bowl of milky cereal, and knew that he was in the right place. He looked for the car. There was an empty parking space in front of the house where he was sure Pavel had left the vehicle. Perhaps he was in the wrong spot. He looked up at the poster to orientate himself and turned back to face the row of dachas. There were two cars parked nearby, but they were parallel to the kerb and neither had the correct number plate. Surely it hadn't been stolen? It was the one outcome London had not bargained for. The dachas on either side of the vacant parking space were locked up. Perhaps an enterprising thief had walked past, seen the solitary car and taken his chances. Kite knew how easy it was to force open the door and hotwire the engine of a Nova; Tony, his instructor at The Cathedral, had shown him how to do it in less than two minutes.

Look, he told himself. *Keep looking*. It was possible he was on the wrong street, that each road had a poster of the cat, that he had taken a wrong turn in the darkness while thinking about Martha. But then Kite recognised a second marker, the dacha with six months of weeds growing in the front garden. It was now beyond question: the Lada had either been moved by Pavel or stolen. But by whom? And why hadn't Pavel come to warn him?

Kite felt himself shutting down, but told himself to look for solutions. *This is what you were hired for,* he thought. This is why they put you through the training. It's a test of nerve. You're in the arse end of Russia in the middle of the night, you need to get three people across the border by sunrise and your car has disappeared. So what do you do?

Within seconds, he knew. Lighting a cigarette, Kite walked back to the dacha, all the while praying that Dmitri had filled up with petrol. He knocked on the door of the house, hearing 'Jeep's Blues' for a second time on the record player. Yuri opened the door. Kite walked past him and checked on Dmitri. He was still passed out on the sofa. Martha was upstairs rearranging her suitcase. Kite asked her for the remaining sleeping pills and she handed him two from the bottle. He then went back downstairs, set the pills by the bookshelf beside a glass of water and began to search Dmitri's pockets.

'What are you doing?' Aranov whispered.

'Car keys,' said Kite. 'Help me.'

The right hip pocket of Dmitri's trousers was empty. They couldn't access the left without moving him. Mouthing a countdown of 'three, two, one', Kite and Aranov rolled Dmitri onto his side until the opening of the pocket was exposed. He could see the outline of a key.

'One more time,' he whispered.

Aranov pulled the snoring Russian closer towards him, freeing Kite to put his hand into the pocket and pull out the key.

'What's going on?' Dmitri moaned in Russian.

Kite picked up the two sleeping pills and the glass of water, slapped Dmitri gently on the face and, whispering in Russian, said: 'Take these, my friend, they'll make you feel better.'

Like a baby in a high-chair blithely anticipating a spoonful of food, the Russian opened his mouth, stuck out his tongue and accepted the pills. Kite held the glass to his lips and Dmitri drank from it, water dribbling onto his Spartak Moscow football shirt.

'Why do we not go?' Aranov asked.

Tania was in the sitting room ready to leave. She had put on make-up; it looked as though she was preparing to go to church.

'Car won't start,' Kite told them. There was no point alarming him unnecessarily by saying that the Lada had been stolen. 'We need to take Dmitri's.'

He went to the back of the house. Lev was still passed out. Kite went outside onto the street, walked up to Dmitri's car and opened the driver's door.

The interior had the ubiquitous Russian smell of cigarettes and old clothes. The engine started first time. Kite saw that there was only half a tank of petrol left, not enough to get them as far as the border. He swore under his breath, engaged the Lada in first gear and drove the short distance to the front of Yuri's dacha. The noise of the engine was so loud it sounded to Kite as though a Cessna was landing in the street. He noticed a strong smell of oil as he switched off the engine. It seemed to follow him as he walked back to the house.

'Ready?' he asked. Tania and Aranov were standing side by side in the sitting room next to two small bags. 'That's all you have?'

'All we have,' Aranov replied.

Kite was struck for a moment by what they were leaving behind. Martha was there too, evidently anxious but doing her best to appear calm. She had carried Kite's bag down from the upstairs bedroom.

'Have you got a knife?' he asked quietly, his voice smothered by the music. 'A sharp kitchen knife?'

Aranov translated the request to Tania, who produced a four-inch knife from a drawer near the sink. Kite indicated that they should go outside.

'If we are stopped in Voronezh,' he said, 'we are going to the hospital because Tania is feeling unwell.' He touched Tania's stomach. She nodded quickly and said: '*Da.*'

It was time to leave. Aranov took a last look at Dmitri and shrugged; it was an odd sort of reaction, as though the slumbering truck driver encapsulated everything he was going to miss about Russia. Tania did not seem to give her snoring house guest a second thought. Kite briefly held Martha's hand then indicated that she should go to the car. They left Duke Ellington turning on the record player.

There were only a few lights on in dachas at the far end of the street. Nothing stirred. Kite walked along the side of the house, clicked his cigarette lighter and located the hose that Aranov had earlier been using to water the garden. There was enough light from inside the house to see what he was doing. He sliced through the rubber tubing leaving about three metres of hose. He cut another separate length of about a metre, looped both around his arm and returned to the Lada.

Tania and Aranov were already in the back seat. Martha was about to close the boot. Kite stopped her and laid the hoses and the knife next to their bags.

'What are those for?' she whispered.

'Precaution,' he replied.

At the last moment he had another idea. As Martha was getting into the passenger seat, he went back into the dacha, crept past the sleeping Dmitri and picked up four of Tania's jars of homemade jam. Clutching them unsteadily in a wobbling column against his chest, he walked back outside.

'Take these,' he said to Aranov who had opened the back door. 'Presents for your in-laws.'

The Russian looked baffled. Kite glanced down the street a

final time and climbed in behind the wheel. He half-expected the stolen Lada to turn into the road ahead of them and block their escape.

'Sounds like a go-kart,' Martha muttered as Kite started the engine.

'It's all we've got,' he replied, and they pulled away from the house.

30

Kite made it to the first corner and turned towards the highway wondering how far the car would take them. The fuel level was steady at halfway, but the smell of oil unsettling. Looking in the wing mirror, he saw that the left-side indicator was not working. Martha struggled with her seat belt until Aranov leaned forward and told her that nobody ever used them in Russia.

'Why we go now?' he asked, sounding worried. 'Why we go at night? It's not safe.'

'You know why.' Kite did not expand on his answer. He was still looking in the mirror to see if they were being followed. He could hear his own breathing above the rattle of the engine.

'So dark,' said the Russian.

Kite was wound so tight he was ready to snap at Aranov. They moved along the narrow, black roads, the highway a faint glow above the treeline. A car passed them, heading in the opposite direction. Kite felt a strange kind of relief that they were not alone. In the mirror he watched the red tail lights of the car vanish into the night.

'Do you know the way?' Martha asked.

Kite felt that she was speaking solely to soothe his nerves; the stillness in the car, with nothing but the sound of the rattling engine, was excruciating. Aranov said something to Tania in Russian and she hissed at him.

'I memorised the route when I was back in London,' he said. 'Petrol stations, places to stop, that kind of thing. We just take the road out to Kursk, then cut south across country towards Stary Oskol and Belgorod.'

It sounded easy. Perhaps it would be. If nobody had seen them leave, if nobody was looking for Aranov, then they were just four people driving to Ukraine. Martha asked why they had taken Dmitri's car and Kite explained that the Lada had been stolen. Aranov overheard what they were saying and said: 'Fucking thieves. Nothing safe in this country anymore.'

'We'll be fine,' Kite replied, 'but there's not enough fuel to get us to Belgorod. We're going to have to stop.'

'Nothing will be open!' Aranov exclaimed. 'Everything closed, Peter! Petrol stations closed. Surely you know this?'

Tania again urged him to be calm. Kite wondered if she spoke better English than she was letting on. Perhaps it was just Aranov's tone; it was adding to everyone's anxiety.

'There are other ways of getting petrol,' he said. 'Best thing you can do, Yuri, is stay in a positive frame of mind. Remember what I said at the dacha. If we get stopped, it's because Tania isn't feeling well and we're looking for a hospital. Have you explained that to her? Is she ready to pretend?'

'Yes, yes,' he replied and reminded Tania of the plan. To Kite's surprise, she reached out and touched his shoulder saying: 'No problem, Simon Hobson, I do this' in halting English.

'Thank you!' he replied, trying to sound upbeat. 'I'm glad somebody is feeling optimistic.'

They finally joined the highway. There were many more cars heading out of the city than Kite had anticipated. He felt absorbed into the traffic, concealed by it. An ambulance roared past, siren blaring. They were overtaken by a Mercedes with Polish plates. Kite again checked the fuel gauge. The needle hadn't budged. Back at The Cathedral, Tony had warned him that the dials on Ladas were notoriously unreliable; they might have a fuel leak or a broken gauge and you wouldn't know about it until it was too late.

'Are we being followed?' Aranov asked.

'What makes you think that?' Martha asked.

'I don't know. Just a feeling.'

'Maybe keep those feelings to yourself?' Kite suggested. It was hard enough concentrating on the road without Aranov leaking paranoia.

'How much longer?' the Russian asked. They had only been gone ten minutes. Something was sliding around on the narrow shelf behind the back seat. It sounded like a loose cassette though there was no tape player in the car.

'Can you stop whatever that is moving around, please?' Kite asked.

Aranov grunted and turned, removing whatever had been causing the noise.

'Why don't you tell us about growing up during Soviet times?' Martha suggested. Kite reached across and squeezed her hand as a way of saying a silent thank you. 'It's a long way to the border. We'll need something to talk about.'

'What do you want to know?' It was no surprise that Aranov had immediately been taken by Martha's question; given a chance to talk about himself, he would always seize it.

'Anything,' she said. 'What was your school like?'

There was a momentary pause, then: 'Well, I grew up with six other families living in the same apartment. We shared a kitchen, a bathroom, a telephone. There was one bathroom for all of us. All the children went to the same school.'

Kite looked up and saw a sign to Kursk on a street running parallel to the highway; he ignored it. He recalled the hours he had spent in London scrutinising possible routes. He was sure that he was on the right road and grateful that Aranov was talking about something other than his own disquiet.

'Tania will tell you the same thing,' the Russian continued, winding down the window so that the air inside the Lada began to drum. Kite opened his own window to lessen the noise, veering slightly on the uneven road. 'The televisions in the seventies, they took five minutes to warm up.' Aranov adjusted his position in the back seat and complained that Tania was taking up too much room. 'If you wanted to watch a programme at six o'clock, you had to turn the TV on at five minutes to six!'

He was so amused by this observation that he translated it for Tania, who grunted when he reached the punchline.

'And what about films and books?' Martha asked. Kite couldn't tell if she was interested in the answers or just trying to distract Aranov while they made their way out of Voronezh. 'What sort of things were you allowed to see on television, Yuri, once it had warmed up?'

Kite gave her hand another squeeze and, realising he was driving too fast, brought his foot off the accelerator. The last thing they needed was to be stopped for speeding by a stray police patrol.

'Propaganda mostly,' Aranov replied. 'Bullshit about Soviet Union. Bullshit about America. We were great, you were shit, all that crap they tried on us.' Martha took out a packet of Marlboro Lights and lit two simultaneously, handing one to Kite. 'Brezhnev showed same films over and over. We get bored of them. So we read. Permitted books were Sherlock Holmes and Agatha Christie. My mother give me Jules Werner Two Thousand Miles Under the Sea for thirteenth birthday.'

'Jules Verne,' said Kite, anxiety making him pedantic. *'Twenty Thousand Leagues Under the Sea.'*

'Whatever.' Kite's correction made Aranov pause; for a few seconds there was silence in the car. 'Now that was a great story,' he continued. 'Submarines. Giant octopuses. I prefer to be with Captain Nemo now than in this shitty Lada risking my life . . .'

'Fucking hell, Yuri!' It was all Kite could do not to pull over to the side of the road, grab Aranov from the back seat and leave him on the hard shoulder. 'We're all doing our

272

best. We are all risking our lives to save yours. What about a bit of gratitude, huh? What about: 'Thanks, Lockie, thanks Martha, I'm grateful for everything you are doing?'

'Lockie? That is your real name?'

It was a careless mistake, but one that hardly mattered. Kite said: 'Yes, that's my real name. But you call me Simon Hobson for the next twenty-four hours or we're finished. That's the name in my passport. You are who?'

'Konstantin Baburin,' Aranov replied sharply. 'Martha is still Martha. Tania is still Tania. You are Simon Hobson. I get it.'

'Good,' said Kite. 'Now carry on with your story.'

A chastened Aranov continued, speaking loudly against the wind-roar of the open window. 'What more do you want to know?' he asked.

'Food!' Martha replied, suddenly sounding like her mother. 'What did you eat and drink? Blinis? Vodka? Caviar?'

'Blinis, sometimes. Caviar, no. Vodka, always.' Aranov asked for one of Martha's cigarettes and she passed him the packet. It was like trying to keep a child sufficiently distracted and entertained on a long journey. 'We ate boiled carrots, milk soup, rice pudding. Those were the good things to eat. You had peanut butter, burgers, French fries, cookies, bacon. You take these for granted. Our desserts were bread and jam. Fresh fruit? We have these only after the harvest, same now. Nothing has changed. For breakfast we had porridge every day.'

'Coffee?' Martha asked.

'*Coffee?* You know what a kilo of coffee beans cost ten years ago? About twenty rubles, maybe a fifth of my salary in one month. So, no. Not coffee. From porridge and tea at breakfast we went to borscht or *shchi* for lunch. Always the soup. I must have eaten ten thousand bowls of fucking soup in my life. Ten thousand chickens, ten thousand potatoes, ten thousand bowls of macaroni meatballs.'

'That's a lot of meatballs,' Kite muttered.

There was a car in his rear-view mirror. It had been there

for five minutes, following him steadily ever since they had passed the sign to Kursk. Kite kept this fact to himself.

'If you wanted anything nice, anything luxurious in Soviet Russia, you needed *blat*. You needed to be the man who knew the man who could find you a pair of blue jeans from America, coffee beans for your coffee, could get you a nice leather jacket like the one you wear now.'

'Oh you like it?' Martha asked.

Aranov did not answer her question. There was silence again, as if they had all been distracted by something. Kite looked in his mirror, momentarily blinded by the bright lights of an oncoming truck. He blinked away the glare. The car was still behind them, still following at a steady speed.

'What you need to know is that everything was . . .' Aranov searched for a word and said it in Russian, hoping for a translation. 'It was a *vremya zastoya*.'

'A time of stagnation,' said Kite.

'OK, stagnation. Yes. Everything was like this. My feelings about my childhood? My feeling is that I was bored. All my friends were bored. Same for them. Keep your room tidy like a good Communist. Fold your clothes tidy. Do your homework. Obey your mother and father.'

'Doesn't sound any different to my life in Swiss Cottage,' Martha observed, but the quip didn't land. Kite was too busy watching the mirror to laugh. There had been several opportunities for the tailing car to turn off the road or to overtake him, but it was still there, still going at the same speed, tracking him.

'There were good jokes, Martha,' Aranov replied. 'You want to hear good Soviet joke?'

'Sure!'

'What happens if crocodile swallows Leonid Brezhnev?'

'I don't know.' Martha looked across at Kite, sensing that he was worried. 'What happens if a crocodile swallows Brezhnev?'

'It fart medals for a week!'

Only Aranov laughed. Kite decided on the spur of the

moment to turn off the highway, heading down a narrow, ill-lit ramp in the direction of what appeared to be a village. He looked in the mirror. It didn't look as though the car had followed them.

'What are you doing?' Aranov asked. 'Where we going?'

'Just a moment,' Kite replied.

They drove in silence for about three minutes along a narrow, single-track road. Nobody said a word. Kite repeatedly checked the mirror. Still no headlights behind him. They passed two cars, parked side by side in the darkness. Kite slowed and looked back at them. Had they been abandoned? He continued to a junction and turned in a wide circle, almost clipping a tree as he put the Lada back on the road in the opposite direction.

'Everything OK?' Martha asked.

Kite slowed to a crawl and approached the two parked cars, switching off the headlights as he did so.

'What the fuck, Peter?' Aranov whispered. 'Lockie, what the fuck?'

'Shhhh!' Kite hissed, pressing a finger to his lips to indicate that everyone in the car should remain absolutely silent. He switched off the engine and allowed the Lada to drift towards the closest of the two parked cars, coming to a halt alongside it.

Aranov tried to speak but Tania slapped him on the leg, whispering: *'Pomolchi!'* Again Kite gestured for quiet, waiting for the silence of the night to engulf them. He indicated to Martha that she should slowly wind down her window. She did so, the mechanism squeaking as the glass shunted down. Kite narrowed his eyes, trying to focus in the darkness. There was a house about fifty metres from the road, all lights off. He looked for signs of movement inside, but there was nothing.

Very slowly, Kite reached for the door handle and stepped out of the car. It was a warm night with only the distant hum of the highway and the occasional click of a cicada to disturb him. Leaving the door ajar, he walked to the back of the Lada, quietly opened the boot and took out the lengths of hose and an oily rag. He then carried them to the closest of the two parked cars, unscrewed the petrol cap and inserted the long rubber tube, pushing it down as far as it would go.

He could feel the others watching him, Aranov desperate to speak. Kite was working from the light of the moon but it was enough. He pulled at the hose and very soon felt the chill touch of petrol on the hard rubber surface. Good. The tank was almost full. He unscrewed the petrol cap on Dmitri's Lada, stuffing it into his back pocket. He then inserted the shorter length of tube alongside the first and pushed both into the tank of the parked car, using the rag to seal the opening. Kite now blew into the end of the shorter tube until petrol began to flow out of the longer hose, splashing onto the ground beside his shoes.

Quickly Kite placed the hose into Dmitri's tank and allowed the petrol to siphon through from the parked car. The process was excruciatingly slow. He waited for the tank to fill, but more than a minute went by, somebody shifting their weight inside the car, another stifling a sneeze. At last Kite heard the liquid bubbling up to the surface and pulled the hose out of the tank. Taking the petrol cap out of his pocket, he screwed it back on and pulled the other tubes clear of the parked Lada. He had the wild idea of leaving a fifty dollar note wedged under the windscreen wiper as payment for the petrol but thought better of it. Instead, he placed the rag and the two lengths of hose in the boot and returned to the driving seat.

'Jesus, stink,' Aranov mumbled.

'Yeah, sorry about that,' Kite replied. Tania coughed very quietly as she reacted to the smell, like someone smothering a sneeze in a theatre. As Kite started the engine he had a mental image of the car bursting into flames, all lives lost. He rolled down the window, told the others to do the same, and pulled back onto the road.

'So now we have enough fuel for border?' Aranov asked.

'Let's hope so.' Kite felt a surge of exhilaration and turned to Martha. She was looking out at the passing road with an expression of immense tiredness.

'You OK?' he asked.

She looked at him and smiled but she was clearly very worried.

'Well done,' she said, reaching for his hand. 'Where did you learn to do that? Cub scouts?'

'Bloke called Tony taught me,' Kite replied and joined a slip-road leading back up onto the highway. 'One of the courses at the Balmoral.'

31

They drove for another two hours, almost without conversation, arriving in Stary Oskol at around three o'clock in the morning. Aranov finally slept, soundlessly, while Tania tried to make herself comfortable in the cramped back seat. Martha gave her the leather jacket to rest her head, but Aranov was taking up too much room and Tania could sleep only fitfully. With the zeal of a gambler checking a pile of chips in a casino, Kite kept staring at the petrol gauge; over a distance of more than 150 kilometres, it had moved only two or three millimetres. He was hopeful that he had siphoned off sufficient fuel to reach the crossing point at Nehoteevka. They were about an hour from Belgorod, perhaps another two to the border.

Close to the small town of Skorodnoye, Kite pulled into the forecourt of a petrol station which – to his relief – was closed. He did not want to have gone through the complications of siphoning the petrol only to discover that he could have filled up the tank as easily as refuelling in Edinburgh. Both Martha and Tania were awake. Aranov was snoring in the back, his head tipped to one side, but he woke up as soon as Kite switched off the engine.

'What's going on?' he asked in Russian.

'Short break,' Kite replied.

He opened the boot, withdrew the lengths of hose and

threw them into a large metal box at the edge of the fore-court. It was reckless, but worth the risk: he didn't want a guard at the frontier pulling them out and asking questions. A truck passed on the highway leaving behind a trail of silence; there were now very few vehicles on the road. Kite walked around in the strange orange light, occasionally stopping to stretch his calves and hamstrings as though he were about to come on as a substitute in a game of football. Martha smoked a cigarette. He caught her eye in the darkness and she smiled at him. He felt reassured by her presence; it cut through the isolation and strangeness of the journey.

The back door opened and Tania walked unsteadily towards the petrol pumps. Aranov emerged from the opposite side. Suddenly she leaned forward and was sick on the concrete, retching repeatedly.

'Fuck,' Martha muttered, knowing immediately what was wrong. 'Must be morning sickness.'

They walked towards her. Aranov put his hand on Tania's back. She was taking short, hard breaths, vomit gleaming in the eerie artificial light.

'Sorry,' she said in English, looking up at Kite.

'Don't worry,' he replied: '*Ne perezhivai, vsio normalno.*' No problem, it's normal.

'Maybe you caught something from the man who came to the house,' said Aranov, speaking to Tania in Russian. It sounded like he intended the remark as a joke.

'What man?' Kite asked.

'Just some guy came to the dacha tonight.' Aranov stepped back. 'Ask for sugar. Can you believe? At eleven o'clock at night.'

A stone dropped in Kite's gut. As Martha said: 'She doesn't have a bug. She has morning sickness,' he realised that Pavel had been to the house to give the signal to abort.

'Why didn't you tell me?' he said, trying to disguise his concern.

'Why should I? You were out looking for Lada. That is when you found out it had been stolen. He was just a guy

279

from the neighbourhood who needed sugar for his tea. "Buy your own!" I should have told him. This is correct way of saying it, Mister English teacher? "I should have told him?"'

Kite didn't hear the question. He was too busy trying to work out why Pavel had given the signal.

'What is it?' Martha asked, noticing the change in Kite's mood.

'Nothing,' he said, indicating her cigarette. 'Give me one of those, will you?'

She passed him a Marlboro Light from her packet. Kite drew deeply on it, trying to work out what to do. If Pavel had known that the border was closed – or teeming with FSK – he would surely have stopped Kite from driving away? Perhaps he had not anticipated that he would steal Dmitri's car and had therefore allowed him to continue.

Aranov was leading Tania back to the car. He had a bottle of water in his hand and passed it to her, unscrewing the cap. Martha was already in the passenger seat. Kite saw that they all wanted to get on with the journey. The sooner they were at the border, the better.

But Pavel. What had he known? He again inhaled on the cigarette, trying to think straight. He was tired. He needed a cup of coffee to jolt him back to life. Had Pavel moved the car to prevent Kite from leaving, knowing that all routes out of Russia were blocked? Whatever he had been trying to tell him by coming to the dacha, it was now too late. They were trapped inside Russia. Kite could not drive back to Voronezh; that was out of the question. How would he explain a midnight journey out of town in a stolen car? No, they had to keep moving forward. He must take the risk that there would be a way across the frontier, even if it involved finding a different crossing point further to the south or even north towards Belarus. They could not delay; if they booked into a hotel or broke into a deserted house and tried to wait things out, sooner or later they would be discovered. It was all on Gromik. What would he do? Place men at each of the crossings from Izvarino in the south to Katerinovka to the north, or second-guess that Kite would take the most direct route via Nehoteevka? It was impossible to know. There was a good chance their absence had still gone unnoticed; that only now Dmitri and Lev were waking up with sledgehammer headaches, both wondering what the hell had happened to Yuri and Tania. Dmitri was probably wandering around outside trying to remember where he parked his car.

Kite drove away from the petrol station, reassuring his passengers that they would reach the frontier before six o'clock. Tania said that she was feeling better, then drifted off to sleep. Martha also slept, leaving Kite and Aranov to share a packet of stale crisps the latter had found in the footwell of the back seat. There was no functioning radio in the car so they drove in silence along a straight black road. It was a bleak time for Kite. He realised that for BOX 88, the exfil had most likely been aborted. He was effectively alone, with no support on the road, responsible for the lives of people who had never been part of Strawson's original plan.

Eventually he reached Belgorod and passed through the outskirts of the city, avoiding some roadworks on the highway. They were soon on the last stretch of their journey. The sun was beginning to rise as Martha and Tania stirred from sleep, Tania asking for water.

'Don't worry about border,' Aranov announced in English when everyone was fully awake. 'We have problems, we use money. Guards not the same as the guards where Lockie and Martha come from. Not the same at all.'

'It's Simon, remember?' said Kite. 'Don't call me Lockie.'

Aranov chuckled. The sleep had done him some good; he sounded in high spirits.

'What do you mean about the guards?' Martha asked.

'The whole point about being policeman in Russia today – or bureaucrat of any kind – is to use your power to make as much money as possible. These people who patrol the border crossings, you think they care about a scientist defecting to the West? They care about buying the hi-fi from

Germany, the suit from Milan. Their work is dedicated to taking bribes.'

'Is that true?' Martha asked Kite. 'Even if they spot someone like Yuri?'

'Perhaps,' he replied. 'But if there are serious people waiting for us, then no amount of money is going to work.'

'What do you mean serious people? FSK?'

Kite nodded.

'Even FSK fucking corrupt!' Aranov countered. 'They are the only people in capitalist Russia who truly understand capitalism. Why? Because they have lived like capitalists for years!'

'We're not going to be able to bribe them, Yuri,' Kite told him. 'Let's not think about it, yeah? I'm sure we'll all be OK and eating lunch in Kharkiv.'

There was silence. In Kite's imagination, the border had become a fifty-mile stretch of coiled barbed wire, permanent and impassable. He would be Steve McQueen in *The Great Escape*, falling at the final hurdle. He tried to snap out of this sudden cynicism, to be upbeat and positive. Kite kept telling himself that Pavel had only raised the alarm because the Lada had been stolen. They were fine. They were not in danger. To break the silence he said: 'We just needed to get to Nehoteevka.'

'I have crossed there before,' said Tania, a piece of inform-ation on which Kite seized with the desperation of an addict.

'Really?' They were speaking in Russian. 'When?'

'Two years ago,' she said. 'Yuri didn't tell you?'

'No,' said Kite pointedly. 'Yuri didn't tell me.'

'I didn't know,' Aranov replied.

'We need to have papers for the car,' she continued. Martha looked at each of them in turn, wanting to know what was being said. 'Did you know this?'

Kite experienced the same trapped feeling of imminent failure he had felt at the petrol station. He asked Martha to look in the glovebox. She pulled out some official-looking papers which Aranov identified as the correct documents.

'But the papers have Dmitri's name on them,' he said. 'So what do we do?'

'We tell the truth,' Kite replied. 'We say that Dmitri is a friend of yours, that you're borrowing his car to visit your parents in Kiev. We met at a party in Voronezh and became friends. Your name is Konstantin Baburin. You have the passport to prove it.'

'Speak Russian, please,' said Tania.

Aranov translated what Kite had said. Tania observed that only 'stupid' people were arrested in Russia, by which she meant those that either refused to play the game or were ignorant of its rules. Kite was oddly emboldened by this observation and pointed out that arresting somebody for driving a stolen car was not profitable for a badly paid police officer. What *was* profitable was taking fifty dollars from the driver and waving him through the checkpoint.

'Exactly!' Aranov exclaimed, clapping his hands before embarking on a twenty-minute diatribe against Boris Yeltsin and his links with the corrupt KGB officers who had organised the coup against Gorbachev. By the time he had finished, the sun was coming up, illuminating a flat, featureless landscape dotted with poplar and birch. They passed a few tractors, dutifully watching over fields of wheat and corn, veering around the occasional pothole. The engine of the Lada began to sound a different note, causing Martha to look anxiously at Kite, who reassured her – more in hope than expectation – that everything was fine.

'Nearly there,' he said.

He had spoken too soon. As they rounded the next corner, Kite saw the flashing lights of a police car up ahead. A man was standing beside the vehicle wearing the uniform of the GAI.

'Fuck,' he whispered.

'Who's that?' Martha asked.

'Traffic police,' Aranov told her. 'State Automobile Inspectorate. Not police technically, but they can still cause us problems. Maybe he just wants bribe.'

Kite looked for a side road, but there was no way of avoiding what was going to happen. They would have to approach the patrol car. Aranov explained that there would likely be a further problem with the Lada's papers: Dmitri had not given written permission for Kite to be driving the car.

'You're telling me this *now*?' he replied, exasperated. 'I thought we had all the right documents?'

'This is different. This is Russia.'

'So how much do we pay?'

'Hundred dollars too much,' Aranov replied. 'But maybe he doesn't take bribes. Maybe we get the one honest GAI in Russia.'

Kite slowed down. The officer was wearing a sky-blue shirt and trousers with a peaked hat that was too big for his head. He was holding a black-and-white baton, shaped like a policeman's truncheon, which he pointed at the car. With a dramatic sweep across his body, he waved the baton towards his feet indicating that Kite should pull up in front of him.

'Everybody be cool,' said Martha, though she sounded as tense as Kite was feeling. 'This is an adventure. It's not every day we get stopped at a roadblock.'

'Yes,' Kite concurred. 'Everybody stay calm.'

The officer approached Kite's open window. He was about twenty-five with clear skin and very brown eyes. His uniform was neat and pressed. Everything about his demeanour suggested a box-ticking bureaucrat, not an opportunist.

'*Dokumenty.*'

Kite reached into Dmitri's glovebox and pulled out the insurance papers. There was a smell of manure from a nearby field. From the back seat Aranov said a cheerful '*Dobryy den*' but the officer did not reply. In Russian Aranov explained that Kite was a tourist driving on a British licence who barely spoke the language. Rather than winning the confidence of the officer, this revelation served only to make him more suspicious.

'*Dovernost,*' he said.

'What's a *dovernost*?' Kite asked.

'It's what I was telling you about,' Aranov replied, with maddening complacency. 'The document saying you have permission to drive Dmitri's car.'

A bribe was going to be Kite's only option; his papers were all wrong. In rudimentary Russian he explained that he was borrowing the car from a friend who lived in Voronezh.

'We had no idea a foreigner needed a *dovernost*,' Aranov added. 'It's an old Soviet law. I thought we were finished with all that.'

Aranov's remark sounded provocative. As a truck passed them on the road, seemingly the only other vehicle for miles around, the officer stepped back from the door and secured the strap of the baton around his wrist.

'Step out of the vehicle,' he said.

Kite reached for his wallet, his heart pounding. He felt that things were unravelling. He pointedly took out two fifty-dollar bills in full view of the officer. Doing so had no discernible effect; if the young man had any interest in the money, he had not shown it. As Kite stepped onto the edge of the road, Aranov also got out of the car, ostensibly to act as translator.

'You are driving illegally,' the officer told them.

Aranov began to speak but Kite interrupted him.

'I understand,' he said. He continued in basic Russian: 'Look. I am a British tourist. I am here with my girlfriend. We are all going to Kiev for an important meeting. If we have to stop, we're going to be late. How can we sort this out?'

He took the wallet out of his back pocket and tossed it back and forth in his hands. The officer looked at him with disdain.

'What is this?' he said.

'This?' Kite held up the wallet. 'It's a wallet. It's American money. You want to see it?'

Perhaps there had been an error in his grammar because the officer immediately took offence.

'Your journey is illegal. I want to see everyone's passports.'

Kite could not believe that they had come so close to the

border but were going to be stopped on a technicality. If the GAI bureaucrat radioed for back-up, they were doomed. Kite knew that he was going to have to think of some other way of convincing the man to let them through, but he seemed set on causing maximum inconvenience. Martha stepped out of the car and handed Kite her passport, trying to look as relaxed as possible. Aranov fetched Tania's documents. As he spoke to her quietly in the back seat, Kite heard the sound of a vehicle approaching from the north; the way their luck was running, it was surely another GAI patrol on the scent of an arrest. He looked out at the road. A Zhiguli was coming towards them, slowing down to rubberneck what was going on.

'*Molodoy chelovek!*'

The driver had addressed the officer through an open window. He looked stressed and worried. In a moment of distilled consternation, Kite did a double-take. It was Pavel.

'What are you doing here?' Pavel said to the officer in Russian, entirely ignoring Kite and his passengers. He was wearing an open-necked shirt and smoking a cigarette. 'There's been a huge crash three miles back.' He pointed behind him along the road. 'They need help!'

It was as though the officer knew that Pavel was lying. Barely summoning the energy to respond, he shrugged and continued to analyse the passports which Kite had passed to him.

'Hey! I'm talking to you. There's been a bad accident.'

'It's not my responsibility,' the officer replied.

'Not your responsibility?!' Only now did Pavel look at Kite. There was nothing in his glance to indicate that they had ever met. 'What are you doing with these people?' Pavel shouted over the noise of a passing truck. 'Taking a bribe like all your fucking friends in GAI?'

To this neat, self-satisfied patriot, such an accusation was a grave insult. Lifting his baton, he waved it in Pavel's direction and ordered him to get out of the car.

'With pleasure.' Pavel flicked the cigarette onto the asphalt. 'You want me to give you money as well?'

Kite shot Aranov a look, telling him that the stranger was acting on their behalf. Martha had also clocked his face, remembering the guardian angel she had glimpsed in the suburbs of Voronezh. As Pavel stomped towards them, the officer placed the passports on the bonnet of the Lada and turned to face him.

'What are those?' Pavel asked, pointing at the documents. It was a trick of close combat. As the officer looked down, Pavel glanced left and right to confirm that the road was clear, then struck the man hard on the side of the head, sending him crashing to the ground. His ill-fitting peaked cap rolled into the dust. Stunned, the officer tried to sit up, but his legs had gone. Pavel was over him before he could speak, landing another punch on the temple which knocked him out clean.

'Jesus!' Martha gasped.

To see the genial, easy-going Pavel transformed into a man of violence was astonishing. Kite immediately understood what he needed to do. Without saying a word, he propped up the stricken officer as Pavel grabbed his legs. They carried him away from the road, setting him down behind an old wooden fence. The Russian went through his pockets as Kite checked that he was breathing. Then they walked back to the Lada.

'What now?' Kite asked.

'I'll take the keys, break the radio.' Pavel was in a mood of concentrated, disciplined decision-making. 'You go. Keep moving. I have a *dovernost* with me.'

'That's what he wanted,' Kite replied, pointing back towards the fence.

'Problem of driving someone else's car,' Pavel replied. 'Get Yuri to fill it in as you go. You may need it.'

He handed Kite a pen, pulling the *dovernost* from his back pocket.

'What the fuck happened to my Lada?' Kite asked.

'Stolen. I came to dacha to tell you, but you were not there. Then I see you borrow this piece of junk. I think "Clever boy", but I follow you, just in case.'

'Thank God you did.'

'God has nothing to do with it.'

A car was coming towards them from the west. Kite ushered Aranov and Tania back into the car; they barely had time to acknowledge Pavel. Martha thanked him before returning to the passenger seat.

'You're going to keep following me?' Kite asked.

'This is now as far as I can come,' Pavel replied. 'I need to watch him. When he wakes up, whack!' He mimed punching the traffic cop a second time. 'I don't want him coming after you or going back into Belgorod to make phone call. If I can think of another solution, or if something changes, I will come to the frontier. Which way are you going out?'

'I thought the quickest way,' Kite replied, wondering if Pavel would approve of this.

'Nehoteevka?'

'Yes. Is it safe?'

'I don't know. Who knows what Gromik knows?' He opened the door of the GAI vehicle. 'I have been on the road all this time, just like you. You might hit problems, you might get through.'

'But we have no other choice,' Kite asked.

'You have no other choice.'

Kite shook his hand. 'Thank you,' he said. 'I don't know what we would have done . . .'

'You would have been fine. You would have thought of a way.' Pavel winked. He glanced over at the fence as if he had heard the officer regaining consciousness. Another truck passed them from the west, heading deeper into Russia. 'Now go,' he said. 'It will already be busy at the frontier. I wish you good luck.'

32

As Kite set off, he clocked that there were now more cars on the road. Several trucks with European number plates passed in the opposite direction, taking goods to Belgorod and Voronezh, to Saratov and Samara. Once he had finished explaining why Pavel had stopped to help them, silence engulfed the Lada. As the frontier drew closer, the highway cut through a vast forest, then opened up in a manner that reminded Kite of the toll booths on French motorways.

Suddenly they were on a vast concrete apron of queuing cars and trucks, drivers and passengers standing idly in the road, officials of various stripes wandering around holding clipboards and walkie-talkies. Several of them were dressed identically to the man who had stopped them less than half an hour earlier. To the north there was what appeared to be a separate section for freight traffic, a much longer queue of trucks and articulated lorries disappearing into a section of forest. Ahead were five crossing posts marked with the double-headed eagle of the Russian state, each with a lane of traffic. Kite wound the window fully down and a rush of warm air poured into the car.

'Here we go,' he said. 'Remember. I'm Simon. You are Konstantin.'

Just then, a man came out of nowhere and stepped in

front of the car. Tania cried out. Kite hit the brakes and managed to stop. The man had made no effort to get out of their way; indeed his reaction was one of pleasant surprise that the car had not struck him.

'Jesus!' said Kite as Aranov leaned forward and bawled the man out in Russian.

He was about thirty with a tidy, slightly pointed beard. Producing a charming smile, he raised a hand in greeting and proceeded to deliver what was obviously his stump speech.

'My friends, my friends, I am sorry to have startled you.' His Russian had an accent which Kite couldn't place. 'I want to help you. My name is Bogdan. You need papers, I can arrange this. You want to go through the fast lane and avoid the queues, I know all the right people.'

Ordinarily, Kite would have avoided him like a drunk in Leith, but as he looked ahead at the border huts and the armed guards, he knew that this local Fagin might be the key to getting through as quickly as possible.

'Hello,' he said. 'Yes, perhaps you can help us. My girlfriend and I are British tourists, travelling with two friends from Voronezh. We're going to Kiev for a few days. Which is the quickest queue?'

Like a bookie sensing a quick payout, Fagin turned on the charm.

'You are British!' He had switched to a fluent, confident English. 'Hello, my friends, hello.' He bent over to get a better look at Martha. 'Your girlfriend – wow, beautiful.' Then, in Russian, a formal greeting to Tania and Aranov as they watched the show from the back seat. 'My name Bogdan. I can help you with your vehicle papers. You will need to go to GAI, but if you like I can do this for you.'

The thought of seeing another GAI officer filled Kite with dread. He could feel Aranov's urge to take control of the situation. There was very obviously something criminal about Bogdan, but also a certain conviction and panache which spoke of experience in the black arts of border crossings. This was not a chancer on debut; he was evidently operating in his allotted section of the car park and knew the way the system worked.

'How much to get the papers done?' he asked. 'We're hungry and want to get something to eat.'

'Of course, of course!' Bogdan indicated a kiosk to the south selling drinks and hot food. 'You look hungry after your long journey! You leave home early, beat traffic? Very clever, yes.' He peered into the back seat and again switched to Russian as he addressed Aranov and Tania. 'Where are you from?'

'Voronezh,' Tania answered with a forced smile.

'OK, OK. So who is the owner of the car? You are the driver, nice man from England, but you don't own a car like this, am I right? In England you drive a Mercedes!'

Bogdan laughed explosively as Aranov responded in Russian.

'It belongs to my cousin, Dmitri,' he said, a gambit he had not agreed with Kite. 'We have the *dovernost*. Do I need to come with you or can you get it fixed for us?'

Bogdan did the conman's trick of looking crestfallen, suggesting with a dip of the mouth that the effort of having the papers stamped by the correct official would be almost impossible.

'To be honest,' said Kite, 'I'm happy to pay you to do it for us. How much would that cost?'

An instant change in Bogdan's expression told Kite that the papers would no longer be a problem; all that mattered was the price.

'Depends, my friend. Depends. You borrow car, you take it to Ukraine, the GAI do not like this, even if you have *dovernost*.' A suitably dramatic pause. 'But I know the guy who runs office.' Bogdan gestured in the direction of the hutch. 'I will talk to him, maybe we make this problem go away. *Maybe*.'

'Great,' said Kite, talking across Aranov who was about to interrupt. 'How much?'

He expected to be asked for at least a hundred dollars and

was prepared to pay three times that. To his great surprise, Bogdan's opening offer was fifty. Kite was so pleasantly shocked that he almost forgot to bargain.

'Fifty?' he said. 'Christ. I had no idea it would be that much. Can you do it for twenty?'

Bogdan looked as though the bright young Englishman had not only insulted his family and good name, but all of Mother Russia.

'What is your name, my friend?'

'Simon.'

'OK, Simon. Not twenty. Not for this. GAI do not help for twenty. You can do thirty American dollars?'

Kite allowed for a suitable pause, reaching into his trouser pocket where he knew he had several ten-dollar bills in a roll. Taking them out in a clump, he allowed Bogdan to see that there was more money in the pipeline if he continued to help them. Discreetly he passed thirty dollars through the open window, handed over the papers for Dmitri's Lada and asked how long the procedure would take.

'Five minutes, my friend. Five minutes, then I come back. You go with me if you like. But take a coffee. Buy your beautiful girlfriend a tea or nice present from Russia as a memory. I see you soon, yes.'

'Do you trust him?' Aranov asked when he had gone.

'Apparently,' Martha replied in a tone which suggested she had full confidence in Kite and thought Aranov was being unnecessarily suspicious. 'Let's go and get that food. I'm starving.'

The kiosk had an atmosphere of transitory chaos, truck drivers in stained singlets mingling with wannabe Russian businessmen in cheap suits, makeshift entrepreneurs en route to Ukraine to strike the deal which would make their fortune. The ubiquitous babushkas were taking a break from selling dried fish and sunflower seeds at the side of the road; young mothers carried babies in slings tied across their breasts. Kite ferried a tray of coffee and pastries to an outside table where Martha was seated with Aranov and Tania. It amazed him that they were not hiding in the car, that sirens had not sounded on approaching police vehicles or an alarm raised in the corrupted offices of the State Automobile Inspectorate. Were they safe? It felt as though they had got away with it, but Kite was steeling himself for one last problem.

An old man sitting in the morning sun bummed a cigarette from Martha as they walked back to the Lada. Bogdan had reappeared, cheerfully waving the traffic papers, his body language suggesting that his business with the dollar-rich Europeans was not concluded.

'No problems, no problems,' he said, thrusting the papers into Kite's outstretched hand. 'So what now? Fast lane or slow? You want to queue with these idiots all morning in the sun or Bogdan take you through to Ukraine nice and quick, nice and fast?'

'How much?' Kite asked. A mixture of fatigue and nervous energy had reduced his capacity for chit-chat.

'For fast lane?' Martha was standing nearby watching the traffic build up behind them.

'Yes, we want to go through now. I have more dollars.'

'OK.' Bogdan tried to disguise his eagerness. He looked up at the checkpoints. 'There is a way through. I have contact. Maybe we cause some people to lose their patience, maybe we don't make friends with some of the drivers of some of the cars in front of you here. But let's do it!' Having allowed Kite to glimpse the promised land, he duly presented him with the invoice. 'But it is slightly costing more than traffic papers, my friend.'

'How much?' Martha asked. Kite had the feeling she was prepared to pay out of her own pocket, just to get the hell out of Russia.

'Sixty.'

It was almost certainly the exact amount Bogdan had earlier glimpsed in Kite's hand.

'Fifty,' he said, just for the sake of appearances. The deal was struck there and then.

293

'Follow me,' said Bogdan, walking ahead of the Lada and waving them forward like a tour guide in a museum. 'This way!'

It took only a few minutes to reach the furthest of the six crossing gates. Two very young, very bored-looking guards perked up as Bogdan approached; he was evidently known to them as a source of easy money. Kite had driven around at least four parked cars, one of which had sounded its horn in annoyance as the Lada jumped the queue. He was concerned that they were drawing attention to themselves. To be in a hurry was to demonstrate guilt. Perhaps it had been a mistake to allow Bogdan to take control of the situation.

'I should be in the boot,' said Aranov. 'I should be hiding. This is crazy. They see me, I'm finished.'

'Shut the fuck up,' said Martha and a stunned Kite looked across at her.

'Easy for you,' Aranov hissed.

'Let's everybody calm down,' Kite urged.

Bogdan was talking to one of the guards. He was about the same age as Kite, tired and riddled with acne. He looked over at the Lada and tipped his head to one side, as though weighing up whether or not to allow it through. He went into a security hut and remained there, out of sight, for what felt like an eternity.

'He's calling it in,' said Aranov. 'He recognises me. He has been told to look for Peter Galvin, for Yuri Aranov. He knows we punched out that guy on the highway.'

'Keep the faith,' Kite replied, but his heart was hammering, his hands gripping the steering wheel so tightly that the knuckles looked like pearls. 'And stop saying "Yuri Aranov". Start saying "Konstantin Baburin". My name is Simon. Remember that. It's all you need to know. You call me Peter or Lockie and we're finished.'

Kite looked down at the four passports in his lap. It worried him that Bogdan had not yet asked for them. He looked back up. The guard was still inside the hut. His colleague was checking the papers on a yellow Volkswagen with Ukrainian plates. It was waved through.

'Hey, Mister Simon!'

Bogdan had called out to him and was gesturing Kite towards the crossing point. The guard had at last come out of the hut. Martha whispered 'Good luck' as Kite stepped out of the car. He half-expected a phalanx of plain-clothes FSK officers to jump out from the queue of traffic, but nothing changed. He simply walked towards the hut and greeted the guard with a lazy wave.

'*Zdravstvuyte*,' he said.

'You speak Russian?' the guard asked.

'A bit,' Kite replied, breaking his cover. 'Do you speak English?'

This was the man who held their future in his hand. He was so young; it didn't seem right that he had so much power. Kite could hear Strawson's voice in his head. *Breathe*. The guard shook his head and said: 'No speak English.'

'My friend here says we can come through slightly faster than everyone else.' Kite nodded towards Bogdan who, for reasons which were not clear, seemed to have lost some of his characteristic bonhomie. 'Is that possible?'

The guard looked over at the Lada.

'Who is with you? Why you come? Why not your Russian friend?'

'Do you need to meet him?' Kite played the eager public school innocent. He was trying to give off a mood of being slightly out of his depth, keen not to break any rules yet willing to cooperate at any price.

The guard nodded. 'Bring car.'

It felt like a breakthrough. Perhaps Aranov and Tania would be subjected to a quick interview, Martha would be asked to confirm her identity, and then the worst would be over. Kite walked back towards the Lada. Bogdan followed him.

'It's going to be a hundred more,' he said. 'You piss a lot of people off, Simon.'

'A hundred and sixty!' Kite replied, astonished that their

escape across the border appeared to be dependent on the equivalent of about a hundred pounds.

'Yes, my friend. These guys, they ask big commission. You understand? You give me hundred, I give direct to them.'

Kite had the money in his back pocket, but negotiated down to seventy because he could feel the guard watching them. He didn't want to look as though he was too eager to pay up.

'Fine,' Bogdan replied. 'Give me seventy dollar and we drive over.'

The Russian took the cash. With a nod so discreet it was almost imperceptible, he indicated to the guard that the arrangement had been made. Kite started the engine and pulled up to the hut.

The guard peered down, looking into the back seat.

'Why is the Englishman driving?' he asked in Russian.

'My girlfriend is pregnant,' Aranov replied. 'She was sick about an hour ago. I'm looking after her.'

'You take your sick girlfriend to Kiev?'

'Morning sickness,' Tania replied. It helped that she looked relatively healthy. There was colour in her cheeks.

'What about you?'

This to Martha. Kite explained that his girlfriend didn't speak Russian. The guard flicked to the page in Martha's passport bearing the entry stamp from Sheremetyevo.

'You have airline ticket from Kiev?'

Kite used the cover story. 'No,' he said. 'We're both students travelling for the summer. We were planning to go back to Moscow and fly home but then Tania and Konstantin suggested we come with them to Kiev. More of an adventure! Apparently it's easy to exchange the Aeroflot tickets at the airport.'

'Expensive,' the guard observed.

Kite couldn't think of an adequate reply so he merely muttered 'Maybe' and tried to continue looking like a privately educated ingénue who was slightly out of his depth.

'Trunk,' said the guard in English.

It took Kite a second to realise what he was saying. He stepped out of the car and opened the boot, relieved to have discarded the lengths of hose. There was still a very strong smell of petrol but it did not seem to trouble the guard. He indicated that Kite should close the boot and he did so. He had not even bothered to search their luggage.

'OK,' he said. 'You go.'

Kite was back in the driver's seat. As he turned the key in the ignition, he saw Gromik at the next crossing station. He was no more than twenty feet away. If Gromik turned, he would see them. Somehow, even as his heart detonated inside him, he had the presence of mind to put the Lada in first gear and to pull away, telling everyone in a firm, quiet voice to wind up their windows and to look down at their shoes.

'Why? said Aranov casually. 'What's problem?'

'Gromik is behind us.'

Kite could sense that Aranov was going to turn and check and hissed at him: 'Don't fucking look back', hoping that the noise of the engine would smother his voice. Martha recognised Gromik's name. She let out a gasp of despair and said: 'Oh fuck no, please' as Kite moved towards the second crossing point on the Ukrainian side. He was soaked in sweat, unbalanced by vertiginous fear.

'It's OK, it's OK,' he said, trying to locate Gromik in the rear-view mirror.

'But he will have photograph. He will show it to guard!' said Aranov.

'We will get across,' Kite told him.

There was a space up ahead behind the yellow Volkswagen. Like the last gasp of air before a drowning man sinks beneath the surface of the water, Kite could see fragments of the Ukrainian countryside beyond the security area.

'Quicker,' Aranov urged.

He pulled up behind the Volkswagen. He had no idea what arrangement existed between the two countries; would Gromik have the power to call them back now that they had left Russia? Would he simply drive into Ukraine and follow them? There was no time to think about it. The Volkswagen had been waved through the barrier by a female guard who beckoned Kite forward.

'Everybody breathe,' said Kite. 'Stay calm. We have come this far. Let's all be nice and friendly.'

'*Zdravstvuyte*,' said the guard. There was a three-pronged trident on the peak of her cap, thick locks of blonde hair tied in a ponytail behind her neck. '*Pasport pozhaluysta.*'

With the engine still running, Kite thrust the passports through the window and produced a benign smile. He turned to check that Tania and Aranov were looking suitably relaxed. To his astonishment, he saw that Tania was crying.

'What is it?' Aranov asked her.

'Russia,' she whispered. 'I will never go there again.'

'Nonsense!' said Kite, hoping that the guard wouldn't notice her tears. 'You'll be back, I promise.'

He noticed that the guard was staring at Martha. Martha nodded back, allowing her to take as much time as she pleased. The guard appeared to be checking the various stamps in her passport.

'Why did you come here?' she asked in Russian.

'She only speaks English,' Aranov replied, leaning forward and speaking across Kite. 'She's from London. Came here as a tourist. We're going to Kiev together.' Kite wanted to push him back but had to trust that Yuri wouldn't blow the whole operation. 'Is there a problem?'

The guard found the question strange and looked at Kite, as though he might be under duress or in some way compromised by his Russian passengers in the back seat.

'First time Russia?' she asked in English.

'Yes,' he replied quickly. 'And our first time going to Ukraine.'

'There could be problem,' the woman replied. The last of Kite's resilience fell away with those words and it was all he could do not to drive forward and smash through the barrier.

'Problem?' he asked.

'You come through quick.' The woman indicated the lane on the Russian side through which they had passed. Had Gromik sent out an alert about Aranov's defection to officials on both sides of the border? Then suddenly it dawned on him: she knew he had paid to jump the queue. Was that all this was? She wanted money, just like the rest of them.

'Yes. We came through quick.' He switched to Russian, taking the risk that a bribe was all it would take. 'Can we arrange the same thing with you?'

There was an awful moment of waiting, an atmosphere of plate glass inside the car. It was clear that the guard understood. Furtively she turned to see if any of her colleagues were watching.

'Jacket,' she said quickly.

'Excuse me?'

She pointed at Martha's black leather jacket. This was to be the price of safe passage to Ukraine; a piece of clothing bought from a second-hand store in Finsbury Park.

'*Konfiskovano*,' the guard explained. Martha understood that it was obviously the Russian word for 'confiscate'.

'You want this?' she asked, already shuffling out of the jacket.

'Yes,' the guard replied, then, more quietly: 'With fifty dollars.'

Kite helped Martha to pull her arms out of the sleeves. He didn't want to look as though they were in a hurry. She removed her purse, a cigarette lighter and a few coins, then she handed the jacket to Kite, who stuffed a fifty-dollar bill into an outside pocket before thrusting it through the window.

'Can we go now?' Martha asked impatiently.

'Yes,' the guard replied. 'You go.'

She turned and pressed a button on a panel and the barrier to their freedom was raised. With a feeling of almost mystical relief, Kite gave a polite nod, wound up the window and drove forward into the West.

33

'So you made it,' said Azhar Masood.

A day had passed since the news of Evgeny Palatnik's assassination had reached BOX 88. Masood and Kite were walking along the southern perimeter of the Serpentine, Cara Jannaway between them, going over some of the details in the Voronezh files. It was a Monday afternoon of picnics and crowds, Hyde Park glittering in bright sunlight.

'We made it,' Kite replied. 'Skin of our teeth.'

'Must have felt good,' said Cara in a wistful tone, as though she were craving an adventure of her own.

'It didn't feel bad.'

Kite remembered the silence in the car for the first few kilometres, the dread of a siren behind them, the worry that an FSK team might grab Aranov on the road and take him back to Russia. Michael Strawson and Rita Ayinde had been waiting for them at the safe house in Kharkov, parents anxiously waiting up for their children to get home from a party. There had then been the long drive to Kiev and an RAF flight to Brize Norton. Aranov, refusing to get on the plane, had eventually been sedated and carried on board by Kite and Strawson, earning him the nickname 'Mr T' at The Cathedral. The Russian had woken up in an Oxfordshire farmhouse twelve hours later to fried eggs and bacon and the all-new sounds of an English summer. Martha spent two days with Rita Ayinde coming up with a cover story for what had happened to her in Russia, while Tania Tretyakova adjusted to the luxuries of life in her adopted country: the private obstetrician; the racks of clothes from John Lewis; produce of all kinds in vast, gleaming supermarkets. Strawson, conscious that Kite had beaten the odds despite risking everything for the sake of an affair with a pretty girl, balanced praise with condemnation, lauding Kite's chutzpah in success-fully bringing Aranov across the border while castigating him for falling into what might have been a very obvious, very dangerous honeytrap.

'You've always had your dick about five feet in front of your brain, kid. What is it about you and women? A beautiful girl shows up in your language class, you can't keep it zipped up for even a few weeks? I know you're young, but you risk your job, you risk the operation, you risk everything just to get laid? That strike you as smart or does that strike you as really fucking dumb?'

Kite had protested his innocence, pointing out the incon-testable fact that Oksana had *not* been a honeytrap, but simply an intelligent, ambitious woman who had found herself unwittingly embroiled with a British spy. If he was going to apologise for anything, it was for lying to her, seducing her, making her think they had a future together when in fact there had been no future at all.

'We were relieved as much as anything,' he told Cara and Masood, leaving out much of this. 'I'd taken a lot of risks, not least in bringing Martha across. Anything could have gone wrong. But in your twenties you have that extraordinary sense of self-belief, don't you? There's no context for your actions. You just go ahead and do things because there's no reason not to. You're right about absolutely everything and anybody who dares to question you is either old-fashioned or stupid.'

Masood caught the twenty-seven-year-old Cara Jannaway's eye, not to check the veracity of Kite's claim, but because he was wondering why the boss wasn't being more effusive about his achievement.

'There was a welcoming committee for you in Kharkov,' he said, recalling what he had read in the file. 'It says that Strawson was angry. Bit much, no? You were the conquering hero, Lockie. "You did it, George. All your life, fantastic." Wasn't there a bit of that?'

Masood was quoting lines from *Smiley's People*. Kite recognised the reference and pictured Alec Guinness standing in the wet Berlin night; Cara, who had grown up on Jason Bourne and *24*, looked bewildered.

'It was Martha,' he replied. 'He was angry that she was involved, frustrated that I'd told her about my work. Thought it would have been easy enough to stage a row at the Brno and send her home as soon as she appeared.'

'And you disagreed with that?'

Kite hesitated. He didn't want to make it sound as though he had fallen out with Strawson or that BOX 88 hadn't been appreciative of what he had accomplished. The Aranov exfil was still talked about at The Cathedral. It had made him a star.

'It was complicated. I didn't disagree exactly. Michael and I had spoken about making Martha conscious. He was just annoyed that I'd done it without first getting his authorisation.'

'Doesn't sound like you had much choice,' said Cara. She was wearing an ill-fitting linen jacket borrowed from Masood to protect her pale skin against the sudden summer sun. 'Your girlfriend shows up, you immediately send her home, Gromik might have smelled a rat.' She thrust her hands into the pockets and sounded another note in defence of Kite. 'And how were you supposed to ask for permission? It's not like there were mobiles in those days. You couldn't just ping him a WhatsApp.'

'That's how it felt at the time,' Kite replied, oddly grateful for her understanding. 'Later on, Michael admitted he was angry that nobody had kept tabs on Martha's movements, that her flight to Moscow was missed. It was an oversight. That was what had pissed him off.'

'How could they possibly have known?' said Masood. 'Especially in those days. There wouldn't have been a reason to listen to her phones, keep tabs on her, find out her intentions for a gap-year summer.'

'Which was exactly the point I made to Michael.'

Kite looked out over the Serpentine. Usually there would have been pedalos and rowing boats on the water, dating couples trying each other out for size, but everything had been tied up for the summer, moored by Covid.

'Sooner or later we all have to tell our husbands, our wives, that we're not who we say we are.' Kite stopped and looked at Cara pointedly. She returned his gaze. He realised that he knew nothing about her private life, only that she had been single when they met and occasionally messed around on Bumble and Tinder. Ten years ago, before Isobel, single in his late thirties, he might have been rash enough to make a play for her; now he was interested only in saving his marriage. 'It was the way I'd allowed my private life to become entangled in my operational life. That was what he objected to.'

'He was a perfectionist,' said Masood.

'With a Puritan streak,' Kite added. They had started walking again, returning in the direction from which they had come. 'Michael wasn't sanctimonious, he wasn't a moraliser. He just believed that sex always got people into trouble. It was better to be a one-woman guy – or one man.'

'That's me done for then,' Cara muttered.

The pale wide path flared in the sunlight. A pair of sweating, black-clad rollerbladers weaved between them, a sudden flash of summers gone by: no masks, no helmets, not a care in the world.

'There are football managers like that,' Masood observed, picking up a suddenly landed Frisbee and flicking it back across the grass towards its owner. 'They want to get their players married off nice and young so they don't go to nightclubs and drink too much.'

Kite recalled that Masood was a passionate Arsenal fan,

lived with his partner in a flat in the old Highbury stadium, a chunk of turf from the pitch sealed in a plastic box in the freezer. 'Yes, that sounds like Michael,' he said, remembering the dying Strawson reaching for his hand in hospital and urging him to marry Martha. 'He wanted me tucked up in bed with a Tom Clancy and a cup of Horlicks by ten o'clock. But I was twenty-two. I'd spent five years in an all-male boarding school trying to dodge the wandering hands of my housemaster, four more in a long-term relationship with Martha Raine. It wasn't going to work.'

Neither Masood nor Cara responded, perhaps surprised that Kite had spoken so candidly about his personal life.

'There was also the worry that Martha had inadvertently exposed my identity to Moscow,' he continued. 'But we discovered through Pavel that Gromik had buried the story. Didn't want to be associated with it. Aranov's defection was forgotten. Gromik swept everything under the carpet and pretended it had never happened. One of the first things we asked MOCKINGBIRD was whether or not there was a file on me at the Lubyanka. Answer came back no. Which is why Galvin and JUDAS 62 is such a mystery.'

'What about Aranov?' Cara asked. 'Is he still alive?'

'Oh very much still alive, very much on our radar. Lived in the States for ten years or so then moved to Andover, took a job at Porton Down. At the last count there had been three divorces, two daughters, one grandchild, at least five girl-friends . . .'

'. . . and a partridge in a pear tree,' Cara sang quietly. 'So Tania had a baby girl?'

'The following January, yes.' One of the men playing Frisbee made a running catch and celebrated like a wide receiver at the Superbowl, hopping up and down in an imaginary end zone. 'She's called Anastasia. Now twenty-six, if you can believe it. Who knows where the time goes?'

'And Gromik?'

Masood's question cut to the heart of the matter. Kite

slowed his pace. This was the moment to tell them about the tape.

'For a while, he was just a background figure.' He took out a cigarette but did not light it. 'Gromik was the local FSK honcho, no more than that. Nobody at BOX gave him a second thought. Until the package arrived.'

'Package?' Cara asked.

Kite could tell from her expression that she had sensed what was coming; there had been a change in the atmosphere of the conversation. They passed the entrance to the Diana Memorial Fountain. Like the rowing boats and the pedalos, it too had been mothballed by Covid; strips of blue plastic were strung across the fencing like tape at a crime scene.

'A video was sent to the house in Wokingham,' Kite told them. 'A parcel for Miriam Galvin.'

'And therefore rerouted to The Cathedral,' Masood added.

'Exactly.' Kite lit the cigarette. 'Gromik knew it was a false address, that anything sent to the Galvin home would be passed to whoever had been running me.'

Kite took a moment to compose himself. Cara must have sensed that he was unsettled because she said: 'What was on the tape?'

'The very worst thing,' he replied.

34

Kite could still remember every detail of the meeting with Strawson. He had been summoned to his office in The Cathedral, a place he always associated with hearing the news that Billy Peele had been killed. Jock Carpmael had wheeled a colour television and video recorder into the room. Kite was invited to sit down on a sofa facing the screen and Jock told that they were not to be disturbed. Strawson had then pressed 'play' on a remote control.

'I'm sorry you have to see this,' he said. 'But you should know what happened to her.'

'To who?' Kite had asked.

Suddenly the bloodied, beaten face of a young woman appeared in close-up on the screen. There was no sound. The damage to her features was so severe that it took Kite a moment to realise that he was looking at Oksana. There were cuts on her tear-streaked face, a blackened gap in her mouth where a tooth had been punched out. Her hair was matted with dried blood. She looked terrified.

'Jesus Christ,' said Cara, listening to Kite's description.

'It got worse,' he told her.

The image of Oksana disappeared. For some time there was silence, the blank screen occasionally flickering. Strawson shifted awkwardly in his seat. Then Kite heard the awful, shattering cries of a woman being assaulted. A voice could be heard over her screams, unmistakably Gromik's.

'This is what we do to women who protect British spies.'

The blank screen suddenly cut to blurred footage of a naked woman being held down by two men whose faces could not be seen. Oksana was being raped by one of them. Kite watched as the body he had held, the skin he had touched, was violated by Gromik's thugs. He was convulsed with shock. Strawson put a hand on his back, but Kite was inconsolable. He shouted at the American to switch off the tape.

'Where is she?' he demanded. 'Why did you show that to me?'

'These are the people we're dealing with, kid,' Strawson replied. He had muted the sound but the tape, like a reel of grisly underground pornography, was still running. 'This is Mikhail Gromik. These are the tactics of the new FSK. They are the same as the tactics of the KGB. Nothing has changed.'

Seeing that Strawson had no intention of switching off the tape, Kite had yanked the electricity cord out of the wall. The screen went blank, the video recorder clicked off.

'Is she alive?' he demanded, overcome with horror. 'What did you find out? Where is she now?'

Strawson's shrugged, non-committal response enraged Kite.

'We have to get her out of Voronezh,' he demanded. 'We have to go back for her.'

Very slowly, with an eerie, almost detached calm, Strawson placed the remote control on the sofa and gestured at Kite to sit down.

'Collateral damage,' he said.

'*Collateral damage?*'

'You couldn't have known. These are animals we're dealing with. Sadists. No better than the Russian soldiers raping women in '44. I'm sorry, kid. I thought you needed to know.'

Kite had left The Cathedral without saying another word.

He had walked for hours around west London, trying to think of all the ways that he could get himself back to Russia while all the time knowing that every one of them was denied to him. The life into which he had fallen was as unforgiving as it was ruthless; there would be 'collateral damage' along the way and young Lachlan Kite would somehow have to get used to it. The price of stopping a terrorist attack in New York had been the death of Billy Peele; the cost of bringing Yuri Aranov to the West so that his grisly biological secrets would not fall into the wrong hands had been the assault and rape of an innocent Russian woman.

Kite's instinct was to go to Martha, but she was out of town with her family. Even if she had been in London, he knew that he would not have been able to confide in her. He would have to live with the secret forever, sleep with the guilt, and hope that Oksana might somehow recover and make a life for herself. He felt powerless to help. Hardly a day had gone by in the many years since when Kite had not been haunted by the punishment meted out to Oksana.

'How awful,' said Cara, putting her hand on Kite's back when he had finished relating the story. 'I'm so sorry.'

'Did you ever find out what happened to her?' Masood asked.

Kite shook his head. 'I tried. For a long time. But it was impossible to get any meaningful information. I assumed – I hoped – that she had left Russia and changed her name. In 2004 somebody from BOX was doing some work in Voronezh. I had him gumshoe around, but nobody knew anything about her.'

'What about Gromik?' Cara asked.

They had reached an avenue lined with plane trees. A pigeon flew low over Kite's head, obliging him to duck. He stopped beside a bench.

'Never saw him again.' He turned to face them. 'Over the years I found out whatever I could. Discovered he'd been recruited into the KGB in '82, spent a year at the Red Banner

Institute in Yurlovo, then went to Dresden where his boss was none other than Vladimir Vladimirovich himself.'

Masood's calm demeanour rarely changed, but for once he looked stunned.

'*Putin?*' he exclaimed.

'The very same.' Cara looked astonished. 'Before our paths crossed in Voronezh, Gromik had been setting honeytraps for businessmen and politicians visiting East Germany, blackmailing them, bankrolling the dregs of the Baader-Meinhof gang. Real charmer. After running things in Voronezh for three years he rejoined Putin in St Petersburg and their old pals act continued. Gromik is what they call a *silovik*, one of dozens of former KGB officers who have formed part of Putin's inner circle for the last twenty years. In a mafia movie he'd be a "made man".'

'Service the queen bee,' said Masood.

'Precisely. Make sure Putin gets a cut of whatever enterprise you're involved with and everybody's happy. Unlike most of the *siloviki*, Gromik stayed in the FSB long after the others had gone on to bigger and better things. Green-lit the Litvinenko poisoning, became the Kremlin's go-to guy for black ops. Effectively ran the JUDAS list for the better part of two decades. Hoped he'd make it to the top but found his route blocked by Makarov.' Alexander Makarov was the serving chief of the FSB, another Putin enabler from the old days. 'Still, don't feel too bad for him. He and his pals have made a fortune through money laundering, smuggling, extortion, stripping Russia to its bones and parking the proceeds offshore.'

'Offshore meaning London?' Cara asked. She had worked at MI5 long enough before joining BOX 88 to know that entire departments were directed at FSB influence operations in the UK, most of them looking at the dirty money washing through British banks.

'Principally London, yes, but the money goes everywhere.'

Masood asked if Cara would pass him his linen jacket so that he could get something from the pocket.

'Sure,' she said, taking it off.

Masood searched one pocket, then another, pulling out a photograph which he passed to Kite.

'Take a look at this, boss.'

Kite studied the picture. It was a recent surveillance photograph of Gromik, apparently taken in high summer. His slicked-back hair was jet black, evidently dyed, and he wore a silver chain around his neck. He was seated on the terrace of a sun-drenched seafront restaurant enjoying a shellfish platter and several bottles of Miraval Rosé. The intervening years had been kind to him: the deals he had cooked up on a nod and a wink from Putin had secured a Rolex Oyster on his wrist as well as the attentions of two bikini-clad, collagen-enhanced Barbie dolls, both of them younger than Cara. As he studied the photo, the rage Kite had felt twenty-seven years earlier was instantly revived.

'Ghost of Christmas past,' he said, looking up at Masood. 'Still looks much the same, give or take the dyed hair and the suntan.'

'Lifestyle choices,' Masood replied.

'Where was this taken?' Kite showed the photograph to Cara. 'Skegness in February?'

'Dubai. Last year, pre-lockdown. Been living there since 2018 under some kind of blind-eye diplomatic arrangement with the Emiratis. They think he's retired from the FSB. I spoke to Mark Sheridan about him last night when Gromik's name cropped up in your report. He says Gromik is still across JUDAS. CIA has him as the brains behind what happened in New Hampshire.'

'Who's Mark Sheridan?' Cara asked.

'SIS Head of Station in UAE, Controller Middle East.' Kite sometimes had to remind himself that Cara was new to BOX 88 and still learning the ropes. 'Coming our way when he retires in a year's time.' He thought of Galvin's name on the JUDAS list but still could not work out why Gromik had waited until now to put it there. 'I didn't know Gromik's move out of Russia was permanent,' he said. Kite looked at the photograph again, thinking of long ago operations in Dubai. 'Must be pushing sixty now.'

'Fifty-seven,' Masood replied. 'According to Sheridan he's now the Kremlin's point man in Dubai. 'Directorate of International Cooperation'. Translation: Putin's eyes and ears in the Gulf, making contacts, crossing appropriate palms with silver, eradicating anyone who gets in their way. Gromik has a teenage son, Mischa, currently studying at UCLA. No wife, a lot of girlfriends.'

'Perhaps this is the right moment to pay him a visit,' Kite suggested. If his own personal safety was to be guaranteed, Gromik had to be removed from the playing field.

'Oooh. Does that mean we're going after him?' Cara rubbed her hands together and puckered her lips. 'I could just do with a holiday in Dubai. I mean, sorry, work trip. Assignment. Operation.'

Something clicked in Kite's mind, the next move in his plan to avenge Palatnik and, finally, Oksana too. Gromik's involvement in the poisoning was too good an opportunity to ignore. Masood saw that he was deep in thought.

'What is it?' he asked.

'Just putting some pieces together.' Kite looked at the photograph one last time. 'Hot in Dubai this time of year. Too hot to operate effectively for any length of time.'

'What are you saying?' Cara asked.

'I'm saying we wait. We plan. We set a trap and we go in September. It's time BOX put a stop to the JUDAS programme once and for all. And it's time that piece of shit got what's coming to him.'

35

Kite called a meeting in the secure speech room in Chelsea early the next day. Rita Ayinde sat to his left, picking at a pain au raisin; Masood and Cara Jannaway were on the right, both armed with plastic bowls of fruit salad from the local Pret a Manger. Facing Kite at the opposite end of the table was Jim Stones, the British Special Forces officer who had been part of the four-man team which had raided Kite's Sussex home earlier in the year in the operation to free Isobel.

'If what I'm proposing succeeds,' Kite told them, 'BOX 88 will undermine Russia's standing in the Middle East for a decade. At the same time, we could see Mikhail Gromik swapping his penthouse on the Palm for a prison cell in Al Awir or – better still – a burial plot in the Kuntsevo. That would certainly be a bonus.'

'What's the op?' Stones asked.

'Ever heard of Mahmoud al-Mabhouh?'

'Rings a bell,' said Rita.

'Rings nothing,' admitted Cara.

'Palestinian terrorist,' Kite told them. 'Sort of person Jeremy Corbyn would invite round to his house for a glass of mint tea and some lentils on the basis he was misunderstood.' The room hummed to the sound of a portable air conditioning unit. 'In 1989, Mabhouh and one of his fellow travellers in Hamas dressed up as Orthodox Jews, kidnapped and murdered two Israeli soldiers, took photographs of their mutilated bodies then buried them in the Negev Desert.'

'Nice,' said Cara.

'Eight years later, Mabhouh moves to Syria and makes contact with the Iranian Revolutionary Guard. Started running long-range missiles into the Gaza Strip. As you can imagine, with a CV like that he had caught the attention of the Mossad. They put him on their equivalent of the JUDAS list, missed him with a drone strike in 2009, decided to finish the job in Dubai a year later.'

'Dubai,' Masood echoed quietly.

'He was going there all the time, using it as a hub to meet contacts, screwing, drinking, the usual. The Mossad obtained details of Mabhouh's hotel and dispatched a twenty-seven-man assassination team to take him out.'

'Christ, was it as many as that?' Masood recalled incredulously, the details of the operation coming back to him.

'Why such a large team?' Cara asked.

Kite shrugged. 'The more, the merrier?' He removed his jacket, draping it over the back of a chair. 'Two of the team accessed Mabhouh's room, injected him with a paralysing agent then suffocated him. Official cause of death was brain haemorrhage, but the UAE authorities quickly became suspicious. They found out Mabhouh was Hamas, realised he'd most likely been assassinated. Unfortunately for the Mossad, it didn't require Hercule Poirot levels of detection to work out whodunnit.'

Rita indicated with a wave of her hand that she had remembered an aspect of the story.

'Wasn't there something about a credit card company owned by someone in the Israeli army?'

'Exactly right,' Kite replied. 'All of them were paying their expenses using a brand of prepaid card which was virtually unknown in Dubai. So when Poirot was walking the cat back, all he needed to do was find out who had used the card in the build-up to Mabhouh's assassination and obtain their phone records. Turned out the Israelis were routing mobile calls through a cut-out in Austria so that they could communicate with one another off-grid. Poirot just had to cross-reference who had been dialling the number in Vienna and join the dots.'

'And something about tennis rackets?' Masood added, screwing up his face as he tried to recall more details of the operation. 'Am I remembering that correctly?'

'You're remembering that correctly, Maz. On the day of the killing, two men were in the hotel lobby dressed for tennis, sitting around waiting for Mabhouh to come back to his room. When Poirot got hold of the CCTV, something didn't look right. The rackets were out of their cases. No tennis player would sit around drinking iced tea indoors without first protecting his racket. Lo and behold, those same two men then got into the lift with Mabhouh and followed him up to his room. Bingo. Now Hercule can identify the assassins. One of them then helpfully came down in the lift still wearing a rubber glove.'

'Sloppy,' said Cara.

'So Hercule has them bang to rights. He calls a press conference.' There was a plate of biscuits in front of Kite, a mixture of Hobnobs and old school Digestives which nobody ever touched. He picked one up and rolled it on the table like a wheel. 'Poirot held up photographs of eleven suspects in the killing, demanding justice. Suffice to say, there were red faces at the Mossad, not to mention rolling heads. So we need to avoid such pitfalls. We need to be lean and we need to be smart.'

'Hang on a minute,' said Cara, all the playfulness in her face suddenly vanished. 'If you're the kind of people who just go around carrying out unsanctioned black ops in foreign countries, then sorry but I'm out. No hard feelings, but it's not what I thought I was getting into.'

'That's not what I'm suggesting,' Kite told her, disappointed that she had rushed to judgement. 'You should already know enough about what we do to realise that we are not unlicensed assassins.'

'Just hear us out,' Rita suggested, catching Cara with a reassuring look. To Kite she said: 'What are you proposing?'

'Yuri Aranov is on the JUDAS list, am I correct?'

'Correct,' said Masood. 'JUDAS 61. Went on the same time as Galvin.'

'So we dangle him.'

'We what now?' Stones reacted as if Kite was being unnecessarily euphemistic. But the others had grasped it. A look of satisfaction came over Azhar Masood. He might have been watching a particularly artful exchange of passes in the Arsenal midfield.

'A trip to Dubai using Aranov as bait,' he explained. 'We're going to go fishing for Mikhail Gromik.'

36

BOX 88 had changed Yuri Aranov's name, of course. The scientist who had crossed into Ukraine in the summer of 1993 was now Professor Alexander Labukas, an identity he had used for the best part of three decades. He lived alone in a semi-detached new-build in Andover, working variously at Porton Down and Manor House with occasional visits to the most secret corners of Westminster whenever Her Majesty's Government required expert advice on the threat from chemical and biological weapons.

The Tuesday roads were quiet and open, nobody going anywhere, the country still working from home. Kite reached the outskirts of Andover by midday and parked a block from Aranov's house. Two boys were kicking a football in the street, one of them pretending to be Harry Kane, the other Marcus Rashford. Across the road a couple were unpacking the boot of a 4x4, a toddler strapped in the back seat staring at an iPad. Kite thought of Ingrid, as he almost always did whenever he saw a child, and wondered if his plan to spend several weeks chasing Gromik in Dubai was just a way of avoiding the crisis in his marriage.

The house was at the end of a long street, as bland and nondescript as every other three-bedroom property on the road, noticeable only for the absence of any stickers or pictures in the front window offering support to Black Lives Matter or proclaiming in rainbows the wonders of the NHS. Kite rang the bell and stepped back from the porch, looking up at the first-floor windows. In the next house he saw a figure drop to the ground, like a child trying to conceal himself in a game of hide and seek. There was the sound of a man's voice calling out, then footsteps and, finally, blurred movement behind panels of frosted glass.

'Peter Lockie Galvin! What a sight for my sore eyes! What are you doing here? Come in!'

To visit Yuri Aranov was to encounter a rare level of domestic chaos: unwashed pots and pans; filthy, torn carpets; a smell of cooked onions and damp clothes absorbed into the walls and furniture. On this occasion Kite was confronted by an odour of faeces and perfumed nappy sacks. He wondered if Aranov's latest girlfriend, Magda, had given birth to a baby about which BOX 88 had not yet been informed.

'Sorry about smell,' said the Russian. 'Anastasia stayed at weekend. She has new baby, baby make a mess, what can I say? How are you, Peter Lockie? How long has it been?'

'A long time, Yuri Alexandrovich.' It was a game they played: if Aranov was going to be incautious about Kite's cover, Kite would be glib in return. 'Congratulations on becoming a grandfather again.'

'Fucking depressing.' Aranov shook his head in mock despair. 'I am past sixty and now I have two of them. Two nails in the four corners of a coffin.'

Kite realised that the smell – the mulchy, composted odour of nappies – would be the same in Ingrid's nursery in Sweden. The thought filled him with an odd sense of nostalgia for something he had not yet known. He took his eyes up to the first floor. 'Who's next door? I saw someone in the window.'

'Romanian family.' Aranov had the émigré's intolerance for foreigners. 'Three children. Dole money benefits. Either they sit in front of TV all day or make noise in garden. Father gone. Mother never home. What do they live on? Food from tins? Pot Noodles?' He broke off to give Kite the once-over.

'Look at you, Peter Lockie. You changed so much! You got old! What happened to your hair?'

'Gee thanks.' Kite was vain enough to be stung by the observation, but he knew that the years were indeed starting to show: his hair was slowly turning grey, the skin around his jaw slackening seemingly with every passing day. It didn't help that Aranov had one of those faces which never seemed to age. 'You look just the same as always, Yuri. Haven't changed a bit.'

'I know,' the Russian replied, as pleased with himself as ever.

From the next house came the sound of a woman shouting at her children in Romanian.

'So what are you doing here, huh?' Aranov asked. 'Why do I suddenly get a visit from the great Mr Galvin? Nothing else going on in your world, you make a tour of old friends?'

'Not a tour,' Kite replied. 'A special trip, just to see you, Yuri. Wanted to talk to you about something.'

Aranov did not appear to be particularly intrigued or flattered by this revelation. Turning around, he led Kite into a messy, open-plan kitchen where the stench of nappies was slightly less overpowering but the smell of onions more concentrated.

'When did I see you last?' he asked, collapsing into what appeared to be a brand-new sofa. Everything around it – the lamps, the bookshelves, the rugs – was on its last legs.

'I think the last time was Skripal,' Kite replied. 'You were understandably concerned.'

Aranov, making himself comfortable in the centre of the sofa, absent-mindedly picked up an empty mug and stared into it, like a seer studying tea leaves. He hadn't yet invited Kite to sit down nor offered him anything to drink. It was his way.

'Can you blame me?' he exclaimed, with sudden exasperation. 'Every day I wear gloves when I open front door. I never drink with strangers. Somebody comes up to me in street, in the park, I walk away. And even though I do this,

318

in May I still catch fucking coronavirus. In bed ten days, feel like death.'

'I'm sorry to hear that,' said Kite. He thought about Palatnik tipping his head back and opening his eyes to administer his own execution. He wondered what medications, if any, Aranov was taking. How might the Russians choose to kill him once they had run him to ground in Dubai? 'But you're better now?' he asked. 'And immune, which is a good thing.'

'Immune, yes. Probably. Better, yes. Definitely. Happier, no. I still have to watch everywhere for FS fucking B.'

'It's hard for you, I know,' Kite acknowledged. 'I get that. But perhaps one of the benefits of the lockdown has been the knowledge that the Kremlin was very unlikely to send one of its errand boys to kill you while we were all sealed in our homes.'

Aranov gave this theory the contempt it perhaps deserved.

'Give me break,' he said. 'Those monsters come any time, any place. Whenever they choose. I am never safe. I live in fear.'

This might have been the moment for Kite to show his hand, but he decided to wait a little longer. It was always worth indulging Aranov with enquiries about his personal life, to give him the opportunity to talk about his problems, his resentments.

'How are things otherwise?' he asked. 'Are you seeing anyone?'

'Things's shit.' The reply was so emphatic Kite almost laughed. 'I had nice girl. Young. Big tits.' To Kite's regret, Aranov cupped his hands in front of his chest. 'Only thirty-six, can you believe it? Polish. Magda. But she leave me. Say she didn't want to catch coronavirus and then I never see her again. Meets somebody else.'

'I'm sorry to hear that.'

'Work so boring during Covid. I do nothing except read Ian Rankin Rebus, play chess on computer, watch pornography. Same as everyone else. I would like to live somewhere beautiful like Edinburgh where this clever Rebus solves his crimes, but apparently weather in Scotland even colder than Andover. Fucking British climate.'

'That's a bit rich, coming from a Russian.'

Kite was paying close attention to the intensity of Aranov's frustration. This was more than just his usual whinge; it sounded like a plea for help.

'The lockdown affected us all,' he conceded, thinking of Edinburgh and that blissful final year in the aftermath of Voronezh when he had lived with Martha in Leith, buying prosciutto and Chianti from Valvona & Crolla, walking up Arthur's Seat, driving west towards Oban and holing up for dirty weekends at a croft on Mull. 'It was especially hard for people on their own.'

'Yes, but you are not on your own, are you, Peter Lockie? You are one of the lucky ones. You told me you got married.'

'That's right.'

'And how is Martha?'

'I didn't marry Martha. You know that.'

'Of course I know that.' A slightly sadistic smile played on Aranov's lips. 'But I want to know how she is. You ever hear from her? Didn't she also get married, but not to you?'

'That's right.' Kite wondered why Aranov was trying to wind him up. 'Several years ago now. Married somebody else. She lives in America.'

'America finished.' Aranov tapped his neck in the Russian way of indicating drunkenness. 'Whole country go crazy, psychotic. Two cults. One the Trump cult, the other the cult of the self-righteous. You want to know the trouble with America? Bad schools. Nobody gets education. Bad schools and now brainwashing through media, no different to the shit Brezhnev used to ram down our throats. America the beautiful. America the brave. Land of opportunity, land of your dreams. So much bullshit. America is land of guns, land of fear, land of hate. Trump pulled back the scab and now we see the wound. We see how stupid they are, how angry. Millions of people supporting this pantomime gangster! Can you believe it?'

'I think perhaps we hear too much about all that,' Kite replied. 'Social media tends to amplify the noise, know what I mean?' He remembered that Yuri, in common with many people who lived on their own, longed for a captive audience on whom he could test his pet political theories. 'Besides,' he said. 'You're here now. You must be glad to be in England, away from all the madness in Washington.'

'Glad to be in England?' Aranov looked at Kite as though he had lost his mind. 'Are you serious? This country worse than America. People here even more stupid than people in Florida.'

'How so?' Kite poured himself a glass of water and took a seat at the kitchen table. It was going to be some time before Aranov was done. The Russian enjoyed nothing more than railing against the two countries which had protected and provided for him for almost a quarter of a century. If it wasn't Trump, it was Bush. If it wasn't Brexit, it was Blair and Iraq.

'How *so*?' he repeated, making it sound as though the answer was as plain to see as the glass of water in Kite's hand. 'This government is the most stupid government in living memory. They could not take a shit without messing up the bathroom. Every day a new idiot comes on the television, on the radio. Tories learn from Trump that governments can lie and that people will not hold them to account. But what they don't have from Trump is the street cunning, the *chutzpah*. They just have their own stupidity. They are weasels. Corrupt men, selling your country down the river.'

'It's your country too, Yuri,' Kite observed, taking a sip of water.

'Well then I am tired of it.'

Here was the opportunity again, the chance to show his hand. This time Kite decided that he would take it, if only to short circuit Aranov's rant about western decline.

'That's not unconnected to the reason I've come to see you today,' he said.

The Russian moved sideways on the sofa and grimaced as though he had sat on something uncomfortable.

'A political reason?' he said.

'In a sense, yes.' Another sip of water. 'We're in the process of resettling several of our most important agents. Offering them the chance of a new life, a new home, a new identity. On a voluntary basis, of course.'

Aranov looked as if he did not quite trust what he was being told.

'Voluntary?' he said. 'Why? Something happen, Peter Lockie? Am I in danger?'

'Possibly.' There was no truth in Kite's response, but his tone suggested that dark forces were gathering and would soon run Yuri Aranov to ground. 'We've been in talks with the government of the United Arab Emirates,' he said. 'How would you feel about moving to Dubai?'

37

The news that Professor Alexander Labukas had disappeared was reported on page four of the *Salisbury Journal*, a weekly newspaper with a print circulation of around 13,000 copies. The 350-word story was filed by local journalist Paul Richardson, acting on a tip-off from his editor. Under the headline: 'PORTON DOWN BOFFIN VANISHES', and a recent, slightly blurred photograph of Aranov, Richardson revealed that Labukas – an 'unmarried father of two' – had failed to return to his three-bedroom semi-detached house in Andover, having last been seen shopping at the market in Salisbury town centre. Labukas, fifty-nine, was described as a 'former Russian national' who had worked at the Ministry of Defence's military research facility at Porton Down. According to Richardson's report, he had accepted a neighbour's invitation to a summer barbecue but failed to attend. When police entered the Labukas property two days later, they discovered that 'the government scientist' had left his laptop and sundry personal effects at home.

Just after ten o'clock on the night of the *Journal*'s publication, the chief executive of the newspaper group received a personal visit at home from Robert Vosse, Cara's former boss at MI5, now working on behalf of BOX 88. Although it was too late to pulp existing copies of the newspaper, Vosse requested that Richardson's report on the Labukas disappearance be removed from the *Journal's* website as a matter of urgency. It was explained that Mr Labukas was a former Russian intelligence source who had been relocated for his own safety. The chief executive was asked to sign the Official Secrets Act and urged to be discreet. Neither the editor of the *Journal* nor Richardson himself were permitted to speak to the media nor to any third-party individuals who showed an interest in the disappearance. A discussion was subsequently held with the digital editor and the paper's managing director, both of whom understood the need for discretion in the wake of the Skripal poisonings.

Back in London, a BOX 88 Turing presented Lachlan Kite with a report showing that, prior to its removal, the Aranov article had been accessed online 436 times, mostly by readers in the Wiltshire area. However, two of the IP addresses were linked to computers belonging to accredited Russian diplomats; a third was traced to Lydia Kaufman, a suspected SVR 'illegal' living in Richmond. Subsequent analysis of Kaufman's communications traffic showed that she had sent two encrypted WhatsApp messages to Russian cell phones within six minutes of reading the Labukas story. In the next two hours, the name 'Alexander Labukas' was detected in nine search engine enquiries originating in Moscow. Kite instructed the Turings to move to the next phase of the operation. Thirty-six hours after the *Journal* had first hit the newsstands, the searchable term 'Alexander Labukas' displayed no results relating to the alleged disappearance, instead leading search engines to a restaurant in Ross-on-Wye.

Kite was not done. A 'D Notice' was circulated to all UK media outlets stating that 'nothing further should be published' in relation to Alexander Labukas, 'a British citizen under the protection of the government whose whereabouts should not under any circumstances be disclosed'. The Notice had the desired effect. The ruling caught the attention of a sharp-eyed journalist at the popular Russian daily *Londonsky Kuryer* who forwarded the D Notice email to a contact at the Russian embassy. By that same evening, FAPSI, the Russian signals intelligence agency headquartered in Moscow, had obtained access to Labukas's banking and medical records, his private email account and mobile phone number. Though Aranov's Android had ceased to function, FAPSI were able to obtain a list of the numbers he had most frequently contacted prior to his relocation. Surveillance taps were placed on several individuals, including his daughters, Masha, resident in Newcastle, and Anastasia, who lived just outside Reading.

It was a short telephone call to Anastasia which sealed Aranov's fate. Using a mobile phone provided by Kite, he called his eldest daughter from Heathrow airport forty-five minutes prior to departing for Dubai. The conversation took place in Russian.

Anastasia: What are you doing at the airport? Are you going away for work?

Labukas: I'm moving from the UK. I had to leave.

Anastasia: You're *what*? *Why?*

Labukas: There's a threat against me. From the past. They need to investigate it.

Anastasia: Investigate what?

Labukas: They killed a man I worked with a long time ago. Before you were born. Before I came to England.

Anastasia: Killed who? How?

Labukas: In America. It doesn't matter. They're taking me to a nice place. You can come and visit.

Anastasia: *Visit*? How, Papa? Where are you going? Why didn't you tell us*?*

Labukas: I wasn't permitted to tell you. It's the place I always talked about going. Beaches. Very liberal, good for the children. You'll like it.

Anastasia: I like Reading! I like visiting you in Andover. I don't want to go to the Middle East. It was *you* that always talked about going there, not us.

Labukas: Please, don't speak to your father in this way. Show some respect.

Anastasia: I'm sorry, Papa. I'm just upset. It's a big surprise. Are you in danger? How will we know how to contact you?

Labukas: They'll find a way. We just have to trust them. MI6 are very clever. I'm not in danger. They look after me very well. They gave me a ticket in Business Class!

Anastasia: You mean they'll look after you the way they looked after Litvinenko? The way they looked after Skripal?

Labukas: This is different. *I* am different. I am not like those other men. Besides, they've learned their lesson.

A transcript of the conversation was circulated to the relevant desks in Moscow. Using a source at Heathrow who regularly provided information relating to passengers transiting through London, the FSB were able to obtain CCTV footage of Aranov making the call. 'Labukas' had been standing between Gates 37 and 38 in Terminal 5. It did not require sophisticated levels of detection to discover that a British Airways flight to Dubai had been scheduled to take off from Gate 38 less than an hour later. The FSB now knew where the target had gone in the Middle East. Furthermore, by securing a copy of the passenger manifest, they were able to obtain the names and passport numbers of the seven male passengers flying to the Emirate in an almost deserted Business Class cabin. Two were government officials from Kenya; three were British citizens under the age of forty. That left two men who might have been Aranov: an Emirati citizen who turned out to be a significant figure in the Abu Dhabi Investment Authority; and Mr Sebastian Glik, a fifty-eight-year-old travelling on a Polish passport.

Now they knew his name.

38

Kite's plan was straightforward: to put Aranov up in a five-star hotel in Jumeirah, to make him think that MI6 needed three weeks to finalise the details of his residency with the UAE authorities, and to use that time to monitor Russian SIGINT and local activity for any indication that Moscow had taken an interest in his arrival. The trail of breadcrumbs had been laid from the streets of Andover to the skyscrapers of Dubai. Thanks to Covid and the heat of late summer, hotels were running at 40 per cent capacity: discovering where 'Sebastian Glik' was staying would have taken even the most sluggish operative at FAPSI no more than a few hours of deskwork. Glik was registered as a guest of one David Higgins, a businessman travelling on an American passport who had taken adjoining rooms at the Faleiro Beach Resort in Marina. 'Higgins' was Jason Franks, ex-Navy Seal and Kite's go-to heavy whenever an operation needed some muscle. Rotating shifts with Jim Stones, Franks would be Aranov's first line of defence against an immediate, pre-emptive Russian attack, sticking with him at all times of the day and night.

Kite's instructions to them were simple: they were never to let Aranov out of their sight. They were to watch him if he swam in the pool at the Faleiro, to sit with him in the bar if he took a drink, to accompany him to whichever of the hotel's three restaurants Aranov fancied to eat in. They were not to leave the Faleiro complex – which shared 800 metres of beach and seven acres of gardens with the Méridien next door – unless Kite gave the go-ahead with a prearranged signal sent *en clair* to Jason's phone. Nor were strangers to approach Aranov without first being cleared. Above all, Kite insisted, Aranov was to be kept away from women.

'Dubai is crawling with Russian hookers,' he told them. 'Any one of them could be FSB with a vial of Novichok in her handbag. She could pick him up in the bar, flirt with him down by the pool, flash him a smile in the spa. Before you know it, Yuri will be drinking what he thinks is a glass of mint tea in her bedroom and then, a few hours later, fighting for his life at Citi Hospital. He'll have plenty of time to enjoy himself once he leaves the hotel. We can control where he goes, who he talks to. But while he's inside the Faleiro, there's no nookie. He'll protest. He'll bitch and whine, but – as Cara would say – them's the rules.'

It was the night before Franks and Stones were due to escort Aranov to Dubai. Kite had called a final meeting at the Chelsea offices so that the team – also comprised of Cara, Masood and Rita – could ask any last-minute questions before going their separate ways.

'Our job in those first three weeks will be to identify who comes to the hotel to take a look at Yuri. Jim and Jason's job is to protect him, but also to make it *look* as though they're protecting him. Moscow will realise pretty quickly that they won't be able to get to Yuri while he's at the Faleiro. Even if they could somehow get around our security, there's too much CCTV, too many tourists, avoidable blowback. So they strategise. It's September. Hotels are cheap because it's 35 degrees in the shade and we're still in the middle of a pandemic. They think: "British intelligence is putting Aranov up in an expensive hotel, but they don't have bottomless money, they won't be able to spare twenty-four-seven security forever." At some point, they'll be expecting Yuri to move. They'll know we most likely have a plan to set him up in a safe house somewhere in the city, once we think the coast is clear. Either that or we're using Dubai as a staging post before setting him up in a third country. For Moscow, it's just a question of finding out where that is.'

'And we let them know where that is – or we don't?' Cara asked.

Kite had been sparing in what he'd told her about the overall plan.

'If it comes to it, yes, we let them know. In time there will be a villa where Yuri will be housed and will present as a softer target. But my strong suspicion is that Gromik will want to take him out at a time and place of his own choosing. He may not trust the villa because of CCTV, just as he won't trust the hotel. But anything is possible with these guys. They're reckless.'

Cara's mouth was pursed, moving this way and that as she pondered the variables.

'What makes you think Gromik will come after him?' Stones asked. 'In fact, what makes you think Moscow will even bite? They could smell a rat, walk away, wait two years to take him out. It's not like they have to rush things.'

'True,' Kite conceded. He was leaning on the table, intermittently chewing on the end of a pencil. 'Within a week of Yuri's arrival, we'll have a pretty good idea of Moscow's level of interest via MOCKINGBIRD.' Everybody in the room knew that MOCKINGBIRD was the high-level BOX 88 source inside the FSB. 'They might never come. Moscow could decide to play a waiting game or baulk at the idea of pissing off the Sheikh. Will Vladimir green-light a JUDAS operation in Dubai? Who knows? This time in a month, we could all be back here in London working on something else. But somehow I doubt Gromik will be able to resist.'

'How so?' Jason asked.

Kite glanced at Rita Ayinde. She knew the answer, even if the others didn't.

'Because we have Peter Galvin,' she said.

39

Of all the places Lachlan Kite had plied his trade in thirty years as an intelligence officer, Dubai was the richest hunting ground. Back in 1993, when he had been busy extracting Aranov from Voronezh, it had been not much more than a glorified fishing village; there were a few air-conditioned office blocks on the banks of the Creek and a lone ex-pat watering hole, The Chicago Beach Hotel, six miles out of town in the area now known as Jumeirah. Back then, Dubai was mostly desert, a sticking plaster of land squeezed between Iran and Saudi Arabia exporting small amounts of oil and natural gas and doing a brisk trade in black market gold. Kite first visited for a few days in 1998, as the finishing touches were being put to that great symbol of turn-of-the-century Dubai, the Burj Al Arab hotel. Built for a billion dollars on an artificial island reclaimed from the sea, the building was immortalised by Federer and Agassi trading volleys on the helipad. By the time Tiger Woods had driven a golf ball from the edge of the swimming pool into the depths of the Arabian Gulf a few years later, the Emirate was up and running.

Dubai was low tax, low crime, low morals. No visa was required at Passport Control and there was no authoritarian interpretation of Islam on display to spoil everyone's fun. The sun shone 350 days of the year, the tourists flocked to the beaches and the world's dirty money was washed on a permanent, two-decade spin-cycle of astonishing growth. The historically Indian area of Deira was absorbed into what rapidly became a 3,000-square-mile international playground for the super-rich, stretching from conservative Sharjah in the north to the vast deepwater port at Jebel Ali in the south. Dubai – its skyscrapers and six-lane freeways, its luxury hotels and multimillion-dollar houses – was built on the backs of migrant workers from Bangladesh, India and Pakistan who were paid in a month what certain locals would drop on a pair of Gucci loafers in an afternoon at the Dubai Mall. The Emirate welcomed everyone: corrupt Iranian bureaucrats, whoring Saudi princes, money-laundering Muscovite gangsters and canny African warlords looking to convert conflict diamonds into real estate. Arms dealers, human traffickers, drug smugglers, exiled politicians and wannabe revolutionaries: they all came to Dubai to trade, to plot, to drink and to screw. Prostitution was practically sewn into the fabric of the community: jaw-dropping girls from Rio, Hanoi, Kiev and Kampala could be found in hotel lobbies, nightclubs and bars, extracting money from six-digit salary executives with the sexual mores characteristic of male expatriates the world over. At the same time, Dubai became a legitimate business hub, a leading global tourist destination and a safe, relatively liberal bolthole in an otherwise unstable and dangerous region.

For the likes of Lachlan Kite, it was a playground for spying, the new Vienna, a Berlin for the age of ISIS and 9/11. Dubai was less than three hours by plane from Tehran and Mumbai, only two from Riyadh and Karachi. At a moment's notice, an Iranian military commander could take a fast boat from Bander Abbas across the Straits of Hormuz to meet a contact in BOX 88. An intelligence officer could drive an hour into the desert to the border town of Al Ain to meet a senior member of the Abu Dhabi royal family. If called upon at the last minute to assist in a BOX 88 operation in the Gulf, Kite could take off from Heathrow after breakfast and be eating dinner in Jumeirah by sunset. Dubai drew tourists and athletes and stars from every continent to a desert city crossroads where Kite and his colleagues could blend in among the tourists and the ex-pats, the Indian merchants and the Iranian entrepreneurs, and spy to their heart's content.

Technology had slightly spoiled the party. By the second decade of the new millennium, passports had gone biometric, CCTV cameras were pervasive, number-plate recognition software tracked the movement of every vehicle in the Emirate and mobile phones were tapped to within an inch of their lives. To be a resident in the UAE was to live with a paradox: Dubai was still as louche as ever, but it had become an Orwellian police state in which any conversation taking place within a metre of an Android or iPhone could be scooped by the SIA, the UAE's signals intelligence agency. Anonymity was near-impossible; to travel to Dubai using multiple identities suicidal. Prior to 2011, Kite and his colleagues at BOX 88 had managed to pass themselves off as – variously – television producers, tourists, real estate developers and oil executives. Those days were long gone, not least because of the fiasco of the Mabhouh assassination. No longer could you arrive in Dubai as one person and attempt to leave as another: facial recognition software would see to it that you were hauled off for interrogation at the airport and very probably sentenced to a ten-year stretch in prison. If it was not quite Big Brother who was watching you, it was certainly the case that Dubai's all-powerful rulers had eyes and ears everywhere.

Pulling off the Gromik sting would require Kite's team to use Moscow Rules. They would work separately in Dubai and never meet face to face unless it was necessary to do so. Anybody who had been to the UAE in the previous ten years – that is Kite and Rita and Stones – would have to use the same identities or risk being arrested when they touched down. For Kite and Stones that meant travelling on their own passports; Rita would have to come in on a Ghanaian legend and make regular flights to Moscow in order to service MOCKINGBIRD. All sensitive messages between the team would be passed *en clair* via cut-outs in London and Oman. Phones were to be burned every forty-eight hours and covers maintained at all times. Kite was an oil executive. Cara was to be Sally Tarshish, a young British woman looking for work in Dubai.

Kite arrived three days after Aranov, armed with a PCR test stating that he was Covid negative, his personal mobile phone and a bottle of Konik's Tail vodka purchased in duty-free. He had used his own passport to enter Dubai three times in the previous six years. Nevertheless as he queued with his fellow passengers in the spotless immigration hall, herded into a snaking queue of masked, jetlagged tourists under the watchful eye of Keira Knightley selling something for Chanel, he could not help worrying that his face would be recognised by the cameras as an entirely different individual altogether – a Mr Stephen Flynn, perhaps, travelling on Irish documentation, whom Kite had impersonated during an operation in 2009. Happily, an official in a pristine white *kandura* asked Kite to remove his mask, quickly stamped his passport and wished him a good morning, there apparently being no record of Flynn's face on the immigration database. Within ten minutes Kite was in the baggage area collecting his luggage from the carousel; it contained nothing more incriminating than a strip of sleeping pills and two novels by Lawrence Osborne. His false passport, the package from London, the weapons: all those would come later when the team was settled. Everything now was about cover behaviour; Kite must give the impression that he was no different to any of the other hundreds of white European men pushing their bags through the Customs channel. He bought a local Etisalat SIM card in the arrivals hall, dutifully downloaded the C19 DXB Covid app and sent a WhatsApp message to Isobel telling her that he had arrived safely in Dubai. To his surprise, she replied immediately, telling him to 'Take care' and including a recent photograph of Ingrid asleep in a sunlit window somewhere in the suburbs of Stockholm. It was a useful, if unexpected enhancement to his legend.

Kite walked out of the terminal, hungry and impatient to begin. As the automatic doors slid shut behind him, he was immediately smacked by the blistering heat, almost laughing at the intensity of it, at the speed with which the air closed in around him and his shirt clung to his back. Ducking into a taxi, his forehead already beaded with sweat, Kite gave directions to his hotel and was soon on the endless, looping freeways of Dubai, the great steel needle of Burj Khalifa glittering in the distance. How strange finally to be free of England, back in his old routine of flights and jet lag, of operational adrenaline and the constant mental checklists of running a team overseas. How was Cara doing? Had Rita made it from Ghana or had there been a problem with her quarantine? Thinking about the different members of the team was like thinking about the followers of some rare religious sect, pilgrims converging from all four points of the compass to gather around a shared target: Gromik.

Kite had booked four nights at an Egyptian-themed Sofitel on the other side of the Creek. He quickly fell asleep, waking several hours later with the strange, disorienting sense that Isobel was in the bathroom brushing her teeth. He turned on the light but it was just the noise of a chambermaid chattering in the corridor. He ordered room service and took a shower, then hooked onto the hotel wi-fi and began the mundane but necessary business of being Lachlan Kite: responding to emails from friends and colleagues; confirming meetings in Dubai for the forthcoming week; searching for restaurant recommendations on Tripadvisor and tips on where to find the best beach. He Facetimed Isobel, hoping to be able to see Ingrid, but she did not pick up. Kite then took his mobile phone and credit cards for a walk, buying a pair of swimming trunks and some goggles in Dubai Mall and enquiring about the possibility of a sunset visit to the observation deck at the top of Burj Khalifa. It was vital that he should establish a random, irreproachable pattern of metadata, show his face in environments thick with CCTV, take Ubers on the Kite account and pay for meals with cards registered in his own name.

To that effect he ordered a rib-eye steak and a glass of red wine in Café Belge, a restaurant on the ground floor of the Ritz-Carlton in the Dubai International Finance Centre, known locally as DIFC. He then returned to his hotel just after ten o'clock. Leaving his phone charging beside the bed, Kite went down to the lobby at eleven, walked three blocks and hailed a cab off the street. At that time of night it was an arrow-straight, half-hour journey to Aranov's hotel along Sheikh Zayed Road, the fourteen-lane superhighway which runs down the spine of the Emirate, from Bur Dubai in the north to the glittering skyscrapers of Marina in the south. Kite gave directions to the Méridien Hotel and paid the driver in cash. A security guard at the entrance aimed a plastic thermometer gun at his wrist, indicated that Kite's temperature was normal and gave him directions to the bar. Beneath the gaze of a dome lens CCTV camera, Kite walked through the lobby and went out into the garden at the back of the hotel. A narrow, winding path led to a small clearing between the beach – where a sound system was pumping out 'Saturday Night Fever' – and a building site enclosed by black wooden panels.

Jim Stones was waiting for him at the base of a palm tree wearing pale brown chinos and a loud Hawaiian shirt.

'What's a nice boy like you doing in a place like this?'

'Bang on time, boss,' Stones replied, glancing at his watch. 'How was your flight?'

'Busier than expected.' Kite turned to check that there was nobody behind him. 'I watched *The Big Sleep* but didn't get any.'

'First class?'

BOX had put Aranov in Business, Stones and Franks in Economy. With an apologetic shrug Kite said: 'Business. For appearances' sake. You know how it is, Jim. I have to live my cover. How's our boy?'

The whitewashed walls of the Faleiro glowed in the floodlights. The two hotels were connected by a network of paths; they shared swimming pools and a spa, bars and several restaurants.

'Mariah Carey would be less demanding. Our boy is a pain in the arse.' Stones looked up at the hotel and gestured in the direction of Aranov's room. 'Sleeps till eleven, misses breakfast, says it's too hot to go outside in the afternoons, too cold in his room because of the air conditioning. Complains about wearing a mask inside the hotel and moans about not being allowed out at night. We've only been here five days. Feels like three weeks. Irony being that he spends most of his time reading Nelson Mandela's autobiography, *Long Walk to Freedom*. I pointed out that Mandela did twenty-seven years in a cell the size of a phone box while Yuri is in a suite costing the British and American taxpayer upwards of five hundred dollars a night, full board, with bath, shower, colour TV and twenty-four-hour broadband. He didn't see the connection.'

Partygoers were singing on the beach, the steady thump of music overlaid by an ecstatic chorus of 'Sweet Caroline'. Kite indicated that they should head deeper into the garden.

'I thought you took him for dinner one night?' he asked. 'Wasn't that a nice change of scene?'

Stones put a hand in his pocket, jangling some loose change.

'Yeah. Date night.' He looked down, scuffing his shoes on the path. 'Jase came too because he'd heard the food was good. Massive restaurant just across the water. Everything done up in black and red lanterns, like the monastery in the Himalayas where Bruce Wayne learns how to be Batman. Girls taking pictures of themselves and putting their food on Instagram. It was so noisy you couldn't hear yourself think.'

'Sounds like most of the restaurants in London,' Kite replied, regretting the remark instantly because it made him sound old.

'Get this. They wanted a hundred and fifty quid for a plate of sushi, another twenty for a bowl of chicken soup. Bill for the three of us with a bottle of Rioja came to three thousand dirhams. Do you remember that trend in house music from about twenty years ago, monks chanting over a drum machine?'

Kite lit a cigarette and said that he did; Martha had often ridiculed Xavier for playing the CDs at parties in the early nineties. He remembered the name of the band: 'Enigma'.

'That was the vibe in the restaurant. This huge Buddha on the wall, big as a house, low lighting so you couldn't see your food. Everyone in black walking around in masks. Like a bad orgy.'

'And our boy complained?'

'Of course he complained. He complains about everything! There weren't any women to talk to, we should have left him on his own, he was a grown-up, nobody was going to harm him, etcetera, etcetera. And of course he wonders what happened to nice Mr Galvin. "Where is Peter Lockie? Why doesn't he contact me? When will he come to Dubai?" On and on he goes. Jase said we should just get him into dead ground somewhere and throw him into a canal.'

'I'm sorry it's been so difficult,' said Kite. 'You getting any time off?'

'Not needed.' Stones indicated that he was perfectly happy. 'It's not that bad, boss. Yuri's a pussycat. I've known worse. Me and Jase very happy here, thank you very much. Sunshine, good food, just a shame your man is such a pain in the arse.'

A young Filipino wearing a Méridien uniform drove past in an electric buggy weighed down with cases of Estrella and Heineken. He was heading in the direction of the beach.

'What about the guest who was looking at him? Inarkiev. Any more on him?'

Within twenty-four hours of Aranov's arrival in Dubai, a reservation had been made at the Faleiro by one Valentin Inarkiev, resident in Dubai, a Russian citizen whom The Cathedral suspected of links to the FSB.

'Pretty sure he was what you said he was,' Stones replied. 'Single man, couldn't have been over thirty. Didn't dress like someone who could afford to stay in this part of town. Packed light, hung around the hotel with nothing much to do. Never saw him talk to anyone, never saw him leave. When Yuri and Jase went swimming in the evening three days ago, Inarkiev the mystery Russian appeared at the pool ten minutes later. Had a quick dip, decided he didn't want to stay in the water, went back to his sunbed. Had a phone with him, took a lot of video, long sweeping panoramic shots of the hotel, the pool.'

'Subtle,' said Kite. It was the first tickle on the line, a little tug in the water. 'Then what?'

'Well then obviously we wanted to take a closer look at him.' Stones trapped a mosquito on the back of his neck, wiping the remains on the sleeve of his Hawaiian shirt. 'Decided to take Yuri for a wander, see if anyone followed. Dubai Mall. I went with Yuri in a cab, Jase waited behind in the lobby, didn't see Inarkiev, wondered if we were making an unnecessary journey. I'd messaged Toby, told him to go to the mall and wait near the entrance to the aquarium. Once we'd put eyes on each other, off he'd go. Me and Yuri drifting around the shops, Toby following, seeing if we had a tail.'

'And did you?' Kite asked.

Stones nodded with a strange solemnity.

'We did. Older couple, late forties. Bloomingdale's bags. There's a branch in the mall but the bags looked used. Bird was quite hot, husband out-of-shape. Fat, badly dressed, didn't buy anything except a latte at Starbucks. According to Toby they tracked Yuri and me for about fifteen minutes, same business with the mobile phones. 'Oooh look, they sell Rolex. Oooh look, there's a giant squid.' Filming all the time, panning left and right, getting footage of Mr Glik and yours truly.'

'But didn't bump you?' Kite asked. It was now more than a nibble; the fish were rising to the surface.

'Not that I was aware of. Closest they came was when we were getting a snack in a cheesecake place on the ground floor. Russians looked at the menu, decided against, that was the last time Toby saw them.'

'And Toby was clean?' Kite asked. 'No tail?'

It was the fear of every surveillance team; that the watchers doing the watching were themselves being watched. Kite knew that Toby Landau, a BOX 88 officer living under natural cover in Dubai, would have called in Rita Ayinde to keep an eye on him. It was how the team had been set up.

'Not that Rita noticed,' Stones replied, confirming that Ayinde had indeed completed her two-week quarantine and was now settled at her apartment in Dubai. 'Followed him around the mall, nothing suspicious, just the two Russians on Yuri and me.'

'With Inarkiev at the hotel,' said Kite. 'Jason confirms that?'

Stones shrugged. He was at the end of what was certain and what was speculation.

'We haven't seen him again.'

'For the last two days?'

'According to Toby, he checked out yesterday.'

The reason was obvious enough. Aranov's presence in Dubai had been confirmed; there had been no need for Inarkiev to waste any more time or money at the Faleiro. It was now just a question of waiting for the FSB to make their move.

40

The young woman stared at the photograph in her crisp new passport, at the false name and the inaccurate birthday, reflecting that she was now almost six months older, a Scorpio, not an Aries, a British citizen called 'Sally Josephine Tarshish' looking for a job in the United Arab Emirates, not 'Cara Mary Jannaway', a former MI5 officer seconded to BOX 88 and taking part in the operation to put Mikhail Gromik behind bars.

Cara had arrived on a steaming Saturday evening. She checked into a Holiday Inn in Shindaga feeling wired and jumpy. The city was not what she had expected. The Dubai of her imagination had been a glass and steel metropolis of sports cars and skyscrapers, catwalk models in miniskirts emerging from canary yellow Lamborghinis, social media influencers and off-season athletes hashtagging the good times in branches of Nobu and Gucci. Yet her hotel turned out to be located in a run-down, low-rise neighbourhood closer in atmosphere to Delhi or Islamabad. The corridors of the hotel smelled of stale tobacco. There was a mock British pub on the ground floor with pictures of Sherlock Holmes and Amy Winehouse on the walls; bored Indian men played pool and watched Twenty20 cricket on beIN Sports. A bangra nightclub across the lobby seemed always to be empty yet kept thumping away until three o'clock in the morning. There was something seedy about the place. The pavements outside the Holiday Inn were scattered with cards advertising the services of prostitutes, and the spa on the top floor seemed only to cater to the needs of men; when Cara had asked the rotund Thai woman behind the counter for a massage she had been turned away, even as a male guest slipped into the waiting room behind her.

For the first two days she had been given nothing to do. The Cathedral had arranged a job interview in Marina with a public relations company, another for a waitressing position at a restaurant in Downtown.

'Just for cover,' Kite had explained. 'To give you a sense of the layout of the city and a purpose while we wait for Gromik. Then on Tuesday you meet Toby Landau at the Starbucks in Trade Centre Second.'

Landau was the BOX 88 wonderboy running, of all things, a fish farm in Jebel Ali, using the job as cover for all manner of nefarious purposes to which Cara was not yet privy. Kite's ruse was to set them up as a couple, though neither party would be expected to do anything other than perhaps hold hands for the benefit of any Russians or CCTV cameras who happened to take an interest in them. Cara had arrived at the branch of Starbucks fifteen minutes early, ordering an English Breakfast tea and sitting at the back just as Kite had instructed, waiting for Toby to turn up and to show an interest in her.

He had been late, but he had also been a pleasant surprise, younger than Cara had expected, tanned and good-looking with a twinkle in his eye that had briefly made her forget their professional obligation to one another. He was wearing a tailored suit which somehow managed to make him look as though he was on his way to an exclusive party, despite the fact that it was not yet eleven o'clock in the morning. Sauntering over with a double espresso and a copy of the *Financial Times*, Landau had settled down close enough to start what appeared to be a spontaneous conversation between strangers. Where are you from? How long are you in Dubai? Can I take your number? Calling herself Sally, explaining that she was in Dubai looking for a job and laughing when Toby had told her that he supplied fresh fish to thirty per cent of the restaurants in the UAE, Cara had agreed to go out on a date with the charming Englishman and watched him leave with a pleasant feeling that her time in the city was going to be far more interesting than she had anticipated.

Then there was more waiting. Another twenty-four hours before the next text came through, a message from Rita, routed via The Cathedral to disguise its origin, purportedly sent by a neighbour in London.

Hi Sally. Sorry for the delay in getting back to you. The package eventually arrived at 315 this afternoon. Nothing broken. Thanks for everything. Bev.

The meaning was simple enough: Rita was confirming Azhar Masood's imminent arrival in Dubai and passing on the number of the room which had been booked at the hotel in Deira.

It was dusk. Cara returned to the Holiday Inn and sliced the Pakistani passport from the lining of her suitcase. Turning to the back page, she added the digits '315' to the phone number of a family member 'to be contacted in the event of emergency' then sealed the passport in an envelope. Leaving her phone in the room so that metadata would not place her near the souk, Cara set out on foot for the Creek, stopping for a glass of mint tea in Al Seef, the development of restaurants and cafés on the southern bank where she had eaten on her first night in Dubai. Families were strolling in the cooler evening air in what she supposed was a local version of the *passeggiatta*; many of the women were veiled, their children laughing and eating ice cream, tourist dhows flashing garish lights on the dark water.

Cara was anxious to get things right: she thought of Stones and Maz, of Rita and Jason, each of them vastly more experienced than she was. She did not want to be the weak link in the chain, to lose the envelope or to take it to the wrong shop in the souk. In her heart, she felt that what the team was doing was reckless: it could lead to Kite's death. He was going up against the man who had most likely put his name on the JUDAS list. They were meant to be luring Mikhail Gromik into a trap, but what if it was the other way around? What if the FSB knew Kite was coming?

Leaving a ten-dirham note for the tea, Cara walked north and found a jetty from which she could make the short crossing to the northern side of the Creek. Young men in worn clothes cast her quick, inquisitive looks as she queued behind them for the boat. They were not lascivious looks; perhaps it was just that it was strange to see a woman travelling alone at night, nervously clutching a handbag. Cara knew that the chances of the bag being snatched were almost non-existent; petty theft was rare in Dubai. Yet as she stepped onto the deck of an ageless, low-slung *abra* she held the bag tight, fearing that it might fall into the water. Settling down on a hard wooden seat, she was soon chugging across the narrow channel in a cloud of exhausted diesel.

It felt like an ancient way of travelling, a throwback to the Dubai of yesteryear, before the bling and the noise, before Burj Al Arab and the luxuries of Marina. The evening wind blew across the deck and light moved in fragments on the surface of the Creek. Cara felt absorbed by the night, anonymous, a western spy wedged between unshaven dock workers and teenagers bent over mobile phones. She was not concerned about being followed; it was impossible to imagine that anyone had taken an interest in her. She would not allow herself to be distracted by the anxiety of operational paranoia. The captain's assistant, a young South Asian man not much older than seventeen or eighteen, walked the perimeter of the deck taking coins from the passengers, inches from the water but oblivious to the risk of slipping in. It cost Cara two dirhams, the equivalent of just forty pence, to cross from Al Seef. Holding the handbag in both hands, she thanked the skipper and stepped onto dry land, walking through a busy outdoor café towards the freeway which ran the length of the Creek on the Deira side. She put on a fresh mask – the last one was soaked in sweat – and hailed a cab, heading south at first, then looping back towards the souk at the next junction. She asked the driver to drop her at the St George Hotel, which Kite had explained was just a few minutes' walk from the shop.

'Closed,' said the driver as he pulled up outside. 'No tourist, no customers.'

Cara saw that the hotel was indeed boarded up, the lights off, a sign on the door in Arabic which she did not understand but assumed was referencing Covid. She reminded herself of her cover, rehearsing the basics like a mantra: *You're here to make a new life for yourself. You're exploring the city. You're going to the souk to buy gifts for your family*. The narrow, dusty streets were still warm from the heat of the afternoon. In the bright light of a tailor's shop a man was working a sewing machine. The window of a travel agent advertised flights to Peshawar and Kabul. There were no women on the streets, only men pushing rattling metal trolleys piled high with nuts and spices, cars driving with their headlights switched off. Wishing that she had a phone with which to orientate herself, Cara was instead pulled this way and that along the narrow, switchback lanes of Al Ras, eventually reaching the entrance to the shop in the bright lights of the gold souk. A bell rang as she opened the door. Cara was immediately caressed by the blissful chill of air conditioning.

'Hello, madam! Hello, yes! Please come in!' The shopkeeper was just as Kite had described, a lean, handsome man of about forty with narrow eyes and a purple-black lump on the side of his neck the size of a thimble. 'Yes, lady,' he continued. 'Can I help you? What do you look for? Where are you from, please?'

There was another customer in the shop, a middle-aged Arab woman who left almost as soon as Cara walked in.

Pieces of gold jewellery were set against white plastic panels under bright lights. There was a strong smell of cinnamon.

'Hello,' she said, approaching the counter with a smile unseen behind her mask. 'I'm from Edinburgh.' It was the first part of a pass phrase, though Cara could already sense that the shopkeeper knew who she was. 'Angus told me to come here.'

'Angus is a good friend,' the shopkeeper replied. 'You have a design you wanted to show me?'

Reaching into her handbag, Cara withdrew the envelope and placed it on the counter. She could feel the weight and outline of the passport against her fingers. A portrait of Sheikh Mohammed bin Rashid Al Maktoum, the ruler of Dubai, stared down at her in apparent disapproval. She then removed a brochure from H. Samuel and spread it out between them.

'One of these,' she said, pointing at a random ring on the page as the shopkeeper slid the envelope beneath the counter. 'Would you have something in that style?'

'I apologise, lady,' he replied, shaking his head with great solemnity. 'We have nothing like this. I am sorry for wasting your time. Perhaps you should try next door.'

41

The man who emerged from the dhow had a heavy beard partly concealed by a sweat-stained face mask. He wore torn denim jeans and a dirty black T-shirt and looked to be in his late thirties. He carried no phone and no means of identification. His only belongings were a cheap wristwatch and a dark canvas bag which never left his side. He slung the bag over his shoulder and walked down a short flight of wooden steps to the concrete pier.

He could see that the van was waiting for him, the back doors open. He felt a wave of relief. If something had gone wrong, if the chain of command had failed, he would have been forced back onto the ship for the return voyage to Karachi. Instead the man helped the crew load boxes into the back of the vehicle, pretending to be just another worker on the busy dock. When it was done, he picked up the bag and sat in the van, waiting for the driver to join him. The oven heat of the cabin quickly enclosed him and he wound down the window. A feeble breeze blew in from the Creek. In the distance he could see the faint outline of the skyscrapers in Downtown, Burj Khalifa piercing the morning smog.

'You're ready?' the driver asked in Urdu. He had a large wart on the side of his neck which stuck out like a thimble.

'As long as you are,' the man replied. They looked towards the small blue Customs hut at the southern end of the pier. 'Everything's OK?'

'All OK,' the driver replied, starting the engine. 'They know we are coming.'

Though he was reassured by this, the man was nevertheless aware that things could still go wrong. If the correct official was not at the Customs post, if a guard searched his bag and found what he was carrying, then he would go to prison and it would be many years before he was released. This was the scale of the risk he was taking.

'Glovebox,' said the driver. 'Take it.'

The man pushed the catch and took out an envelope from which he removed a passport. It was weathered and bent out of shape, the photograph taken in London four weeks earlier. As the van pulled up to the Customs barrier, he handed the passport to the driver, who exchanged a few words in Arabic with a tall guard wearing a high-viz jacket. The guard made a cursory inspection of the passport, looked into the cabin and made eye contact with the man. He did not ask him to remove his face mask. The man took this as a sign that everything was going to be fine. The guard then wished both of them a good day, signalled that the barrier should be raised and waved the vehicle towards the traffic on Baniyas Road.

'What did it cost in the end?' the man asked. His heart had been pounding with nerves, now displaced by a giddy feeling of relief.

'A thousand,' the driver replied, meaning dollars not dirhams. Given what he was carrying, it was a small price to pay for the cooperation of the guard.

Within minutes they were in the souk, stuck behind a line of cars and an old man manoeuvring a wooden cart into a narrow alley. Shoes were collected on the steps of a mosque. A small basket of turmeric had toppled over in the window of a shop. The driver lit a cigarette and smoked as he inched through the traffic.

The entrance to the hotel was hidden in the neon and bustle of the crowded street, but the man recognised the concrete arch with the blue lettering in English and Arabic: Galaxy Premier Hotel.

'Thank you,' he said. 'I'll get out here.'

He picked up the canvas bag from the floor of the van and stepped out onto the street. The driver did not respond. The man walked directly into the lobby of the hotel and approached the reception desk. An elderly Pakistani, crouched over a keyboard beneath a faded black-and-white map of Deira, looked up. At first he seemed startled by the man's appearance, but happily agreed to let him a room for two nights with breakfast included. The man handed over the passport and watched as the elderly Pakistani copied the details onto a form. A vehicle blasted its horn in the street behind him.

'Have you got water in the room?' he asked in Urdu.

'Of course,' the manager replied.

There was a lift to his left. Holding a thick metal key bearing the number 409, the man rode the lift to the fourth floor, emerging into a deserted corridor which smelled of curry powder and disinfectant. Immediately he walked down the switchback stairs to the third floor.

Room 315 was at the end of the corridor. He knocked. Somewhere a dog was barking. The man heard footsteps inside the room and the rattle of a key. Then the door opened.

'What a charming hotel,' he said, walking inside.

'Welcome to the Ritz-Carlton, Maz,' Lachlan Kite replied. 'How was your trip?'

42

An hour later, Kite left Azhar Masood alone in the room with a suitcase of fresh clothes, a razor blade and several credit cards in a snakeskin wallet containing three thousand dirhams in cash.

'No way I'm sleeping here,' Masood had told him, testing the squeaking springs on the hard double bed as a baby screamed in the next room. 'Quick shower, quick shave and I'm off to the Hyatt.'

He had brought a clean identity for Kite: a British passport in the name 'James Justin Harris' with an iPhone and wallet litter to match. The vital object he had couriered from Porton Down was sealed inside a lead-lined box, about the size of a Rubik's cube and packaged in Fortnum and Mason paper. Kite took it out, weighed it and turned it over in his hands. Though he had helped to design the box and had last seen it in the Chelsea offices just two weeks earlier, he was nevertheless unsettled by it. The contents were the fulcrum on which the operation would succeed or fail; Kite was effectively holding the future of BOX 88 in the palm of his hand.

'This ends somebody's career,' he said, placing the box on the bed. 'Ours or Gromik's.'

'Or maybe nothing comes of it,' Masood countered. 'Maybe the Russians don't bite, we get word they're not interested, Gromik is too busy screwing and spending his money to care.'

The room had been cramped and hot, Masood's clothes giving off the funk of long nights at sea in the *dhow*. For a moment nothing was said. Kite tracked the progress of a fly as it buzzed around an air-conditioning unit, eventually settling on the corner of a stained curtain. The noise and chatter of the street was suddenly so loud it was as though the window had been thrown open. Kite unlocked the iPhone and scrolled through the apps. The Cathedral had filled it with messages and photographs tailored to Harris's legend. It was a standard operational tactic, but Kite was well aware that no alias would withstand meaningful scrutiny from the UAE authorities.

'I've got to get this somewhere safe,' he said, resting a hand on the box.

'Toby still taking it?'

Kite nodded.

'He's made contact with Cara? They're up and running?'

'Love's young dream,' Kite replied. He put the box in Masood's canvas bag and looped it over his shoulder as he stood up. 'That was a considerable risk you took, Maz.'

'Worth it if it gives us what we want,' Masood replied. 'Besides, you would have bailed me out of a Dubai prison, right?'

'Eventually.'

It took Kite an hour to reach Jebel Ali, the economic 'Free Zone' where Toby Landau plied his trade at Jambiri, a $60 million, air-conditioned indoor fish farm built on five acres of concrete at the southern tip of the Emirate. The farm was the brainchild of a Danish scientist who had employed the young Englishman for his quick mind and commercial *chutzpah*, oblivious to the fact that he needed professional cover for his primary career as an intelligence officer. Jambiri sold 5,000 tonnes of sea bream, shrimp, kingfish and Atlantic salmon every year. It was a lot of seafood, but Landau had hungry clients across the Gulf. When he wasn't operational in Dubai, he was driving south to Abu Dhabi or north to

Muscat, boarding planes to Riyadh and Jeddah, always with a legitimate reason to be on the move and therefore of negligible interest to the region's security personnel. Kite had met Landau only once before, at a party in London to celebrate the engagement of a colleague at The Cathedral, and had not been involved in his recruitment. The technical side of the Gromik operation was being handled by a small group of Turings in Oman who reported to Landau twice a day. Landau was the cut-out between Kite and The Cathedral. Much of the early workload of the operation had been placed on his shoulders.

'Mr Harris!' he exclaimed, striding towards Kite's taxi as it pulled up in front of Jambiri headquarters in the heat of the midday sun. It had been arranged that Kite would show an interest in expanding the company into China for the benefit of any staff with whom he came into contact inside the building.

'Mr Landau,' he replied, bumping elbows with his host as though they were perfect strangers. 'You're a long way out of town.'

They were at the sea's edge amidst a flat, concrete expanse of pylons and cranes. The only colour in this bleached industrial landscape came from the sides of the ship containers piled high on the quays like giant children's bricks.

'We certainly are,' Landau replied. 'Next stop, Abu Dhabi. Come in out of the sun. They'll take your temperature at the desk then we can talk inside.'

Landau was short and lean but physically strong, with a deep desert tan and hair shaved close to the scalp. Looking at him playing the role of the sharp, thrusting executive, Kite felt an almost paternal sense of pride in his young employee, remembering the early years of his own career and the many parts he had played as a fledgling spy. Like Kite, Landau was a boarding school survivor; unlike Kite, he had skipped university altogether to flourish on his wits and ambition. There was no Martha Raine in his life, in her absence a reputation for womanising.

'Do you live near here?' Kite asked.

'Further north.' Landau pointed along the coast in the general direction of Marina. 'How well do you know Dubai?'

'Not well at all.'

'Well thank you for venturing out all this way.' A security guard in a black face mask aimed a thermometer gun at Kite's wrist and pronounced him safe to proceed. 'Come into the body of the kirk.'

Kite climbed two flights of air-conditioned stairs and was led along a carpeted corridor hung with framed scientific photographs depicting various genres of fish. Landau had a sports jacket draped over his arm and a sweat patch on the back of his white linen shirt. The occupants of several glass-doored offices stared at Kite as he passed.

'It's a relatively quiet time of year for us,' Landau explained, guiding Kite to a small conference room where he was handed a bottle of water by a solicitous Filipino. 'A lot of the restaurants and hotels are still opening up after the summer. Make yourself comfortable.'

Kite put the canvas bag on a vacant chair, waited for the Filipino to leave the room, then removed the box.

'A gift from London,' he said. 'Something from Fortnum's.'

'How very kind.' Landau took the box and placed it on the table in front of them. He had been told never to open it, to place it in the safe at Jambiri as soon as possible and to present it to Cara only when Kite gave the signal. If the operation failed and the team was obliged to return to London, Landau was to lose the box in the ocean. 'I'll open it later.'

Their conversation continued along predictable lines for some time. How was life in the UK now that the lockdown was over? Did Mr Harris think that Sweden had taken the most enlightened approach to the coronavirus pandemic? Were schools now open again or were children continuing to be taught online? Landau informed his guest that at the height of the crisis in Bur Dubai and Deira, trucks had driven past every fifteen minutes ordering citizens by megaphone – in Arabic, English and Filipino – to remain indoors.

'How fascinating,' said Kite, hoping that any eavesdroppers at the SIA had by now lost the will to live. 'We never went quite that far in London.'

In due course Landau indicated that Kite should leave his mobile phone on the desk and follow him out into the corridor.

'Let me give you the grand tour,' he announced loudly for the benefit of any passers-by. 'Follow me through here. I'll show you what Jambiri is all about.'

Landau opened a heavy door and entered a vast, prefabricated warehouse containing dozens of fibreglass tanks. The warehouse was much cooler than the conference room and drenched in noise. Men in shorts and flip-flops moved between the tanks on raised steel walkways; others stood at the base of emptied containers guiding tiny fish into buckets with handheld nets.

'Built by Ernst Stavro Blofeld,' Landau shouted over the sound of a generator. 'All we need is a tank full of piranhas.'

Kite assumed it was his customary joke for visitors and smiled accordingly. They proceeded to a quieter area where Landau had set out two chairs.

'It's so hot in the summer I sometimes work in here, Mr Harris,' he said. He had put on a face mask for the short journey from the conference room and pulled it down below his chin. 'Bit noisy but not as humid. Would you like some more water?'

'No need, thank you,' Kite replied.

He had liked Landau in London and he liked him now. There was a sharp-eyed toughness about him allied to an informal, almost languid nature which put people at ease. He knew him to be a good talker, fast on his feet, proficient for one so young but ready to take on new experiences and responsibilities without getting overwhelmed. In common with the best intelligence officers, Landau was possessed of a superb memory. Nevertheless it was to a piece of paper that he turned as they settled in their seats, retrieving it from the inside pocket of the jacket he had put on against the chill of the air conditioning. There was no change in the rhythm and tenor of their conversation; anyone observing the two men would assume that they were still talking about the possibility of Jambiri expanding into China.

'This is a list of all the accredited diplomats at the Russian embassies in Muscat and Abu Dhabi as well the consulate here in Dubai,' he began, passing the piece of paper to Kite. Though he did not appear nervous, it was obvious that Landau was keen to make a good impression on the boss. Kite suddenly felt old before his time; revered and passing out of fashion. 'Each of them is obliged to carry a national ID card fitted with a radio frequency identification device for passive surveillance by the SIA. Obviously they tend to leave those at home when they're out and about being naughty, but if one of them comes anywhere near Yuri, the Turings in Oman should know about it within minutes. Same applies to the number plates of all diplomatic vehicles registered to Russian consular and embassy staff in the region, the Serbs, the Bulgarians, etcetera, etcetera. The Turings are plugged into local ANPR as well as the tags in all UAE vehicles registered for electronic tollgates. If they get within five hundred metres of Glik, alarm bells will sound. The two bozos I followed around Dubai Mall work here at the consulate in Dubai.'

'And Inarkiev?' Kite asked.

Landau folded up the piece of paper and returned it to the jacket.

'None of us had seen him before. Flew in and flew out. Now back in Moscow. Got to assume he's reporting on Glik. How high up is MOCKINGBIRD?'

'High enough,' Kite replied. Landau knew only that MOCKINGBIRD was a source inside the FSB who was to play a vital role in the plan. 'If the Kremlin bites, we'll know. If they sense a trap, we'll get that too. When's Inarkiev due back?'

Landau shrugged. It was another thing Kite liked about him: when he wasn't certain about something, he didn't waste time speculating; he admitted to the gaps in his knowledge. Cara was possessed of the same quality.

'Maybe he doesn't come back. Maybe they do it locally with Tweedledum and Tweedledee from the mall, or send specialists from Russia.'

'Specialists like Boshirov and Petrov? Lugovoy and Kovtun? Let's hope so. Makes our job a lot easier.'

The suspects in the Skripal and Litvinenko poisonings were generally considered by the intelligence fraternity to be laughably incompetent, despite the relative successes of their operations.

'And Gromik?' he asked.

'Nothing.' A member of staff walked past in a pair of waders, nodding respectfully at both men. Once he was out of earshot, Landau continued. 'Oman has had eyes on his comms for the past week. Nothing unusual, nothing about the Faleiro or Glik. There's a rumour he's got corona and is isolating. May have gone to Europe. Nobody has seen him around town for several days. I'm friends with a guy he plays tennis with but I don't want to push the relationship until it's necessary.'

'There's still plenty of time,' Kite replied. He wondered if Gromik had left Dubai on a passport that BOX 88 knew nothing about. 'And the girl?'

It had been arranged that Landau would find a young Russian woman in Dubai who was amenable to the idea of becoming Aranov's girlfriend. Landau looked momentarily confused. In that slight hesitation, Kite saw that there were complications in the younger man's private life.

'The girl for Yuri,' he explained. 'London said you have somebody suitable?'

'Ah that.' Landau had indeed been thinking about someone else. 'I thought you were talking about Sally Tarshish. We had coffee at Starbucks. I'm taking her for a date on the Creek tonight. Liked her a lot.'

Kite was unexpectedly taken with memories of Oksana Sharikova. That same paternal sense of pride he had felt for Landau was now a protective shield around Cara. For the purposes of the operation it was important that their relationship should look legitimate, but Kite did not want Cara getting hurt.

'I'm very fond of her, too,' he replied. 'It's good that you two got on. Makes things easier. More plausible.'

He wanted to warn Landau with his eyes – *Don't mess her around, this is business, not pleasure* – but knew how easily and how often spies fell into bed with one another. The thrill of the shared secret, the aphrodisiac of playing a role; it was always too hard to resist, particularly overseas so far from the watchful eyes of home. He told himself that Cara was a grown woman, that she was more than capable of looking after herself. If anything, it was Landau who should be wary of losing his heart to her.

'As far as Yuri is concerned, yes, I've got the perfect person,' he said. 'Natalia Kovalenko. Russian, twenty-six. We've worked together before. Cathedral vetted her two years ago for a different job. She's from Buynaksk, visits Dubai on rolling three-month visas, has an MBA but occasionally turns tricks to make ends meet. Mostly trying to find a husband in Dubai and always happy to help me out when I come calling.'

'Buynaksk?' said Kite, struck by a historical coincidence. In 1999, the FSB had planted a bomb in an apartment block in the city, blaming the subsequent explosion on Chechen separatists. Landau saw that Kite had recognised the name.

'Yes. Lost her parents in the '99 attack. They were in the building. Killed instantly. She was eight. Hence her willingness to do anything that will fuck Putin. She's posed as my girl-friend, as a client, a personal assistant. Always reliable, tough, smart.'

Kite did not ask how they had met nor if they had them-selves been romantically involved; he would read the vetting report, trusting that Toby's judgement was sound enough to give Natalia the leading part in the play he had written about Gromik's demise.

'Blonde?' was all that he asked, because blondes were Yuri's type. Rita called them 'blow-job blow-up dolls'. One of the women with whom Aranov had enjoyed a three-year relationship was a wannabe Diana Dors from Gdansk whose husband had walked out on her.

'Looks a bit like an upmarket Madonna,' Landau replied. 'Not as in the mother of our dear Lord Jesus Christ. As in "Material Girl", "Vogue". That Madonna.'

'I see. But not too feisty?' Kite knew that when it came to women, Yuri preferred them passive and biddable, acquiescent to his demands.

'Fantastically feisty, but don't worry. She understands men like him. Can bat her eyelids and play dumb with the best of them. She'll tolerate Yuri's idiosyncrasies if the job requires it. And he'll go for her, no question.'

'She needs to be good enough to get a relationship going. Can't be a one-night stand.'

'Believe me, she's great company. And there's things this woman does in bed which will make Yuri think he's died and gone to heaven. No man walks away from that.'

Kite wanted to say: 'But you did' because it was obvious that Landau had slept with her. He thought of Cara again, worrying about what she might be getting into. He saw so much of his younger self in these quick-tongued, fearless spies; Landau was possessed of the energy and crazy self-belief necessary to thrive at BOX 88. He remembered his own ceaseless yearning for the company of women, the greed of his desire right through from eighteen to his early forties.

'What does she know about what you do?' he asked.

'This,' said Landau, gesturing at the tanks and the metal walkways and the men trudging around the warehouse with their buckets and waders. 'But she's not stupid. She knows I have other irons in other fires. She knows that what I'm asking her to do is political. She also knows that if she's successful she'll make enough money to sit on the beach for five years.'

'We'll need everything looked at again. Her apartment, phone, laptop. Has all that gone to The Cathedral?'

'Of course.' Landau managed to seem slightly offended that

Kite had asked the question. 'Whatever they say to one another, whoever comes near her, wherever she goes, Oman will be on top of it.'

'And you think Yuri will go for her?'

Kite was being uncharacteristically apprehensive partly because Natalia was the only member of the team he had not personally screened, but also because he was all too aware of Aranov's mercurial character.

'Trust me.' Landau produced a wolfish smile. Kite saw how easily he could seduce and entice. There were vast appetites in those eyes of his, greed and charm and cunning. 'She's gorgeous,' he continued. 'He won't be able to believe his luck.'

'Good. We need him to like her or we'll have to come up with another line of attack. They will get to him through her. It's all about Gromik's people believing what's put in front of them.'

'And if they don't?' Landau pulled his mask off entirely and stuffed it in the outside pocket of his jacket. The fabric had left a small ball of black fluff in his beard; it was as though a fly had settled there and suffocated.

'They will,' Kite replied. 'These people are thugs. The girl is the easy way in and the easiest way in is the route they always take. We just have to hope Moscow takes the bait.'

43

In Moscow it was almost as though they had heard what Lachlan Kite had said and were determined to deny him his triumph.

'We don't take a risk of this kind in the United Arab Emirates,' FSB director Alexander Makarov pronounced with a finality which suggested that Yuri Aranov would be left at peace to live out the rest of his days under the Dubai sun. 'Russian investments in the region, Russia's prestige in the Gulf, our relationships not only with the ruling families of Dubai and Abu Dhabi but also with the leaders of Bahrain, Israel and Saudi Arabia – all would be set back by a generation if there was a Novichok liquidation in Dubai. No, we have to let this snake survive.'

Valentin Inarkiev, who had travelled to FSB headquarters to give his report in person to the director, as well as to three members of the Special Technology Centre, remained quiet as General Vladimir Osipov of the Criminalistics Institute suggested that Aranov might be removed without resort to chemical or biological agents. Again Makarov baulked.

'Any type of assassination – by chemical agent, by firearm, by strangulation, by throwing this Aranov off the top of Burj Khalifa – they all achieve the same result. We do not benefit. Russia suffers. It's not like striking at the British or Americans, whose habit is to turn the other cheek. There will be a reaction from the Arabs. It's their culture. We would be dishonouring them. They would be obliged to retaliate with stringent commercial and diplomatic penalties. They have made us welcome in the Emirates, they have allowed Russia to do business, to invest, to assist in improving the security of the region. It would be an insult to Sheikh Khalifa, to the Crown Prince and to Mohammed bin Rashed. They would lose face. And the one thing you cannot allow in this region is for the sheikhs to lose face. The response would be crushing.'

Though Makarov's conjecture seemed somewhat melodramatic to Inarkiev, he continued to keep his counsel, listening respectfully as the director continued.

'That's why I don't share Ivan Ivanovich's theory that Aranov's appearance in Dubai is a trap. Sure, the newspaper article in England was clumsy. Admittedly, Aranov was somehow allowed to telephone his daughter before boarding the plane to Dubai. But these things happen. Surely the British understand that we would never take the risk of assassinating an enemy of the Russian state on Emirati soil? We are not fools.'

And so it was that any prospect of a state-level attack on Yuri Aranov wilted in a stuffy secure speech room at the Lubyanka. Invited to comment, Inarkiev wondered if the surveillance around Yuri Aranov should continue so that the FSB might at least determine whether or not he was staying in Dubai permanently or was instead in the process of being moved to a new location. Makarov thanked him for his contribution and confirmed that Inarkiev should return to Dubai to observe Aranov's movements. Whether or not 'Sebastian Glik' left Dubai or settled at an address in the Emirate, it would nevertheless behove the FSB to keep tabs on him.

Only when Inarkiev and the three men from the Special Technology Centre had left the meeting did Leonid Deviatkin, a young, exceptionally gifted officer from the Seventh Directorate, enter the room. He had been listening to the meeting in his office via a set of headphones. Makarov greeted him with a grunt.

'So that's that,' he mumbled. 'Aranov is not a target.'

'There may be a small problem, sir,' Deviatkin countered.

The director looked up. His doughy face was pale and expressionless.

'A problem? How so?'

Deviatkin made his pitch. He knew that everything would depend on the director's reaction to his proposal.

'As you know, Mikhail Gromik lives in Dubai. Indeed, I believe he flew back there last week after dealing with the fallout from PARASITE.' PARASITE was the Service codename for Alexei Navalny, the political activist whose assassination had been botched by the FSB six weeks earlier. 'As you also know, we recently discovered that Gromik was intimately associated with Yuri Aranov's defection in 1993. If he somehow discovers that Aranov is living on his doorstep, that we knew about this but failed to inform him, there could be consequences at a high level.'

Following a long but not particularly illustrious career, Director Makarov had risen to the top of the intelligence tree thanks to an almost supernatural ability to detect, and thus to avoid, the many traps and pitfalls which had accounted for the demise of dozens of his contemporaries in the large, viciously secretive and entirely corrupt bureaucracy of the FSB. He therefore instantly understood the warning implicit in Deviatkin's remark: Mikhail Gromik was a personal friend of the president. Therefore Gromik must be informed, pandered to and kept fully abreast of the situation. A senior officer should be dispatched from Moscow as a matter of urgency to give him a full and comprehensive briefing.

'Perhaps I should go to Dubai and speak to Gromik personally?' Deviatkin suggested, pouncing on the opportunity. 'We can't send Inarkiev. It needs to be somebody of appropriate rank or there's a risk that Mikhail Dimitrovich's ego will be . . . how can I put this tactfully?'

Makarov nodded his head in wearied understanding,

saying: 'Yes, yes. You are right.' A sip of sparkling water, a glance at Deviatkin and the decision was made. 'Go out there. Tell him that JUDAS 61 has been moved by the British to the United Arab Emirates. Make it very clear that there is no appetite in Moscow for a reprisal attack unless Aranov is relocated to a third-party country.'

'And if Gromik objects?'

Makarov produced a broad, seemingly indifferent shrug.

'Then he will be defying the will of the Russian president. You will make it clear to him that this decision has been taken at the very highest level. You are informing him of operational matters out of courtesy and respect for his long service to our country.'

It was more than Deviatkin could have hoped for. Obtaining a negative Covid test from his doctor, he returned home to pack his bags and boarded an Aeroflot flight to Dubai that same evening.

44

Friday brunch at the Royal Continental Savoy in Jumeirah was the social highlight of the week for Dubai's Russian community, a chance for old friends to meet, for families to spend time together, for oligarchs to show off the width of their wallets and the Melissa Odabash bikini adorning their latest mistress.

Deviatkin knew the hotel well. At least two of his former associates regularly holed up there, sometimes for three or four months at a time, paying around $15,000 per night for a suite. Their bills, which ran into the millions, would often be settled in cash. Typically, wives and children turned up during the school holidays before returning home for the start of a new term; at that point, a girlfriend would move in, making full use of the hotel's spa facilities and the Rolls-Royce shuttle service to the Dubai Mall. In lieu of payment for their time and company, the girls would return to their lover's suite laden with shopping bags from Tiffany and Cartier. Many of the Russian plutocrats who made the Royal Continental their home away from home would insist on round-the-clock security, not because there was any active threat to their safety, but because having a couple of muscled-up former Spetsnaz tailing you at a distance of five metres as you strolled along Jumeirah beach was both a status symbol and a means of projecting power. Deviatkin had a visceral loathing of ostentation and greed, of which there was more in Dubai than almost any place on earth. What he observed in the Russians who frequented the Royal Continental was everything he despised about his country's new elite: the greed, the vulgarity, the posturing. He learned from a friend that staff at the hotel were trained to recognise the difference between a wife, a mistress and a prostitute: the phenomenon was known internally as the 'multiple family scenario'. Mistakes were sometimes made. On one occasion, a chambermaid had mistaken the wife of a Russian tech billionaire for a Ukrainian call girl who regularly breakfasted in his suite, resulting in a divorce settlement estimated to have cost the errant husband upwards of $650 million.

It had been more than a year since Deviatkin and Gromik had last spoken, though the two men knew each other well. Deviatkin had worked under Gromik in the early stages of his career when Mikhail still smelled of patchouli oil and dressed like an extra in *The Sopranos*. That was before the money started rolling in: the shares in an oil concession which had made Gromik an overnight dollar millionaire, a reward from Putin for excising his enemies from the JUDAS list. During all this time, Deviatkin had successfully given the impression that he considered Gromik to be something of a mentor and guiding spirit; for his part, Gromik viewed Deviatkin as one of the brightest and most efficient intelligence officers at the Lubyanka. He had no doubt that his protégé would one day go on to run the FSB.

'You've chosen the perfect place to meet,' he said, surveying the lavish buffet spread before them in the main dining room of the Royal Continental. There was sushi and king crab, foie gras and spit-roasted lamb. Indians attending the brunch could enjoy a range of dishes from the subcontinent; Chinese guests would feel at home with dim sum and the finest roast duck in the Emirate. 'I never know what to eat,' Gromik conceded. 'A man needs a stomach the size of Bahrain to fully enjoy himself.'

Deviatkin laughed appropriately as he helped himself to a

plate of sashimi. Beside him, two striking African girls – neither of them wearing masks – were discussing how much of the limitless champagne to enjoy before heading back to their rooms for a massage. Though it was only one o'clock in the afternoon, both were wearing high heels and designer dresses.

'So we eat,' said Gromik, heading for a table on the terrace with a view over the gardens. 'We eat and then we talk.'

Families flanked them: to the left, a group of solemn Chinese, their children engrossed in tablets; to the right, four generations of impeccably dressed Pakistanis eating in near-absolute silence. The patriarch was a fat thug with slicked-back hair whose party trick was to verbally abuse the inexperienced Filipino waiters for failing to attend to his every need. One poor boy was almost in tears, doubtless fearing for his job as he raced off to fetch a correctly chilled bottle of Chablis or room-temperature San Pellegrino. Gromik did not appear to notice what was happening: doubtless he was inured to the casual cruelties of Dubai's super-rich.

Much later, after several plates of food and a good deal of vodka, the two men took a walk on the beach. Deviatkin decided that this was the opportune moment to broach the subject of Yuri Aranov's arrival in Dubai; in doing so, he felt a little like a cat bringing a dead mouse to its master in search of approbation. The revelation certainly shook Gromik from a state of post-prandial stupor into one of near disbelief.

'How long has he been here?' he asked, astonished to discover that JUDAS 61 was secreted in a hotel not two miles from where they were standing.

'Less than two weeks,' Deviatkin replied, preparing to depart from his brief. 'Director Makarov considers that this is too good an opportunity to ignore, particularly in light of the failure of the PARASITE operation.' Gromik had been only tangentially involved in the Navalny fiasco; indeed, his absence from the planning stages was considered inside the Kremlin to be one of the principal reasons why the operation had failed. By mentioning it, Deviatkin was playing on

Gromik's considerable vanity. 'Both the director and the president are anxious that the Service restore some of its prestige. They've asked if you would be prepared to coordinate a rapid strike on Aranov from your base here in Dubai. I would act as liaison. Anything you need goes through me. That way neither party is compromised. As is always the case, of course, the president and Director Makarov can indicate – and if necessary prove – no active knowledge of the operation.'

It had become an uncharacteristically cloudy afternoon in Jumeirah. Both men were wearing long trousers and polo shirts, the uniform of male guests at the Royal Continental brunch. Gromik's designer sunglasses were pushed up over his head. The rush and draw of breaking waves was like the sound of his mind as it worked over the implications of what Deviatkin was proposing.

'What manner of attack?' he asked.

A wince and a sharp exhalation of breath from Deviatkin, who declared that a chemical or biological operation in the UAE was out of the question.

'It would have devastating consequences for Russia's standing in the Middle East. Instead Director Makarov asks that we do this in what you might call the American way.' A man walking barefoot in denim jeans and a T-shirt passed them on the sand and they were briefly silent. When he had passed, Deviatkin said: 'Low risk, maximum effectiveness.'

'With locals?' Gromik asked.

'Too risky for you.' Deviatkin wanted to give the impression that Gromik was the object of veneration at the Lubyanka and that his security was of paramount importance to FSB senior command. 'I will supply the men, arrange cover identities, fly them in, fly them out. We would need no more than two for the job. You will coordinate surveillance using local networks. All I need from you is a time and a place and a way for my men to get to Glik. Dubai is your town. I figure you can work this out better than I can.'

'You think it can be done, given the security arrangements at the Faleiro?'

'Undoubtedly. The British can't keep him there indefinitely. Sooner or later he'll be moved to a secure address and the muscle around him will evaporate. There'll be cameras at the residence, no doubt alarms and perhaps a guard monitoring the building. But with enough understanding of his routines, it should be, well, extraordinarily easy to remove him.'

Gromik gave no indication that he disagreed with his younger colleague's assessment. He wanted immediately to engage with the specifics of the operation.

'I'll need Glik's phone,' he said. 'That's vital. Also the names of everybody with whom he comes into contact.'

'It goes without saying, Mikhail Dimitrovich.' Feeling the sudden warmth of the sun as a bank of clouds dispersed above them, Deviatkin knew with a feeling of deep satisfaction that Gromik had been hooked. 'If you are happy to proceed, I suggest we work closely together and spend the rest of today establishing communication protocols, strategies and so forth.'

'I have all the time in the world.'

They had started to walk back in the direction of the hotel. Deviatkin touched Gromik's back, causing him to come to a halt.

'There is just one other piece of business.'

Gromik understood from the tone of Deviatkin's voice that whatever he was about to be told was highly sensitive.

'Go on,' he said.

'In order for me to proceed with the operation against JUDAS 61, it was necessary to familiarise myself with the details of Yuri Aranov's defection. Until I read the files, I was not familiar with the name Peter Galvin. You may know him as JUDAS 62.'

The name detonated something inside Gromik. He looked out across the water but said nothing.

'Why is Galvin on the JUDAS list?' Deviatkin asked, feeling as though he was pushing his luck. 'He isn't Russian. Why target a British intelligence officer?'

'I didn't put him there,' Gromik replied tersely. 'Interest in Aranov's defection was only revived in the last year. I assumed the director wanted to make a point to colleagues as well as to MI6.'

'A point?'

'That western spies are no longer safe from reprisals. If they protect Russian traitors, we will target them. Isn't that it?'

'Perhaps,' Deviatkin replied evenly. He knew that in order to protect his career, Gromik had kept his role in the Aranov defection a secret; that his involvement had only recently come to light was plainly a source of embarrassment to him. Indeed, killing Sebastian Glik might go some way towards restoring the damage to his reputation.

'Did you ever find out Galvin's real name?' Deviatkin asked.

There was a moment of silence. A man ran past chasing a giggling toddler as a seagull banked in the sky.

'For a long time Galvin was a ghost,' Gromik began, his words so faint they were almost carried off on the wind. 'He was never identified. Never seen again.'

'You never got a name?'

'Never tried.'

It sounded like a lie. Surely Gromik would have wanted to know the identity of the young British spy who had humiliated him all those years ago? Perhaps he had wanted to erase the experience not only from the Service's files, but also from his own memory. Yet to pursue Galvin would have been to draw attention to his own failures and inadequacies. Best to bury the story.

'Whoever he was, he's probably retired by now,' Deviatkin suggested.

'Retired or dead,' Gromik added.

'He had a girlfriend who visited him in Voronezh, am I correct?'

'Martha, yes.' Gromik's answer was instant. 'I forget her surname. Raymond? Raven? Rain? Again, I don't know what became of her.'

Deviatkin could sense his craving for revenge, the hope

that he might at last extinguish the humiliation of that distant summer morning twenty-seven years earlier. But how to do that when Gromik knew nothing of Galvin's whereabouts and had lost all trace of Martha?

'So perhaps after the Aranov operation we can make efforts to find her,' he suggested.

Gromik turned to him. There was the flicker of a smile on his face as he said: 'I would enjoy that very much.'

45

Five hours later, having established with Gromik the lines of communication with which they would run the attack on Yuri Aranov, Leonid Deviatkin returned to the Mandarin Oriental hotel, wrote up his account of the meeting, used a clean phone to call the secure number in New York and gave the details of his return flight to Sheremetyevo. At the same time, he enquired if the Hard Rock Cafe concession in Terminal Three would be open at three o'clock in the morning. The woman who took the call had an American accent and assured him that the restaurant was open twenty-four hours, despite recent restrictions imposed by Covid. The next day, having attended to other FSB-related business in Dubai, including a four-hour meeting at the consulate in Umm Al Sheif, Deviatkin set out for the airport to catch an Emirates flight to Domodedovo scheduled to depart shortly after five o'clock in the morning.

Having cleared security, he purchased a bottle of Lagavulin in duty-free as well as a scented candle from Jo Malone for his wife, who had developed a fondness for the brand after visiting the United Kingdom as a student. Just before 3 a.m., Deviatkin entered the branch of the Hard Rock Cafe, dutifully cleansed his hands using a bottle of sanitiser proffered by the maître d', and was seated in a four-person booth next to a guitar which had once belonged to Jesse Carmichael. Deviatkin detested the music of Maroon 5. His nine-year-old daughter, on the other hand, loved them. He duly sent her a photograph of the instrument as well as a picture of a pair of silver lamé bootleg trousers, secured behind glass, which – according to a sign inside the case – had been donated to the Hard Rock franchise by Shakira in return for a donation to her charitable foundation.

At two minutes past three o'clock a middle-aged African woman, magnificently attired in a turquoise Ghanaian *kaba*, entered the restaurant. She was carrying several bags of duty-free and wheeling a carry-on suitcase. Spotting Deviatkin, she asked to be seated at a table adjacent to his booth, placing the larger of the three carrier bags on the seat beside her. The restaurant was very noisy and surprisingly busy given the earliness of the hour. A Dire Straits concert from 1985 was playing on a flat-screen television and there were constant interruptions from public service announcements detailing the imminent departures of flights to the four corners of the earth. Deviatkin ordered nachos and a glass of red wine, his heart rate pounding as he extracted the copy of *The Economist* from his briefcase and set it down on the table in front of him.

Twenty-five minutes later, his belly full, his bill settled and his adrenaline tempered by the wine, the Russian rose from his seat. The middle-aged woman in the turquoise *kaba* had her mouth full, but managed to swallow what she was eating as she gestured towards Deviatkin's table.

'Have you finished reading that?' she asked in a pronounced Ghanaian accent. She was pointing at the copy of *The Economist*.

'What? This?' Deviatkin picked up the magazine and passed it to her. 'Please. Be my guest.'

'You are very kind.' The woman produced an engaging smile and dabbed at the corners of her mouth. 'I left my book in my suitcase. I will go to the shop after this to buy a new one.'

With these few words, their brief exchange ended. Leonid

371

Deviatkin made his way to the departure gate for his early morning flight to Moscow. Rita Ayinde flicked through the pages of the magazine, saw that the agent known to BOX 88 as MOCKINGBIRD had secured an envelope midway through the Business section, and turned to the back page. She then pretended to read an obituary of Ruth Bader Ginsburg as her own heartrate returned to normal.

Within an hour Rita was on her way to Oman, within six she was in Muscat with the Turings, sending Kite the news by encrypted message:

> Hi. So the Lanes aren't going to make an offer on the house. Too risky in this climate. But Lee has spoken to the Lanes' son directly – he is very interested and keen to move quickly. He also has no idea where to find Peter or his girlfriend. Let's discuss with Lee how best to proceed. Sounds promising. Sis x

46

Within two hours of receiving Rita's message, Kite was back at the Méridien.

Employing the same route that he had taken for the meeting with Stones, he joined the connecting path between the two hotels and was soon in the lobby of the Faleiro making his way to a bank of lifts in the north corner. Wanting to leave a productive trail of metadata for Dubai State Security, Kite had on this occasion brought his personal phone; when the operation was over, it was important that the elusive Lachlan Kite should be seen to have made at least one visit to Yuri Aranov during his time in Dubai.

Jason and Stones were waiting for him in Jason's room dressed identically in shorts and white T-shirts. It was as though they had plans to go downstairs immediately afterwards for several sets of tennis. Kite left his phone in the bathroom and joined the two men on the balcony. An alarm sounded on a crane two hundred metres to the west. Far below children were splashing around in the Faleiro pool.

'So what's the news?' Franks asked.

'Gromik is buying in.'

The two Closers looked at one another.

'So we're leaving?' Stones had grown so accustomed to his incarceration that he looked almost crestfallen at the prospect of three weeks of luxury living coming to an end. 'Yuri moves into the villa and goes solo?'

'Soon. Depends how tonight goes.'

'Tonight is the girl?' Franks asked.

'Tonight is the girl.' Kite looked out at the ocean. 'But it's a dangerous moment. Gromik knows that Aranov is staying here. Once you two have left his side, it's going to be open season. We'll be reliant on MOCKINGBIRD warning us of any imminent attack.'

'How do you think Gromik will want to do it?'

'Novichok?' Stones suggested.

Kite shook his head. 'Off the table. The hit will be old school. Guns and ammo, or Yuri gets pushed off a balcony. Gromik has a yacht, maybe he tries to take him offshore and do it there. Who knows? Your job is to make it look as though you've skipped town. Then you sit on Yuri until Gromik makes his move. The Turings are across all the information MOCKINGBIRD is feeding into Oman. Toby has a network of Falcons out here who are watching the couple from Dubai Mall as well as keeping an eye on Comrade Inarkiev.'

'He's back in Dubai?' Franks asked.

'Staying next door at the Méridien.' Kite had received a follow-up message from Rita with details of Inarkiev's recent movements. 'He's orchestrating Gromik's response.'

'Is that secure?' Stones looked concerned.

'If it wasn't, they wouldn't be risking it. FSB works on the same silo system as BOX. MOCKINGBIRD has operational control from Moscow with Gromik running things on the understanding that everything has been cleared by their superiors.'

'And if Gromik happens to pay Makarov a visit, or vice versa, and finds out that MOCKINGBIRD is taking them for a ride, what then?'

Kite felt that he did not have to answer that question. The implication was obvious. Deviatkin would be tried as a western spy and executed.

'It won't happen. Gromik is as worried about DSS technical

surveillance as we are. He doesn't want to be calling up the director of the FSB to discuss the imminent assassination of JUDAS 61. All the way through his career – Litvinenko, Skripal, Palatnik – Gromik has made a point of staying in the background, sending others into the fight on his behalf. Lugovoy and Kovtun were his creatures. He was always careful to keep his fingerprints off the paperwork. It'll be the same with Yuri. MOCKINGBIRD will send two men to Dubai to take him out. Inarkiev will assist them and Gromik will take the credit.'

'And you know how to prevent that?'

Franks shot Stones a look. Neither of them had been made privy to the full details of Kite's plan.

'I know how to prevent that,' Kite replied.

47

It was a short walk to Aranov's suite. Kite saw the shadow of the Russian's face pass across the eyeglass and heard the surprise in his voice as he saw who had come to visit.

'Peter Lockie Galvin!' he exclaimed, opening the door. Under normal circumstances the two men might have embraced, but Aranov was a cautious man and stepped back because of Covid. 'At long last you come to visit me. I've been here so long I almost turn into Arab.'

'Good to see you, Sebastian.' Kite closed the door behind him. 'Sorry it's taken me so long to get here.'

'No problem. You are busy man in England.'

Over the course of the previous three weeks, Aranov's living space had been transformed into an Aladdin's cave of books, magazines, DVDs and wilting flowers. His clothes were strewn across every available surface. Two trays of congealed room service blocked the short passage between the door and the master bedroom.

'I bet you're popular with the chambermaids,' said Kite, switching on the television and opening the windows so that the same din from the construction project filled the room. 'Looks like you've made yourself at home.'

He was astonished by the clutter Aranov had managed to amass during his stay. Struggling to identify a space where he might sit down, Kite eventually pulled a chair inside from the balcony and sat by the open window. A wall of heat soaked him in sweat.

'Where have you been?' Aranov demanded, sitting on the edge of his vast double bed. 'Almost a month I'm waiting in this fucking hotel with no word from you.'

'I've been in London,' Kite told him. 'Flew in late last night. I'm sorry you've not been happy here. Hopefully things are about to change.'

Aranov did not appear to be listening because he immediately embarked on a rant about his imprisonment at the Faleiro.

'What has been the point in me being here so long?' he demanded. 'I only leave the hotel once for a dinner with your bodyguards. I can't walk the streets on my own. I can't meet the women you promised me. I don't even get to take a taxi to fucking Dubai Mall. Most times of the day it's too hot to walk in the garden but too cold to be inside because hotel manager makes air conditioning like fucking fridge. I never thought I would say this, Peter Lockie, but I miss the shitty weather in England. At least I had friends there. At least I was a free man.'

'As I said,' Kite responded patiently, 'all this may be about to change.'

Again Aranov failed to listen. Isobel had a phrase for such people: 'Always on transmit, never receive.'

'There is no threat to me in Dubai,' he continued, 'so why do you give me three weeks of round-the-clock security, no space to breathe?'

Kite tried to cut him off. 'I explained this,' he said. 'Before you left . . .'

'Yes, yes. MI6 protocols.'

'We needed to find you somewhere permanent to live. We needed to be certain that your arrival in the UAE hadn't been noticed by the wrong sort of people. I didn't want you being placed in any danger, Yuri.'

'Who is going to place me in danger?' Aranov picked up a knife from yet another tray of half-finished room service and waved it in Kite's face. 'I come on new identity, using new passport. Sebastian Glik. Maybe people know I have left England, but I could be in a thousand places, a hundred cities. Yuri Aranov has disappeared.'

'That's right.' Kite wiped the sweat from his face. 'But we needed to watch the ether, listen to Russian conversations, wait to hear back from our sources in Moscow.' It occurred to him that he ought to feel more shame at lying so brazenly. 'You know the drill. And you knew the risks, however small they may have been. My absolute number one priority has always been to protect you.'

With that he walked out onto the balcony and looked down at the swimming pool. A lone bather, braving thirty-five degrees of mid-afternoon sunshine, dived in wearing goggles and a white cap. On Kite's first day at the Sofitel a child had burned the soles of her feet on the white hot tiles by the pool, screaming so loudly and for so long that a small crowd had gathered to watch the incident unfold.

'Why can't we go out? Just the two of us?' Aranov's voice was a low-frequency whine. 'Your men can keep an eye on things, make sure we are safe. I have eaten every meal on the menu in this fucking place, read every book you give me, watch every show on TV. I want to start this new life I have been promised. I want to see my daughters, my grand-children.' A sudden pause, then the coup de grâce: 'I want to fuck.'

'All this can happen, Yuri.'

At last Aranov heard what Kite had said and understood that there was light at the end of the tunnel.

'You are serious?' he asked. His despondent, cantankerous mood instantly switched to one of near-euphoria. 'I can leave hotel? I can meet women at night?'

'Better than that,' Kite replied. 'We've found you a nice villa in a quiet suburb not far from here. Umm Suqeim. You can move in over the next few days. I thought you might like to go out and celebrate?'

'With you, Peter Lockie?' Aranov sprung off the bed. 'I

would love this! I buy you dinner! I buy you all the food and drinks you want!'

Kite had arrived at the edge of his lies; he could not be seen with Aranov in public without Gromik realising that Peter Galvin was in Dubai.

'Unfortunately I can't do tonight,' he said, turning around as the din from the construction site increased in intensity. Wherever you went in Dubai there was the same incessant noise of vast machines moving sand and slamming concrete. 'David can take you to the Royal Continental at Jumeirah. There's a restaurant where you can eat dinner alone, a bar on the roof where he can leave you to your own devices. Lots of girls to look at, lots of new friends to be made. You can go together so that you have company or you can be alone. It's safe now, so whatever you prefer.'

'Alone!' Aranov replied without hesitation. 'You think I want to spend another night in the company of your soldiers?' It was the response Kite had anticipated. 'No, if I can't be with you, Peter Lockie, then I want to be solo. Can I have a telephone finally, call my daughters?'

'I'm afraid that's taking things too far. We're in the process of providing your family with a secure number which you can use to reach them. They know you're here, they know you're safe.' This much at least was true. 'London is working on it, but it'll take a few more days. I can certainly give you a local mobile which you can use to contact us, on the strict understanding that you don't try to call anyone in the UK or speak about your situation. That happens and we take you back to Andover.'

'Of course.' In his excitement, Aranov was prepared to consent to any small restriction. 'I don't need to speak to anyone. I just want to be out in Dubai, to feel free.'

'And free you will be. You've put up with a lot over the past few weeks. But now it's all over. The world can start to revolve again. Dubai is your oyster, Yuri.'

48

Afterwards it was reported by the Turings in Oman that Yuri Aranov's departure from the Faleiro Hotel caused no fewer than four Russian intelligence officers to drop what they were doing and to trail Sebastian Glik's taxi as it sped along Sheikh Zayed Road. A car registered to the Russian embassy in Muscat passed through three electronic tollgates en route to the Royal Continental Savoy. Valentin Inarkiev followed in an Uber accompanied by an unidentified female who had materialised at the Méridien. Jana Shvets, the woman who had been spotted tailing Aranov at the Dubai Mall, took a taxi to the Royal Continental and managed to get a last-minute reservation at Goya, the exclusive – and immensely expensive – Spanish restaurant where Glik was booked in for dinner. It had taken less than forty-eight hours, but Gromik already had tactical control of a team of FSB and SVR personnel, each of them with instructions to report back on what Glik ate and drank, whom he spoke to, where he went after dinner and what his tastes were in women.

Meanwhile Aranov was in seventh heaven. Finally free of the constraints of the Faleiro he was a lone wolf in a new city at liberty to explore and to enjoy. Suddenly the Dubai about which he had heard so much – the slick, top-tier metropolis, the Shangri-La of sports cars and Salt Bae, of nightclubs thronging with beautiful women – was spread before him like the glittering horizon. Having finished his meal, he walked through the lobby of the Royal Continental, delighting in scents of sandalwood and eau de cologne before enjoying a Romeo y Julieta cigar and a balloon of Hine in a smoking room overlooking the gardens. Later he strolled down to the beach and even took his shoes and socks off so that he might enjoy the feeling of the warm sand between his toes. Looking up at the night sky as he drew on the last of the cigar, Aranov felt an intense sense of satisfaction, fortified by a Negroni and the two large glasses of Ribera del Duero he had enjoyed at dinner.

A striking Arab woman, no older than thirty, passed him on the beach. She was talking hands free on a phone. Aranov craved female company and remembered a bar Jim Stones had spoken enthusiastically about on the eighth floor of the hotel. Having briefly sat on a lounger so that he might dust off the soles of his feet and put his shoes and socks back on, the Russian made his way back to the lobby and asked a member of staff to direct him to the bar. Within moments he was entering a lift which would take him to the roof.

Just as the doors were shutting a young, smartly dressed Englishman called out: 'Can you hold that please?' and rushed towards him. Aranov pressed a button so that the lift doors remained open. The young man walked in, thanking him effusively. He was accompanied by two women, both in their twenties: one almost certainly British with an hourglass figure and shoulder-length chestnut hair; the other a tall, extraordinarily beautiful blonde in a strapless green dress who – despite her mouth being covered by a face mask – gave him a look of such yearning and intimacy that Aranov immediately understood she was for sale.

'Saved our bacon,' said the Englishman. He was tanned and well-dressed with close-cropped hair. 'Lifts here always take ages. The bar gets so busy this time of night.'

'It is no problem,' Aranov replied.

'You're Russian?' the shorter girl asked. He had been right. Her accent was British.

'*Da*,' Aranov replied, using his native tongue. The lift had almost arrived at the eighth floor. 'How could you tell?'

'*Ya tozhe Russkaya*,' said the blonde, blinking at him provocatively. *I am Russian too.*

'You are?' Aranov felt his chest contract. 'Where from?'

'Dagestan,' she replied.

The lift doors opened onto a scene of some chaos. Half a dozen guests were gathered around a reception desk, behind which a masked hostess was consulting an iPad in an effort to find them a table. A bouncer, standing close to the lift, asked Aranov to step to one side and to wait his turn. Meanwhile the hostess informed the group in front of him that they would have to wait until a table became available. Reluctantly the guests stepped aside, muttering about going to the Four Seasons. It was Aranov's turn to try his luck.

'I'd like to have a drink,' he announced.

The hostess looked him up and down.

'Do you have a reservation, sir?'

Stones had not said anything about booking a table. Through a narrow window above the reception desk, Aranov could see waiters carrying trays of cocktails across a crowded, moonlit terrace. A group of women were drinking glasses of champagne at a circular bar overlooking the gardens. He wanted to be among them, enjoying the release and excitement of a night out, yet it looked as though a simple organisational oversight was going to deny him.

'I don't,' he said, feeling old and out of touch. 'Is it necessary?'

The hostess said that unfortunately it was absolutely necessary; numbers inside the bar were being restricted because of Covid and the terrace was already full.

'We have a reservation.'

This from the Englishman, speaking over Aranov's shoulder. At first Aranov was annoyed by this and about to tell the young man to wait his turn when it suddenly became clear that he was being invited to join them.

'You're on your own, right?' he asked, flashing Aranov a

friendly smile. 'You're welcome to sit with us. Shame to come all this way and not get in.'

The hostess, who had recognised the man and greeted him with a fond kiss, seemed to think that this was an excellent solution to the problem and encouraged Aranov to accept the man's invitation. The masked blonde and the British girl also seemed happy with the outcome. Aranov was delighted.

'Are you sure?' he said. 'That's very kind of you. Very thoughtful. Let me buy you all a drink. It is the least I can do.'

A waitress appeared and led the group to a table overlooking the gardens. As Aranov waited for the ladies to sit down, he again thanked the man for his kindness and hospitality.

'What's your name?' he asked. 'I'm Sebastian. Sebastian Glik.'

'Toby Landau,' the man replied, vigorously shaking Aranov's hand. 'This is my girlfriend, Sally Tarshish, and our good friend, Natalia. Are you here in Dubai for business or pleasure?'

49

Cara admired how calmly Toby controlled the situation, timing their approach to perfection, making easy small talk with Aranov in the lift, then saving the day with the hostess. Being with Toby, playing the part of his new girlfriend, was much easier than she had anticipated, not least because in the short time they had known one another they had forged a genuine connection. Was that something Kite had anticipated? Did he understand both of them so well that he had known they would be attracted to one another? From the first moment of their supposedly accidental meeting at the coffee shop, something had clicked. When Toby had taken Cara on the Creek for a cheesy romantic cruise, originally intended purely for purposes of backstory and metadata, they had fallen for one another in a way that felt completely sincere. They didn't have to pretend to be comfortable in one another's company; the chemistry between them was as intense as anything Cara had ever felt, and all the more exhilarating for being forged in an atmosphere of secrecy.

Coupling up had been one of Kite's first ideas, a way for both of them plausibly to be able to work together in Dubai without rousing local or Russian suspicion. Cara had to keep reminding herself that the relationship was a mirage, an operational necessity, not anything real or meaningful, even as she kept going back to Toby's apartment and sharing his bed every night. She liked the way he talked candidly about his job, as if she were a shrink, a priest, a best friend he could confide in. At last, he said, somebody had come along who understood the tightrope stress of the double life, but also the thrill of secret work, of playing a game for the highest stakes. They had gone for long walks in Business Bay and Marina, talking for hours about their experiences, Cara telling Toby about her recruitment into MI5, Toby describing growing up in the UK, his mother dead at forty-three, raised by a father who only understood how to put a boy into boarding school at eight, fetch him ten years later and hope that the experience had turned him into a man. They spoke about the buzz they got from pushing people's buttons, reading situations, pretending to be one sort of person when in fact you were quite another; both of them acknowledged that there was something addictive about the secret world which would very probably be damaging in the long term.

Cara knew that it was important not to lose sight of the reason they were together, not to forget that Toby had a life in Dubai, a cover career and a network of agents invaluable to the smooth running of BOX 88 in the Gulf. Within a few weeks she would be back in London and obliged to return to The Cathedral to resume her training. What had passed between them would be nothing more than a memory, a distant summer fling looked back upon with affection in years to come. But when she made Toby laugh or he fixed coffee for her in the morning or woke her in the small hours of the night to make love, it was hard to imagine that their relationship would not outlast the Aranov operation. It was Cara's secret hope – a crazy professional fantasy of the sort she had been trained to resist – that Kite would relocate her to Dubai so that she could remain with Toby and they could both continue to work for BOX 88.

The conversation in the lift at the Royal Continental was Cara's first encounter with Aranov, the man who had dominated her working life for the better part of three months. Settling beside him on the terrace, it was all she could do not to stare as she might have done in the presence of a famous actor or musician. He was more immediately likeable than she had expected, with sympathetic eyes and an impish grin. Kite and Rita had complained so often and so entertainingly about his mood swings that Cara had expected a grouchy, entitled bore. Yet as Aranov regaled them with stories of his Russian childhood, lied surprisingly well about his reasons for moving to Dubai and happily bought consecutive rounds of wildly expensive cocktails – albeit on Kite's dime – Cara found herself warming to him.

They were there to use Natalia as a honeytrap, luring Aranov into a quasi-relationship which – it was hoped – would come to the attention of Gromik and his band of disciples. That, at least, was Kite's plan and so far it was working better than any of them had dared to expect. Granted, Natalia had arguably overdone it with the come-to-bed eyes in the lift, but when she removed her mask at the table after sitting down, Aranov had looked, in Toby's later description, like a dog in a cartoon with his eyes popping out on stalks, his tongue flapping on the floor. Thereafter he was relaxed and gregarious, a man liberated from the shackles of confinement and determined to enjoy every second of the evening.

'Do you know the story about the avocados?' he asked, by now well into his second cocktail and happily taking centre stage. 'A British diplomat told it to me. Very funny.'

Cara wondered if the 'British diplomat' was Kite. She laid a bet with herself that she would have heard the story before.

'No!' she said, encouraging Aranov to continue. 'Tell us more.'

The Russian leaned forward. He had a cheeky, conspiratorial look in his eyes.

'In Soviet times, as I have said, it was very difficult to get hold of basic goods, especially food, foreign whisky, clothes, this sort of thing.'

'*Da*,' said Natalia quietly, though she was far too young to remember the deprivations Aranov was describing.

'A British businessman living in Moscow drove to London

in the early 1980s and packed his car with luxuries to take back to Russia. Scotch whisky. French wine. Cheeses and Parma ham from his favourite delicatessen in Knightsbridge. But the thing his wife loves more than anything else in the world is avocado pears.'

'Avocado pears?' Natalia asked, seeking a Russian translation.

'*Avokado*,' Aranov replied quickly and for a split second Cara was concerned that he might think she was stupid.

'OK, OK,' said Toby, urging Aranov to continue.

'So this businessman he takes a tray of two dozen avocados in his car and arrives at the Soviet border two days later. The guards want to give him hard time. They check what he is carrying. They find the whisky, they find the wine, they find the cheese. All this they allow to pass because it is legal. But then they see the avocados. These young guards are hungry. It's the end of winter. They are jealous of all the food the foreigner is bringing into Russia and they know that these pears, which they have never seen before in their lives, must be incredibly delicious if he is prepared to drive them all the way from London to Moscow!'

A delighted laugh from Natalia, echoed by Cara. She had indeed heard Kite tell the story before, although it seemed to be the first time Toby was hearing it.

'So they tell the businessman that the avocados look dangerous. Like grenades. They could contain drugs or explosives. They are going to confiscate them.'

'No!' Cara exclaimed.

'His wife she will be sad,' said Natalia.

'Exactly!' Aranov was on a roll. 'And the British man is furious. He tells them they are not drugs, they are not dangerous, he protests at the confiscation. But nothing works. The guards take the tray out of the car and put it in their hutch. The businessman then drives off.' Aranov paused for maximum effect. 'But!' – he raised a finger, catching Natalia's eye – 'at the last second, just as the barrier is raised, the guard runs up to his car and knocks on the window. The man slowly lowers the glass' – Aranov mimed this, turning his hand over as if sitting in the driver's seat of a car – 'and he asks the guard what the problem is. Guard says: "These avocados. How do you cook them please?" And you know what the man replies?'

'Go on,' said Toby.

'"You boil them very slowly for three hours."'

Pandemonium. Toby laughed explosively. Cara reacted as though she had never heard the anecdote before and almost fell off her chair. Natalia saw that she was expected to follow suit and giggled delightedly. Aranov felt that he had them in the palm of his hand.

'Oh, Sebastian!' Cara exclaimed. 'What a wonderful story!'

'You tell it so well it's almost as if you were there,' added Toby.

'Do I look this old?!' Aranov replied and for a moment Cara saw a flash of his vanity and quick temper. Yet the Russian was so keen to make the right impression on Natalia that he quickly withdrew the question and ordered another round of drinks. Cara seized the opportunity to excuse herself to the bathroom, inviting Natalia to come with her.

'Do you like him?' she asked as they walked away. Natalia was being paid by the hour and was hardly likely to want to turn down such a lucrative assignment, yet it would be operationally beneficial if her relationship with Aranov looked as genuine and as heartfelt as possible.

'He is fine,' she replied. 'At least he has energy. He is cultured and intelligent. Do you think he also likes me?'

Natalia was astonishingly beautiful and so naturally seductive that Cara could hardly believe she had asked such a question. There was something almost touching in her self-doubt.

'Babes, I've never seen a guy so interested in a woman. It's like he's got a sign round his chest saying: "Take me". I'm surprised he hasn't proposed. Yes, he likes you. Don't worry.'

There were other girls in the bathroom, most of them in

heels and figure-hugging dresses. One of them recognised Natalia and greeted her in Russian.

'So I wait for him to invite me?' she asked.

'Sure. Toby is probably talking to him about it now.'

Cara was right. As soon as they had left the table, Aranov had asked Landau if Natalia was single. Bending the truth for moral as well as professional reasons, Landau confided that his friend was indeed available and keen to find a man who would 'keep her in the manner to which she was accustomed'. He revealed that Natalia liked older men, that it seemed obvious she was attracted to him and that perhaps Sebastian's best course of action would be to take her number and invite her out to dinner.

'She doesn't want to be paid,' he promised. 'She's not like some of the other girls here this evening.' Toby indicated a South American woman on the city side of the terrace who had been making eyes at him all night. 'Just take her out somewhere nice. Lots of good restaurants in the city, I can recommend several. You know what Russian women are like. They want to be spoiled. Good food, champagne, the high life.'

'I can provide this,' Aranov replied quickly. Cara and Natalia were coming back from the bathroom.

'Here they are,' said Toby, shooting him a man-to-man wink. 'May all your wishes come true, Sebastian. I think this is the beginning of a beautiful friendship.'

Sitting on the other side of the terrace sharing an £80 bottle of Gavi de Gavi, a salmon tartare and some Maki rolls, Azhar Masood and Rita Ayinde watched the denouement of the Natalia meet-cute trying to figure out which of the other guests in the bar were working for Mikhail Gromik. Rita had a hundred dirhams on the badly dressed Dolph Lundgren lookalike who had arrived half an hour after Toby and Cara. Maz was convinced that the middle-aged couple drinking mineral water and smoking Vogue cigarettes were local SVR who had staked out the bar while Aranov was eating dinner on the expectation that he would pop upstairs for a nightcap after settling his bill.

It turned out they were both right. When Toby and Cara stood up to leave shortly after one o'clock, Dolph called for his bill and followed them downstairs where a car was waiting for him. He tailed them back to Toby's apartment. Meanwhile the middle-aged couple smoked another Vogue and waited on the terrace until Aranov and Natalia had settled their bill, then split up to follow them. The man followed Aranov to the Faleiro, the woman housed Natalia to her apartment block in Bur Dubai.

It was a pattern which was to characterise the next six days of the operation. Whenever Toby drove to work, or Cara maintained cover by attending a job interview, or they met in the evening for a drink on the roof of the Jumeirah Beach Hotel, they were followed. At Deviatkin's suggestion, Gromik had also put two officers on Natalia. They witnessed three subsequent meetings with Sebastian Glik, the last of which concluded in his suite at the Faleiro. By the time the couple were observed at the Dubai Opera, shopping in the Mall of the Emirates and dining at Avli, it was widely understood that they were in a relationship.

All this was reported back to Kite via MOCKINGBIRD. Very quickly he concluded that the time had come to strip away the security around Aranov and to move him out of the Faleiro. Only when he was sure that Glik's MI6 protection had left town would Gromik consider mounting an attack.

50

The property Kite had chosen for Aranov was a discreet three-bedroom villa in Umm Suqeim, a beachside suburb favoured by diplomatic families and businessmen who preferred to keep a low profile. The neighbourhood, which was not far from Burj Al Arab, had none of the cramped bustle of Deira nor the high-rise glamour of DIFC and Marina. Indeed, there was something of the time capsule about it: this was surely what Dubai used to look like, before the march of progress threw up two hundred skyscrapers in fifteen years and the city became the playground of the super-rich.

Aranov's rented house was built in a simple suburban style on a grid of quiet, dusty streets; it had a small garden planted with date palms and jasmine, canvas chairs in which Yuri could relax in the shade of a magnificent frangipani and a communal swimming pool a stone's throw from the back gate. The sea was a five-minute walk. To the team's amusement, it was discovered that the closest stretch of sand was known as 'Kite Beach'. It was exactly the sort of quiet, discreet place that a Russian scientist, hunted by the FSB, would be housed by his masters at MI6. The day before they were due to check out of the Faleiro, Jim Stones drove Aranov to his new home, showed him how the panic alarm could be activated in every room, demonstrated that the locks on the doors and windows were secure and reassured him that there were no active threats to his safety from any branch of the Russian government.

'Mr Galvin wanted me to confirm that none of our sources inside the FSB and GRU have any idea that you've been relocated to Dubai. London has been watching Russian communications traffic, analysing the behaviour of SVR personnel here in the UAE, and confirmed that you're home and dry.'

They were in the master bedroom on the first floor, sounds of children splashing in the pool, a smell of bleach emanating from the en-suite bathroom. Aranov was seated on the edge of a queen size double bed, gently bouncing up and down on the patchwork quilt. Stones imagined that he was testing the springs for Natalia.

'Where is Peter Lockie?' he asked. 'Why doesn't he tell me these things in person?'

'You'll see him again,' Stones replied. 'He's a busy man. Back and forth to London. Covid has thrown a spanner in the works. The fact that he's not in Dubai tells you how relaxed he's feeling about your new life here. He's even checked out Natalia. She's clean as a whistle. All yours, Seb.'

In a rare moment of self-criticism, Aranov took it upon himself to apologise to Stones for his erratic behaviour.

'I owe you both my gratitude,' he said. 'I know I have been pain in ass. It's because I get stressed. Because I miss my family. Sometimes I allow impatience to drive my mood. I have always been like this. I have temper.'

'It's OK,' Stones replied, surprised – and oddly affected – by Aranov's *mea culpa*. 'You've kept us entertained. It's been an honour looking out for you.'

Aranov continued to express satisfaction with his new digs. He was not to know that security cameras had been installed in every room, feeding live audio-visual images to the Turings in Oman. Nor was he aware that Kite had rented a second house, just four doors down, where Stones and Franks would live for as long as it took Gromik to call in his Moscow assassins.

Though Kite was convinced that the FSB would not risk an attack on the villa itself, preferring instead to carry out the assassination in an environment over which they had absolute operational control, it was nevertheless vital that BOX 88 were aware of Aranov's movements at all times. Natalia knew about the blanket surveillance at the house: Toby had told her where the camera was located in the bedroom so that she could throw an item of clothing over the lens to protect her privacy.

'Do I get a car?' Aranov asked.

'You don't need one,' Stones replied. 'Take Ubers, order taxis. Plenty to go around. Maybe you want a bicycle? People around here use them all the time. It's nice and flat, good exercise, quick way of getting to the beach.' Aranov was poking around in the spare bedroom. 'In time your family can come out and stay. Your grandchildren can enjoy the pool. Anastasia might like to go shopping. You'll have an allowance, a housekeeper coming in three times a week. And of course Natalia is welcome to move in. You'll just have to persuade her.'

'So when do I come?' Aranov asked.

'Mr Galvin says tomorrow.'

51

Mikhail Gromik had sent a flash message to Moscow requesting trace information on Natalia Kovalenko. Who was she? Where did she come from? How long had she been living and working in Dubai? What was the nature of her relationship with Toby Landau and how long had she been friends with Sally Tarshish?

Leonid Deviatkin had been aware for some time that the tragic circumstances of Natalia's childhood in Buynaksk would make it highly unlikely that she would cooperate with the FSB, but it had to look to Gromik as though she held no personal animus against the Service. She must also present as the sort of opportunist who would happily betray her foreign lover in return for money. With this in mind, Deviatkin doctored Natalia's records, moving her place of birth from Buynaksk to the nearby city of Makhachkala on the shores of the Caspian Sea. It was recorded that her parents had been killed not by a bomb attack but instead in a car crash on the outskirts of Kaspiysk. Deviatkin changed the name of the high school Natalia had attended, but in every other way preserved the facts and idiosyncrasies of her early life in Dagestan. In forwarding the report to Gromik, he made the obvious but nevertheless important suggestion that Natalia's nascent relationship with Sebastian Glik could be used as a means of obtaining access to JUDAS 61.

'Let's see if she can be useful to us,' was Gromik's encouraging response, reported immediately to Toby Landau via a BOX 88 officer in Moscow who received a copy of Deviatkin's report in brush contact at Prospect Mira metro station.

As soon as Landau had obtained the document, he arranged to meet Natalia for dinner at La Petite Maison, an upmarket mock-French brasserie in DIFC frequented by recuperating athletes, social media influencers and Dubai's idle rich. He had invited Cara and Aranov along for cover, but had deliberately told Cara to arrive half an hour late. Natalia had given the same instruction to Aranov so that she and Landau would have time alone to discuss the next phase of the operation.

'Somebody from the Russian side is going to approach you,' he told her as they set their menus to one side over a candlelit table separated from its neighbours by screens of Covid-protecting plastic. 'We don't know where. We don't know when. It could be tonight, might be two weeks from now. Gromik put in a trace request in your name and a report has come back. Certain details about your childhood have been changed which you need to be aware of.'

She was wearing an off-the-shoulder dress which had made every man – and most of the women – in the room stare at her as she walked in. Landau outlined the biographical changes while trying his best not to think about the nights they had spent together at his apartment, the long weekend they had enjoyed in Lamu courtesy of a BOX 88 operation in Kenya. His memories of Natalia were vivid and carnal. He often wondered if she thought about him in the same way.

'So otherwise I am the same woman with the same past?' she asked.

'Almost exactly the same. The only difference is you grew up in Makhachkala, went to a different school and lost your parents in a car crash. The chances of anyone asking you about this are slim, but it's best that we're careful.'

They had ordered a bottle of Canard-Duchêne, Natalia's

champagne of choice. It sat in a bucket of ice at the side of the table. Landau preferred wine but never said so in her company.

'How's it going with Sebastian?' he asked.

'How is it going with Sally?'

That look she had: a little jealous, a little combative, certainly playful. For a moment they were oblivious to every sound and movement in the restaurant, playing the game they always played.

'You go first,' Landau replied.

He knew that she cared about his private life only in the way that certain women held on to a memory of being pursued and adored. When they had first met, he had been transfixed by her. Then time had passed and they had moved on into new lives, new relationships. What remained was a strange kind of friendship – a mixture of mutual respect and professional opportunism – which suited them both.

'Is she going to stay out here after this is all over?'

'I don't think so.'

'Would you like her to?'

Landau took a sip of champagne, let it fizz in his mouth for a second before swallowing it. He was reluctant to talk about Cara, not because he was protective of their privacy, but because there was a part of him – the scoundrel opportunist – which wanted to leave open the possibility that Natalia might one day sleep with him again. Lust was the flaw at the centre of his character. He was still too young, and too entranced with the pleasures and excitements of his rarefied life, to want to do anything about this.

'She's great,' he said. 'Smart, funny. But too young for me. And wants to be in London.'

It looked as though Natalia had believed only the portion of Toby's response which was true; the part about London was plainly a lie.

'Is that so? She prefers Brexit Britain with Covid than life in Dubai with Toby Landau and La Petite Maison?'

'Apparently.'

Now it was Natalia's turn to drink, to look away as she surveyed her fellow diners, to pretend that she had not noticed Toby's knowing look nor sensed the force of his desire. She knew that he was a womaniser, that a man like Toby would never settle down with a Russian girl who had sold her body in the nightclubs of Dubai. It would be shameful. No, the woman he would eventually marry would be uncomplicatedly adoring and almost certainly British. Natalia knew that he liked to think of himself as a hedonist, but that his true nature – beneath the charm and the intellect and his undoubted courage – was conservative and controlling. She did not mind this about him. Her own personality was not dissimilar.

'What about Sebastian?' he asked.

The question sounded absurd in light of their discussion. Very obviously Sebastian Glik was little more than a business opportunity, a man she was seeing because she was being paid to do so. Nevertheless Natalia had been surprised to find him stimulating. She was never bored in his company. But he was typical of local men in his attitudes to the opposite sex; women existed purely to serve his needs.

'Everything fine,' she replied. 'He is sympathetic, intelligent.' Her eyes went to the entrance of the restaurant. 'And he is here.'

Landau looked up. Sure enough, Aranov, wearing his favourite Panama hat and what could best be described as a safari suit, was engaged in animated conversation with a member of the restaurant staff. He had taken off his Roy Lichtenstein face mask for the purpose and was pointing at the screen of a mobile phone.

'So he is,' he replied, standing up and gesturing towards him. 'Sympathetic. Intelligent. And dressed for a game drive in the Serengeti.' He looked down at Natalia. 'So you remember what I told you? Born in Makhachkala. You went to Shkola 12 in Kaspiysk.'

'I remember, Toby. Please do not worry. I know exactly what it is that you want from me.'

52

Two days later, Natalia Kovalenko was leaving a yoga class in Al Quoz, hungry and unshowered, her hair still damp with sweat, when she heard someone calling out her name. She looked up to find a man wearing Gucci loafers and a Lacoste polo shirt walking towards her in the reception area. He was about sixty, tanned and physically fit, with dyed black hair and a silver chain around his neck. Her first instinct was that he was a former client, someone she had met at the Hyatt or Ritz-Carlton, but he had used her real name and precisely matched the description Toby had given her of Mikhail Gromik. Though she had long expected this, she was not only startled but suddenly very frightened by what might be about to happen to her.

'Can I help you?' she asked. She did not want to betray any nervousness. Perhaps the rush of blood to her face could be explained by her recent workout.

'Good yoga class?' he asked.

'Who are you, please?' Natalia replied.

'I want to be a friend to you.' Gromik moved close enough to the main door of the studio that it opened automatically. Natalia felt that she had no choice other than to walk outside. Gromik followed, saying: 'Tell me about "vinyasa flow". What is this? And bio oxygen? Sounds interesting. You have classes under infra-red lights? Perhaps I should come here and find out what yoga is all about.'

'What do you want?' she asked, standing quite still on the pavement outside. 'I don't know you. You're disturbing me.'

Natalia had played out this moment many times in her mind. Toby had talked about how it might happen, who would approach her, what might be said. She dreaded being dragged into a car or physically harmed; certainly Gromik's supercilious manner was deeply unsettling. She knew that his easy, harmless way with her disguised a coiled brutality.

'I don't mean to disturb you,' he said. 'Please forgive me. My name is Andrey.'

Gromik offered to shake Natalia's hand but she declined, saying: 'I am not clean. I've just worked out. I don't want to touch a stranger.'

'Of course.'

She could sense that he was reading her all the time. *Is this girl a British agent? Is she whore or spy? Will she be persuaded to work for me?* Natalia knew that it was important to give some indication of her strength of character, an instinct for survival; she did not want Gromik to think she was weak.

'How do you know who I am?' she asked.

'I know a lot about you, Natalia Petrovna. I know where you were born. I know that you left Dagestan when you were just seventeen years old to – how can I put it politely? – make your fortune in Moscow, Zurich and Dubai. I know that you live in an apartment on 5th Street in Al Hudaiba which costs you perhaps more than you can afford in these difficult times for, well, working girls . . .'

Toby had told her that Gromik brought young Thai and Vietnamese women to his apartment, sometimes two at a time. She detested his moral hypocrisy, the little smirk on his lips and his sarcasm.

'How do you know so much about me?' she asked. 'Are you police? Have I done something wrong?'

'No, no. Not at all.' She had walked away from him, but

he was following her. 'I wanted to talk to you only because there is an interest in your boyfriend. If you cooperate you will be quite safe.'

'Boyfriend?' Natalia came to a halt beside a busy coffee shop. She could hear the chatter of families, the easy laughter of men. 'I don't have a boyfriend.'

A smile from Gromik, false as a mask.

'Surely Sebastian Glik would be disappointed to learn that you feel this way?'

Though she had been told to expect this, Natalia's heart still turned over. She felt as though she had lost a breath. A child chasing a balloon ran past her, brushing against her leg.

'Sebastian? What do you know about him? He's just a friend. I hardly know him.'

'And yet you have spent many days with him since you met last month at the Royal Continental. Restaurants, shopping expeditions, nights at the Faleiro Hotel. Sounds to me like you are growing close.'

'What I do with my time is not . . .'

With a practised expression of indifference, Gromik raised a hand to her objection.

'I don't care how you choose to make a living, Natalia Petrovna. I am a man of the world. I know Dubai. Believe me, I want to protect you. If you can introduce me to Mr Glik, that's all I care about. There will be no other problems.'

She felt that it was better not to respond. Her silence encouraged Gromik to continue.

'Tell me about the men he has around him.'

Natalia Kovalenko had always possessed a facility for lying. She could set her face and tell a man whatever he needed to hear and he would believe her.

'What men?' she asked.

'The Englishman and the American. His security protection. Tell me about them. Where did they go?'

'I don't know anything about that.' Every detail of her expression supported that assertion. 'When I see Sebastian,

I see him on my own or with friends. There is never anyone else with him. What are you talking about?'

'What friends?'

This was where Natalia had to be careful: she knew that a word out of place, the wrong gesture or glance, might betray Toby's involvement in the deception.

'What does it matter?' she asked. 'My friends are my friends.'

'Where are they from?'

'They are English.' She assumed that the FSB had already established as much.

'English?'

'British. How do you say it? What's the difference? They are boyfriend and girlfriend. Not Russians.'

'And they know Sebastian?'

'Mind your own business,' Natalia replied, walking off. 'Leave me alone or I will call the police.'

He took hold of her as she stepped away, the pressure on her arm strong enough to detain her yet not so aggressive that it drew the attention of passers-by.

'Be careful,' he whispered. All of the easy charm in Gromik's sun-weathered face had suddenly fallen away. 'We know all about you, Natalia Petrovna. All about what you do here in Dubai. If you fail to answer my questions, if you fail to cooperate, it will take one phone call to my friends in Immigration and you will be thrown out of the Emirate.'

Indicating that she was prepared to concede to Gromik's demands, Natalia freed her arm. The muscle above her elbow ached but she knew that she had played her hand skilfully. With seeming reluctance she explained what had happened at the bar, telling Gromik that Sebastian had failed to make a reservation and that Toby had invited him to join their table.

'So perhaps he can come along too,' Gromik replied. 'What did you say was the name of his girlfriend?'

'Sally.' Natalia screwed up her face. 'Come along where?'

'I am organising a little party.' Gromik was looking at her in the way that the men in the nightclubs of Dubai sized her up before asking her to come back to their hotels. 'I want Mr Glik to be the guest of honour.'

53

The snows were coming.

Leonid Deviatkin waited at the perimeter of the chess pavilion in Gorky Park, feeling the thinness of the cold air against his cheeks, reckoning Moscow would be in the grip of winter within five or six days. These, then, were the final carefree moments of autumn. The old men with their chess clocks and bags of plastic pieces would soon be gone, back to their apartments and local cafés, hoping that Covid wouldn't take them before Christmas. These might be the last times that some of them saw one another. Though he was not yet forty, the thought made Deviatkin feel old.

A man in a red sweatshirt, another in a brown leather jacket, approached him from the west. The taller of them was Zatulin, recently returned from America with a pot belly and a late summer tan. Laptev was in the sweatshirt looking like he had come straight from the gym.

'You're late,' Deviatkin told them. 'Let's walk.'

Their business was murder. In 2014, on his first operation, Andrei Laptev had been one of a seven-man team responsible for the death of Timur Kushaev, a human rights activist and politician opposed to the Putin government. Kushaev had been found dead in Nalchik with an injection mark under his left armpit. The official cause of death, much to the amusement of Laptev's colleagues in the Lubyanka, was recorded as heart failure. A year later, Laptev was given responsibility for the assassination of Ruslan Magomedragimov, a political activist in Dagestan. The injection mark left by Laptev on the victim's neck was found under autopsy, but it was arranged that the cause of death would be given as asphyxiation.

Zatulin specialised in poisons. He had discovered that Evgeny Palatnik suffered from glaucoma and proposed – with the approval of Mikhail Gromik and Director Makarov – that his Xalatan eye medication be switched for an A-234 Novichok. Zatulin had also successfully poisoned Nikita Isayev, an opposition activist, on a train from Tambov to Moscow. It was this attack which had made his name. Makarov was of the opinion that if Zatulin had been involved in the summer's attempted assassination of Alexei Navalny, PARASITE would have arrived at Sheremetyevo in a bodybag.

It was nevertheless the first time that Laptev and Zatulin had worked together. Deviatkin told them that they would rarely enjoy such an easy, risk-free assignment. He explained that Sebastian Glik had once been a scientist with Biopreparat. At the instigation of Evgeny Palatnik, Glik had agreed to work as an agent for the British Secret Intelligence Service, which had lured him to the West in 1993. Glik was therefore a traitor who had abandoned his colleagues and his country in return for money.

'This is where the tide turns for him,' Deviatkin continued. 'As a reaction to the triumph of the Palatnik operation, Glik has been moved by SIS to the United Arab Emirates. Unbeknownst to him, he has entered into a relationship with a whore from Makhachkala who is under the control of Mikhail Gromik. Glik is on the JUDAS list. Gromik wants him dead.'

'How does he want to do it?' Zatulin asked, removing the leather jacket and looping it over his arm. 'Is there a weakness we can exploit?'

As always, Deviatkin was struck by the single-mindedness of the men trained to kill by the Russian state. Not for them a discussion about the rights and wrongs of killing a British citizen on foreign soil. Not for them an assessment of the political risks of carrying out an assassination in the UAE. Just the facts of the case. How do we get to the target? What are his weaknesses? What is the best way of removing him from JUDAS?

'It can't be the same method as Palatnik,' Deviatkin replied. 'Too complex, too risky. Director Makarov will not authorise the use of chemical or biological agents in an operation of this kind. Instead there will be an apartment, a balcony. Glik will be invited to a party by his whore, he will find that he is the only guest. You are there to assist Mikhail Gromik in any way that he asks. If there is to be an injection, he will oversee the technical side. If you are to throw Glik to his death from the twentieth storey of a Dubai high-rise, so be it. Mikhail Dimitrovich will make all the necessary arrangements. According to your files, neither of you has visited the United Arab Emirates in the last ten years. Is that correct?'

Both Zatulin and Laptev confirmed this. Laptev, who was known as 'Baby Face' by his colleagues on account of his unusually smooth complexion, looked intrigued by the prospect of travelling to Dubai for the first time.

'You fly in. You do the job. You fly out,' Deviatkin told them. 'This is an opportunistic strike. Intelligence indicates that Glik could be moved by SIS at any moment. I have arranged cover identities which you will collect in the usual way. You will be staying at the Regal Plaza hotel in Deira. It's discreet. Close to the airport in the Indian section of the city. You keep a low profile. No girls, no drinking, no trouble. Gromik will meet you at the Kana Cafe in Business Bay at midday the day after your arrival. All of these details are in the package left for you at the airport in the usual location. From now on you communicate only with Gromik, never with me or with any other member of the Service. Is that completely understood?'

Deviatkin took their silence for assent. Both men were well aware of the embarrassment caused by a colleague who had been duped by Alexei Navalny into discussing details of his assassination on a phone call which was recorded and subsequently disseminated on the Internet.

'Remember that in Dubai you are always being watched,' he warned. A woman who reminded Deviatkin of his late mother passed them on the path. 'Trust Gromik. He knows the environment, he will instruct your behaviour. You're tourists, you're there to buy gold in the souk, to see the sights, to visit the beach. You should be home within a week.'

Laptev looked up at the sky.

'There will be snow by then,' he said.

54

At first light, Cara Jannaway packed the outfit in a plastic bag, went down to the gym in shorts and a T-shirt, ran for half an hour on the treadmill then washed her hair in the shower. There were no CCTV cameras in that section of the hotel. Afterwards, alone in the changing area, she put on the clothes, retrieved her handbag and went back up to the lobby.

She had worn an abaya before, walking around Bethnal Green at Rita's suggestion in order to familiarise herself with the feeling of being covered. That had been over a month ago. The experience had made her rage against the men who would oblige their wives, their sisters, their daughters to dress in such a way. A fat Cockney in a Chelsea shirt had muttered: 'Take that shit off your face' as she passed him on the bus. In these initial moments in Dubai, Cara was again dismayed by how powerless she felt, not just hidden but hemmed in, her peripheral vision stripped away. It didn't help that this was the most dangerous moment of the operation, a morning when everything could go wrong. If there was an accident, Kite could end up in hospital; if they were arrested, they would likely go to prison for the rest of their days.

The box. Toby had given it to her at dinner the night before. At first Cara had assumed it was a genuine gift, a present from Fortnum and Mason, but then she had felt the weight of it and seen the look in his eyes. This was no bracelet or watch, no pair of earrings to celebrate how much fun they were having. This was the box Azhar Masood had brought in on the dhow, the box that would seal Gromik's fate.

Cara was anxious. There was no pretending otherwise. She was thousands of miles from home, dressed as a conservative Muslim wife and completely reliant on the team not letting her down. She spoke no Farsi, no Arabic, no Urdu. If anybody talked to her she would have to mumble and shoo them away; if it was law enforcement she would have a job explaining why Sally Tarshish was wandering around Dubai wearing an abaya.

'Just tell them it's research for something you're writing,' Toby had suggested. He reminded her that John Simpson, the veteran BBC reporter, had dressed up as a woman in order to get into Kabul in 2001. 'You wanted to know how it felt to be a veiled woman in this heat, in this culture. During a pandemic.'

'And the box?' she replied. 'How do I explain that?'

'The box is just what it looks like. A present you're taking back to England. Nobody will be interested in looking at it. Trust me.'

Cara thought about what was inside and what might happen if the contents somehow leaked in her bag. One drop would be enough to put her in hospital for weeks; if she touched the liquid without gloves, she would be dead within hours. For once she was grateful for her mask, the anxiety on her face invisible to the guests and members of staff who passed her in the lobby of the Holiday Inn. In these moments, waiting to go outside into the thick heat of the morning, Cara was convinced that Kite's plan was a stupid risk, the entire operation an insane gamble. She had been mad to go along with it. Then she thought of Palatnik and Litvinenko, of Navalny and Skripal, of the dozens of men and women slain by Putin's pitiless thugs, and found her courage again. It was worth it. To avenge their deaths. To teach the Russians a lesson. BOX 88 would at last put the FSB's killers behind bars and make Mikhail Gromik pay for the sins of his despicable career.

The young Kenyan concierge who usually tried to engage her in conversation barely looked at Cara as she walked out of the hotel. The abaya had made her invisible; this, Cara supposed, was its great benefit for any woman who wished to elude the male gaze. It was a typically bustling, humid morning. She saw the taxi parked across the street, the number plate matching a message Rita had sent at dawn. Cara opened the back door and climbed in, putting the handbag on the seat beside her.

'Good morning, miss,' said Azhar Masood, engaging first gear and pulling away from the hotel. He was wearing a beige polo shirt and several days of stubble. 'All set for the day ahead?'

She was surprised by how elated she was to see him. Back in London they had joked about Maz doing the Knowledge; to see him masquerading as a Dubai cab driver helped to ease her nerves.

'Well set,' she replied. 'Love the new look.'

'I'm from Peshawar these days,' he said, smiling in the rear-view mirror. 'Signed up on Tuesday, along with about ninety other guys wiring their wages home. It's an interesting job. You meet all kinds of people.'

She touched his shoulder and gave it a squeeze, wanting to tear off the face mask and to laugh with Maz about all the crazy things that had happened to her in Dubai. She wondered if he knew about Toby; perhaps their fling was common knowledge among the team. As they drove north towards DIFC, Masood told her that MOCKINGBIRD had operational control of the Aranov plot from Moscow, a bonus that nobody on the team had thought possible.

'So things have been made slightly easier. He tells us what Gromik is thinking, gave us full details of the two men who flew out yesterday. Vasily Zatulin and Andrei Laptev. They're staying at the Regal Plaza Hotel in Deira, sharing the same room. Here's your key. You're in 484.' Maz reached into the breast pocket of his shirt and passed a purple keycard over the back seat. Suddenly Cara was working again, no more time for idle chit-chat or catching up. 'Zatulin and Laptev are in 302 – one floor down, opposite side of the hotel. Too bad we couldn't get you closer but that's the way the cookie crumbled on check-in. The layout of the hotel is good for us. There's only one entrance on a busy one-way street. Security on the door and an escalator leading up to the lobby. That's where you'll wait. If the Russians come back, you'll see them in time to warn Lockie. I'll be on them too.'

'So we don't know when they're seeing Gromik?'

'According to MOCKINGBIRD they have a meeting at midday in Business Bay. Kana Cafe, on the Creek. We're across Gromik's comms, recording everything he sends and says. The language suggests he's going to talk them through what he's got planned for Yuri. It's going to be a party. Natalia invites him. He goes up, they push him off a balcony. Job done.'

'Nice and simple. Make it look like an accident.'

'Exactly. They should be leaving any time in the next few hours, could be the meeting gets delayed until this afternoon, could be they take the entire day off and go to the top of Burj Khalifa like good Russian tourists.'

'They love a spire, that lot,' Cara replied, trying to sound more like her old self. 'Salisbury Cathedral. Burj Khalifa . . .'

A pedestrian in a business suit tried to flag the cab from a traffic island. Masood drove past him.

'Where's Lockie?' Cara asked.

'Had a breakfast meeting at eight.' Masood glanced at the clock on the dashboard. 'He's waiting to get the signal that Laptev and Zatulin are on the move. Soon as he does, we pick him up in Festival City, take you both to the Regal Plaza, then it's the Cara and Kite show.'

'What about CCTV in the hotel? Did the Turings take care of it?'

'Turings have control for as long as we need it. Lobby cameras will pick you up, but Oman can loop and erase the activity outside the rooms. If the hotel gets suspicious, it's made to look like a Russian attack, Moscow trying not to leave evidence their boys were ever there.'

'And my room?'

A car cut across the taxi and made a fast right turn into a quieter stream of traffic. Masood hit the horn, coming to a halt at a red light.

'Same thing. No snail trail. There's a change of clothes for both of you in 484. Once Lockie's done you meet him there, just as we arranged in London. You'll need your keycard to work the lift. He'll want to shower, clean up. Don't touch him. Don't touch his clothes. The gloves will go in a bin liner, ditto the shoes, everything he was wearing. Suitcase goes in the boot of the cab, I drive to a building site, toss it. You remember, right?'

A message buzzed into Masood's mobile phone.

'I remember,' Cara replied. This much was true. She had rehearsed the morning in her mind a hundred times. 'Is that Rita?'

They were both looking at the phone. Masood glanced down at the screen.

'Russians just left the Regal Plaza,' he said. 'Lockie waiting. Here goes.'

55

Kite was waiting for them at the prearranged point in Festival City. He was overdressed for the weather, wearing denim jeans, a long-sleeved shirt and walking boots purchased in a branch of Timberland the previous afternoon. It was as much personal protection as he could plausibly explain without walking into the Regal Plaza wearing a hazmat suit. A Nike baseball cap was both a shield against the fierce morning sun and a further layer of defence for CCTV. In his back pocket he had a pair of latex gloves and a second mask, in his mind the unsettling feeling of taking an operational risk greater than any he had ever contemplated.

The mission was at the point of no return. To go to the Russians' hotel room with the isotope was to set in motion the final stages of the plan. Gromik had contacted Natalia and invited her to an apartment in a DIFC high-rise the following evening. She was to make sure that Sebastian Glik was with her and would be permitted to leave as soon as she had delivered him to the Russians. For her assistance, she would be paid $100,000, her silence guaranteed by the threat to her life from the FSB.

The taxi pulled up in front of him, right on time. Kite saw Masood at the wheel, Cara shrouded in her abaya in the back seat. She shuffled over as he climbed in, saying 'Hi' very softly.

'Always knew you'd end up driving cabs, Maz,' he said. Kite knew it was important to sound relaxed. 'How's every-body feeling? No Covid? No last-minute requests?'

'Still no Covid,' Masood replied, pulling away from the kerb. 'We're about ten minutes away. You confirmed Rita has the Russians?'

Kite took off the baseball cap. There was a smell of old cigarettes in the car and a strange, almost surreal atmosphere of intrigue and disguise.

'Confirmed. One of Toby's guys walked them out of the hotel after breakfast. Rita and a second vehicle are on them. Zatulin in blue shorts, white polo shirt, Laptev in beige chinos and a red polo shirt.' He looked at Cara, who would need to remember what the two Russians were wearing so that she might recognise them if they came back to the hotel. 'Looks like the meeting at Kana is going ahead. Toby has someone on the terrace, more eyes inside, with any luck we'll get photographs too. We have perhaps an hour.' Kite turned to Cara, unnerved by her stillness. 'You OK?'

'All good,' she said, repeating Kite's description of what the Russians were wearing and confirming that she had been sent photographs of both men by The Cathedral. She reached for her handbag. 'It's in here. I hope it's safe.'

Kite took the box and placed it inside his rucksack.

'Please don't worry,' he said. Kite didn't think that Cara was having second thoughts about the isotope, but his own nerves needed settling so he explained, as much for his own benefit as for hers, what was going to happen. 'The box is lead lined, the bottle protected by a material that will have absorbed any leak in the highly unlikely event that the glass smashed between here and London.' Cara nodded encouragingly, adjusting her face mask. 'What's in there is only about two milligrams of caesium-137. The rest is water. I don't fully understand the science but even if something goes very badly wrong, we won't be causing a public health problem. There's no risk to staff or guests in the hotel, not even to Zatulin and Laptev . . .'

'I know, I know,' Cara replied quickly. 'We went through everything. I just want you to be safe. I want everything to go smoothly.'

'And it will,' Kite replied, thinking again, for the hundredth time, of Isobel and Ingrid and the risk he was taking with his own health. 'The water will evaporate into the carpet leaving a trace of radioactive salts. I'm not going to put it on the sheets, on the towels, where a chambermaid might touch it. Inside their luggage, yes. Dirty clothes, yes. But nowhere that anybody innocent gets harmed. If Gromik's goons grow a hairy back or start melting at three o'clock tomorrow morning, fuck them, they got what's coming to them.' Masood laughed. 'There was radiation all over the bathroom used by Lugovoy and Kovtun because they didn't know what they were handling. They took showers, shaved, brushed their teeth. Ten minutes after putting the polonium in Litvinenko's tea, Lugovoy was encouraging his own son to shake his hand. The fucking teapot went through a dishwasher and was used the same day to serve customers in the bar. Even after that performance, everybody survived. It'll be the same for us. You have to ingest this stuff in decent quantities for it to kill you.'

'See Palatnik for details,' said Masood, joining a busy highway running parallel to the Creek. They were heading north into Deira, five minutes from the Regal Plaza. 'If you could put this shit into Gromik's eyes, I'd happily help you do it.'

Kite was surprised by the force of Masood's response and put it down to nerves.

'Hell of a disguise,' he said to Cara, touching the sleeve of her abaya. 'Wish I could say it suits you.'

'Genuinely don't know how women put up with this shit,' she replied. 'It's baking hot, you can't see anything, you walk around and people either stare like you're a leper or look in the other direction. If I was forced to have this on twenty-four-seven, I'd go mad.'

'How's Natalia?' Kite asked. 'She seem OK? Gromik offered her a hundred grand, we don't want her head turned.'

'Toby says she's fine. She's spoken to Yuri, he's excited about the party, thinks it's an international crowd of her friends, no Russians.'

'He should still have cleared it with us,' said Masood, coming to a halt at a set of lights. 'If we weren't looking out for him, he'd be dead in a week.'

'Sooner than that,' said Kite. He needed to double-check that they were both absolutely clear about the next phase of the operation. 'So. One last time. Maz, you drop Cara at the hotel, she hands you some money, walks inside, takes the escalator to the lobby and sits down with her phone. You and I drive another couple of hundred metres, check that the Russians are at Kana, I get out, walk back to the Regal Plaza, head directly upstairs with the isotope. You got my key?'

'We're in 484,' Cara replied as Maz passed Kite the second of the two access cards. 'Zatulin and Laptev in 302.'

'Radios are in the glovebox,' said Maz.

Kite leaned into the front seat, popped the glovebox and retrieved two handheld two-way radios with which Kite and Cara would communicate.

'We're on channel 7 with the privacy code 12,' he said. 'Run the signals with me.'

'Successive clicks, abort,' Cara replied. 'I get the same from you, it means you've finished and I'll make my way upstairs to our room.'

'484,' said Kite, as they both tested the radios. The clicks were clearly audible; there would be no mistaking them for squawk or feedback.

'484,' Cara confirmed. 'Bad guys in 302.'

The air conditioning in the taxi was struggling. Kite wound down a window in the back seat and was hit by a humid wall of exhaust fumes.

'Don't forget to text me after you get out of the shower,' said Masood. 'I'll be driving around the block. Cara, there's a suitcase in the room containing the phone and everything else you need. Wrapping paper, Sellotape, new outfits, Lockie's shoes. Put the dirty clothes inside it, the gloves, the masks, walk outside and I'll pick you up. Lockie goes his own way.'

Suddenly a siren behind them. A police motorcycle was coming in from the right on a road running perpendicular to the highway. Kite saw the muscles in Masood's shoulders tense. Cara whispered 'Christ'. They were all on edge. Kite turned in the back seat to see not one, but two police cars on their tail, sirens blaring. It was inconceivable that the UAE authorities were onto them; the team had exercised extreme caution in every aspect of their tradecraft. An arrest now, with the box in the rucksack, would be catastrophic.

'I'm sure they're not for us,' he said. 'Could be anything. We're all just a little bit jumpy.'

Kite was right. The first of the two tailing police cars had nosed far enough through the traffic to come within a few metres of their taxi, but now accelerated through a gap on Masood's side and was soon heading towards the new city. The motorcyclist at the intersection seemed to have been staring directly at Masood, but now faced the oncoming traffic and gunned his bike in the direction of the Creek.

'I need a drink,' said Cara. 'And a holiday. And a shower. And a new fucking outfit.'

'All good things come to those who wait,' Kite replied.

'We're almost there.' Masood indicated the entrance to the Regal Plaza up ahead. Kite put the baseball cap on and pulled the mask back over his face. 'You guys ready?'

At exactly the same time they both said: 'Ready.'

56

Kite entered the lobby to find Cara seated alone on a low leather sofa with line of sight to the escalators. She had a plastic bag at her feet, an iPhone in her hand, looking for all the world like a bored Muslim wife waiting for someone to join her. She did not look up as Kite passed. There was another, much older woman in the lobby, seated in an armchair closer to the reception desk. A man with chalk-white hair was beside her, talking to a member of staff. Kite did not think they posed a surveillance threat.

Using his knuckle he pressed the button for the lift, touched the keycard to the panel and rode to the fourth floor. The cabin was glass-fronted: Kite could see down into the lobby where Cara was staring at her phone. Every inch of his progress through the hotel was being covered by CCTV, but the Turings would erase whatever they found as soon as Kite and Cara were clear of the building. The footage would be replaced with film clipped from earlier security recordings.

He emerged onto the landing. A Chinese man was standing in front of a vast window overlooking the swimming pool. He was making a telephone call. Kite walked away from the lifts into a strong smell of fenugreek and cumin in the deserted corridor. Plastic water bottles and cartons of half-eaten food had been left in bags outside several of the rooms. There were no members of staff nor any other guests visible in the corridor. As he approached 302, he put on the gloves, took the room key from his pocket and pressed it to the door. Kite heard a click, saw the tiny green glow on the panel above the handle and walked inside. He placed the card in the slot to activate the lights and saw that the room had already been cleaned. Following protocol, he put a Do Not Disturb sign outside the room and turned the bolt so that he was locked in.

Kite was aware of his heart pumping fast, of sweat gathering in the palms of his gloved hands. There were two suitcases in the room, both carry-ons, one of them open, the other zipped up. The closed case was on a raised luggage rack, the other on the floor by the window, bulging with clothes and personal effects. Kite looked in the cupboard opposite the bathroom and found what he was looking for: some shoes and a hotel laundry bag containing dirty clothes. He turned two of the shoes over so that their soles were facing up and opened up the laundry bag. He put his radio on the bed, opened the rucksack he had been carrying and took out the box.

The air conditioning in the room had reactivated but the stale, uncirculated air was still very hot; the edges of Kite's mask were damp with sweat. He could not take it off and risk inhaling vapour from the isotope. He told himself to breathe normally, to take his time. If there was any problem – a knock on the door, clicks on the two-way radio – it would be easy enough to get out of the room and head downstairs without raising further suspicion.

Kite broke the seal on the box, pulling off the tape and putting it in his trouser pocket. His latex glove caught on the pocket as he pulled his hand out; he had to roll a section of the rubber back down over his wrist. He raised the lid of the box. A small glass bottle was nestled in the grey foam moulding, innocent as a perfume. Taking another deep breath, and holding it, Kite removed the bottle, suddenly worried that it would fracture in his hands. It looked so fragile. He unscrewed the lid, put the bottle on the desk and drew some of the liquid into the pipette.

Radiation is exposure over time, the Einsteins at The Cathedral had told him. *You must limit the amount of time the bottle is out of the box.*

He let out the breath and walked to the cupboard, allowing a single drop of the caesium to fall onto the soles of each of the two shoes before turning them back over. He had practised this in London with saline; the flow rate of the isotope was near-identical. More confident now, Kite squeezed three drops onto two items of clothing in the laundry bag, set the pipette on the ground and pushed the bag back into the corner of the cupboard where he had found it.

The sound of someone in the corridor. Kite froze, dreading the sound of a keycard in the door, but the footsteps passed. Taking a breath, he went into the bathroom, inserted the tip of the pipette in the grid of the plughole and squirted several drops of the caesium solution down the drain. He looked around. There was a wet shaving brush on a shelf beside the sink, a bottle of breath freshener behind it. His job was to leave a trail for the Dubai police, not to kill or maim, and Kite returned to the bedroom without adding to the contamination in the bathroom. The sweat under his latex gloves had caused them to cling ever tighter to his hands. Though the air conditioning had begun to cool the room, he was still extraordinarily hot. He badly wanted to remove his mask and take a deep, cleansing breath but to do so was impossible. He returned to the open bottle, very carefully drew more caesium into the pipette and looked over in the direction of the beds. Kite told himself that he would be finished within two or three minutes if he kept to the same rhythm, leaving spots and trails of radioactivity which would light up like a starfield.

Then he heard a crackle on the radio.

57

Cara had looked up to see a man matching Zatulin's description getting off the escalator in the north corner of the lobby. He was about thirty-five with shapeless black hair and a small pot belly. But was it the Russian? His face mask made it impossible to be sure. He was wearing beige chinos and a red polo shirt. Cara could not remember if Zatulin had been wearing blue shorts or chinos. Was Laptev the one in the red polo shirt? She wished that she had triple-checked the descriptions but had been so distracted in the car and determined not to seem nervous or out of her depth that she had kept her mouth shut.

The man was already past her. He looked Russian. Christ, if it was Zatulin they were finished. *Laptev in blue shorts, white T-shirt, Zatulin in beige chinos and a red polo shirt.* Was that right? Was that what Kite had said? Surely both men were still at Kana Cafe? Someone in the team would have warned her if there was a problem.

Cara had no time to hesitate. She knew that if she radioed Kite and she was wrong, the operation would end in failure; he would never get a second chance to go back to the hotel room. But if she failed to warn him that Zatulin was coming up, Kite was finished.

Cara stood up and followed the man to the bank of lifts, lingering behind him as he waited. He noticed her and turned around. His eyes were shy and kind. Cara was near certain he was Zatulin. A lift opened to their right and he gestured at her to take it. Taking a wild risk, Cara decided to test his accent.

'Please,' she said, trying to sound like an Arab who spoke only a few words of English. 'You here first. You go.'

'No, no,' Zatulin replied. He spoke in English but his voice was as Russian as Tolstoy and Chekhov. 'Please, you take it. I wait.'

Without another word, Cara stepped inside and touched her room card to the sensor, heart pounding. She pressed '4' and the lift pulled away from the ground floor. Through the glass-fronted cabin she could see Zatulin waiting patiently in the same spot. Reaching into her abaya she found the radio and tried to locate the power switch so that she could turn it on with one hand. There were four lifts in the hotel, one of which was out of order. Cara looked up and saw two cabins above her: one was being held on the second floor, the other on the third. She prayed that they were busy or that they would be called to higher floors before returning to collect Zatulin. Time was everything. Kite would need at least a minute to clear out of the room and find somewhere to conceal himself.

The dial on the two-way radio clicked in her pocket. The radio was on. She turned up the volume and pressed the communication button again and again. But surely it was now too late? Cara thought about going down to level 3 and interrupting Zatulin as he got out of the lift, but what could she plausibly say or do to detain him? She wasn't wearing the right clothes; a trained intelligence officer would smell a rat if the same veiled Muslim woman tried to engage him in stilted conversation twice in the space of a few minutes.

She took the iPhone out of her pocket. Only now did she see the message sent by Rita half an hour earlier and somehow inexplicably delayed by a glitch of technology.

Your brother isn't feeling well. He's decided to come back to the hotel. Just to let you know he's on his way.

58

Kite heard the warning clicks and froze. For an instant he was caught between wanting to finish the job and the vital requirement of getting out of the room as fast as possible.

He opened the suitcase on the ground beside him, pulled back a handful of clothes and let several droplets of caesium fall onto the lining. Moving quickly, he closed the case as he had found it, screwed the pipette back into the bottle, laid it in the moulded case and shut the box. He picked up the radio from the bed, switched off the power, put the box and the radio in his rucksack and stood up.

What the hell had happened? He took a last look around, ensured that he had left nothing behind, removed the keycard from the activation slot and unlocked the door.

Silence outside. Kite held the door open with his leg, removed the gloves, dropped them into the rucksack and glanced outside. There was nobody in the corridor, just a chambermaid's trolley four rooms to the left. Allowing the door to close slowly behind him, Kite walked towards the trolley. He walked away from the lifts; he could not risk passing the Russians if one or both of them had come back to the hotel.

Only when he had reached the trolley did he remember the sign. 'Do Not Disturb'. He would have to go back to remove it and take the chance that he would be seen. Without hesitating, Kite turned and walked back towards the room. There was a sound at the end of the corridor: he was sure that it was the lift doors opening. Kite reached for the sign, tore it off and walked back in the direction of the trolley, ducking into the open door of a room on the same side of the corridor.

There was nobody inside. The sheets had been stripped from the bed and there was a vacuum cleaner plugged in by the window. Remembering Martha and the hotel room in Voronezh, Kite touched the door with his foot so that it swung shut behind him. He walked into the bathroom, leaving the door ajar. At last he removed the mask and took a deep breath, wiping his face on a towel which he then dropped to the floor.

What had gone wrong? He was now trapped while he waited for the Russians to come back. Cara would not have warned him to abort without making a confirmed sighting of either Zatulin or Laptev. That meant they were on their way up.

Movement outside the room. The chambermaid was coming back. Kite heard the click of the passkey and some muttered words. Had the Russian greeted her? The door swung open. In the reflection of the bathroom mirror he saw an African woman enter the room and walk towards the bed. She switched on the vacuum cleaner and moved out of sight. Putting the mask back on, Kite slipped out of the bathroom and walked out into the corridor, half-expecting to see Zatulin or Laptev coming towards him as he headed in the direction of the lifts.

He passed '302' slowly. He could hear someone inside the room. Would they notice that the air conditioning had been left on? Kite was sure that it wouldn't matter; they would think that the chambermaid had only recently finished cleaning.

He waited for a lift and rode up to the fourth floor. When he reached '484', he tapped on the door and Cara let him in.

'What happened?' Kite asked, taking off his face mask.

'Zatulin came back,' she said. 'No warning. Nothing. Rita sent a text from the café, but for whatever reason it didn't go through. I only saw it when he was in the fucking lobby.'

She was still wearing the abaya. There were latex gloves on her hands.

'Doesn't matter,' Kite told her. 'I did enough.'

'And you were safe?' she asked. 'No problems?'

'All safe.' Kite put the rucksack on the ground and took off his baseball cap. 'Let's get going.'

59

They moved quickly.

Kite went into the bathroom and took the phone and the box out of the rucksack. He wiped them down with a damp towel and put them outside in the passage leading to the bedroom.

'Ready,' he said.

Back inside the bathroom, he took off his boots and the baseball cap and stuffed them in a bin liner along with the rest of his clothes. He put the rucksack inside a second liner and put both bags in the room.

'Bin night,' he said.

All of this was precautionary. Kite had been extraordinarily careful with the pipette; there was a vanishingly small chance that any of the caesium had touched his boots or his clothes. Nevertheless he switched on the shower, scrubbed his face thoroughly in hot water and washed his hair. He emerged five minutes later with a towel around his waist. Cara had put the bin bags inside a suitcase and was busy wrapping the lead box in coloured paper.

'Not quite Fortnum and Mason,' she said. If she was surprised by Kite's half-naked appearance, she did not show it. 'Now my turn.'

A dormant part of Kite woke up to the fact that he was in a hotel room with an attractive young woman, but it was a feeling of nostalgia, of vanished years, not of desire. A decade earlier – stung by the loss of Martha, his private life in chaos – he might have tried to make something of the moment, but that part of his nature had abated. Standing in his towel he felt no different to a man changing into a pair of swimming trunks beside a pool; to make a pass at Cara would have been absurd.

She walked past him in the abaya, saying: 'Clothes on the bed.' She was carrying a holdall containing her own outfit. She had laid a pair of chinos, a bottle green Lacoste polo shirt and some underwear on the covers. Kite had given her a pair of his desert boots in London; she had brought them over in her luggage and they were on the ground beside the television. He dressed, listening to Cara singing quietly in the shower, thinking of Isobel and Martha, of all the days and nights he had spent with them in hotel rooms in every corner of the world.

Then he looked at his phone. There was a text message from Rita.

A couple of the boys not coming home. Heading to the villa instead. Mum and Dad are still there. We'll catch up with them.

Kite wondered how long it had taken for the message to come through. It was as simple to interpret as it was disquieting. Laptev was not coming back to the Regal Plaza; instead Gromik was taking him from the Kana Cafe direct to Aranov's villa.

According to surveillance, Natalia had spent the night with Yuri in Umm Suqeim. Natalia was 'Mum', Aranov was 'Dad'. Was it possible she had betrayed the team to Gromik? MOCKINGBIRD had insisted that the assassination would take place in the apartment in DIFC, yet there was nothing to stop Gromik mounting a pre-emptive attack if he thought Laptev could get away with it. He would be in and out of the villa inside five minutes, injecting Aranov and leaving him to die. If the right local palms were crossed with the right amount of silver, cause of death would be given as heart failure. There would be no point in Kite alerting the DSS to the caesium footprint at the hotel; Zatulin and Laptev would be back in Moscow within twenty-four hours.

Kite formulated a reply which Rita would understand as an instruction to get Aranov and Natalia out of the house.

Do the boys want to get into the villa? Maybe ask
Mum to bring Dad to the beach so they don't cross
paths.

He sat on the bed as Cara came out of the bathroom. She was wearing a blue summer dress and white trainers, her hair wet from the shower.

'Everything all right?' she asked.

'Could be nothing. Could be something,' he replied. 'All we can do is wait and see.'

60

Rita Ayinde waited for Kite's reply.

She could not risk ordering Aranov to leave the villa. If he became aware that there was a threat against his life, it would throw the operation into chaos. Nor could Stones or Franks show their faces; if Gromik saw them, he would know that he had been tricked. She had to trust her instinct that the Russians were heading towards Umm Suqeim not to kill Sebastian Glik, but merely so that Laptev could take a look at the villa and familiarise himself with the neighbourhood. Nothing coming out of Moscow or Oman indicated that Natalia was communicating with Gromik about anything other than the timing and location of the party. Furthermore, why would a man as experienced and as thorough as Gromik countenance putting men into an MI6 property over which he had no control without apparent preparation?

Yet still Rita had doubts. The Russians had left Business Bay in two vehicles, Gromik in a new Mercedes, Laptev in a Lexus registered to the Russian consulate with Inarkiev at the wheel. Rita and Toby Landau were tracking the Lexus; one of Toby's Emirati boys was close to the Mercedes on a moped. It was a dangerous follow; they would have to abandon the pursuit long before they reached the outskirts of Umm Suqeim: Aranov's neighbourhood was too quiet for a discreet tail.

'Pull over,' she told Toby.

'You serious?'

'It's not safe. He'll make us.'

At that moment, at long last, Kite replied to her message.

Do the boys want to get into the villa? Maybe ask
Mum to bring Dad to the beach so they don't cross
paths.

'Lockie says we should call Natalia, get her to move Yuri out of the house. Can you do that?'

'What if she spooks him?'

'Do you think she would?'

Landau shrugged. He had left Sheikh Zayed Road at the English College and pulled over next to a strip of private houses on 35th Street. There were no easy options. Warn Natalia and Aranov might smell a rat; allow the Russians to reach the villa and there was a danger Laptev could walk in and finish the job.

'I don't think we need to worry,' Landau told her with the infuriating self-confidence of youth. 'They're not going to do it now. We should relax.'

'Never tell a woman to relax.' Rita looked out at the white-washed walls of the houses, blinding sunlight on the windscreens of passing cars. 'Gromik's people have a history of opportunistic strikes. Maybe the plan has changed and MOCKINGBIRD isn't across it.'

'Maybe, maybe.' Landau's tone was slightly insolent. He glanced at his watch. 'Look, there's no time. Even if I call Nat, suggest she takes the old man for a walk, by the time he's agreed to stop watching TV, pulled on his trousers, found his face mask and applied some Factor 30, Laptev will be at his door. We've had a good run up to now. We've been thorough and we've been lucky. Something like this was bound to happen. There's nothing we can do to stop it without blowing the whole thing.'

'Fuck that,' Rita replied. 'I'm getting out.'

61

Within three minutes Rita had hailed a taxi on Sheikh Zayed Road, within ten she was pulling up in Umm Suqeim on a quiet street running parallel to Aranov's villa. Before her stood a row of suburban brick houses, each one identical to the next. If she could find a passageway between them it would lead her to the shared swimming pool in the centre of the block. With luck, she could then reach Aranov's back gate in time to prevent any attack.

She was dressed to be ignored: in a faded cotton blouse and denim skirt, the off-duty uniform of a sub-Saharan house-keeper. Rita tried a side gate to the nearest house but found that it was locked. She walked to the next property and tried again. A dented metal door rattled but would not open. At the third attempt, she tried a wooden gate separating two houses similar in design to Aranov's villa. The gate opened and Rita found herself in a small, overgrown garden. She joined a dusty path which led her through a grove of trees to the swimming pool.

A man was half-submerged in the shallow end. He was reading a paperback book and looked up at Rita without acknowledging her. Doubtless he thought she was a maid from one of the neighbouring houses. A child's coloured beach ball was wedged under an oleander. Rita bent down and picked it up. Aranov's back gate was only twenty metres away; she could tell where it was by the position of the tall palm tree growing alongside it. A fence separated the back garden of Yuri's villa from the pool. Rita walked up and peered over it.

No sound or movement inside the house. She opened the gate and walked into the back garden. The French windows were open and there were two empty glasses on a table in the centre of the verandah. For an awful moment Rita thought that she was too late. Laptev had been and gone, entering the villa through the back garden and vanishing as quickly as he had come. But then she heard a voice.

'Hello?'

It was Natalia. She was leaning out of the bedroom window. Rita looked up, shielding her eyes from the sun.

'Found a ball,' she said, adopting the same Ghanaian accent she had used at the airport with Deviatkin. 'Is it yours please, madam?'

'No,' Natalia replied. It became apparent that Aranov was behind her, asking who she was speaking to. 'We don't have children. It is not our ball.'

It was the first time Rita had seen Natalia since the bar of the Royal Continental. She had spent most of the evening with her back to Aranov's table and indeed Natalia showed no indication of having recognised her. With a friendly wave, Rita asked if she might leave the garden via the front gate and Natalia happily gave permission.

'Of course,' she said. 'Hope you find the owner!'

With a feeling of relief, Rita made her way to the front of the house. There was no traffic on Al Woushar. She looked up and down the street. Two large plastic dustbins had been left at the edge of the road. She opened one of them and threw the ball inside: a stench of rotting food reared up at her. She crossed the road, walking towards a section of waste ground littered with bottles and shattered blocks of concrete. She was heading in the direction of a bus stop, wondering what had become of the Russians, when she saw the Mercedes. Gromik was heading for Aranov's villa. Laptev and Inarkiev were directly behind him in the Lexus. Rita kept walking. None of the men looked at her as they drove past.

A young, smartly dressed woman was coming along the pavement towards her, pushing a pram. Adjusting her hair as though she wished to make a good impression, Rita gestured at the woman to stop.

'Excuse me,' she said, staying with the Ghanaian accent. 'Do you live around here?'

In a European city, the woman might have ignored her and walked on, but this was suburban Dubai – safe, quiet, international – and people were generally friendlier.

'I do,' she said. She had a posh English accent. 'Can I help?'

Rita moved to one side so that she could look down the street while continuing the conversation. The two vehicles had slowed on approach to Aranov's villa.

'I'm going from door to door,' she said. 'I am nanny. Looking for work.'

Rita put on a pair of sunglasses and continued to watch them. The young mother summoned a look of profound empathy.

'Oh I'm so sorry,' she said. 'We already have somebody living with us.'

'Do you have any friends with children looking for help?' Rita asked. Neither vehicle had stopped. 'I can cook for them. Clean. Babysit.'

'I really am terribly sorry.'

The Russians were not getting out of their cars. Gromik carried on to the next block, swung the Mercedes around in a wide loop and started back in Rita's direction. The Lexus did a three-point turn outside the villa.

'OK, OK,' Rita said. 'Nice talking to you. Thank you for stopping.'

'Absolute pleasure,' the mother replied. 'Good luck with your search!'

The Mercedes passed them at speed, tailwinds throwing up a cloud of dust which caused the mother to curse and

432

pull a muslin over her pram. Rita walked up to the corner of the street, saw Inarkiev drive past with Laptev in the passenger seat, and tapped out a signal message on her mobile.

Nothing to worry about. Boys didn't want to go inside after all. I saw Mum and Dad. They're both well x

Kite's reply came through a few seconds later.

Glad to hear it. I'm off to that place on the Creek we talked about. Time to speak to the manager x

62

Kite presented himself at the whitewashed gates of the British embassy on Al Seef Street as 'James Justin Harris'. His bag was searched and he was asked to leave his mobile at the entrance. Having placed the phone in a locked box, a uniformed Nepali official directed him towards the reception area. Kite sat beneath a portrait of the Queen flanked by Union Jack-themed posters advertising the capitalised glories of 'GREAT Britain'. A machine in the corner was threatening paper cups of undrinkable filtered coffee. Two tanned young men in immensely tight white trousers were advised by a member of staff that their replacement passports would be ready by the time the embassy closed at 2.30 p.m. Kite imagined they were social media influencers, fans of *Love Island* and *The Only Way is Essex*, visiting Dubai to avoid the tiered lockdowns back home. One of them, a dead ringer for the footballer Rio Ferdinand, nodded at Kite and said: 'All right, mate. What you in for?'

'Lost passport,' Kite replied.

Mark Sheridan was on time. He was the SIS Head of Station, declared to the government of the United Arab Emirates, a fortysomething married father of three who had cut his eye teeth in Iraq and Afghanistan. Kite had tapped him up for a job in BOX 88 two years earlier. Sheridan, attracted by the idea of remaining in the secret world after retiring from SIS, had readily agreed, not least because he would be earning three times his official Foreign Office salary with three sets of school fees covered to the age of eighteen. Dubai was to be his final posting before he transferred to BOX.

'Mr Harris?' he said, casting his eyes around the waiting room. To Kite's amusement, Sheridan first allowed them to settle on the two tight-trousered gentlemen of Essex. 'Mr James Harris?'

'That's me,' Kite answered, rising to his feet.

'Would you come with me, please?'

Kite adjusted his face mask and followed Sheridan out of the waiting room. They made their way along a series of brightly lit corridors soaked in CCTV exchanging pleasantries about the pandemic. Sheridan opened two sets of alarmed doors using a laminated pass and led Kite to a secure speech room in the eastern corner of the embassy. He switched off the automated recording system so that no evidence of their conversation would exist.

'If you're here, I assume it's time for us to act,' he said.

Sheridan was a tanned, thick-set man with a healthy head of hair parted in the centre. There was a slight gap in his front teeth, the only idiosyncrasy in an otherwise ordered, rather bland face. He reminded Kite of the headmaster at his godson's boarding school near Frome.

'The situation is more or less where we wanted and expected it to be,' he told him. 'Yuri fell for Toby's Russian girl, hook, line and sinker. Can't get enough of her, sings about her in his sleep. Gromik was looking for a weakness, saw Natalia as the way in. Approached her coming out of a yoga class last week and applied the necessary pressure. She's invited Yuri to a party tomorrow night in an apartment block in DIFC. We assume the idea is to inject him in the house style or – if they're feeling lazy – chuck him off the balcony. It's conveniently located over a deserted pedestrian square so there'd be no danger of the falling body injuring any passers-by.'

'They think of everything in Moscow.' Sheridan was

wearing a tie. He took it off, rolled it up and set it down on the table. 'What kind of party?'

'Exclusive. Kick-off 9 p.m. Yuri and Natalia the only guests. Canapés and good times. Hudson Park Residencies Tower One, an apartment on the sixteenth floor overlooking the royal palace. Only other guests in attendance Comrade Vasily Zatulin of the Criminalistics Institute and his colleague Mr Andrei Laptev, both Lubyanka Closers with a roll call of dead bodies on their CVs.'

'I assume they're already in town?'

Kite nodded. 'I was in their hotel this morning. The room is ready, just a question of the DSS being alerted to the isotope and sending a team to investigate.'

'How do you want to do it?' Sheridan asked.

'Timing is everything.' Kite had written to Sheridan in advance of his arrival in Dubai but this was the first time they had had the chance to discuss the final stages of the operation in detail. 'I want you to speak to Khalil at 5 p.m. tomorrow, exactly four hours before the party is due to start.' Khalil Albaloushi was a senior brigadier in Dubai State Security and a close friend of Sheridan's. 'Show him the evidence. You tell Khalil that this is a stream of intelligence coming out of Moscow from a highly placed source inside the FSB which must be acted upon immediately. The life of a British citizen is in danger, a radioactive isotope is at large in Dubai, more people stand to lose their lives unless we stop Gromik and expose the JUDAS programme.'

'What about the technical side?' Sheridan smothered a sneeze. 'How much evidence have the Turings compiled?'

'Goldmine.' Kite instinctively reached for his phone before remembering that he had left it at the entrance. 'Oman has everything. The data will be transferred to you as soon as I leave the embassy this afternoon. Phone calls, metadata, photographs of Gromik with Zatulin and Laptev, encrypted messaging between the various members of the Russian team. Certainly more than enough to convince Khalil to act and more than enough to put Gromik behind bars.'

Kite spotted a box of water bottles in the corner of the Secure Speech room. He took two, passed one to Sheridan and opened the other.

'It's all yours. This becomes an SIS operation, a triumph for MI6. But you must impress upon Khalil the importance of waiting until exactly eight o'clock before they seal off the Regal Plaza. If their boys go to the hotel too early and make a song and dance, the Russians will hear about it on the bush telegraph and get spooked. Gromik will pull the plug on the party and his team will disperse.'

Sheridan reached for his rolled-up tie, tossing it between his hands like a baseball.

'Don't worry. Khalil will do as he's told. He knows I've got something in the pipeline.'

Kite was reassured by this but knew there were dozens of components which could fail at the last moment.

'None of this was worth doing unless we get Gromik's head on a plate,' he said. 'He missed Navalny. The next three names on the JUDAS list are all vulnerable. BOX can't protect them, nor can the British and American governments. Gromik will always find a way. We let him go, we'll have their blood on our hands.'

'The next name on the JUDAS list is yours, Lockie.'

Kite hesitated. Sheridan had been told about Peter Galvin on background for the Aranov operation.

'I'm one more target, yes,' he conceded. 'According to MOCKINGBIRD, nobody at the FSB, the Kremlin or anywhere else has ever heard of Lachlan Kite, which makes Galvin's appearance on the JUDAS list all the more baffling. I've always worked on the assumption that we don't go after one another's intelligence officers. It's against the rules.'

'The rules Putin seems so keen to obey?'

Kite acknowledged Sheridan's point but had said all he intended to say about Galvin. They moved on.

'Speaking of MOCKINGBIRD,' Sheridan continued. 'Is he – or she – going to be secure after all this?'

'He,' said Kite. 'We've had nine people servicing his every

need on and off for six weeks. Brush contacts, clean phones, safe houses, hotel rooms, every trick in the book. He's exhausted, has wanted out for a long time. Knows this is his last dance. Tomorrow morning he gets on a plane to Istanbul, ostensibly en route to Damascus for a security conference. A BOX team will pick him up at the airport, take him to Paris.'

'And Makarov has no idea that Gromik is going after Aranov? You're sure of that?'

It was the question Kite had been asking himself ever since Deviatkin and Gromik had teamed up to run the operation.

'Well that was always the risk of MOCKINGBIRD sending Laptev and Zatulin to Dubai,' Kite replied. 'All it would take is one phone call, a chance remark, a sense in Moscow that something is out of place, and our whole house of cards comes crashing down.'

63

Leonid Deviatkin was locking the safe in his office and preparing to leave the Lubyanka for what he hoped would be the last time when there was a knock at the door.

'Come in,' he called out.

Director Alexander Makarov walked in, closely followed by General Vladimir Osipov of the Criminalistics Institute. It was unusual to see the two men together in this section of the building; usually Osipov only visited the sixth floor if he was called to a meeting.

'May I speak to you for a moment, Leonid Antonovich?'

Makarov's tone was so courteous that Deviatkin immediately became suspicious. Had something gone wrong in Dubai? Aranov was due at the party in less than three hours. Had the British team been rumbled?

'Of course,' he said, welcoming Osipov with a friendly nod which was not reciprocated. 'What can I do for you?'

Makarov leaned against a bookcase, distractedly rubbing his cheek. 'Do you know how I might track down Vasily Nikolaiovich?'

'Zatulin?'

'Yes.'

Disguising his concern, Deviatkin landed on a line of questioning.

'Is he not answering his phone?'

'If he was, would I be here?'

'And you need him for a job?'

The question caused Makarov to look over at Osipov, who had taken it upon himself quietly to close the door of the office.

'Not for a job, no.'

Deviatkin knew that his meeting with Zatulin and Laptev in Gorky Park would have been recorded in the diary, so he said: 'I met him in Gorky Park last week on a personal matter. I haven't seen him since.'

'Personal?'

'Personal with a professional twist.' Deviatkin implied with a knowing smile that the meeting had been of no great significance. 'Vasily Nikolaiovich wanted my advice.'

To Deviatkin's relief, Makarov did not immediately ask what Zatulin's problem had been. Instead he wanted to know why Gromik had used his MODIN security clearance to investigate the names 'Martha Rain' and 'Martha Raven' at the consulate in Dubai.

'Martha who?' Deviatkin was profoundly shaken. It was the first time that any of his colleagues had mentioned Martha's name in all the time that he had worked for the FSB. 'Never heard of her.'

'Me neither,' Makarov observed. 'There are no reports on women of that name. Nothing in the files. I wonder what he was after.'

Deviatkin shrugged. It was all he could do; better to feign puzzlement than to add another layer to his existing deceits.

'Have you contacted Mikhail Dimitrovich?' he asked, dreading the answer. Any communication between Gromik and Makarov might potentially expose the existence of the Aranov plan.

'I wanted to see you first,' Makarov replied. 'There are some irregularities in the records. Mikhail Dimitrovich first showed an interest in this Martha after your meeting in Jumeirah.'

'He did?' Deviatkin looked at Osipov, who had maintained

an expression of stony-faced revulsion ever since he had walked in. 'Meaning he went to the consulate and ran the names through MODIN?'

'That is precisely what I mean, yes. Not before. Immediately afterwards.'

'Forgive me, Director, but what is it that I can help you with? What are your concerns? That Mikhail Dimitrovich is operating outside his remit?'

The question seemed to stir something inside both men.

'Do you think he is?' Makarov asked.

Again Deviatkin shrugged, offering an explanation which he hoped would convey the extent to which he revered Gromik and considered him above suspicion in all matters.

'Not at all,' he said. 'Perhaps Rain – or Raven – is somebody Gromik has encountered in Dubai. Perhaps his research on MODIN was unrelated to our conversation at the Royal Continental. Who knows?'

Osipov folded his arms. Glancing at Makarov, he touched the lapel of his jacket. It was probably an agreed signal: either that he believed Deviatkin to be lying or that he was sure he was telling the truth.

'Possibly,' said Makarov. 'I'll have my assistant look into it.'

He picked up a paperweight from the desk, felt the weight of it in his hands and asked: 'What are your plans for the next few days, Leonid Antonovich?'

It felt like the blade being raised on a guillotine. Deviatkin could not know if he was under suspicion or if Makarov's question was merely an innocent enquiry into his probable whereabouts.

'I'm flying to Damascus tomorrow morning,' he replied. 'Via Istanbul. The RSII security conference. Remember?'

'Let's fly together,' Makarov suggested with a warm, enveloping gesture of camaraderie which was quite out of character. 'I have a plane taking me directly to Syria. No need for you to route through Turkey, especially with all the trouble around Covid. Afterwards we'll go down to Dubai and speak to

Mikhail Dimitrovich in person. I'd like to get to the bottom of the mysterious Martha. Something about her doesn't feel right.'

Deviatkin was sure that Makarov was setting a trap. It was possible that he had already spoken to Gromik, that Kite's involvement in the Aranov operation had been exposed and that Deviatkin would be arrested before nightfall. Nevertheless, he was obliged to respond to the director's invitation with a suitable display of gratitude.

'What a kind offer,' he said. 'I would like that very much.' He turned to find that Osipov had stepped forward and was staring at him; it was like stumbling into a cobweb. 'If there's room on the plane, I would of course be honoured to join you.'

64

Natalia Kovalenko emerged from the shower, checked that she was still on time for the party and picked out a dress. Toby had told her not to take anything – a tramadol, a Xanax – because he knew that she sometimes used medication for her nerves. He had said she would need 'her wits about her' this evening, an expression Natalia had never heard before. She stared at the strip of pills on her bedside table. She knew her own mind, how the anxiety inside her could quickly complicate into panic. Pushing a pill from the packet, she swallowed it with a slug of Evian and wondered how long it would take before she felt better about what was going to happen.

The doorbell. Toby and Sally were early. Natalia answered the intercom, found some Van Morrison on Spotify and returned to the bedroom. She lived alone in a one-bedroom apartment in Al Hudaiba with noisy, nosy neighbours and a view across a dusty grid of streets and the docks at Al Mina. Toby knocked on the door as she was zipping up her dress. Holding a bottle of champagne, he swept into the apartment with an ecstatic 'Happy birthday!', complimenting Natalia on the way she looked while miming that they should be wary of microphones. Sally followed, looking like a typical English girl of her generation, dressed down in a cotton dress with white sneakers, no effort made with her hair or make-up. Natalia wondered if Toby minded that. In the old days, when they had partied together, he had told her how much he enjoyed the way Russian women dressed and looked after themselves. He liked being seen with her in public, knowing that he was the man who was going to take her home and 'unwrap her'. Sally was cute and funny and clever, for sure, but there was no devil inside her. Natalia was sure that Toby would soon become bored and move on to his next conquest.

'Happy birthday, Natalia!' she exclaimed, enveloping her in a hug of Coco Mademoiselle. She was holding a bunch of flowers. 'You look amazing!'

'Thank you,' Natalia replied quietly. 'You too. English dress?'

'Yeah. Bought it from London. Vintage.' Sally closed the door behind her as Toby sang along to 'Moondance'. 'Where's your dress from, Nat?'

'Dolce.'

It was then that Natalia noticed Sally's handbag; it was exactly the same as the one she had taken to dinner at La Petite Maison. Was she trying to copy her style?

'Excited about the party?' Toby asked, acting as if everything was normal. 'Where are you taking the old man?'

'Just to a friend's apartment.' Natalia was not as proficient at dissembling for the microphones and felt caught off guard by his questions. 'Small dinner.'

'We're going to Avli,' he replied, so high-spirited and relaxed. 'Do you know it?'

'I have been taken there.'

Sally came towards her with the flowers.

'These are for me?' Natalia asked.

Sally indicated that Natalia should read the card that was tucked inside the arrangement.

Take my handbag to the party. It has a microphone and a camera running.

She looked at Sally, who said: 'I'm really looking forward to it. Toby says it's the best Greek restaurant in Dubai.'

'Expensive,' Natalia replied, unbalanced by what was happening. The note continued:

Also Mace. If you're in trouble, we'll know and we'll come to help you.

Natalia looked at them both and nodded. Sally produced a forced smile and said: 'Good job I'm not paying then!'

Toby took three glasses from the kitchen and popped the bottle of champagne. Two days earlier he had told her that the apartment was clean; MI6 had been watching it and nobody had tried to break in to plant cameras or bugs. Why, then, couldn't they speak freely?

'So guess what we did yesterday?' he said.

Natalia was expecting an interesting story – Toby always told interesting stories – but soon came to understand that he was merely making empty conversation so that their meeting would sound as natural as possible. Natalia picked up the piece of paper, found a pen in a drawer, laid the paper across the glass surface of the table and wrote them a note of her own.

Who is listening?

Sally took the pen from her. Toby was still telling his story, an exaggerated anecdote about going kayaking among the mangroves in Ajman. Sally started to write.

'People think Dubai is just a city of sin,' he continued. 'Dirty money, winter sun, no culture, blah blah blah. But there we were, forty miles from Marina in one of the most beautiful places on God's green earth, all kinds of wildlife, beautiful birds, pink flamingos . . .'

Sally handed Natalia the note.

Possible directional microphone across the street.
To catch the vibrations on the window.
You are doing BRILLIANTLY. Everything will be fine!

Natalia had not heard the term 'directional microphone' before but it was easily understood. She looked at Sally and nodded, aware that she was shaking very slightly. The tramadol had not yet taken hold. They clinked glasses and drank some champagne. Toby was still talking about the mangroves.

'Or if you want culture, there's the Dubai Opera, the Louvre in Abu Dhabi, all kinds of art galleries. Why do people insist on painting Dubai as a kind of Sodom and Gomorrah-on-Sea?'

'Have you quit your job and gone into PR?' Sally asked. Natalia saw the spark between them, that sarcastic sense of humour which bound the British to one another, always to the exclusion of outsiders. 'Why are you banging on about art galleries and Abu Dhabi? We're here to have a drink with Natalia on her birthday.'

'Sorry,' Toby replied, playing the hapless boyfriend. It was a side of him that Natalia had seen many times; the practised deceiver, the actor capable of playing a dozen different roles. 'What time are you off?'

'Soon,' she replied.

In her mind she was running through all the things Toby had told her about the party. To go alone. To text Sebastian Glik when she was almost there, asking how long it was going to be before he arrived. Then to go up to the apartment, just after nine o'clock, and to tell Gromik that her boyfriend was coming separately. Not to eat or drink anything she was offered unless she was sure that they were prepared to eat or drink it themselves.

'Maybe we could meet afterwards?' Toby suggested.

'After what?'

'After it's over!' he exclaimed. 'Is Seb coming here or are you meeting him at the party?'

'At the party.'

In Russia they have a saying: 'He lied like an eye witness.' Toby Landau was just such a man. Looking straight at her, as though everything was easy and stress-free, he said:

446

'So it's settled then. Let's meet up for a proper birthday celebration. Bring Seb if you think he can handle the pace. It's amazing to think that by midnight you'll be twenty-six!'

65

Yuri Aranov could not remember looking forward to something as much as he was looking forward to going to the party with Natalia. For weeks he had been trapped in the Faleiro, eating the same room service food, followed day and night by his bodyguards, forbidden to go out in Dubai. Now here he was living rent-free in an attractive house in one of the most sought-after neighbourhoods in the Emirate. He had a beautiful Russian girlfriend, no nagging ex-wife badgering him for money, and an MI6 expense account which dwarfed his monthly salary at Porton Down. When Aranov read in the newspapers about life in England, the stories painted a bleak picture of damp, deserted town centres, rising Covid cases, the inevitability of a long winter lockdown, chaotic, overcrowded hospitals. He would occasionally check the weather in Andover – rain, single-digit temperatures – and chuckle to himself as he looked out of the window on another glorious day in Dubai. He had not felt so positive for years. No wonder Natalia told him he had the vitality of a man of thirty-five.

The sun was setting over Umm Suqeim. Aranov was in his bedroom on the first floor of the safe house applying a splash of aftershave and checking his reflection in the full-length mirror. He was wearing a blue linen jacket – a favourite of Natalia's – and listening to some U2. Natalia had told him that her friends ranged in age from twenty-five to seventy; some of them had lived in the Gulf for many years, others were more recent arrivals. Aranov wanted to make a good impression on them; more than that, he wanted to look like a man who belonged in Dubai.

So absorbed was he in these thoughts that when he closed the bedroom curtains against the dusk, he failed to see two men moving in the shadows beyond the garden. Humming along to the chorus of 'With or Without You', Aranov walked downstairs to pour himself a glass of wine. He checked his phone and saw that Natalia had sent him a message. She was due to arrive at any moment.

> Baby I'm sorry. Can I meet you at the party? Running late. I went to the beauty salon then Pilates, then Toby and Sally surprised me with a visit. They brought champagne! Forgive me? I'll make it up to you, baby. I promise.

As was always the case with Natalia – in fact with all young women in Aranov's experience – the message was decorated with emojis. This one ended in love hearts and kisses, smiles and winks. There was even a purple devil after 'beauty salon' which made him feel weak with longing. He tapped out a reply.

> Of course, no problem. Just let me know the address. Maybe we can meet outside and go in together?

Natalia agreed that this was an ideal solution and sent Aranov the address of the building in DIFC where the party was taking place. He set the phone down, took a bottle of Muscadet from the fridge and was just about to pour himself a glass when he was startled by a sudden movement behind him.

'Sorry to give you a fright,' said the man. 'It's time we had a little talk.'

66

The Cathedral had found Kite a bedsit on Airbnb in a high-rise adjacent to Hudson Park Tower One. From the living-room window, looking seven floors up, he could see the south-east corner of the sixteenth-floor apartment where Gromik, Laptev and Zatulin were gathered, waiting for Aranov. Kite had checked in using the Harris alias and was looped into the surveillance attack on the party via a laptop, two-way radios and a brace of mobile phones. Natalia was en route to the party in an Uber. Rita was inside the tower on the same floor as Gromik, role-playing a cleaning woman. Toby and Cara were having a drink in the Four Seasons in DIFC, ready to move when required.

Everything was in place but everything could still go wrong. Kite knew that once Gromik became aware that he had been framed, he would attempt to flee. With a network of contacts across the Gulf ready to assist him in his hour of need, he could be out of Dubai by midnight and back in Russia by dawn. It was vital that BOX didn't lose him.

Natalia's Uber was a red dot across a map of central Dubai, looping off Sheikh Zayed Road and pulling up in front of the tower just before nine o'clock. As soon as Kite saw the vehicle he texted Mark Sheridan, giving the signal to provide Khalil Albaloushi with the address of the party. He was to emphasise that the three Russian intelligence officers – Gromik, Zatulin and Laptev – were inside Hudson Park Tower One in Apartment 1662 expecting Sebastian Glik to arrive at any moment. If Kite's calculations were correct, the police would be there within ten minutes.

The take quality from the microphone in Natalia's handbag was as good as Kite could have hoped. On the laptop he could also see reasonably clear images from the miniature camera hidden in the clasp. He heard her thank the driver, the clunk of the car door closing, then watched shaky footage as Natalia made her way to the entrance. She was the one element of the plan over which he had no control; if Gromik tied her to the conspiracy, there was no knowing what he might do to her. Kite had always worked on the assumption that Gromik wouldn't risk harming Natalia, but in truth there was no telling how a man like that might react once he realised he had been cornered and was facing ruin.

A security guard opened the door at the base of the tower and pointed a temperature gun at Natalia's forehead. No provision had been made for her getting Covid; if she was running a fever, so be it, the arrests could still take place. But the guard waved her through and Landau's girl made her way across a brightly lit, marbled-finished lobby towards a bank of lifts at the rear of the building. Once inside the cabin she pressed '16' and checked for messages on her phone.

'She's doing well,' Kite muttered to himself.

On the sixteenth floor, Natalia proceeded along a deserted corridor to the door of apartment 1662. Kite wondered if he might catch sight of Rita at the edge of the frame, vacuuming the carpet or dusting the lights, but she was nowhere to be seen.

Natalia stopped at the door. Kite briefly saw her high-heeled shoes and caught a glimpse of the watch on her wrist. Then a gentle rat-tat-tat as she knocked.

The door opened almost immediately. Kite saw the lower part of a man's chest and the Gucci belt on his trousers. Gromik. He invited Natalia inside and closed the door behind them.

'Where is he?' Gromik asked in Russian.

'He's coming,' Natalia replied.

'You were supposed to bring him with you.' He sounded suspicious but not angry. 'You were supposed to come together.'

'Don't worry.' Kite was amazed by how calm she sounded. A BOX 88 team had searched Natalia's apartment and found some Xanax. Maybe she had swallowed one for her nerves. 'He's looking forward to the party. He's on his way. Some friends came round to my apartment to wish me happy birthday. This way was easier.'

Kite noted that Gromik did not ask which friends had paid her a visit; perhaps he already knew. Natalia had turned so that the clasp of the handbag was facing into the apartment. There were two shadows by the window.

'Who are these men?' she asked.

'My colleagues,' Gromik replied. 'This is Sergei, behind him Anton. They are guests at the party. Friends. Drink this.'

A champagne glass was thrust in front of the lens.

'I don't want anything to drink,' Natalia replied. 'What is your plan tonight? Who are these men?'

Zatulin came forward. 'Take the champagne,' he told her, flanking Gromik. Kite could see the shadow of his pot belly. 'When your boyfriend comes to the door, it needs to look like you're having a good time.'

To Kite's dismay, Natalia took the glass. Surely she knew not to drink anything they gave her?

'I don't trust you,' she said, her words so clear in Kite's headphones she might have been in the same room. 'You drink it. I know what you people are like.'

It was an extraordinarily brave thing to say. At the back of the image, Laptev turned. Zatulin said: 'Watch your mouth' but Gromik calmed him with a colloquial Russian phrase Kite did not understand.

'I'll drink it,' he said firmly and took the glass from Natalia's hand. She pivoted to the right. Kite could see the movement of Gromik's arm as he swallowed the champagne.

'See?' he said, passing the glass back to her. 'We are not monsters. The drink is quite safe. You should not believe what you read about us in the papers. Now where is your fucking boyfriend?'

67

'Sorry to give you a fright,' said Jim Stones. 'It's time we had a little talk.'

Stones and Jason Franks had somehow materialised in Aranov's kitchen. The Russian was so shocked that he dropped his wine glass. It was a long-stemmed plastic picnic glass which bounced on the floor like a child's toy. There was something absurd about the sound it made.

'I thought we told you to keep your back door locked at all times,' said Franks, taking Aranov's mobile phone and placing it in the fridge. 'Now we find out you're going to meet some Russians without informing us.' He touched the collar of Aranov's blue linen jacket. 'What was the point in trusting you?'

'What the hell is this?' Aranov replied. 'Give me back my phone. I thought you were both in England? I thought you left Dubai?'

'Flew home and came back,' Stones replied succinctly. 'Missed you, Seb. Thought you might need looking after.'

'I do not need looking after.' Aranov tried to open the fridge, but Stones prevented him. 'I am a free man. You told me I could live how I liked!'

'Yeah, about that.' Franks guided Aranov towards the living room. 'Afraid we encountered something of a problem.'

'What kind of a problem?' Aranov picked up the plastic

picnic glass on his way out of the kitchen. He looked like somebody clearing up at the end of a party. 'Where did you come from? We said goodbye. Why are you back in my home?'

'That nice girlfriend of yours is not who she appears to be,' Stones told him.

'Not who she appears to be?' Aranov stopped and turned. 'What do you mean?'

'She's a Russian agent, Seb,' said Franks.

The Best of U2 was still playing on Aranov's hi-fi. He tried to switch it off but only succeeded in turning up the volume on 'I Still Haven't Found What I'm Looking For'. In desperation he gestured at both men to leave the villa.

'Absolute bullshit,' he said, spittle flying out of his mouth as he repeated his demand. 'Of course she's not. You're paranoid. Get out!'

'It's not bullshit,' said Stones, turning down the music. 'And we're not paranoid. The party tonight is a trap. Local SVR found out you were here. Chances are you'd have been killed if you'd shown your face. We have to get you out of Dubai in the next six hours. There's a flight leaving at two. You've got to pack right away, only take what you need. There's no time for questions, no more time to argue.'

There was a moment in which Aranov seemed to grasp the seriousness of what Stones had said, but just as quickly he reverted to a toddler-like state of enraged injustice. His mouth collapsed into a gaping sulk, his hands were raised above his head in furious indignation, his voice so stressed that the words came out as a sustained whine.

'I will not go!' he said. It looked as though he might stamp his feet. 'Your information is quite wrong!' He swore angrily in his native tongue. 'Natalia is Natalia, not an agent for SVR. This is shit. Total bullshit. Get out of my house!'

'Your jacket,' said Stones, ignoring him. 'Give it to me.'

'My what?' the Russian replied. 'Why do you want it? Fuck you, no, you can't have my jacket.' Then he saw the two men coming towards him and was suddenly frightened.

'What do you mean I have to leave Dubai tonight? This is crazy. What about my house?'

'No more questions, Seb,' said Franks, indicating that he should remove the jacket. 'SVR needs to think you're on the way to the party. Jim here is going to put on your clothes, your Panama hat and your favourite face mask and he's going to walk outside and get into an Uber. You and I are going out back, through the garden, past the pool, to a car that's waiting on Shilameen. From there we go to the airport. Understood?'

At last Aranov was silent. Every dream he had entertained about the night ahead – the new friends he was going to make, the sparkling conversation he would enjoy, the long night back at the villa in Natalia's lithe, soft arms – had been shattered by MI6. They had messed up. They were amateurs. He had been betrayed.

'No it is not understood!' he exclaimed, the last cry of the incensed toddler. 'Not understood at all.'

Stones now did something which he had been wanting to do ever since he had first set eyes on Yuri Aranov. Grabbing the Russian by the shoulders, he pushed him up against the wall and said: 'This is no fucking joke, mate. What did we say about asking questions? What did we tell you about arguing with us?'

Aranov felt the weight and thickness of Stones's forearm against his chest. It was like being pinioned by a metal bar.

'All right, all right,' he gasped. 'Let me go. I pack. We leave. Don't hurt me. I'll do as you say.'

'There's a good boy,' Stones replied. 'Now give me the fucking jacket.'

68

'Text your boyfriend,' said Gromik, sipping from the glass of champagne. 'Find out where he is.'

Natalia Kovalenko took out her phone and pointed at the screen. WhatsApp had isolated Glik's location to the street outside the villa in Umm Suqeim. The switch in Gromik's mood, the way he menaced her and then turned on the charm, was profoundly unsettling. She realised that her hand was shaking.

'Look,' she said. 'He's on his way. He's coming.' Gromik glanced at the screen and seemed satisfied that Natalia was telling the truth. 'Are you going to harm him?' she asked. 'What are you going to do to him?'

These were the men whose colleagues had murdered her parents. She had to keep driving that thought from her mind or she might lose all self-control. The tramadol hadn't helped at all; everything inside her was tense and fearful. Gromik was standing so close that it felt as though at any moment he might grab her or drag her outside to the balcony.

'We just want to talk to him,' he replied in Russian. It was a glib response; it no longer served him to treat her with any respect. 'Once he gets here, you can go. We know where you live, of course. We can find your friends and any member of your family. You know to keep quiet and never to speak of what happened here today.'

'I swear I will never say a word.' Natalia believed in her soul that there was now nothing Toby or his friends from MI6 would be able to do to prevent Sebastian dying that night. Either Gromik and his accomplices would poison him and make it look like a heart attack or they would throw him off the balcony. It happened all the time, all around the world. The Russian state specialised in accidental death.

'Where is he now?'

The question came from the taller of the two men who had been standing by the window. Natalia looked down at her phone and saw to her surprise that Glik's taxi was already a mile from the villa.

'He's on his way,' she said. 'Do you want me to text him?'

'Would you usually text him when he's about to meet you?' Gromik asked.

'No,' she replied.

'Then don't.'

He walked over to a table in the centre of the living room and picked up a walkie-talkie. He set the channel and lifted it to his mouth. Gromik spoke briskly, in what was obviously a coded language designed to sound benign to anybody listening in. Natalia concluded that there was somebody else on Gromik's team watching the entrance to the tower, waiting for Sebastian to show up.

'What are you going to do to him?' she asked again, tears suddenly springing to her eyes. Gromik gestured at her to be quiet as he listened to a response on the radio.

'How much longer?' said a male voice. Natalia assumed he was asking about Glik's estimated arrival time.

'Within ten minutes,' Gromik replied. 'Join him in the bar if you can.'

What was 'the bar'? The lobby? The lift? Natalia had an image of Glik being injected by this man in the cramped steel confines of a lift. There was nobody who could stop it happening, nobody who could save Sebastian.

'I want to leave,' she cried out. 'He's coming. You don't need me anymore. Let me go.'

'On the contrary.' Gromik placed the radio back on the table. 'This is a moment when we very much need a beautiful woman like you to stick around. Why don't you come out onto the balcony, Natalia Petrovna? The view over Dubai is spectacular.'

69

The fire alarm sounded at the Regal Plaza shortly after eight o'clock, forcing over 275 disgruntled guests and staff to evacuate the hotel over a period lasting around twenty minutes. At the same time, more than a dozen uniformed officers from the General Department of State Security descended on the hotel. Salah Al Din Street was blocked from the Warba Center intersection in the east to the Fish Roundabout at the edge of Al Maktoum Road to the west. Traffic within a two-mile radius was quickly brought to a standstill. As a precaution, officers from the Dubai police ordered and arranged the evacuation of all residents from properties on 29th and 30th streets to the north of the hotel.

A decade earlier, word of the chaos at the Regal Plaza might have taken several hours to filter out into the wider community. Residents in Dubai would have seen a report on the nightly news or perhaps received a panicked phone call from a friend or relative who had heard rumours about the two Russian men staying in Room 302. But in the age of Twitter and WhatsApp, of smartphones and 4G, images of men and women in yellow hazmat suits sealing off the hotel shot around the world in seconds. By nine o'clock the hashtags #RegalPlaza #Caesium #Putin #Skripal #Dubai #Navalny and #MI6 occupied seven of the top ten slots on Twitter.

With bots amplifying the chatter, the Turings in Oman were

able to establish a narrative – later forming the template of reports on news channels around the world – that MI6 had foiled an attempted FSB assassination by radioactive isotope of one Yuri Aranov, a Russian scientist who had defected to the United Kingdom in 1993. Several FSB spies were wanted in connection with the plot and were being sought by Dubai State Security. British intelligence officers on the ground in the UAE were assisting them in their task.

The first wave of the story hit the Russian consulate in Umm Al Sheif at almost exactly the same moment that Jason Franks was guiding a disgruntled Yuri Aranov through the back garden of his villa, past the shared swimming pool – now deserted save for a lone, unclaimed inflatable crocodile – and out onto Al Shilameen Street. A car was waiting for them. The driver – the same man who had taken Azhar Masood from the dock to his meeting with Kite at the Galaxy Premier Hotel – popped the boot, helped Franks to load Aranov's luggage, then texted Kite to let him know that Yuri was safe and well and on his way to the airport.

Meanwhile Jim Stones had taken Aranov's phone from its makeshift Faraday cage in the fridge and used it to book an Uber. When he was sure that the driver was outside, he walked out through the front door wearing Aranov's blue linen jacket, one of his signature Lichtenstein face masks and the Panama hat which he sported at all hours of the day and night. In his right hand, Stones was clutching a bottle of Bollinger, in his left a bunch of tulips which Yuri had thoughtfully purchased from Spinneys earlier in the afternoon as a gift for Natalia. Stones and Aranov were about the same height and build, though Stones slowed his walk and stooped slightly en route to the Uber in a much-practised attempt at mimicking Aranov's gait.

Parked a little over two hundred metres away beside the patch of waste ground where Rita had briefly engaged the young English mother in conversation, the SVR officer known to Kite's team as 'Dolph' saw what he thought was Sebastian Glik leaving the villa clutching a bunch of flowers and a bottle of champagne. He had duly texted Valentin Inarkiev to let him know that Glik was en route to Hudson Park Residencies in a black Lexus SUV. Dolph provided the number plate and proceeded to follow it out of Umm Suqeim onto Al Wasl Road.

Inarkiev heard Gromik's callsign on the radio. He was sitting inside a hire car parked on the ramp leading up to the main entrance of Hudson Park Tower One. In a brief conversation, during which he received instructions from Gromik to follow Glik into the building once he arrived and to accompany him in the lift to the sixteenth floor, Inarkiev saw his mobile light up with half a dozen notifications from at least three separate numbers. He put the radio down on the passenger seat and picked up the phone.

There were two messages from colleagues at the consulate and one from Inarkiev's girlfriend in Moscow. They all told the same story and they were all asking the same questions. What the hell was going on? What had happened in Deira? Was there any truth to the rumours? Without looking at social media and before he had even switched on the radio to hear the news reports on Dubai Eye, Inarkiev knew with a feeling of nauseating certainty that their simple and carefully organised assassination plot had been exposed. Somebody in the chain of command had messed up; was it *him*? He opened Twitter and saw a blizzard of posts relating to the evacuation of the Regal Plaza. In astonishment, he scrolled through rumours about a caesium attack in Dubai and concluded that Gromik – against all common sense – had instructed Laptev and Zatulin to bring a radioactive isotope into the UAE. It was a catastrophe.

Abandoning the usual protocols, Inarkiev called Gromik on an open line. Time was of the essence.

'We have a very serious problem,' he told him. 'The Regal Plaza has been raided and sealed off. It's all over Twitter.' Gromik was silent yet his consternation was somehow audible on the line. Inarkiev said: 'The world knows.'

At that moment, two police cars passed him on the ramp

on their way to the entrance of the Tower, sirens blaring. In the distance, Inarkiev could see the flashing lights of more vehicles approaching.

'The cops are here,' he said desperately. 'It's over. They're coming for you, Mikhail Dimitrovich. You need to get out of there as quickly as possible.'

70

Gromik put the phone back into his pocket and walked towards Natalia.

When he struck a woman he liked to use the back of his right hand because there was a chance that the ring on his middle finger would crack the cheekbone.

'You fucking bitch!' he yelled and sent her crashing to the floor. 'You fucked us. You told the police.'

Gromik saw that he had knocked her out. He turned to Laptev and Zatulin, telling them to stay put and to wait for his return. With the habitual cunning of a lifelong predator, he knew that his chances of survival depended on abandoning the two of them to their fate. Both men were trained to deny whatever accusations would be thrown at them; FSB *omerta* guaranteed that they would never betray him. All Gromik had to do was get out of Dubai before the authorities found him. Easier said than done. But with enough money, and the right amount of luck, he could be in Russia by the weekend.

'What's happened?' Zatulin asked. 'Is Glik still coming?'

'I'm going to find out,' Gromik told him. 'Stay off the radio. Stay off the phones. I'll be back in five minutes.'

Kite had listened to Inarkiev's call on a two-second delay from Oman. As he was texting Jim Stones to let him know that he should get out of the Uber, he heard Gromik swearing at Natalia and saw her fall to the ground. The lens in her handbag picked up the base of a chair leg and what he assumed were Gromik's shoes. Surely the Russian wouldn't risk harming her any further; everything depended on his ability to flee the scene as quickly as possible and to distance himself from Laptev and Zatulin.

He called Rita on the radio.

'Good guys on their way up,' he said. 'Keep an eye on the corridor. Number One is moving.'

Seven floors up in the opposite building, Rita heard the click of the door on apartment 1662, a brief exchange in Russian between Gromik and another man, then the sound of someone making their way down the carpeted corridor. She switched on the vacuum cleaner and pushed it towards the apartment, spotting Gromik moving quickly towards the bank of lifts. He had pulled a red face mask and a folded-up Yankees baseball cap from his back pocket and put them on. Though she was standing less than twenty feet away and was sure that he had noticed her, Gromik did not look at Rita. Instead he pressed the button for a lift, intending to go up to a higher floor inside the tower. It was the clever move: let the police raid the apartment, sit it out upstairs while they arrested Laptev and Zatulin, then take advantage of the ensuing chaos to slip away. Gromik might even wait until morning when the dust had settled. Rita wondered if the FSB had a safe flat elsewhere in the building where he would lay low.

But where was Natalia? Rita switched off the vacuum cleaner and turned away just as the bell chimed to announce the arrival of a lift. Gromik stepped into the cabin. The doors closed. Moments later, another lift opened from which four armed soldiers emerged, surging towards Apartment 1662. Leaving the hoover in the corridor, Rita opened a fire door, walked up towards the seventeenth floor and radioed Kite.

'Number One is inside a lift going to a higher floor. No sign of Two or Three. No sign of the girl. Locals going in.'

The stairwell was thick with trapped heat. 'Call the lovebirds,' she told Kite. 'Our boy could stick around for a while, could go for the car.'

The car was the vehicle in which Gromik had driven to the Hudson Park Residencies, a Jaguar I-PACE belonging to a Brazilian girlfriend who had loaned him the keys while she was out of town. Gromik had used it in order to circumvent ANPR cameras which would otherwise have pinpointed his own vehicle to the location of Aranov's planned demise. The Jaguar was parked in a quiet street on the opposite side of Al Mustaqbal Street, not far from the eastern perimeter of the royal palace.

'Watch the exits,' Kite told the team. 'A lot of ways out for Number One. Unless he's got an apartment in there, he's on CCTV. If it was me, I'd leave the building.'

Standing on the concrete stairwell between the sixteenth and seventeenth floors, Rita listened to Kite's message just as she heard a fire door opening several floors up. Was it Gromik? Surely it was too soon to risk leaving the building? She had been sure that he would bide his time on a higher floor yet it sounded as though he was going to make an attempt to reach his car. There were dozens of exits to choose from; it wouldn't be possible for the Dubai police to cover every one.

She removed her shoes. Moving swiftly and quietly, Rita ran down to the fifteenth floor, opened a fire door and emerged into a carpeted corridor identical in design and layout to the one she had vacuumed upstairs. Looking back into the darkness of the fire escape stairs, she waited. Gromik passed moments later.

Rita sent a message.

'Number One heading down the north-west fire escape. Yankees baseball cap. Red face mask. Must be going for the street.'

As soon as Gromik had left the apartment, Zatulin had gone onto the balcony and looked down towards the ground.

Apartment 1662 was on the opposite side of the Tower to the main entrance; it wasn't possible to see the two police cars which had passed Inarkiev moments earlier, only to hear the distant sound of sirens.

Laptev was kneeling, attending to Natalia, who had regained consciousness. She tried to sit up.

'What did you do?' he asked her. 'Did you talk to the police?'

In shock, her head throbbing, her vision blurred, Natalia wordlessly indicated that she was innocent.

'Help me,' she muttered, touching her badly bruised cheek. 'Please. Don't hit me . . .'

Zatulin closed the balcony doors and picked up Natalia's handbag which had fallen to the ground.

'We should leave,' Laptev told him. 'Sitting ducks here.'

'I need her phone,' Zatulin replied.

With that he reached into Natalia's handbag, took out her iPhone and pointed it at her face to unlock the screen. But as he tapped in Inarkiev's number, Laptev saw a tiny fragment of light glinting off the surface of the lens concealed in the handbag.

'Bitch has got a camera!' he hissed and reached to strike Natalia. He grabbed a fistful of her hair, yanking her towards him as the door of the apartment collapsed inwards, so violently that Laptev instantly released her and cowered back in an effort to protect himself.

'*Shurta!*' a man shouted. He was one of three armed police officers in uniform brandishing assault weapons. '*La tataharak!*'

Jim Stones was the first to spot Mikhail Gromik on a busy intersection to the east of the Hudson Residencies. He was wearing a Yankees baseball cap and a red face mask and had somehow found a way out of the building via the basement in Tower Two.

Stones had been on the point of getting out of his Uber; now he waited, anticipating that Gromik would hail a cab off the street and try to disappear into the night. Yet the Russian kept walking, ignoring the chance to get away. Informed of this, Kite concluded that he was going for the Jaguar; one of Sheridan's local moped boys had tailed it to the Tower. Gromik's route to the car would likely take him across a stretch of wasteground north of the royal palace and west of Al Mustaqbal Street, an area largely devoid of people. As the Dubai night screamed to the sound of police sirens, Kite watched the live feed from Oman updating the Russian's position. Gromik had not yet dumped his phone, presumably so that he could instruct Inarkiev to shred and delete all files relating to the Aranov assassination and warn Deviatkin that the operation was blown. Did he already suspect that one of them had betrayed him? It was surely a possibility.

Stones saw Gromik drop the phone as he crossed Al Mustaqbal; it was crushed beneath the wheels of a passing truck. The Russian then made his way along a quiet residential street, heading for what he supposed was the relative sanctuary of his borrowed Jaguar. He turned only once, checking that he was not being followed, but Stones had left him to his fate. He knew what was coming.

There was a taxi parked across the road from the Jaguar, a bearded man at the wheel. Gromik paid him no attention; he assumed he was waiting for a passenger to emerge from one of the nearby houses. Opening the door of the Jaguar, he climbed into the driver's seat.

'I have a gun pointed at your heart,' said Jason Franks, rising from the darkness of the back seat to press the barrel of a Sig Sauer P239 into Gromik's spine. 'Let's see you put your hands on the wheel, nice and slow.'

'CIA?' said Gromik, his voice catching.

'Something like that, buddy,' Franks replied as a needle punctured the Russian's bicep, filling him with 80 milligrams of ketamine. 'Something like that.'

71

Leonid Deviatkin had no time to answer his phone, no opportunity to look at social media or otherwise to be made aware of the unfolding chaos at the Regal Plaza. He knew only that he was under suspicion and that his encounter with Director Makarov and the malign Vladimir Osipov had left him with a feeling of profound disquiet. It had never been his intention to go home that night, but nor had Deviatkin considered that it would be necessary to fly the escape signal and to follow the precise protocols established by Lachlan Kite to ensure his safe exfiltration from Moscow.

Deviatkin had left the Lubyanka shortly after five o'clock and cleaned his tail with half an hour of anti-surveillance in the narrow, switchback alleyways of Kitay-Gorod before taking a taxi north to Prospekt Mira where again he tried to flush out Makarov's watchers. He was certain that he was not being followed, yet that certainty only served to make Deviatkin feel more paranoid; the moment he believed he was home and dry would be the moment that Makarov's men grabbed him. Boarding a train at Alekseevskaya, he rode the Metro to Begovoy, twice switching trains and direction in an effort to throw off his possible pursuers. As the news from Dubai was filtering through to every Directorate of the FSB, Deviatkin was retrieving the cached phone from the restaurant on Leningradsky Avenue and calling the third number listed in the directory. A man answered.

'*Privet?*'

'Hello. Do you speak English?'

There was a pause. Then:

'Yes, sir. I speak English. How can I help you?'

Deviatkin used the exact words Kite had given him.

'Am I connected to the Hotel Metropol?'

'I'm sorry, sir. You have the wrong number.'

The line went dead. Deviatkin waited, somehow expecting that somebody would call him back. He was standing on a busy pavement in the warmth of the evening sun, still in the suit he had worn to work. It had been his habit in the summer months to wear thick-rimmed sunglasses and a beret, not to protect his head from the sun but so that he might more easily conceal himself from the pervasive CCTV cameras across central Moscow when the time came to elude capture. The pandemic had added another welcome layer of camouflage, Deviatkin altering his appearance with a bulky patterned face mask. Now, with winter imminent, he had switched the beret for a woollen hat but his eyes were exposed to surveillance. He was one of only two or three people on the street wearing a mask. Deviatkin waited for a bus which would take him back into the heart of the city. Despite his makeshift disguise he felt exposed, as if at that very moment he was being watched and studied by men in cars, at pavement cafés, in front of banks of computer screens in the bowels of the Lubyanka.

The bus came. Deviatkin found a seat at the back, watching to see who had followed him. He noticed a middle-aged woman carrying a shopping trolley who had boarded at the last moment. Was she part of a surveillance team? Had they known about the dead letter box at the restaurant? Everyone was a threat. Deviatkin could smell the stale funk of unwashed clothes; the stench was so intense that people were moving away from him, taking different seats in the bus. Was it his own sweat? Then he saw that a bearded man to his left in

470

torn rags was asleep against the window. Deviatkin turned away, looking out at the passing street. He was suddenly aware that this would be the last time that he ever saw Moscow; it was like turning his back on a sick friend that he could no longer do anything to help.

Twice he switched buses and at last reached the stop on Sakharov Avenue. It had started to rain. Deviatkin had no protection against the sudden storm save for his woollen hat. A taxi slowed down but he waved it on, suspicious that he was being set up. He waited until another had passed, getting soaked in the rain, then hailed the third. He was convinced that he had seen the driver walking the corridors of the Lubyanka. Surely this was only his mind playing tricks on him? Deviatkin gave the address of the apartment complex in Lefortovo, surrendering to the inevitability of capture, only to observe the driver following the correct route to Shosse Entuziastov as he cheerily listened to house music on the radio. MOCKINGBIRD realised he was going mad with worry; nothing in the long history of his double life – no secret meeting, no dead drop, no brush contact – had ever filled him with such anxiety. He felt like the lone survivor of some awful natural disaster who, on the point of being saved, is suddenly lost to a cruel twist of fate.

Yet nobody came. Deviatkin waited in the shadows, growing cold in the concrete chill of the car park. Having no phone, he checked his wristwatch, only to see that it was still exactly nine o'clock. Had the watch stopped some time ago? Had the MI6 team been and gone? If so, what now? He had missed them. They wouldn't come back. He would have to find somewhere to spend the night and then attempt to make contact in the morning. But the snow was coming; you could feel it in the air. He had money for a hotel, but he would not be safe there.

Then, a car. The sound of an engine being switched off in mid-motion but still coasting towards him in the dead ground. Deviatkin stepped back so that he was pressed against the wall. The car stopped and the driver lowered the window.

'Back seat. Trunk,' he said in Russian.

He was much older than Deviatkin had expected, a man in his late sixties with an easy smile and a calm, almost jovial manner. He could have passed for a taxi driver, a politician, a retired schoolteacher. He looked like everybody and nobody. Deviatkin opened the door and climbed through the crawl space in the back seat until he was lying on his side in the boot. The old man turned and pushed up the seat so that Deviatkin was suddenly shrouded in darkness.

'My name is Pavel,' he said, his voice barely audible. 'Don't worry, my friend. I've done this many times before. I will get you out of Russia.'

72

When Mikhail Gromik regained consciousness, he found himself in a spacious living room on the ground floor of what appeared to be a private house. He was lying on a sofa beneath a picture depicting four Bedouin men seated around a fire in the desert. It was strangely quiet. He sat up and rubbed his arm, dimly remembering what had happened in the car. He was thirsty and reached for the bottle of water which had been placed on a table beside him.

Four people walked into the room. A black woman wearing jeans and a red blouse, followed by two stocky, well-built men in their late thirties. Finally, a bearded Pakistani carrying a tripod and a video camera. They had evidently been waiting for Gromik to wake up.

'Where am I?' he asked.

'Still in Dubai,' the woman replied. She had a British accent. Gromik was sure that he had seen her somewhere before but could not place her. The tripod was set up in front of him and the camera switched on. When he attempted to stand up and walk out of shot, one of the men pointed a Sig Sauer at him and told him to sit down. He was American. Gromik recognised his accent from the Jaguar. The woman said: 'State your name.'

'My name is fuck you,' Gromik replied. 'What's yours?'

'You know why you're here,' said the American.

'You've been a naughty boy, haven't you, Mikhail?' his friend added. He had a British accent and was slightly sunburned. They both looked like ex-soldiers. Gromik knew the type. 'We want you to tell us all about it.'

'I tell you nothing,' he replied. 'I'm a free citizen. I don't know you people. I don't know what it is you want.'

'What we want is answers.' This from the woman. 'Why did you bring Andrei Laptev and Vasily Zatulin into Dubai with a radioactive isotope?'

Still groggy from whatever had been injected into him in the car, Gromik nevertheless understood what the woman had said and was able to separate the two accusations: British intelligence knew that he had planned to kill Yuri Aranov, but they were going to frame him for a far graver crime. The realisation settled on him with the suddenness of a fever.

'You know I didn't do that. You know that you brought whatever it was into Dubai.'

The woman laughed, repeating sarcastically: 'Whatever it was.' Gromik was aware of the video capturing every pixel of his response. He knew that he should give an impression of being in control of the conversation. 'Let me tell you what it was,' she continued. 'Let me tell you what Dubai State Security found in Room 302 of the Regal Plaza Hotel this evening. They found traces of caesium-137 on articles of clothing, on the soles of shoes, on the carpets and in the bathroom. Ring any bells, Mikhail?'

'This is bullshit. This is all CIA. This is MI6. You have planted this evidence against me.'

'That's convenient, isn't it?' This from the Pakistani, who was standing beside the camera, occasionally checking the screen. 'Always somebody else's fault with you lot, isn't it? Navalny poisoned himself. Litvinenko ate some bad sashimi. Tell me, was it the CIA who switched Evgeny Palatnik's eye medication for an A-234 Novichok?'

Gromik did not respond. The woman came closer. She was holding up a file.

'This is a report into the Palatnik assassination drawing on intelligence from a source inside the FSB. Yes, that's right, we have somebody telling us what you planned out here, moment by moment. He places Vasily Zatulin in Lake Placid on the same weekend that General Palatnik was killed. He accuses you of orchestrating the plot. That same source inside the FSB, a man well known to you, has told us that you planned and executed the attempted assassination of Yuri Aranov. You ordered Zatulin and Andrei Laptev to Dubai in possession of enough caesium-137 to kill most of the people in Jumeirah.'

'Leonid Antonovich,' Gromik whispered, the realisation that he had been betrayed by Deviatkin pulsing through him. 'Jumeirah?' he asked. 'That's where I am?'

'You're in a pickle, that's where you are,' said the sunburned soldier. Gromik did not understand what he meant; it sounded like a supercilious remark.

'Tell you what,' the Pakistani continued. 'Why don't we introduce you to an old friend? Someone from way back who might be able to help clear your mind?'

Still reeling from the nausea of Deviatkin's treachery, Gromik unscrewed the lid on the bottle of water and drank greedily. Yet he could not quench his thirst. He was cornered, humiliated, knowing that even if he could escape this place it would only lead to his arrest. He was being held by the British because it suited them; either they had cut a deal with the Emiratis or they wanted something. Gromik did not know what that could be. Surely they were not intending to try to recruit him?

'Sit over here, please.' The American pulled a chair from the corner of the room and placed it on one side of the sofa. 'In this chair.'

Gromik wanted to preserve his strength. He knew that there was no sense in defying their instructions. Rising from the sofa, he sat in the chair and placed his hands on his knees. He was suddenly extraordinarily tired.

'What old friend?' he asked finally. 'What are you talking about?'

'Peter!' the woman called out, turning towards the door through which she had entered. 'You can come in now. We're all ready for you.'

73

It is an iron law of interrogation that the first lie you tell must be the lie that you stick to. It was this simple commandment that sealed the fates of Vasily Zatulin and Andrei Laptev.

They were tourists, they said, old friends from Russia who had come to Dubai to escape the first weeks of the Moscow winter. They had wanted to go to the top of Burj Khalifa, to shop for their wives, to swim in the ocean (even though neither man had thought to pack a pair of swimming trunks). A friend of a friend had loaned them the apartment in Hudson Park Tower Residencies. No, they didn't have his name; some keys had been left in the lobby. The girl they had invited up to the sixteenth floor was a Russian citizen, going by the name of Natalia, who was going to spend the night with them and had promised to bring a friend. There was no third man in the apartment who left just before the police arrived. Natalia was lying about that. It had always been just the two of them.

The men were kept in different cells. When Zatulin was asked why they had chosen to share a room at the Regal Plaza, so far from the sights and sounds of the city, he said that it was because they didn't know any better; they hadn't realised that Deira was across the Creek. Laptev contradicted this by insisting that they had wanted to save money. Dubai hotels were expensive, even during the pandemic, and they needed to pay for the girls. Time and again the men told different stories. Zatulin had never heard of Mikhail Gromik; Laptev admitted that he had met him for coffee in Business Bay. Zatulin insisted that they were scheduled to leave Dubai at two o'clock that morning because it was the cheapest available flight; Laptev said that he had an important business meeting to attend to in Moscow which had come up at the last moment. They were going to entertain the girls, he said, then pack their bags and head to the airport.

At first, the DSS interrogators, assisted by Mark Sheridan of the British Secret Intelligence Service, said nothing about the radioactive isotope. Instead they presented the Russians with evidence of their complicity in the murders of Ruslan Magomedragimov, a political activist from Dagestan, and Timur Kushaev, a political opponent of the government of Vladimir Putin. Wasn't it the case, they argued, that Laptev and Zatulin, far from being innocent Russian tourists enjoying some much-needed RnR in Dubai, were in fact FSB assassins working on the orders of General Vladimir Osipov of the Criminalistics Institute and FSB director Alexander Makarov? If they were mere tourists, how could they account for the dozens of phone messages exchanged with an individual identified in Laptev's phone as 'Chief' discussing the fate of a certain 'Y' and his girlfriend 'N'? Surely 'N' was Natalia Kovalenko, the woman who had come to Hudson Park Tower One on the night of the arrest and with whom 'Chief' had communicated on no less than nine previous occasions? Indeed metadata had placed 'Chief' outside a yoga studio in Al Quoz earlier in the month. Did they realise that this was the same yoga studio where Natalia exercised up to three times a week? Furthermore, could they explain why Kovalenko had a cut and a bruise on her left cheekbone? Which of the two men had struck her? Zatulin claimed that Natalia had fallen over when the police stormed the flat; in the next room, Laptev admitted on tape that it was he who had hit her on the assumption that she was working for a criminal gang who intended to rob them. That last excuse caused DSS Colonel Khalil Albaloushi to laugh out loud and shake his head in disbelief at their brazen lies.

When finally confronted with the evidence from their shared room at the Regal Plaza, both men strenuously denied bringing a dangerous radioactive isotope into the United Arab Emirates. Having no knowledge of BOX 88's existence, Laptev claimed that they were being framed by MI6; Zatulin laid responsibility at the door of the CIA. Their shoes had been taken as a precaution as soon as they arrived at the detention centre. Analysis carried out in a laboratory within an hour of the arrests demonstrated dangerous levels of radioactivity on the soles of Laptev's boots, radioactivity which had left a trail from Deira to Downtown and potentially placed tens of thousands of lives at grave risk. Again the men denied all knowledge of the conspiracy. They had never heard of Yuri Aranov or Sebastian Glik. Mikhail Gromik, with whom both Laptev and Zatulin had been photographed enjoying brunch at Kana Cafe, was just an old friend from Moscow. No, they had no idea he had once been a senior officer in the FSB. They continued to insist that they were just tourists in Dubai who wanted to go to the top of Burj Khalifa. The whole thing was a grotesque misunderstanding.

'If only your government could confirm that,' said Albaloushi, leaving Zatulin to stew in his cell at dawn. 'But they deny all knowledge of you. The Russian consulate in Dubai claims that you and your friend Andrei are CIA officers travelling under false Russian passports with the express purpose of bringing shame on the government of Vladimir Putin. We need to find Mr Gromik. Maybe he can help to clear up all these mysteries.'

74

Lachlan Kite walked into the living room.

'Hello, Mikhail,' he said. 'Long time no see.'

Gromik did well to hide his consternation; it was almost as though he had been expecting him.

'Galvin,' he said. Masood glanced at Rita. 'So it was you. All this was your *revenge*?' The two men stared at one another. 'You look much older now. You used to be so handsome. All the girls in Voronezh, no? Now look at you.'

It was the sort of clever insult that only a vain man could have conceived; Kite admired it.

'Revenge is of no interest to me,' he replied. 'We're just trying to protect Yuri Aranov. What concerns me is why it took you almost thirty years to come for him.'

'I didn't come for him.' Gromik frowned as though Kite had made a basic mistake of understanding. 'You put him in front of me. You brought Aranov to Dubai. You brought the caesium. I sat on my boat drinking coffee and smoking cigars. I retired long ago.'

'Of course you did.'

Kite was carrying a canvas bag. The others were silent as he reached into it. He pulled out a small box. Placing it on the table in front of Gromik, he lifted the lid, indicating a tiny glass bottle nestled inside the moulding.

'You recognise this, I assume?'

'I've never seen it before in my life.' Gromik stared at Kite with what might, in different circumstances, have been construed as a look of pity. 'Whatever it is, it has nothing to do with me.'

'That's odd.' Kite looked up at the others. 'We found it in the boot of your car. It's a Novichok identical to the one used against Evgeny Palatnik. Alongside it was the consignment of caesium-137. What was the deal? You were going to use both on Yuri?'

'You lie. You put them there.'

'Maybe the CIA did,' Masood replied.

'Or maybe they came with the car,' Stones suggested. 'Optional extras.'

'It's not my car. Belongs to friend.'

'We know,' said Kite. 'Betise. Brazilian. Very stylish woman, by the looks of her. Does she know why you were using her car tonight?' Gromik did not reply. 'Did you tell her you needed it so that there would be no radioactive trace in your own vehicle? You have to admit. It's going to look suspicious when the locals join the dots.'

'You planted this. You used the caesium to contaminate the hotel room. Stop this game.'

Kite sat on the arm of the sofa, opened a bottle of water and drank from it.

'It's strange to hear you talk like this, Mikhail. To deny the truth. Perhaps this is the time we're living through, an era of contradictions. Nothing can be proven. Nothing is right and nothing is wrong. Hypocrisy and lies are just normal everyday occurrences. A president with three wives and a penchant for porn actresses can be proclaimed by his supporters as a man of God. That same president can accuse his opponent's son of corruption while his own children enrich themselves in full view of the American people. In my own government, a top adviser can claim that he went for a fifty-minute drive during a national lockdown in order to test his eyesight. The key is to be as brazen as possible, isn't it? Never apologise. Never admit fault. Say what you like and play the virgin nun if anybody has the temerity to criticise you. Come out fighting and accuse the other side of even graver sins. Cynicism is the hard currency. You yourself illustrate the problem perfectly. You sit here in this house and tell us that you didn't plan the assassination of Yuri Aranov, that you didn't bring a Novichok and a radioactive isotope into Dubai. You claim that it was the British. Or was it the Americans? I've lost track. The remarkable thing is that you believe it. I can see it in your eyes, Mikhail. You've become so used to lying that you can't even see the truth anymore.'

'I will not play your game,' Gromik replied. His immense arrogance and his long relationship with power made him seem very calm. 'What do you want?' he asked. 'If you're so convinced of my guilt, why don't you just hand me over to the Emiratis?'

'Maybe I don't trust them. Maybe I worry that you have friends in the DSS. You could slip one of them a Rolex or the keys to your yacht and they'll let you get away. Isn't that how things are done with you lot? A nod and a wink and a few million wired to Turks and Caicos? No, what I want from you is answers. What I want is a guarantee.'

'You have them,' Gromik replied with a lazy shrug. 'Plainly I have no choice.'

'Well, that was easy.' Kite looked at Rita, who rolled her eyes. 'You don't even know what it is we need.'

'Get on with it.'

'Why is Peter Galvin on the JUDAS list?' Gromik's composure cracked. 'Why did it take twenty-seven years for Yuri Aranov to be targeted?'

'Deviatkin told you about JUDAS?'

Kite looked at Masood, who said: 'We've known about the JUDAS list for a long time.'

Gromik was silent. He studied Masood as he might have examined something which had become attached to the sole of his shoe.

'Who the fuck are you?' he asked eventually.

'I'm the one whose friends have guns,' Masood told him, indicating Franks and Stones. 'You should be nice to me.'

Kite stood up. 'Again,' he said. 'Why Galvin? Why now?'

The Russian looked at Stones, then twisted round so that he was facing Rita. A car drove past, the only vehicle to come near the villa in more than an hour. At this time of night, in Umm Suqeim, it was as quiet as the Highlands of Scotland.

'That's why you did all this?' Gromik asked. 'Because of the JUDAS list?' Nobody in the room answered him. He glared at Kite, shaking his head. 'You're worried about saving your own skin?' Warming to his theme he settled back in the chair and crossed his legs. 'Or is it about the girl? I can't even remember the bitch's name.'

'Why don't we remind you,' said Masood. 'Her name was Oksana Sharikova.'

Gromik looked up at him with contempt. 'That's right. She was one of yours. She paid the price.'

'She was never one of ours,' said Kite. 'Oksana was innocent. You knew that, yet you assaulted and raped her. Then you covered it up.'

'Believe what you want to believe.' Gromik tried to stand, but Stones stepped forward and pushed him back into the chair. The Russian seemed momentarily startled by his strength.

'What happened to her?' Kite asked. 'You buried the details of the Aranov defection. You removed every record of Peter Galvin's time in Voronezh. You stuck the file away so that nobody would know you'd fucked up. Did you dispose of Oksana too so that there would be no loose ends?'

'Believe what you want to believe,' Gromik repeated.

'Tell me what happened to her.'

The Russian shrugged. 'I really have no idea. She was just a whore. Who knows what happens to whores? She got married, she grew fat, she had kids. How should I know?'

Kite had to take a moment to compose himself. He made a silent pledge that he would use every resource at his disposal to find Oksana. He had left it far too long.

'To my original question,' he said, edging closer towards Gromik. 'Why now? Why were you looking for me?'

'Ask them in Moscow,' Gromik replied. He was picking at a patch of dried skin on his cheek. 'I didn't put you on JUDAS. I don't even know your real name.'

Rita glanced at Masood. They both understood that this was the vital piece of information which Kite had been seeking. Gromik had revealed that his identity was secure.

'What about the girl?' Kite asked.

The Russian looked confused. 'What girl?' he asked. 'You talking about Oksana again?'

'The girl who came to visit me from London.'

Kite studied every tic and nuance of Gromik's response. The Russian looked by turns bored and puzzled, as though his time was being wasted and he had better things to be doing.

'Mary?' he said, seemingly struggling to recall her name. 'No, that's not right. I remember now. *Martha*.'

It was the response Kite had dreaded: if Gromik remembered Martha's surname, it would have been all too easy for the FSB to discover her connection to the young Lachlan Kite.

'Is she safe?' he asked.

Gromik laughed. 'Your little girlfriend from thirty years ago? Safe? Is she even alive today?'

'Yes she is.'

'Then why wouldn't she be alive tomorrow?'

'Because of the JUDAS list. Because of Navalny. Because of Salisbury. Because of Litvinenko. Because you people will never stop.'

'All of this you're talking about was lies exaggerated by the fake news,' Gromik replied, a remark on which Rita pounced.

'Exaggerated? An innocent woman died because her boyfriend picked up your vial of poison, thought it was perfume and gave it to her as a gift. How much contempt must you have for human life to conduct yourselves as you do? You call yourselves intelligence officers. You call yourselves patriots and professionals. You're fucking murderers. Pure and simple.'

'Who is this black bitch to talk to me like that?'

No sooner were the words out of Gromik's mouth than Franks raised the Sig Sauer to strike him, but Kite – appalled by what he had heard – indicated that Gromik should be left unharmed.

'Long time since anybody spoke to me like that.' Rita was superbly calm; there was no indication that Gromik's slur had upset her. 'It's the key to you people, isn't it? A woman in power makes you feel threatened. A *black* woman in power makes you feel unmanned. It's the same with the so-called traitors you target. Litvinenko. Navalny. Magnitsky. These men are the last vestiges of your moral conscience. They make you aware of the corruption at the centre of your soul, the sickness in Russian political life. They make you feel inadequate. They embody what needs to change, so you have to erase them.'

'If you say so,' said Gromik.

'She does say so,' said Kite.

'Is she a psychiatrist?' The Russian gestured at Rita. 'A shrink? You have her around so you can talk about your problems?'

'I'd say you were the one with the problem, Mikhail.' Kite touched the lead-lined box. 'You know what this stuff can do. You're an expert in chemical agents. You're aware that even a few drops of this will likely kill you?'

'That would make you a murderer, Peter Galvin.'

'A murderer like you, Mikhail Dimitrovich? Like Lugovoy and Kovtun? Like Boshirov and Petrov? A murderer like them?' Kite reached into his back pocket for a pair of latex gloves. 'So I take it you disapprove of your own methods?'

'I say again . . .' Gromik had been unsettled by the direction the conversation was taking. He was suddenly struggling to find the right words. 'What do you want?' he said, staring at Kite's gloves. 'You spoke of guarantees?'

A nod was all it took for Stones and Franks to act. Within

485

seconds they had seized Gromik's hands, tied them behind his back and secured his legs against the chair. At the same time, Masood switched off the camera and moved the tripod closer towards them.

'Let's make a new film,' said Kite. 'Let's see how brave you are when the boot is on the other foot. Let's see if you're prepared to die in the same way that an old, defenceless man like Evgeny Palatnik was made to suffer. Can you take what you dish out?'

Panic flooded Gromik's eyes. He saw that Franks and Stones had put on balaclavas to conceal their identities. Kite was also covering his face.

'Wait!' Gromik begged, his voice slightly hoarse. 'What the fuck are you doing? You're going to kill me? You're going to put that shit in my eyes?' He swore in Russian, words of rage and disbelief. Franks placed a gag in Gromik's mouth and grabbed his face in a headlock. At the same time Stones untied the Russian's left hand, rolled up the sleeve of his shirt and held up his bared arm. Gromik tried to draw it back by bending the elbow, but Stones was too strong for him.

Kite looked through the balaclava at Masood, who indicated that the camera was again recording. Very carefully Kite removed the glass bottle from the box, drew some of the liquid into the pipette and walked forward.

'Five or six drops of this on your skin and you'll be dead by morning,' he said. Gromik's body had gone limp. He was no longer putting up any physical resistance. There were tears in his eyes. Through the gag he said: 'Please! Please, sir!'

'Will you tell us everything you know about Director Makarov and the JUDAS programme?'

Gromik was not ready to concede to such a demand. He closed his eyes. Kite could see that he was trying to summon a kind of dignity; he might yet choose to die rather than cooperate.

'Give me his arm,' he said to Stones.

Stones lifted the arm. Again Gromik fought against this, trying to draw it back towards his body. He was strong but his efforts were hopeless. Sweat had broken out on his brow. He was screaming through the gag.

'Wait!' he cried, the word barely audible.

Kite indicated to Franks that he should remove the gag. Gromik tried to catch his breath.

'You would murder me?' he asked, looking at Kite in bewilderment. 'What do you want to know?'

'A guarantee that all attempts on the lives of British and American citizens come to an end. That the name Peter Galvin is removed from the JUDAS list. And that you do not try to find Martha.'

'I forgot Martha!' Gromik replied. 'I told you this! Everything was destroyed.'

'Is she safe?' Kite demanded. 'My family. Will they be targeted?'

'Of course not!' Gromik looked desperately at his exposed skin. 'Anything you want. Anything you need. I can guarantee this for you. I can give you names, programmes. I can reassure you that Moscow knows nothing about you. If they did, they would have put your true name on JUDAS.' He was breathing very fast, sweat falling down one side of his face. 'This has all gone too far. You took it too far. Please, don't harm me. I beg you.'

It was a pitiful sight, a once proud man – disdainful and forbidding – reduced to pleading. Kite had expected Gromik to fold, but not this quickly and with so little dignity. Beneath the designer clothes and the year-round suntan he was still the low-level thug from Voronezh, cruelty hanging around him like the stench of his favourite patchouli oil.

'Did you get it?' he said.

'Every word,' Masood replied.

Kite removed the gloves and turned his left hand over so that the palm was facing the ground. He held the pipette over the skin and allowed several drops of the liquid to fall onto his knuckles.

'Saline,' said Masood.

In his final humiliation, Gromik stared at the camera,

wanting to retract his promises, to erase his pitiful confessions. He tried to break free of Stones and Franks, but they continued to hold him.

'You fucking bastards. So now you throw me back, yes? To the police? This was all for nothing?'

'Not for nothing,' Kite told him. 'Who knows what happens next? The Emiratis might release you. You could persuade them you had nothing to do with the Aranov assassination. Maybe you know somebody in the ruling family who can have a quiet word with the Sheikh and get you home to Russia. We just wanted to make sure you knew what was at stake.'

Rita produced a photograph from her pocket. She held it in front of Gromik's face. It was a picture of his son, Mischa, taken in California over the summer by BOX 88 surveillance.

'Just in case,' she said. 'You break your word and two things happen. We send this film to the Lubyanka so that your colleagues will know how cheaply and how easily you gave them up. And if Peter here so much as suspects that somebody is coming after him, or his friends and family are in any way threatened, your boy dies. This black bitch will see to it.'

75

They were at the airports when the pictures of Deviatkin came through. Franks and Stones had checked in at the British Airways counter in Dubai, Kite and Rita had taken a car to Abu Dhabi and were flying out on Etihad.

Kite looked down at his phone. The photographs, taken only moments earlier, showed Deviatkin standing on the waterfront in Helsinki, Pavel beside him holding up – of all things – a cricket ball. Kite had no idea how the ball had come into his possession in Finland on a chill October morning, but smiled at Pavel's sense of mischief nonetheless. For years, whenever work had brought them into contact, the Russian had found a way of referencing cricket in their communications, a private joke which had run since 1993. Pavel was now almost seventy and might easily have chosen to live out his final years without risking life and liberty for BOX 88. Yet he refused to walk away.

'I loathe Putin even more than I loathed the Communists,' he had told Kite. 'At least Khrushchev tried to change things. Brezhnev, the others, they had no choice. They were locked into a system. Putin and the *siloviki* were free to choose and they chose to take away the future we fought for. We are still watched. We are still threatened. They murder and steal. They paint the schools and the hospitals to make them look good, but there is no money to pay for books or medicines – it is all stolen. The best people – the scientists, the doctors – have left because why would you stay in a country that is so rotten? Meanwhile the *siloviki* have their football teams and their private jets, their super yachts and Caribbean islands. They have their women, most of them younger than their own children. They are scum.'

As if to contradict his point, at that very moment Mikhail Gromik was sitting alone in a humid cell in Al Aweer Central Jail wearing only a thin white smock and some flip-flops, a disposable paper face mask and a pair of plastic gloves. His mobile phone and Rolex Oyster had been taken from him. Thanks to Covid, Gromik had been denied a visit from his lawyer and was permitted to communicate with the outside world only via video conferencing or public payphone. Nobody from the Russian consulate had attempted to contact him. He did not know who else had been arrested in connection with the foiled assassination plot nor how the story was playing out in the international media. He had received no written communiqués from Moscow and could not risk trying to contact Makarov on the prison phone. Sound-proofed rooms were set aside for inmates to speak online to their family and friends, but Gromik knew that anything he said would be eavesdropped by the DSS. Since arriving at the prison, he had eaten only a fatty mutton stew and some boiled rice. He had no bed to sleep on, only a torn, bug-infested mattress and a blanket which itched his skin and stank of stale sweat. The communal showers at the prison were infested with insects, the toilets so filthy Gromik gagged when he used them. It was not just the deprivation he found hard; it was the knowledge that he had fallen for Galvin's deception and brought shame on the FSB. That Deviatkin had betrayed him was no defence; he had been played for a fool. To live with that knowledge was like living in the early stages of a wasting disease.

A desire for vengeance burned inside Gromik yet he could not act. Even if he waited, biding his time in a Dubai jail until he was released and his son returned safely to Moscow, there was still the film. MI6 could release it and demonstrate Gromik's cowardice to the world. He could see no way out of his predicament, no way of convincing the authorities that he had no knowledge of the radioactive isotope. Who would believe him? Laptev and Zatulin had surely been arrested and were also claiming to be innocent of the charges. Gromik assumed they were languishing in some other section of the same prison. The Emiratis had kept them apart so it had been impossible to get their stories straight; doubtless each of them had already compromised the other.

Such thoughts turned over in Gromik's mind as he waited to face the public prosecutor. He could see no way out of the trap Galvin had set for him and into which he had fallen so lazily. If only he could get a message to Inarkiev, smuggle it out by bribing a guard. There had to be a way of targeting Galvin without jeopardising Mischa; they must expose the nature of MI6's plan, find the proof which would show the world that the FSB was innocent of the charges brought against it. Perhaps there was a way of doing what he should have done in 1993: finding the visa application filled out by Martha and running her to ground in London. But where to begin to find such paperwork? Nothing back then was computerised. Gromik had shredded everything. He could not think of a way of saving himself. And why should Inarkiev help? Chances are he had already been recalled to Moscow or was himself being questioned by the Emiratis.

It was impossible to see a way out. Every avenue was closed to him.

76

Cara Jannaway was the last one left, the only member of Kite's London team yet to have returned home. The others had departed as they had arrived. Unnoticed.

On the night of Gromik's arrest she had been too tired to go home with Toby and had instead returned to the Holiday Inn, sleeping until almost midday. By then Natalia had been released by the authorities, Mark Sheridan informing the DSS that she had been working on behalf of MI6 and was not involved in any criminal conspiracy. Toby had also gone home, making a promise to take Cara for a celebratory dinner at Zuma. She was due to fly back to London at the weekend; it was to be their penultimate night together.

She had wanted to stay in Dubai, no question, but Kite had never spoken about it, there had been too many problems to solve and Cara Jannaway's personal life, understandably, was not at the top of anyone's list of priorities. Toby had made it clear that he would fight for them to become what the CIA called 'a tandem couple'. The Aranov operation had been a triumph and Cara had played her part. If she stayed in Dubai she could learn from Toby and continue to be an asset to BOX 88. If there was another global lockdown, having another officer on the ground in the Gulf might prove advantageous. These were the arguments they had rehearsed whenever they were together. Yet Cara was sceptical about her chances. She was still at a very early stage in her career. Kite might want to keep her in London, not least because she could prove to be a distraction to Toby if she remained in Dubai. Packing up her room at the Holiday Inn, she went for a final swim in the rooftop pool, then texted Natalia to see if she was OK.

No response. Voicemail said that the phone was switched off. Cara sent a WhatsApp message but the display showed only a single grey tick. She assumed that the DSS had confiscated Natalia's phone so that they could examine its contents. Concerned about her friend's wellbeing, Cara hailed a cab from the rank outside the hotel and gave directions to her apartment in Al Hudaiba. In their desire to leave Dubai as quickly as possible, Kite and the others had done very little to ensure that Natalia was in good mental health; it was possible that she had been badly shaken up by her ordeal and needed some TLC. Responsibility for that lay primarily with Toby, but he had been at Jambiri all day, keeping up his cover. He didn't have the time to look after her.

A woman was coming out of Natalia's building as Cara approached the main door so there was no need to buzz the apartment. Armed with a bunch of flowers, a bottle of white wine and a packet of her favourite Vogue cigarettes, Cara climbed the stairs to the third floor. She was about to knock when she heard the low murmur of a man's voice on the other side of the door. Natalia answered in English, sounding in good spirits. Cara wondered if she had a client in her bedroom, a tourist paying by the hour for her time. Surely not. She had made too much money out of Sebastian Glik to have to go back to her old ways. BOX 88 had bought her out of that lifestyle.

Then the man's voice again, unmistakable. It was Toby.

In a fleeting instant, Cara felt excited that he was there, that she was going to see him. She almost knocked and called out his name. Then she heard him say: 'I'm coming back to bed' and the moment collapsed around her.

Cara backed away from the door. Of all people, she thought

of Oksana Sharikova, seduced and abandoned by Lachlan Kite all those years before. She had been left alone in Voronezh to wonder why she had given her body, her mind to a man who had cared so little for her. Why was it so hard for these men to be satisfied by one woman? What were they chasing that they needed to leave a trail of destruction in their wake? Landau's ruthlessness and entitlement disgusted her. The affection Cara had felt for Natalia evaporated into numb anger.

She might still have knocked and confronted them, but did not want the mental image of their entwined bodies to haunt her in the weeks and months ahead. Instead, dazed and humiliated, Cara walked downstairs, returned to her hotel and took a taxi to the airport. By the time she had left Dubai, Landau had sent several messages to her phone and called four times, as if he sensed that something was wrong.

Cara Jannaway never saw nor spoke to him again.

77

Lachlan Kite sat by the window in his office at The Cathedral, looking out over Canary Wharf. There were two boats on the water, a handful of pedestrians walking between the towers. The city was otherwise motionless beneath a vast Wedgwood sky. He had come to headquarters to retrieve some files and to make a secure call to Ward Hansell in New York. The office was deserted. Scattered on his desk were the latest newspaper reports on the foiled assassination in Dubai. Most of the stories and comment had already been relegated to the foreign sections; Covid and the royal family had regained their customary slots on the front pages. He had left his lucky silver box in a desk drawer and took it out, opening the lid to read the inscription inside: *To Lachlan, From Da.*

'Lockie?'

Kite was drinking a cup of coffee. He set it down and turned. Cara Jannaway was standing in the doorway. She was wearing jeans and a black leather jacket, her hair cut short in a bob.

'You again,' he smiled. 'Your pass is still working, I see.'

They had seen one another only once in Dubai; Kite sensed that something had happened to change the atmosphere of their relationship.

'Gromik is dead,' she said.

'I know.'

'You think they poisoned him?'

'How?' Kite asked. 'He wasn't allowed visitors.'

'Inarkiev saw him.'

This was new information. Kite had learned about Gromik's death on his way back from visiting his mother at the care home in Wimbledon, but Sheridan – who had called with the news – had said nothing about Inarkiev making a visit.

'Was it taped?'

'Their conversation?' Cara was still standing by the door, as if reluctant to walk in. 'Assume so. Hope so.'

'I'll tell Sheridan to get on it.'

'He's already there. DSS called Inarkiev in for questioning three hours ago. Mark's sitting in. He wanted you to know.'

'You could have told me that over the phone,' Kite replied, gesturing at Cara to come into the office. 'Why are you here? Something else.'

'Yes, I'd like to have a chat.' She closed the door behind her. 'When it's a good time for you. When it's convenient.'

Her teasing, careless way with him was a thing of the past; Cara was more serious now, as though Dubai had taught her something about herself, something about the world.

'You're doubting your own future,' he said, remembering his own reservations and battles with the secret life at almost exactly Cara's age. 'You're wondering if it's all worth it.'

'Is it?' she asked. 'Will I have to keep going through all this?'

'All what?'

Kite saw that Landau had betrayed her. And he understood how: a post-operational euphoric night with Natalia for old time's sake and screw the consequences.

'Toby?' he asked.

'So you already knew?'

Cara looked ashamed, as though everyone was laughing about it behind her back.

'I just assumed.' Kite thought of Martha, of Oksana, of too many broken hearts. 'I'm sorry. You didn't deserve that after everything. You were brilliant in Dubai.'

The compliment appeared to revive her slightly. Cara picked up the silver box from Kite's desk and turned it in her hands.

'I'm not here for a shoulder to cry on,' she said. 'I'm here for career advice.'

'Good.' Kite's reply was sharp and to the point. 'Ignore what happened with Toby. Sex is sex. It's an offshoot, a corollary of what we do. Also a function of being a relatively interesting person.'

Cara laughed contemptuously, the way the younger generation could look at an older person, size them up and dismiss them almost in the same breath.

'Fuck's that mean?' she said. 'So spies cheat? It's in our nature, so we get a free pass? You don't qualify unless you commit adultery?'

'I didn't say that.'

There was silence. They watched each other. Cara seemed to be thinking: Should I invest the next twenty years of my life in you, or are you as full of shit as everyone else? Kite was wondering: Is it worth this woman making the sacrifices she will inevitably have to make in order to be as good at her job as I think she can be?

'Look,' he said finally. 'There are two problems facing the world and therefore two problems facing BOX. They're going to be around for a long time yet. The first is information. Where do people get it? Is it authentic? Do they trust that information? What effect does it have on policy and what effect does it have on mass behaviour? Think of China. Think of Russia. Think of America. In all those places information is a problem. It's not just a question of who controls it. It's already out of control. It's a question of whether people are smart enough to realise that they're being manipulated. Film clips. News stories. Rumours. What looks like the truth and what looks like a lie?'

Kite saw that he had Cara's attention. He kept going.

'The second problem is greed. For money. For power. To all intents and purposes they are the same thing, because if you're running China, if you're running Russia, if you're in the White House or even Number 10, by definition you have both. Therefore you want to do everything you can to remain in place. To obtain more power, to obtain more money. It was ever thus. Our challenge at BOX, and the reason we need people like Cara Jannaway to stick around and learn the ropes – is to make it as difficult as possible for corrupt people and those who serve them to remain in power and to manipulate the truth. If we stop doing what we're doing – if you leave here today and go off and make television programmes or dedicate your life to organic farming – you'll make it easier for greed and the sickness of misinformation to undermine our society. That's my speech. That's my pitch.' Kite finished the last of the coffee. 'I want you to stay, Cara.'

'Never said I wanted to leave,' she replied.

'But you were thinking about it.'

She allowed him this insight, nodding her assent. Kite stood up and walked towards the window, looking out over the quiet docks.

'So are you in or would you rather have a quiet life?' he asked. 'There will still be Toby Landaus in the real world. You can still betray someone and break his heart, only you'll have the luxury of being able to tell your friends about it.'

Cara looked at Kite with a mixture of fondness and intense curiosity.

'You've been doing this a long time,' she said.

'True.' *My whole life*, he thought. It felt as though it was all he had ever known. 'That's why I'm still here. To try to get better at it.'

'So what's next?'

She put the silver box back on the desk. Kite picked it up and slipped it into his pocket. There and then he decided to give it to Ingrid as a Christening gift.

'I'm going to take you to lunch,' he said. 'We're going to find a place that will sell us a sandwich, we're going to eat it down by the river and talk about Yuri Aranov's new life in Edinburgh. After that, you're going to go home and take a week's holiday.'

'And you?' she asked.

'Me?' Kite smiled. 'I have a tradition of buying a painting every time I finish an operation.' He looked back at the gleaming towers of Canary Wharf. 'If I can find a gallery that's still open, I'll pay them a visit. After that I'm going to Stockholm.'

'Stockholm? How come?'

'My wife is there. And my daughter. Time I got them back.'

Acknowledgements

Charlotte Hobson's wonderful memoir, *Black Earth City*, took me to Voronezh in the early 1990s, vividly describing a period she had spent there as a student. Charlotte – now Marsden – was also kind enough to read an early draft of the manuscript and to offer incisive, patient criticism. Henry Virgin taught English as a foreign language in Rostov-on-Don at about the same time Peter Galvin was plying his trade at the Dickens Institute. You can read about his experiences in Henry's fascinating book, *Exit Rostov*. *Everything is Normal* by Sergey Grechishkin, *One Steppe Beyond* by Thom Wheeler and *Snowdrops* by A.D. Miller also acted as time machines of one sort or another.

I owe a huge debt of gratitude to Mark Franchetti for reading the first draft and to Catherine Goncharov for patiently responding to my endless enquiries about post-Soviet Russia. Owen Matthews, author of two superb Cold War thrillers, *Black Sun* and *Red Traitor*, walked me through the joys of flying Aeroflot thirty years ago and had some useful tips for crossing into Ukraine. He also did a forensic edit on the manuscript, for all of which I am immensely grateful. My thanks to Sheila Sim for her memories of Voronezh and to Gus Wilkinson for tips on teaching English. *Putin's People* by Catherine Belton, *Biohazard* by Ken Alibek and Stephen Handelman, *The Skripal Files* by Mark Urban, Luke Harding's

A Very Expensive Poison, Dubai: The Story of the World's Fastest City by Jim Krane and *Persian Roulette* by Oscar King were all very helpful. Dan Kaszeta, author of *Poison*, gave me several masterclasses in chemical and biological weapons and kindly allowed Evgeny Palatnik to adopt his surname when he moved to America.

I would have stumbled badly in Dubai without the help of the redoubtable Ben Higgins. Edmund Broad showed me around his fish farm and gave permission for Toby Landau to work there. My thanks also to Otto Penzler, Rose and Vita, Patrick Forbes, Natalie Amos, Chris St George, Christina Bruce and Hamish Adam, Henry Weldon, Kate Mallinson, Peter Frankopan, Dan Fesperman, Maria Bizri and Reehan Baig, Nick Lockley and Panos Nicolau, Henry Carpenter, Ed Clowes, Gus Maguire, Mira Manek, Prakash, Olivia Davies, Martin R, Will, YT, TC, WT, Munim and Al.

As always, I am indebted to Julia Wisdom, Sarah Gabriel and Will Francis for their wisdom and tireless assistance, and to my wife, Harriette. Grateful thanks to Kathryn Cheshire, Roger Cazalet, Ann Bissell, Kate Elton, Anne O'Brien, Claire Ward, Stephen Mulcahey and everyone at HarperCollins.

C.C. London 2021